FROM THE COLORFUL WHARFS OF SAN FRANCISCO TO THE CHILL BEAUTY OF REMOTE ALASKAN BOOMTOWNS

🌹　　🌹　　🌹

Beautiful, brazen young Cordelia Stewart withstands the dangers and uncertainties of the frozen frontier to follow the romantic dream burning deep within her.

Her father's sudden death has left her with a devastating dilemma. In order to claim her inheritance she must marry Donald Earle, her father's right-hand man at Stewart's Shipyards. Rather than marry a man she does not love, Cordelia flees north to search for Avery Curran, who abandoned her when he was smitten by Klondike fever.

Braving extreme hardship and the fiendish pursuit of Earle, who has sworn to capture her fortune and her beauty at any cost, Cordelia befriends Quade Hill, a rugged young newspaperman who comes to the Yukon to avenge a personal tragedy, a tragedy that will propel them into a hellish web of danger and deceit—and into each other's arms.

WILD ROSES

JULIA GRICE

AVON
PUBLISHERS OF BARD, CAMELOT AND DISCUS BOOKS

WILD ROSES is an original publication of Avon Books. This work has never before appeared in book form.

AVON BOOKS
A division of
The Hearst Corporation
959 Eighth Avenue
New York, New York 10019

Copyright © 1980 by Julia Grice
Published by arrangement with the author.
Library of Congress Catalog Card Number: 79-55390
ISBN: 0-380-75069-4

First Avon Printing, January, 1980.

AVON TRADEMARK REG. U.S. PAT. OFF. AND IN
OTHER COUNTRIES, MARCA REGISTRADA, HECHO EN
U.S.A.

Printed in the U.S.A.

For Michael and Andy, two very special people

But the North was a mirror, reflecting the horror or beauty a person brought with him.

—David B. Wharton

Among my greatest aids in researching this book were the colorful photographs taken by E. A. Hegg, well-known photographer of the era, to whom I owe a tremendous debt. He photographed the Yukon under adverse conditions and so left a record of what happened there for all of us to see. I was also lucky to find some interesting first-hand accounts written by people who actually went north. Among these are Mont Hawthorne's book, *The Trail Led North*, told in "Uncle Mont's" salty language and humor. Basil Austin's *The Diary of a Ninety-Eighter* is full of wry quips, and Angelo Heilprin's 1898 guide to the Yukon, *Alaska and the Klondike*, was most informative.

For a very lively overall picture of the "last stampede," I used David B. Wharton's book, *The Alaska Gold Rush*. Also, for information about Alaskan rivers, I read Richard Mathews *The Yukon*, the story of that great waterway.

Needless to say, all of the people in this book are completely fictional and are based on no living persons. Although the names of most of the steamers, such as the *Alki*, *Nora*, *Ora* and *Hannah*, were real, their captains and crew are completely fictional.

The quotation by David B. Wharton is from *The Alaska Gold Rush*, published by Indiana University Press in 1972, and is reprinted with their permission.

I would like to thank the members of the Detroit Women Writers, especially Vera Henry and Margaret Duda, for their warm encouragement. My father, Will Haughey, gave me help with the boating scenes. Thanks are also due to my agent, John K. Payne, of Lenniger Literary Agency, for everything he has done, and that includes getting me started writing historical fiction in the first place.

🌹 Prologue 🌹

The man crept up the back staircase of the office building, lugging his awkward burden, careful not to spill it. His throat burned as he sucked in great, nervous gasps of air.

His heart slammed inside him, almost making him sick with its strange, pulsating excitement.

He would show them. By God, he'd show them . . .

He heard a noise. His heart leaped; the inside of his chest convulsed as if he'd been shot. Then, controlling himself, he looked furtively around.

Nothing. It had been nothing but a creaking in the old boards of the building, that was all. No one had seen him. And, if he were careful, no one would. Not until it was too late . . .

Ila Hill leaned back in the dusty old chair in the back room of Papa's office and narrowed her eyes at the room's one tall window.

She wasn't supposed to be here, she knew, but she didn't care. She was filled with tight, sharp anger. No matter how big a fuss she caused, she would refuse! She would *not* make a debut and join the crowds of other girls, hundreds of them, who followed the old traditions as meekly as sheep. And Mama could huff and puff as much as she pleased about it.

A blast of air made the window molding rattle. From

below on State Street arose the clatter of a cable car, the clop of horses' hooves. More faintly came the cries of the little boys who hawked matches from boxes strapped around their necks.

The sounds all seemed cold ones, December ones. Ila closed her eyes and shivered. She shouldn't have come here, of course. More and more often these days Mama told her how selfish and willful she was. "Secretive" was the word Mama used most often, staring at Ila with a puzzled expression, as if she had reared a changeling and was just now discovering it.

Yes, there was constant clashing between herself and Mama; it never seemed to stop. Ila felt constrained, smothered by her life and bursting with her hidden anger. She had to get away, had to go somewhere to be alone and think. Fortunately it had been easy, this morning, to filch the office key from Papa's dressing table, to persuade Cardovan, Papa's driver (he had more than once eyed her brilliant auburn hair) to drive her downtown. And today was Saturday; Papa dismissed his office staff at twelve. So she had all afternoon, and as much privacy as she could wish.

Impatiently Ila reached out and tapped one of the keys of the new Remington typewriting machine which Papa temporarily stored here in the back room. The machine was black and shiny, and smelled faintly of machine oil. It was a pleasant, rather masculine odor that made Ila think of business, the outside world and freedom.

I, she typed. *Ila.* Then she slid the chair forward so that she could reach the keys more easily. *Ila Hill, your correspondent,* she typed painstakingly. *Ila Hill, writing this article to you from Paris . . .*

Abruptly her right forefinger slipped and five of the metal keys were clumped together. Ila stared at the typewriter in dismay.

"Damn," she said. It was a word Mama loathed. "Damn, damn, damn." She reached out and gave the mass of metal a hard prod. Then, when the keys still would not separate, she flung herself out of the chair in a swish of taffeta underskirts and stood by the window.

"Silly old typewriter," she muttered to herself. "Doing that to me." She gave a little kick at the table that supported the machine, and had the satisfaction of seeing it wobble precariously.

Well, it didn't matter, she assured herself. She had broken the machine, she was almost sure she had. But Papa could always buy another one, couldn't he? Papa was rich. He owned one of the biggest barge shipping businesses on Lake Michigan; he shipped lumber just about everywhere. Surely he could afford one stupid type-writing machine.

She looked out at the street below. Even on Saturday, State Street, lined with formidable baroque-style build-ings, was ceaselessly busy. Men swinging briefcases half-ran to be out of the wind, or jaywalked along the brick pavement bisected by cable-car tracks. Women shoppers were bent forward into the moisture-laden Lake Michi-gan wind.

The corner of State and Madison was one of the world's busiest corners, Papa said. Often traffic snarled up here into a fearsome mélange of trolleys, drays, bug-gies, spring wagons, horses and people. But this was also the world, she reminded herself fiercely. Things hap-pened here. Real things.

While she, Ila Hill, whose brother was a journalist and traveled all over the world, had to be content to settle meekly for a debut and a "season" and meeting carefully screened, proper young men from whom she would be expected to choose a husband.

I won't, she thought again. Anger still pushed through her, hard, cold and yet helpless, for she did not know where to direct it. At her mother? At Chicago society, so hidebound in its dullness, its rules and traditions? Or at Quade, her brother, who could escape from it all and do exactly as he pleased simply because he was male?

Her eyes focused on the figure of a fashionably dressed girl disappearing beneath the awning of a millinery shop across on Madison. The shop had a fanciful gilt eagle suspended on wires over its doorway. Two elegant glass display cases topped with scrollwork sat on the sidewalk outside.

Where are you going, you foolish girl? Ila called si-lently to the hurrying figure. *Are you going to buy a pretty hat for your coming-out ball? Are you going to*

dance the night away in someone's arms? She laughed to
herself, harshly.

It was then that she heard the noise.

It came from the room opening off the typewriter
cubby-hole, a larger office which held big wooden cabi-
nets filled with the voluminous account books and records
of her father's business. There was also a big table on
which work could be spread out, and an enormous curtain desk for Papa's clerk, with fifty pigeon holes, each
stuffed with papers.

The sound was an odd one, almost as if liquid were
being sloshed out of a bucket or container. A stealthy
noise, evil somehow, and hasty.

Ila stiffened, one hand clutched to her chest, her fingers
splayed against the cameo brooch which she wore pinned
at the high neck of her white shirtwaist blouse. Instinctively she knew that whoever was making those noises
must not have heard her at the typewriting machine and
thought himself alone in the office.

The gurgling, splashing noise continued. Footsteps
creaked on the oak flooring as if the person—whoever
he was—was moving about, pouring fluid on the floor.

Pouring liquid! The sound was so foreign, so grotesque,
that Ila could not believe she was really hearing it. Her
heart froze as she thought of what Papa would say when
he found out. *Careless,* he would accuse her. *Careless girl.*
First the typewriting machine, and now this, letting someone steal into Papa's office to pour water all over it.

Or was it water? *And what was that smell?*

Of course it was water, she admonished herself, pushing away the horrible thought that began to come to her.
This was all merely a practical joke dreamed up by someone who had a rather eccentric sense of humor, and
who—

No, she thought. It wasn't a joke at all. This was a
cold December afternoon; there was snow on the wind.
Anyone with any sense was hurrying toward buggy or
cable car, toward home and to tea and warmth; not playing pranks.

She should go and see who was there, she thought
numbly. But she didn't want to. She didn't want to do that
at all. She stood paralyzed, torn between looking out the

window, with its view of State Street and normality, and thinking about the outer room, from which the sounds came. Her hands were perspiring now, and her right forefinger dug into the raised edges of the cameo, which depicted a woman's face carved in serene, enchanting repose.

The sound of pouring stopped. Then there was a sharp scrape. It was a noise Ila knew well, for Papa smoked a pipe and refilled it frequently. Then there was another noise, one she had never heard before, a whooshy, licking, frightening roar.

And then came another sound, that of a bubbly scream. It was her own.

The terror, which had been clogged in her like wax, suddenly liquefied. It poured like hot grease through her veins. In one gasping, wild, convulsive movement, Ila Hill ran toward the doorway.

A man stood there. He was bent forward, clawing frantically at his right hand, which was on fire. He was, Ila saw with nightmarish clarity, Papa's office clerk. And ringed about him in a semicircle was a belt of orange-red flames, cutting off her passage to him.

She was trapped.

"Oh, God."

She sucked in some air. Her fingers cut into the brooch. *Fire!* This wasn't supposed to happen, one corner of her mind cried. She was Ila Hill. Things like this didn't happen. Not to her.

The man clawed again at his burning hand, then buried it in the fabric of his high-collared white shirt and snuffed out the flames.

For a moment, against the eerie orange flicker of flames, their eyes met. His pupils were wide; huge black circles filled with . . . *lust?* Oh, God, it couldn't be, but it was . . .

"No!" Ila screamed. It was as if she could see herself dead . . . Oh, God, he was taking it away from her, all of it, the future, the world, everything, everything . . .

Hatred filled her, filled up every crevice of her body, welling upward from her toes like a powerful river, flowing onward and onward . . .

"No, no!" she screamed as the flames bridged a gap

and leaped toward her, as her hem caught fire. *"Nonono . . . oh, God, not me . . . no . . . I hate I hateIhate IhateIhate . . ."* The fire came for her.

Later, when Cardovan, the surrey driver, climbed the stairs and identified her body, her charred fingers were still clutched around the peaceful figure on the cameo brooch.

Part 1

❧ Chapter 1 ❧

The man stared at her, his eyes bold and calculating.

He was mentally undressing her; Cordelia Stewart was certain of it.

She flushed, nearly dropping her camera as she moved it on its tripod to get a better view of the milling activity on the waterfront A brisk bay wind whipped at the folds of her dove-gray skirt, showing the frothy edge of a cambric petticoat trimmed in Valenciennes lace.

Was it, she wondered, the camera which had caught his attention? It *was* unusual for a woman to be here alone at the waterfront, lugging around a big folding camera as if she knew exactly what to do with it.

Or was it the rumpled condition of her hair? The focusing cloth did tilt her rose-trimmed straw hat askew. She felt awkward and disheveled, not at all certain she liked the boldness of that stare. Or, lounging by a shabby black buggy, the man himself, short and paunchy, with pale, unhealthy skin, as if he never saw the sunlight.

Still—she knew that she did make a charming picture, dressed as she was in her walking suit and elbow-length cape trimmed with black satin braid. The flared, elegant skirt for its entire length was lined with romain silk which made a voluptuous rustle when she moved. It was the latest fashion, of course, for Papa was generous with his clothing allowance and, in one of his fond moods, had

2

called her his "extravagantly lovely Miss Princess Cordelia."

Not that she was *that* lovely, of course. Papa in his joviality tended to exaggerate. Still, it was pleasurable to be called beautiful, and she was aware that her rich chestnut hair was alive with golden highlights. Piled high on her head in a pompadour, it gave her finely chiseled features a look of fragility.

Her golden-brown eyes—wickedly slanted, Papa said—were feathered with dark lashes and arched over by brows like two delicate wings. Her mouth was full and a bit willful, but could curve into a warm smile. She looked a lot like Papa, people said.

The dove-gray wool stylishly nipped in at her trim waist and flared out generously at bust and hip, making her figure a curved hourglass.

She was on San Francisco's waterfront, the wharves a picture of hectic confusion. Three squat steamers bound for the Yukon were moored in a row, their round smokestacks blackened with soot. The decks of two of them—the *Topeka* and the *Willamette*—were filled with men at work. More men, antlike in dark coats and hats, pushed and shoved to get closer to the ships. There were a few women among them, Corrie (that was her nickname) saw, and they were shoving just as hard. The scene before her would make a good photograph.

She stole another look at the man.

He was still there, staring, a short, rather unpleasant person who looked, Corrie decided, like one of the city's night denizens. Although he was dressed respectably enough, Cordelia observed, his trousers were unpressed and his waistcoat spotted with food.

How dare he eye her like that? What did he want? Well, she would ignore him, she decided . . .

Only half an hour ago, she and Avery Curran, her fiancé, had climbed out of the buggy Avery hired and stood gazing out at the turbulent waterfront scene. Men pushed and shouted. Some lugged huge bags of provisions. Carriages careened among them, their drivers cursing.

"Look at them!" Avery had drawn in his breath

sharply. "Pushing and shoving in order to get to the Yukon. Gold. Think of it, Corrie. All that gold!"

Corrie smiled. Papa, too, talked of gold. In his younger
days Cordell Stewart, owner of the well-known Stewart
Shipyards, had photographed half of the Comstock Lode,
using the old wet-plate process. He still kept a nugget of
gold in his library as a paperweight.

"Did you read in the paper about the man with the
forty-ounce nugget?" Avery asked.

"No, I didn't."

"I heard it was as big as a grapefruit. Bigger." Avery's
expression was glazed, entranced. Corrie's eyes could
not help being drawn to his good looks. With his high,
aristocratic cheekbones, full mouth and cleft chin, his
dreaming gray eyes, Avery was the sort of man women
stared at. Even older women of forty and fifty eyed him
hungrily, as if they would adore to caress him or to stroke
his fine, flowing, blond, luxurious mustache. Avery had
the lean, graceful body and beautifully carved features
of a young god. Or of a knight in an old painting.

Was it his fault that he was so good-looking? Was that
why Papa objected to him so violently?

"Can you imagine it, Corrie? A nugget that big?"
Avery was saying. "Can you imagine what it would feel
like to hold it in your hands?"

But Corrie was barely paying attention to Avery's enthusiasm. Instead, she was thinking of the day when she
had met him. It had been at Madeline DeMoro's wedding. Avery was a distant relative of the bridegroom's, a
student at Harvard Law School. Naturally, every woman
at the big reception had turned to stare at the wildly
good-looking young man with his arresting dark eyes and
aristocratic features. But Avery had eyes only for her.
Cordelia had been immensely flattered when he asked
her to dance.

Defying convention, he danced every dance with her.
He was charming, telling her of his struggle to put himself through college, making it all sound like a rather gay
escapade, hardly work at all.

"Oh, he's a beautiful man," Madeline DeMoro had
whispered to Corrie when they stood near the punch
bowl as the reception was ending. "And his family was

rich—once. But now they're all dead, and he owes pots and pots of money, and it's going to take him years to get his law practice started. Be careful, Corrie!"

"Oh, I will," Corrie promised blithely, making up her mind then and there that she wouldn't be. Avery was exciting, she had never met anyone like him before, he could make her shiver just by looking at her . . .

"Corrie! Cordelia Stewart!" Avery's voice interrupted her. "You haven't been listening to a word I've said!" He turned to her, his dreamy look gone now. "Well, anyway, enough of that. I've got to go now. I've some business to transact."

"So soon? But I wanted to take some photographs! And then I thought we could go and have tea somewhere."

"I don't have time, Corrie. And listen. Tomorrow don't bring that accursed camera with you, all right? People gawk at it so."

An odd pain shot through Corrie. She was a photographer! Didn't Avery understand that? But she pushed aside her hurt feelings.

"Let them, then! Haven't they ever heard of women using cameras?"

"Probably not. And I feel like a fool, tagging along after you and that ugly old black leather box of yours."

"It isn't ugly! Oh, very well," she added, flushing. "I'll stay here by myself then, and get the pictures I want."

"But—"

"Nothing will happen to me, Avery—and besides, I want to take some pictures of this to show Papa."

"Be careful, then; that's my lovely Cordelia." He tilted up her chin with his forefinger. For one shimmering, wild moment she thought he was going to kiss her, right there in public. But then he didn't. "Take a cab home," he advised. "And I love you, Corrie Stewart. Remember that."

She did remember it; how could she possibly forget? But that had been half an hour ago. Avery was gone now, and the little man was edging closer to her. He staggered slightly. Had he been drinking? Uneasily she inserted a new plate and pulled the black focus cloth over her head to shut out the light. She tried to concentrate

on the picture she would take, a three-quarter view of
the *Topeka*.

"Say, miss, how's about takin' a picture of me? How
much you charging for it?"

The voice, loud and close to her, was slurred with
drink.

"I don't take pictures for hire."

"Aw, sure you do. Sure you do!" He lunged closer to
her, his body smell pungent in her nostrils as he knocked
against the leg of her tripod.

"Watch out! Oh, do be careful; that's expensive equipment!"

"Is it, now? Is it as expensive as you are, honey? I
seen you near Sansome—taking pictures in one of the
houses there, you was. I seen you."

"You most certainly did not! I was never on Sansome
Street in my life!" she gasped, taking a step backwards.
Sansome Street was one of the boundaries of the "Barbary Coast" section of San Francisco where, it was whispered, women could be bought for a pinch of gold dust.
Dance halls, "cribs," bawdy houses and worse were there,
places whose evil Cordelia, at eighteen, could not even
imagine. Papa had flatly forbidden her to go near this
area, and he had not minced words in explaining why.

"Weren't you now? I thought I seen you at the Goat
and Compass." The man edged closer, his voice a musky
confiding whisper. "All nekkid and rosy pink you was,
with that there camera of yourn, taking pictures of what
they was doin' on the floor, and then afterwards you lain
down on the floor, too, and then you . . . "

Naked—pictures—Corrie took another step backwards,
her ears not taking in the full meaning of the man's
words, but only the sniggery, oily menace in them, and
the fact that he had taken her for a woman of easy
morals.

"I . . . I'm not what you think at all. And I don't wish
to be bothered any more. Would you please leave, sir?
Or I'll start screaming. I swear I will!"

He moved closer. His hand gripped her upper arm in
a hold surprisingly strong. "Will you, now? And do you
think any of them will hear you?" He gestured toward the
crowds of hurrying men. "They got gold on their minds,

honey, not anything so pretty as you. But me—now, me, I'd notice a pretty girlie. With or without your clothes, I'd have knowed you anywheres."

Suddenly, without warning, he thrust his left hand under the short semicircle of her cape. He began to knead her breasts, his fingers digging at her nipples and pulling at them in an ugly, disgusting way.

It was a violation so abrupt that Corrie could only stand there, frozen and unbelieving. Never had anyone touched her like this. Not even in her bath had she touched her own body so.

She jumped back, trying to twist out of his grip. She opened her mouth to scream, but nightmarishly, no real sound emerged, only a high, frightened squeak.

The man threw back his head and laughed. "Aw, I didn't mean no harm, girlie! You sound like a mouse, you do. Some pretty little mouse! Say, why don't you come on down to Osgood Street with me, eh? I got a place there, I'm gonna open it up, and we could use a girl like you with all that brown goldy hair to give us some class . . . "

"*No!*" Fury and terror welled up in Corrie as she pushed at him, fighting her encumbering skirts to stamp down on his toe with the substantial heel of her kid boot. "Get away from me, get away!"

The man yelped, and Corrie lifted her foot for another kick. This one landed on his kneecap, stinging her toe as much as it hurt him.

"Ow! Dammit, you little whore-bitch! I'll teach you to—"

Corrie looked frantically about for help. No one seemed to have noticed her predicament at all. Men still thronged toward the steamers, lugging bags and packages. Carriages and buggies cut through the crowd, narrowly missing pedestrians. Someone's bag spilled open on the ground to reveal a jumble of clothes.

Again Corrie tried to scream, but her mouth was dry.

"You rotten little whore, I'll teach you to kick! I'll drag you back to my place and I'll put you to work whether you want to or not . . . " The man took a wild swing at Corrie, causing her to dodge backwards, her shoulder smashing into the corner of the camera.

"Leave me alone! Oh, just leave me be!" Now she *was* screaming. Her voice was shaking and unrecognizable. Oh, why didn't someone notice her? What was wrong with all of these hurrying people?

Whiskey smell enveloped her as the man pushed at her, again knocking her into the camera, which began to tilt on its tripod. Frantically Corrie grabbed for it. The Empire State camera had cost her twenty-four dollars, and she'd spent months learning how to use it. No one was going to wreck her camera!

"What the *hell's* going on here?" The voice came from behind her. Corrie felt someone righting the tripod and then a hand beneath her elbow, supporting her. She caught a whiff of cigar smoke and a fainter, indefinable, musky male odor.

Her attacker's glance traveled upward and then his eyes widened. Then, like one of the big, gray wharf rats, he scuttled away, the tail of his coat flopping behind him.

Corrie turned to see who had rescued her.

A pair of bright blue eyes glared down at her, crackling with anger.

"You little fool! What in the name of all that's gracious were you doing down here on the wharf exposing yourself to the likes of that creature?"

Again, Corrie stood stunned, frozen, unable to speak. He was big—nearly six feet four—and muscular and rangy, his huge shoulders nearly bursting out of his dark wool cheviot suit. He had a wide, craggy face with a nose which had once been broken. His forehead was broad and the entire bone structure, from wide jaw to heavy, carved cheekbones, gave the impression of stubborn strength.

Yet his mouth was sensitive, with smile wrinkles around it and at the corners of his eyes, suggesting the man laughed often.

He was certainly not laughing now. With one swift motion, he grabbed for Corrie's camera. To her shock, he began to dismantle it, folding the tripod, plainly intending to put the camera back in its carrying case.

"What are you doing?" Her voice was a squeak. "You can't—you have no right to touch my camera—"

"Maybe I have no right, but someone's got to look out

for you. Obviously you're not capable of doing it yourself." He half-knelt to manipulate the camera case, his hands moving efficiently. Corrie noticed the fabric of his suit strain across his shoulders.

Corrie rushed at him, beating at his hands. "I can look after myself perfectly well, thank you, without any assistance from strange men I meet on the streets! I'm a photographer!" she raged. "I'm accustomed to carrying my camera about, and I've been doing it for quite some time now, with no help!"

He did not seem to hear her, but continued to pack the camera into its case, methodically fastening the leather strap.

"There," he said. His intensely blue eyes glinted, as if he was amused at her. "All packed away safely."

"But I don't want it packed away! I want to take some more pictures of the Yukon steamers! I promised Papa I'd take them! I— Oh, damn you!" she sputtered, in her helpless fury calling on her father's vocabulary.

The man stood up, one corner of his mouth twitching. He picked up the camera case, hefting it as if it weighed very little. "Come, come. Where did you learn to speak such disgraceful language? You, my dear, in addition to being foolish and reckless, are certainly no lady."

"What? Why, I certainly am! I'm more of a lady than you are a *gentleman*. And I don't want my camera picked up, and I don't want—"

"You don't want to do anything, do you? You're a very stubborn girl, aren't you? And very opinionated, I'd say." He linked his left arm through hers and urged her toward the street, where a number of surreys and buggies waited with horses stamping their hooves restlessly.

"No!" she cried. "No, I don't want to go! And I won't!" She tried to drag her feet, but he was pulling her along firmly, his arm half lifting her. "What are you doing? Where—where are you taking me? I don't want to go anywhere, I tell you. I haven't finished my pictures—"

"You've finished them for today."

They were at the row of black buggies parked along the street. One of them, drawn by two matched chestnut mares, stood empty. It was watched over by the driver of a beer delivery-wagon.

"Thanks," Corrie's captor said, tossing the man a coin. "In you go, girl. And home as fast as I can get you. Unless you'd like to try taking a photograph of the interior of a brothel on Kearny Street. Would you enjoy that accomplishment?"

To her dismay he easily lifted her into the buggy as if she weighed less than the camera. He shoved the camera case in after her. "Keep it steady," he ordered. "We don't want to damage it."

"Damage it?" Never had Corrie felt so angry, so helpless to assert herself. "We're not going to damage it because I'm not going home with you! I've not finished my work! I'm going to get out right now, and—"

"No, you're not."

With a swift, easy movement, the big man swung himself into the buggy, lifted the reins, and clucked to the horses. Instantly they were moving along the uneven street, twisting in and out of the crush of carriages, vans, wagons and surreys, aiming to where the city occupied its hills, gray and cream houses marched upward in rows of planes and angles.

Cordelia Stewart gave the man a sidelong look. Sitting next to her, he appeared even bigger than before. His wide shoulders took up a great deal of room against the padded buggy seat-back. He was so bulky and muscular that he made Corrie, who was a relatively tall girl, feel small. He would, she thought furiously, make Avery Curran look underfed.

And yet—she eyed him again—oddly his mouth was gentle, and his hands were sensitively formed and well-shaped, the hands of a gentleman.

"I live on Nob Hill," she said in a low voice. "Since I see that you're determined to take me home no matter what preference I might have."

"And what's wrong with being taken home? Sounds like a good place for you today."

He flashed her a wide grin that creased his whole face and gave him an appealingly boyish look.

"But I don't *want* to go home!" She touched the camera case, assuring herself that all was well with it. Then her hand flew to her chestnut-gold hair, pushing its fine, soft looseness up under the dubious confinement of her rose-trimmed hat.

"Your hair looks fine," the man said maddeningly. "And its color blends magnificently with those beautiful, tawny eyes of yours."

"Indeed. I'm *not* worried about my hair!"

"Aren't you?" The blue eyes gleamed with mischief as he spurred the mares up the gradual slope of the street. "A true lady would always have perfectly kept hair, even when she is being approached by gentlemen of the streets who are not gentleman at all."

She gave him a sharp look. Then, in spite of herself, she felt some of the tension leave her body. She sank back against the padded seat, beginning vaguely to enjoy herself. This man was teasing her. Well, she could cope with that. Papa was an incorrigible tease, and over the years had tested her often.

She would ignore him, she decided. Let his taunts fall off her like rain off a fur coat. Anyway, she assured herself, she would soon be home and rid of him.

"It is kind of you to be so interested in the welfare of a girl to whom you haven't been formally introduced," she said at last, tartly.

"Quade Hill, journalist, at your service." He made her a mock bow, his lips twitching again as if he were trying to force back another wide smile.

"And I'm Cordelia Stewart." Did she see his eyes narrow slightly? "Most people call me Corrie, though. We live on Mason Street."

"Near the Crocker home?"

"Yes, close enough."

She had been named after Papa, Cordell Stewart, who wanted a son and had to be satisfied with a girl. But Mama had thought "Cordelia" sounded too grown-up for the harum-scarum little girl she had been, so it became Corrie. Though her mama was dead, her nickname remained.

They were both silent for a moment as the buggy jogged over the rough-textured brick. As the carriage hit a bump, Corrie felt the bulk of his shoulders press against her. Again she was uncomfortably aware of his bigness, his vitality.

"And did you enjoy your encounter with Rabbit-foot McGee?" she heard him ask.

"Rabbit-foot McGee?"

"Yes, the gentleman whose foot you were trying to squash into jelly."

"Oh!" She recovered herself. "No, I didn't enjoy it. But that's never happened to me before. No one has ever bothered me like that before."

"Then you've been lucky."

They were at California Street now. Expertly he guided the buggy around a cable car which clattered upward past them on its tracks, laden with dark-coated men sitting decorously within. The street, lined with heavy Victorian buildings bristling with turrets, bay windows and gazebos, seemed to flash before Corrie's eyes. The tilt of the street had become more pronounced and the mares strained against the harnesses. A skid or a wrong step could send horses, buggy and occupants careening disastrously downward. But this was a fact Corrie seldom thought about. She had grown up on steep streets, and took them for granted.

Quade Hill leaned toward her. "Watch your camera, so it doesn't tilt out of the buggy."

Her fingers tightened on the black case.

He added, "I'm surprised that you've never run into anyone like Rabbit-foot before. That is, if you make a habit of wandering about with your camera as you did today."

"What a strange name," she said.

"He got it because he carries a rabbit's foot about with him, of course. He thinks it brings him luck. He'll need a lot of luck to open his next place; I understand that his last one burned down just at the height of the festivities one night. Two of the lady occupants were angry at each other and tried to tear each other's hair out by the roots. Someone knocked over a lamp, and poof! Four people were killed, I believe. Rabbit wasn't among them, worse luck. Now he's hit hard times, and is trying to make a come-back."

"How do you know such things? Are you a friend of this—this Rabbit-foot man?"

"Friend? No. But I do happen to know, Miss Stewart, that a man like Rabbit-foot McGee is a very dangerous person to be around if you are young and pretty and wearing a little hat trimmed with yellow roses. He eats

up pretty young women! Haven't you any conception of
that, you little idiot? There are Chinese girls over on
Grant Avenue who are kept virtual slaves—*slaves*, do
you hear me? And any lovely woman who is unwary
might find herself in a similar situation. Don't you realize what he was saying to you? He could have put you
in his buggy and dragged you back to that place of his,
Miss Stewart. He could have thrown you down a stairwell somewhere, and locked you in a room, and . . . "

He stopped. Corrie saw that his face was flushed with
anger.

"Oh, I didn't realize . . . " She remembered the man's
whiskey stench, the way his fingers had kneaded and
pulled at her nipples. Abruptly a cold fright washed over
her, a fear more vivid than when she had actually been
facing him.

"I'm sorry. I shouldn't have been so explicit. Your face
is practically white."

"No, I— That's all right."

She sat rigid in the buggy, not seeing the gray and tan
and yellow of the solid mansions with their gingerbread
ornamentation, not seeing anything. He had been right,
she thought numbly. After all, he had been right.

She didn't look at him again. They drove in silence until they reached her father's house.

🌹 Chapter 2 🌹

Susan Raleigh, Corrie's aunt, sat by the bay window, overhung with trailing plants, of the second-floor sitting room. She looked up from her cut-work embroidery in time to see Corrie alight from the buggy with a strange man.

The man—big and rather formidable-looking, although dressed like a gentleman—handed the girl her camera. Then he bowed and sat in the buggy watching appreciatively as Corrie rushed up the walk, both hands clutched around her camera as if someone were trying to take it from her. Corrie's cheeks, Susan noticed, were flushed with hectic color. Her full skirts almost flew as she ran. And she barely glanced at the man, not even stopping to thank him for the ride.

What now? Susan thought, suppressing a smile of amusement. Many years ago, she herself had been a wild beauty like Corrie, full of high, irrepressible spirits. She had had a twenty-inch waist and deep auburn hair. She smiled to herself, thinking of all the tongues she had set to wagging, the gossip she had generated.

But that was long ago. Now her waist was thicker—although not by much—and her hair was salt-and-pepper, streaked with gray. Susan was forty-eight and widowed. Five years ago she had come to San Francisco to live with her elder brother, Cordell, who had recently lost his own wife, Gwen, and was left with a motherless thirteen-year-old daughter to rear.

And it had all worked. She herself had always wanted

a child to mother. Corrie had taken to Susan immediately, and the feeling had been mutual. Young Corrie was a warm, loving creature, full of laughter and enthusiasm.

Yet despite her exuberance, the girl was obedient as well. And it was not her fault that her father allowed her to roam about the city as if she were a boy.

Once Susan had tried to discuss this with Cordell Stewart. Her brother laughed in her face. "I'm glad she's independent, Susan. I wouldn't want a daughter who was like some of the simpering little beauties I've seen."

"You've always wanted a son, haven't you?" she retorted. "Well, Corrie isn't a son, and can't ever be. She is a very pretty and desirable girl. You can't take her and—"

"Enough. I can do exactly as I please with her. And she suits me as she is. I'll thank you to see she's properly dressed and fed and has decent manners. You can teach her to paint watercolors and play the piano, if you wish. As for the rest, leave it to me."

So, secretly admiring her brother's stand, Susan endeavored to teach the headstrong girl the proper manners of a young lady. Now, putting aside her embroidery, Susan hurried downstairs. She could hear voices coming from Cordell's first-floor library. He had gotten out of bed today and had someone with him. By the loud shouts penetrating the heavy oak door, Susan knew that—as usual— Cordell was disagreeing with his guest.

She came upon Corrie in the foyer. The girl had set her camera case down and had turned to the ornate, gilt-edged mirror. She was leaning toward the glass, inspecting her own face as if she had never seen it before.

Susan caught her breath. Her niece—as yet—had no real conception of her own appeal. True, her face did not have the smooth, oval, soft prettiness so much in fashion today. Instead, Corrie's face possessed a boldness in the cut of the cheeks and jaw, a delicate sensuality. Her coloring was high and exquisite, her tilted eyes a smoldering amber that would challenge any man.

Soon enough, Susan thought with a sigh. *Soon enough.*

"Corrie. Who was that man who dropped you off?"

Her niece looked up, eyes blank.

"Pardon me, Aunt Susan?"

"I asked who was that man who dropped you off in front of the house? Have we met him before?"

"No, Aunt," Corrie said resignedly, clasping her hands together and preparing for the interrogation that was to come.

"Had you been introduced to him, then?"

Corrie hesitated. "Yes . . . in a way . . . "

Susan knew Corrie never lied, but had been known, on occasion, to omit part of the truth. Before the girl could explain, a bellow came from the library where Cordell Stewart was entertaining his guest.

"Coffee, Susan, coffee! Where is that consarned Li Hua this morning, anyway? Keep a houseful of servants and then try to find one when you want her! Where have they all gone, anyway, out on a boat in the Bay? Susan, would you see if you can find— Oh, and we want some brandy too. Brandy would be just the thing . . . "

"Yes, Cordell." She expelled her breath in a long sigh. Bea Ellen, the laundress, was sick today. So Susan had set Li Hua, the upstairs maid, to pressing petticoats and ruffles. Where was the girl? Giggling with the ice man again? If so, she would . . .

Susan hurried off down the polished, wallpapered corridor, intent on the whereabouts of Li Hua. She forgot the problem of Corrie. She did not see her niece step again to the mirror and inspect herself in it, her mouth straight and somber and trembling slightly.

Corrie stared into the glass, her eyes focused on the girl who gazed back at her. Her cheeks were flushed apricot and her golden-brown eyes looked dark and frightened. Gradually she brought her quick breathing under control. She reached up and unpinned the hat, then smoothed her heavy chestnut-honey hair drawn up into its fashionable pompadour, and reset the pins and combs that kept it in place.

She shouldn't have accepted a ride from that impudent man, she told herself. Why on earth had she? She should have insisted on being let out. Now she had arrived home shaken and upset, with most of her photographs untaken.

She pressed her lips together, biting the lower one until it stung. Something about that Quade Hill—his bigness, his rough, vital energy—had been vastly disturbing. He

was so very male and confident. Too confident, she
thought. To sweep up a strange girl the way he had done,
to practically kidnap her into his buggy, to drive her
home against her will, and, worst of all, to frighten her
with hideous stories of what could have happened to
her if he *hadn't* done all that.

She was only thankful she was not planning to marry
a man so domineering and unpleasant. Avery's manners
were smooth and impeccable. Even though he was as yet
only a struggling law student, Avery was a real gentleman. Never, she told herself, would Avery Curran sweep
a girl into a carriage and drive away with her as if she
was a sack of wheat!

As her fingers adjusted the last hairpin, she became
aware that voices were coming from her father's library.
So he was up today, she thought. The pains from what
he insisted was his chronic indigestion were getting worse
each day. Although both Corrie and Susan had begged
him to consult a physician, he had refused.

"I don't need one of those foolish bleeders and pokers
to shake his head at me and tell me I've been drinking
too much for the past forty years. If I want that kind of
advice, I can give it to myself, dammit!"

By the time Corrie had her hair smoothed and her
face under control, she had nearly forgotten the outra-
geous man in the buggy. The incident was finished and
she would never see him again; why bother to think about
it? She left her camera by the base of the staircase and
decided to go to the kitchen to see if Mrs. Parsons, the
cook, had saved anything for her luncheon.

She started down the corridor, her fingers pulling at
the fastenings of her cape and tossing it on a chair. As
she passed the door of her father's library, the voices assailed her. Some of the words were distinct.

" . . . big business, syndicates. They are the people
who moved in and made the money in California and
Colorado and Nevada, and they are the ones who'll be
making the money—the real money—in Alaska too!" A
young man's voice, loud and intense.

"Big business, my hind foot. It's the little man who's
going to find the nugget as big as his head, dammit. I
should know that; I spent enough years in Virginia City.

As for big business, I need you to be right here in San Francisco, not thinking about the Klondike. I've got ships to build, sailing ships! Ships to take the men where they want to go!"

That was her father. His companion was Donald Earle, manager of the Stewart Shipyards for the past year, and an employee there for the previous four.

An involuntary smile crossed Corrie's face, then quickly faded. Despite his protests, she knew that Papa yearned to go to Alaska himself. He kept track of every headline in the papers that screamed *gold*. But if he could not go, then he didn't want anyone else to go, either. And especially not Donald, his hand-picked successor in the shipyard.

Donald was thirty-five years old. Five years ago he had presented himself at the Stewart Shipyards, announcing his willingness to work hard at anything. "Work hard" was a phrase guaranteed to appeal to Cordell Stewart, who could toil like a team of horses himself and expected the same behavior from everyone else. Donald had stayed. And he worked, if anything, harder than Papa. Two years ago he had pushed Papa aside just as he was about to be overrun by a pair of bolting dray horses. Papa had never forgotten that. Now Donald had her father's trust, and was as close to him as anyone not his son could be.

Now Corrie brushed on past the door to the library, trying not to listen further. Most girls thought Donald good-looking, she knew, with his suntanned complexion and dark eyes, muscular body and confident walk. But to Corrie, his skin seemed too red and blotchy, his lips too full and stubborn and the look in his black eyes too intense. She found him rather fat around the waist and thought he walked with an overbearing brashness.

Corrie continued on into the kitchen area. In the back of the house were the big pantries, the storage rooms, the laundry and housekeeping office. But the center of it all was the kitchen, with its big steel range and warm odor of baking rolls.

Mrs. Parsons, the cook, was in the housekeeping office, making out orders. Corrie sank down at the kitchen table and thought about Donald, how he looked at her in such a disturbing way. He never did it when Papa was about, but then, he had a sly way of getting around Papa, of charming him. And last week Donald had begun hinting to her of something even worse: marriage.

The thought made her squirm. Marriage! But it was impossible, of course. Avery Curran was the man she loved, not Donald.

She finished her luncheon, a cold roast beef sandwich made with crusty French bread, and some apricot cake which she washed down with fresh milk. On her way toward the front stairs, she paused in the foyer to pick up her camera when Donald Earle came bursting past her.

His tanned face was reddened with annoyance, his stubborn mouth twisted. As usual, his stride was forceful, and he tossed his glossy black hair out of his eyes impatiently. Today, it seemed, had not been one of his days to charm Papa.

"Corrie!"

"What do you want, Donald?"

She lifted the camera and gave him a level look. For five years now (it seemed those monthly dinners were a fixture in her life) Aunt Susan had been urging her to be more civil toward Donald. But she couldn't pretend something she didn't feel. And it seemed that her very coldness spurred him on.

"Corrie, come for a walk with me!"

"Now?" She was dismayed. "No, thank you. I have to go up to my darkroom and develop these plates. I just took them and they need——"

Donald gave an impatient shrug, and his big shoulder muscles wriggled under the smooth serge of his coat.

"Oh, surely you have time for a short walk. Your pictures can wait. I don't see why you bother with them, anyway. You don't get paid for them and nobody else wants them. And it's a wonder you don't get into trouble when you're wandering about with that camera——"

"Oh, be still! I don't care!" she snapped, stung. First Avery and then that Quade Hill man. Now here was Donald, continuing the same theme. Today's incident had badly scared her. She didn't want to be reminded of it any further.

"I'm going upstairs to develop my photographs," she repeated.

"Corrie. Listen, Corrie—" To her surprise, he was gripping her by the arm, his fingers squeezing into her flesh.

"Stop that; you're pinching me, Donald Earle!"

He let go of her. "Sorry. It's just that I must talk to you, Corrie. Something has come up. There's something I've wanted to say to you for a good long time now. And you've got to hear me out."

"Donald, I really haven't time—"

His black eyes flashed, his full lips twisting. "I have something to talk about, and I certainly can't do it here. I'd like our discussion to be private."

Corrie sighed. "Very well." She reached for her cape and wrapped it around herself, quickly closing the black satin strap fastenings. Rapidly she pinned on her hat. She wouldn't walk long with Donald, she told herself. Just long enough to hear what he had to say, and tell him no.

As he held the front door open for her, she saw that he was looking down at her, his eyes full of heavy, demanding desire.

"I want you to be my wife," Donald said.

They had been walking downhill for some minutes now, the city spread out before them, sunlight glancing off brick and stucco, peaked roofs, towers and baroque balconies. But Corrie had seen all of this before and barely noticed it; all she could think of was Donald's shocking statement.

I want you to be my wife. Waves of dismay radiated through her. And yet, she told herself wildly, she should have expected this. She had known for a long time— years, really—that Donald was attracted to her.

"Marriage?" She said this slowly, wondering how to frame her refusal.

"Yes, marriage! What's wrong with that? I want you, Cordelia. I've wanted you ever since the day I first met you. How old were you then, thirteen? But even then you were showing signs of becoming a woman, and I knew that I'd have you, that one day you'd be mine."

Corrie could only stare at him. The young men she knew did not talk this way. And she was chilled by the thought of Donald looking at her and desiring her while she was still in the innocence of childhood.

"You can't be serious," she managed. "I—I was only a child . . . "

"A little girl, yes. But ripe. Already ripe." Again Donald's eyes filled with heavy-lidded desire, and he took her arm with a sensuous movement. Uneasily, Corrie moved away.

"Don't touch me!" If only this were Avery, she was thinking. How eagerly she would submit to his caresses.

Donald's face darkened as he let his hand drop to his side. "You've always been cold to me, haven't you, Corrie? When I came to dinner, you pretended that you didn't notice me, that you didn't care much for me. But that doesn't matter now. Marriage will change you, my dear, and you'll be only too happy to have a real man who can teach you what life is all about."

"But I don't want to learn about life from you! I'm already—" However, before she could go on to tell him of her engagement to Avery, he had stopped in the center of the sloping sidewalk and pulled her to him, ignoring the stares of a gardener setting plants in a window box across the street.

"Donald!" she gasped. "Please—not in the street. You know it's bad manners to—"

"To hell with bad manners. I want you, Corrie, and I mean to have you. Have you any idea of what it's like to come to your house once a month and to see you there, marriageable and ready? Ready, Corrie, ready! You're a woman now, you're eighteen, and I've waited five years for that. And I'm the one who's going to have you, not some—"

"You are *not!*" With furious effort Corrie pushed at him and succeeded in loosening his grip around her, although his arms still clasped her.

"Oh, I'll have you, all right. One way or another, Corrie. And I'm willing to wait for that privilege. Not, of course, that I'll have to wait for long."

"What do you mean?" she whispered.

"I mean that your father approves of my marrying you. He's fond of me; he's come to accept me almost as a son. I think he would like to have me in the family. And since he only has one daughter—well, I think the conclusion is obvious, don't you?"

"No, I don't! Papa would never—why, he'd never encourage me to marry someone like you, someone I don't even love. You're talking utter nonsense, Donald Earle. And I've heard quite enough. I want to go home. I'm going to turn around and go right now."

"No." He had taken her arm and was pulling her down a narrow side street. The wooden frame houses were close together, casting a dark shadow into the street itself. "No, Corrie, I haven't finished our talk yet. And I don't intend to take you home until I do."

"But I'm finished!" she cried. "I've told you that I don't want to marry you, and that should finish it. What more is there to say?"

"Just this: I want you, Corrie Stewart, and I've always wanted you. I've dreamed of nothing but you for the past five years, and I plan to have you, whether you wish it or not. And I will have you. I'm very close to it right now."

"What do you mean by that?"

"Just what I said."

"You're lying! I'm going to go and tell Papa what you've said to me. I'll tell him—"

"You'll do no such thing." Again Donald's hand roughly encircled her arm. His face glared down at her, twisted with anger—and, yes, with pleasure, too. Pleasure in the little game they were playing, in the distress and shock she was showing, in her futile efforts to wriggle out of his grasp.

"I will so tell Papa!" she stormed. "I'll tell him anything I please! After all, he's my papa, he loves me, and he'll listen to me. All you are is his employee," she went on recklessly. "*I* come first with him!"

"Do you?" Now Donald was openly laughing, his eyes narrowed, and Corrie felt a stab of real fright.

"What are you saying? What do you mean?"

"In the first place, little girl, I think you'd better know something. Your father is dying. That so-called 'indigestion' he's been complaining about is a tumor in his stomach. I've been told that on good authority by a competent physician."

"No, you're wrong!" She felt as if he had lifted up a hammer and slammed it down on her skull. She felt dizzy; the old frame buildings seemed to whirl about her. "But . . . dying?" she thought. "He can't be! Donald's wrong. Oh, not Papa. Not Papa."

As she took deep, gasping breaths of air, she collected her thoughts. "How do you know that? Papa's always refused to see a doctor."

Donald's black eyes glittered. "He didn't have to. Last week he took me to a saloon after work and while he was drinking he confided to me that he's been having severe pains in his belly and has been coughing up blood. The next morning I went to a doctor I know and I told him what your father had said. He made a diagnosis. It was that simple. Your father only has a month or so to live."

"But how could a doctor diagnose Papa when he hasn't even seen him? Oh, this is all preposterous!" Corrie floundered on, her voice high and shaking.

"Do you doubt the truth? I'd wager your father has lost twenty pounds in the past month. He looks terrible. He's been in bed more than he's been out of it. That man is dying, and there isn't a thing anyone can do about it."

Corrie stared at Donald, at the expression of satisfaction on his face. "Why, you're happy about it, aren't you? You're *glad.*"

"Nonsense. I feel as badly about it as you do."

"You're lying!" There was a hard, unyielding lump in Corrie's throat, telling her that Donald was right about one thing, anyway. Papa was very ill. He had lost weight. But he certainly wasn't dying! No, that just was not true. Cordell Stewart was too alive, too vital, ever to die.

She went on shakily, "I should go home and . . . "

"And what? Tell your father he's dying? You won't do that, Corrie. And you won't go home and tell him anything else I've said, either. Do you know why?"

Donald had pulled her close again and she could see every small detail of his face: the full, determined mouth, the hard, black eyes, the squared, rigid jaw, and the glossy black hair.

"Because, Corrie, he doesn't want to believe he's dying. And he won't believe anything you say to him about me. He likes me. He depends on me. You don't know how hard I've worked to achieve that. And nobody is going to ruin it now. Do you hear that? Not you and not anyone. Because the doctor told me that any shock, any emotional shock, could kill him. And you don't want to be the one responsible for killing your papa, do you?"

"No! Oh, no, don't even suggest such a thing!"

"This doctor told me that with the amount of bleeding and pain your father has, it's only sheer courage that has kept him going this long. Anything could kill him now. That's why you're going to go home like a nice, sweet young lady, tell him about our engagement, and you're not going to utter one word of complaint about me to him. Not one."

For long minutes they continued to walk while Corrie tried to recover from the shock of what she had just heard. Donald wanting to marry her. Her papa dying. Oh, it was a nightmare!

She struggled to get feelings of panic and fear under control. "You're using my father's health to threaten me," she said at last, her voice so low and flat that she didn't recognize it.

"Am I?"

"Yes, you are! And I don't intend to let you. I have no plans to marry you, no matter what happens. Whether Papa lives or dies."

"You will marry me."

"I've told you, I won't!"

For answer, Donald reached into his waistcoat pocket and pulled something out. It was a small object that winked and glittered even in the shadowed street, catching the afternoon light and throwing it back in glittering shards. It was, Corrie saw numbly, an engagement ring, a large diamond encased in a heavy, ornate setting.

She stared at it, feeling as if this were all a dream. Any minute now she would wake up and discover that she was lying on the bed in her own room, that she had been napping. No, this wasn't real. It couldn't be. It was Avery Curran she loved, Avery. She had her wedding all planned . . .

"This is yours," Donald said. "Go on. Put it on. I bribed your maid to measure your ring finger one night while you were sleeping. So it should fit." He thrust the ring into her hand.

"No." Her eyes would not leave the winking, somehow evil beauty of the ring. "I don't want it. I won't wear it."

"You'll wear it. Oh, you'll wear it happily enough."

But before Corrie could force her stiff lips to reply, Donald had wheeled about on his heels and was striding on ahead of her, cutting across the dirt and down another side street. He was gone.

Corrie's fingers tested the hardness of the ring, the faceted, almost oily surface of the diamond.

She hesitated.

Then, impulsively, she raised her right arm and threw the ring as hard as she could. In a flash of reflected light, it flew across the street and landed in the midst of a heap of refuse piled near a doorway.

🌺 Chapter 3 🌺

You'll wear it. Oh, you'll wear it happily enough.

For one wretched instant Corrie stood staring numbly at the heap of trash into which she had thrown the ring. Suddenly it was as if she could hear Aunt Susan's sweet, measured voice in her ear. *To throw away a valuable ring is wasteful, my dear. Criminally wasteful.* And she could see Donald's face, too, swollen with anger. *You'll wear it . . .*

Corrie drew a deep breath. Abruptly, she ran across the street. Choking back tears, she knelt in the dirt and began to push through the garbage and dust, wondering where the ring could have gone. Had it somehow fallen into the neck of a broken beer bottle? Or into some crack in the damp earth? And why couldn't she have been content to toss the ring away and forget it, as Papa would have done?

She choked back a half-hysterical laugh. Five years of being raised by Aunt Susan had made its mark on her after all. In spite of herself, she was being sensible.

With increasing desperation, she turned over the moisture-soaked bits of newspaper, the gummy glass bottles, the stained, unspeakable rags. But she did not find the ring.

You'll wear it. Oh, you'll wear it happily enough.

Now, this is ridiculous! she told herself angrily, brushing away the tears that half-blinded her. She had seen the ring fly over here. She knew exactly where it had landed. It was impossible that it should not be here.

26

Surely in a second or two she would find it. She would take it home and send it to Donald by Li Hua, wrapped up in a small brown parcel. Inside the parcel she would include a message: No, she couldn't marry him. She was sorry, but she couldn't even consider such a thing.

She heard a noise and looked up to see a stray dog approaching her from the other side of the heap of refuse. Its whiplike body plainly showed its ribs. It was quivering and growling low in its throat at her.

"Nice doggy," Corrie said. She eyed the animal.

It took a step closer and now she saw the bloody scabs on its ears where evidently it had injured itself in a street fight. If the beast had been fed properly, its black coat would be as shining and lustrous as the dog-fur coats which many men, to Corrie's horror, considered fashionable. But in its present state, not even a dog catcher would want it.

The animal growled again, from deep in its throat. This time the sound was more menacing, and Corrie realized that it, too, wanted to poke among the odd scraps of food and meat. It was hungry; *she* was the intruder. For the first time she became aware of how desperate and ridiculous she must look, on her knees scrabbling through the trash in her stylish dove-gray skirt and cape.

Another growl sent her scrambling to the feet. As the dog approached stiff-legged, she began to back away.

"Please . . . I didn't mean to intrude . . . Please, good doggy . . . "

She could never get the ring now, she told herself despairingly. Even if the dog would let her, it was inextricably mixed up with the trash. Whatever would Donald say? What would he do?

Leaving the animal to its meal of scraps, she fled home in a confused daze. Her mind whirled with ugly questions which could not be answered. *Was* her papa really dying, as Donald insisted? Why did Donald think that he was "very close" to having her? And what would he do when he learned that she had thrown away his ring?

Somehow this last thought frightened her the most.

She arrived home out of breath, the knees of her gray skirt stained with dirt. In the gilt-edged mirror she caught a glimpse of herself, her rich, chestnut-gold hair tumbling out of its pins and her cheeks stained a hectic pink. *Avery*, she thought, looking at herself. *Oh, God, Avery.*

But fortunately only Li Hua, who had answered the door, noticed her arrival.

"Is Papa still in the library?" Corrie asked the maid.

"No, I think he's back upstairs in his bed. He looked very tired." Li Hua herself seemed subdued; had Aunt Susan scolded her? Corrie cast her a look of sympathy and gave her arm a quick squeeze. Li Hua had a small, oval face as pale as porcelain, and lush blue-black hair pulled up into an attractive pompadour. Her figure was fragile, clad in the trim, black serge uniform and white lawn embroidered apron Aunt Susan insisted that she wear. She was a third-generation American and her name meant "Pear Blossom." She was two months older than Corrie, and had been a servant since she and Cordelia were both thirteen. Since Li Hua's mother was dead, as was Corrie's, the two girls shared a common bond.

"Oh, dear," Corrie said.

"Do you wish your hair redone, Corrie?" Li Hua asked tactfully.

"No. No, I— Yes! Why not?" Corrie said, changing her mind. She had to talk to Papa, so she had better look her prettiest. For all of his free-thinking ways, Papa liked to see her looking good. No matter how sick he was, she told herelf, *that* would never change.

She sat impatiently while Li Hua's small, slim fingers flew over her hair and transformed it from dishevelment back to the fashionable pompadour, puffed becomingly, with soft little curls at her temples and ears. She could tell that the servant was curious, and on the verge of asking questions.

"Oh, Li Hua, would you mind hurrying?" she asked quickly, hoping to forestall them. "I have such a headache. And I did want to go and talk to Papa."

The girl nodded, but she gave Corrie a sharp look. Corrie suppressed a surge of annoyance. If Li Hua hadn't measured her finger, she thought, none of this would have happened. She wouldn't have received the ring and she wouldn't have lost it.

What would Donald do when he learned it was gone?

The thought had continued to occupy her, growing more forbidding with each passing minute. Surely he would be furious. Would he tell Papa what she had done? Would he demand repayment? Abruptly Corrie remembered the way Donald's hands had dug into her upper arm, the way he had seemed to enjoy her fear, and she grew even more frightened.

"Shall I get you your black taffeta skirt, Corrie?" Li Hua was asking.

"Oh, I suppose so. I tripped in the street and soiled my gray skirt."

Li Hua's dark almond-shaped eyes glinted, and Corrie knew that she didn't believe one word of it.

She shed her dirty skirt and slipped into the clean one, her mind in a turmoil. Papa ill . . . but of course he wasn't! That was only one of Donald's lies. Still, there was Donald's proposal. And the ring lost through her own fault . . . Her belly felt tight with anxiety; her statement about a headache had been the truth.

"Would you like a clean shirtwaist, too?"

"No, I—oh, I don't care! And would you please go now, Li Hua? I've got to think. My head is pounding." Then, seeing the stricken expression on the other girl's face, Corrie added, "I'm sorry, I didn't mean to be sharp. It's my . . . headache. I had some trouble with my camera this morning." She stopped, too numb to continue. Nothing seemed real today except the terrible things that Donald had said.

Three minutes later she was knocking on the door of her father's two-room suite.

"Come in, come in. Is that you, Corrie?"

She entered the room; her taffeta skirt, its black velvet bottom trimmed with scalloped silk, rustled entrancingly.

Immediately her eyes went to the bed where her father sat propped up on three pillows and surrounded by clutter: the San Francisco *Chronicle,* books, a huge ashtray crammed with cigarette butts and a still-smoldering Cuban cigar. He sat in the midst of this disarray like an oriental lord. To Corrie's immense relief, he looked as healthy as ever.

"Hello, Princess," he greeted her. "You look lovely today. Just right for setting some young man's heart aflutter."

Did he mean Donald? Corrie felt herself freeze.

"Oh, Papa, you're a tease, aren't you? But a nice one."
She forced herself to smile as charmingly as she could.
She knew that she looked her best. The taffeta skirt was
elegant. And the white lawn waist she wore, trimmed
with open-work embroidery and Valenciennes lace, emphasized the firm grace of her breasts, yet gave her a
demure look, too. It was for that reason she had chosen
to wear it.

"Have you read the paper yet?" Cordell Stewart demanded. "Congress just appointed a board of inquiry.
How do you like that? Me, I think the whole thing was
done by Spanish agents!"

He went on with more speculation about the recent
sinking of the U.S. battleship *Maine*.

Cordell Stewart was a big man with the weatherbeaten
complexion and wrinkles of one who is often in the sun.
His eyes, too, so like Corrie's, seemed washed by the sun
until they were pale amber. As he spoke, his hands
gripped the folded pages of the *Chronicle* and he jabbed
at the lead article with his index finger.

Corrie waited until he had finished his tirade and then
spoke in a low voice. "Papa . . . "

"What? Well, how did your pictures go this morning?"
he asked jovially. "If I hadn't been laid up with this
damned stomach of mine, I'd have been down there on
the docks with you, showing you how it's done." He held
up one of the photographic prints which also littered the
bed. "I've been looking at these photographs I took in
Virginia City. You can say all you want to about these
new dry plates and roll film; we took some pretty good
pictures in the old days with wet plates, even if it was
hell to develop 'em right on the spot."

"Papa. I have to talk to you."

"Talk?" He laughed again, this time less heartily, and
lifted the print to his face to peer closely at it. "Look at
the quality of this picture, Cordelia. Can you see the sign
on that saloon at the end of the street? I swear you can
read every damn sign on the s—"

"Papa! Would you please put down those pictures and listen to me?"

"All right, all right. What is it, then? Do you need a raise in your allowance? If you want one, all you have to do is ask. The shipyard is making plenty, and if I can't spare a little bit for my own daughter—"

"Papa! It isn't that. It's not money. It's . . . " She felt his eyes on her and faltered.

"Well, do you have a debt you want me to pay for you? You know all you have to do is come to your Papa for that. I've always paid all your—"

"No, Papa, it isn't that," she cried. "It's—Donald. And more."

"I thought so," he said. "Yes, I thought you had something on your mind besides photography."

"Papa, why does Donald Earle seem to think that you would encourage his marrying me? He seemed to think that you would want that. It isn't true, is it, Papa? Because I don't want to marry him—not in the slightest! I'm going to marry Avery Curran, Papa. We're going to be married in August, as soon as you give your permission. We're going to buy a pretty house . . . oh, we've planned it all, and Avery *will* be able to support me, Papa, because he's working very hard to pay for his schooling, and—"

Corrie knew that she was babbling. But she could not seem to stop. Papa *would* like Avery when he knew him better; of course he would! It was only a matter of time. Unfortunately, after meeting him at Madeline DeMoro's wedding, Papa had not been impressed.

"Oh, he's handsome enough, Cordelia, if you like decorative young men, which I don't. I just don't want you mixed up with him."

"Papa!" she'd protested, angered by the unfairness of it.

"Don't 'oh, Papa' me! I want a man of substance for you, Cordelia, a man who knows what real work is, not some puppy who might evaporate right along with the fog."

Today Papa's voice held that same stubborn, angry conviction, and she knew that his opinion had not changed.

"Now, wait a minute, Cordelia. Just wait. What's all this about that puppy Curran?"

Corrie licked her lips. "Papa. I want to marry him."

"No. You most certainly will not! And what's more, I don't want you seeing him again. Is that clear?" Papa leaned forward and pointed one finger at her, his expression formidable. "Do you hear me?" he added.

"Papa—" But then Corrie sighed, knowing that she was defeated, this time at least. "Yes, I hear you. But it's Donald who worries me at the moment," she hurried on. "He asked me to marry him. Or, rather, he *demanded* that I marry him! He seemed to think that he had some inside advantage, that you would favor having him in the family!"

"Oh."

To her surprise and dismay, her father sank back onto his pillows. He lifted the photograph and stared at it intently. A minute ticked by, marked off by the black and gilt ormolu clock that stood on the dressing table.

"Papa! Please talk to me! Do you mean to tell me that there is some truth in Donald's claims? That you *do* approve of him marrying me?" Corrie's voice rose.

Her father continued to examine the print of Virginia City as if he had never seen it before.

"Well, Cordelia, I didn't mean to tell you exactly like this. I was planning to wait until a better time, when you got that wastrel Curran out of your system."

"Avery is not a wastrel! Papa, how can you call him that? He's perfectly respectable, and trying so hard, and . . . I love him! He—"

"He is a good-looking, fly-by-night puppy, I'm sure of it. I'm convinced he's living on other people's money and I absolutely forbid you to marry such a man. Dammit, Cordelia, I've had you followed and I know what you've been doing. Meeting the man on the sly. Looking up at him with big eyes and believing all that drivel he tells you—"

"Following me? You had me followed! Oh, Papa! Why? Why do you hate Avery so much?"

"Be still, Cordelia, and listen to me. I want you to marry a mature, responsible man who can take care of you as I've done. I don't plan for you to end up with a

man who'll fritter away all your assets, and I've taken
steps to see that you don't."

"What kind of steps?" She could not believe that she
was really hearing this.

"I've made some changes in my will, that's all. Not,"
he added, "that I don't expect to be around for a very
long time." Did a queer expression pass over her father's
face? "However, in due time, certain things will come
about—"

"Papa." Corrie sank into a carved mahogany chair,
feeling suddenly breathless. "You're not going to die . . . "

"We all die, daughter. And I plan to do it tidily, with
everything taken care of. I don't intend to lie tossing and
turning in my grave, wondering whether Avery Curran or
someone like him is gambling away all your money. So
I've planned for someone to take care of you."

A heavy, frantic feeling pushed against her chest. "It's
Donald," she whispered. "Isn't it?"

"Yes." Cordell Stewart's voice was suddenly feebler,
as if his energy had begun to fade. "Yes, Cordelia, I've
planned for Donald Earle to be your husband. I've written it into my will."

The will was incredible. It was grossly unfair and autocratic!

Corrie lay sprawled face-down on her bed, weeping into the quilted comforter. Her mind was a protesting whirl.
She could not believe that Papa had really done such a
thing. Had he taken leave of his senses? But the will had
been written, signed and witnessed. A copy of it now re-
posed in his attorney's office, with another copy in the
library safe. It was all official, and had been accomplished
without consulting her.

The terms of the will were simple. If Cordelia married
Donald Earle within eighteen months of Cordell Stewart's
death, she and Donald would share full ownership of the
Stewart Shipyards and all of the other Stewart properties,
which were considerable. They included a number of
stocks and bonds, a mine in the Black Hills, a lumber
mill in British Columbia, and two dry goods stores.

If, however, Corrie did *not* marry Donald, then she
would only inherit twenty percent of the Stewart holdings.

Donald would receive another twenty percent and the rest would go to charity. If she, Corrie, died before she could marry Donald, then Donald would get sixty percent of the estate, with the remainder going to charity. An annuity had been set aside for Aunt Susan, with smaller bequests to the household servants.

The effect of all this, as Cordell Stewart pointed out, was to force her and Donald toward marriage. They could only achieve full ownership if married to each other. If Corrie did not wed, or married someone else, she could only expect a small portion of the estate, enough to keep her comfortable, but no more.

"But that isn't fair!" she gasped. "I don't want to marry Donald. I don't love him! I—"

Her father's face suddenly looked tired. "Love, Cordelia, is at its most healthy when well greased with money. I like Donald. He's bold, plain-speaking and aggressive. He reminds me of the way I was at his age. I would have been pleased to call him a son. This way I can make him my heir and take care of you at the same time."

Then he slumped back onto his pillows. "Now, go, Cordelia, will you? I've tired myself out. I plan to take you to the Tivoli tomorrow night, and I'd better rest up for it. *Shamus O'Brien* is playing. You'd enjoy that, Princess, wouldn't you?"

In answer Corrie jumped out of her chair and flung out of the room, slamming the door behind her.

She lay miserably in her bed. Her father's will explained so much, she thought. No wonder Donald wanted to marry her! If he did, he'd be a full owner of the Stewart Shipyards, with complete control of it. Perhaps this was what he had wanted all along. And, she thought, feeling sick, this also explained Donald's confidence. Her papa *did* approve of him, he wanted to make Donald his heir!

Love is at its most healthy when well greased with money. Had Papa ever said such a cynical thing? Did he really believe it?

Well, her love for Avery did not need to be lubricated with money. She didn't care about Papa's estate. She didn't care if she did not inherit anything at all. As for Donald, he could—go jump off a pier!

She sat up abruptly, remembering the ring. In her shock, she had not mentioned this to her father. *Oh, God,* she thought. Her head was throbbing now, worse than ever. Well, she wouldn't think about it now. She had to talk to Avery. Had to see him, feel his arms about her, hear his assurances that he loved her, that all was still right between them.

She got up, found pen, ink and paper, and began to scribble a note. Then she rang for Li Hua. She would send off the note right away, and she would meet Avery tonight. He would know what to do.

❧ Chapter 4 ❧

San Francisco at night smelled of flowers. The fragrance of roses, heliotrope and rich lemon verbena drifted toward Corrie on the night wind. Faintly she could smell the odor of salt wind and, briefly, the tantalizing whiff of roasting coffee.

From somewhere came the clatter of a late cable car, the clop-clop of horses' hooves and rattle of wheels as a carriage maneuvered the steep streets.

But Corrie barely heard. She was running downhill, a brocaded cape flying about her shoulders, her boots clacking against the pavement. In her haste to slip out of the house unseen, she had forgotten her hat. "Hoydenish," her aunt would have teased. But it didn't matter, she told herself. If she was lucky, no one would see her but Avery.

Breathless, she arrived at the corner where she had said she would meet him. The street was deserted, although the lighted windows of the homes that lined it said that people were here, behind the walls. As if to verify this, a woman's laugh suddenly burst out, full of hilarity.

Corrie pulled the elegantly trimmed cape closer about her shoulders. Somehow that laugh, with its connotations of warmth and sociability, made her feel even more lonely.

She shouldn't have come out this late at night, she knew. Shivering, she remembered the morning on the wharf, and the way Rabbit-foot McGee's hand had touched her. Also, she thought with growing unease, there was the man Papa had hired to follow her. She peered into the darkness. Surely *he* couldn't be about?

Abruptly she shook her shoulders, as if to shrug away such thoughts. She was no shrinking, timorous female, was she? She was Cordelia Stewart, daughter of Cordell Stewart. No, she hadn't been reared to tremble and feel faint just because she was standing all by herself in a dark street.

All the same, she was relieved when Avery's buggy finally pulled up.

"Avery! Oh, Avery!" She lifted her skirts and gave a spring, jumping into the buggy before he could help her. "Oh, Avery, I'm so glad to see you!" She flung herself toward him and felt his arms go around her.

"Corrie, what's the matter? My God, when I got your note I couldn't imagine what had happened. Has something gone wrong?"

She barely heard him, so conscious was she of the feel of his arms about her. He smelled clean. She loved the odor of him, the scent of hair pomade and washed clothing and shirt starch; she loved everything about him. Never would she give him up, ever.

"Corrie, for God's sake, let go of me, will you? I want to start up the buggy. We can't just sit here in the street. Someone might see us."

She felt the buggy begin to move, and then the horses were plodding downhill again. They were not very lively; you did not get spirited horseflesh when you had to rent them, Avery said. But when his law practice was established, he would be able to afford his own pair, and his own carriage, too.

"All right, Corrie, what was that note of yours about? "What was the great urgency?" he was asking her. His profile was facing her so that she could see the perfectly chiseled, patrician lines of his forehead, nose and chin. She had taken innumerable photographs of him; she had studied his face in detail from every angle. But the purity of his profile always had the power to stir her.

"Couldn't we wait till later to talk about it?" she said quickly. "I just want to enjoy being with you. I don't want to think about ugly things."

He turned to look at her. "What ugly things?"

"Oh, Avery, the night is so lovely! Just listen, I can

hear a fog horn on the Bay. Couldn't we just enjoy it for a few minutes before—"

"Corrie, you're being evasive. I think we'd better talk." Avery slapped the reins and turned the buggy to the left. "I'm going to take you to my apartment. We'll have a little privacy there. You won't mind, will you?" He was gazing at her intently.

"Mind?"

"Well, I can see that we have to talk, and I don't care to do it in the streets. We're much too likely to be seen, especially with the theaters ready to let out at any minute."

He lived in a cream and white frame house, with three floors of bay windows. A pair of iron griffins kept guard over the front steps. As if in a daze, Corrie felt herself being whisked toward another door set flush with the pavement. Three steep steps led downward.

"You live in the basement?" Somehow she hadn't quite pictured Avery living below ground.

"Well, yes. I assure you I have a very pleasant view from my window. And this is only temporary, until I get myself situated."

The apartment was nice enough; although the rooms were small, the furniture was polished mahogany and there were faded oriental rugs on the floors. A bay window faced black wought-iron fencing, through which could be seen the street, at thigh level.

"I'm lucky to have this much," Avery told her. "The woman who runs this house must have taken a liking to me, I guess. And I also help her with—" He stopped, abruptly.

Corrie, embarrassed, moved toward the window and stood watching a lone surrey as it clattered by. Poor Avery! He must be helping his landlady with some odd chore, such as carrying out the trash, but was too ashamed to admit it. Well, she didn't care about that. She admired Avery for being willing to work. And he would not be poor all of his life . . .

"All right, Corrie, what was that note of yours about? You were lucky that I was here at all to receive it. I had an engagement tonight which I had to break—"

She felt him come up behind her and put his arms

about her waist. His breathing was soft on the back of her neck, his mustache silky. She felt a stirring deep within her. Only Avery could do that to her, could make her tremble . . .

Her heart pounding, she stepped away from him. "It's Papa. I'm afraid he doesn't approve of our marrying; he's even had me followed. And . . . he has done something else, too. He's changed his will."

Haltingly, she explained the terms of the will. As she spoke, she saw Avery's face grow twisted with anger.

"But that's preposterous!" he burst out. "To stipulate such a ridiculous thing! What could he have been thinking of?"

"He was thinking of my future. I know that, and I suppose I love him for it, but—oh, what am I going to do, Avery? I don't want to marry Donald Earle! I loathe the man, I always have. He makes my skin crawl."

"But if you marry me you'll only get twenty percent of the estate, won't you?" Avery said this slowly. "There'll be barely enough to keep us in clothes and carriages."

"Oh, who cares? I don't care about Papa's money! We can get along without it!"

As if he hadn't heard her, Avery gave an impatient shrug. "The problem is, Corrie, what are you going to do now? Surely you can persuade him to change his mind. If he made one will, he can make another. It would be much easier than . . . litigation later."

Corrie attempted a smile. "I suppose I could *try* to talk to him. But he's very stubborn."

"Tomorrow, Corrie. You'll do it then. You can change his mind. After all, you're his only daughter, aren't you? He dotes on you. You're the little rosy red apple of his eye!" To Corrie's surprise, Avery said this savagely. But then, almost instantly, the anger disappeared from his face.

She plunged on. "Avery, there's another thing. Donald's ring. This afternoon he proposed to me, and gave me an enormous diamond ring. He walked off before I could hand it back to him." She stopped, her mouth dry. "I was so angry at him that I threw it away."

"Threw it *away?*"

"Yes!" She said it defiantly. "I'm sorry, I know it was

foolish of me, but I lost my temper. Then when I went to look for it in the pile of trash there was a big dog, and I couldn't find it."

"You threw a diamond ring into a pile of *trash?*"

"Yes."

"But how could you? Do you know where you threw it? On what street? Perhaps we can find it again."

"No, I don't remember. Oh, Avery, I've been trying all day to think just where I left it. But I can't! All I know is that the street was narrow . . ."

"Oh, God! The waste! Oh, you little fool!"

He strode away from her, pacing the small room, his arms swinging sharply at his sides. His blond brows were beetled together and two heavy frown lines had appeared on his broad, patrician forehead, almost ruining his looks. She had never seen him like this before.

"But it's Donald I'm worried about," she heard herself go on numbly. "When he finds out what I've done—"

"Oh, God. My God, Corrie." Avery had stopped pacing. "Well, there's only one thing to do. You can go right back to your papa sitting there in his rich house and you can ask him for the money to buy another ring. That should take care of it. Of course, you and I will never see any of that money . . . "

Rich house. She stared at him, thinking of the luxuries of her father's home. The billiard room, the small, elegant ballroom, the greenhouse, the two parlors and two dining rooms. And her home, she knew, was not by far the most lavish on Nob Hill.

"Money," she said. "My father's money. Is it really that important to you, Avery?"

"Yes." For an instant Avery's gray eyes seemed to harden. Then he was smiling at her as usual. "Corrie. I suppose I seem crass to you, don't I? Crass and money-hungry."

In one step he had reached her and had his arms about her again. She didn't question it; she just accepted the warmth of him about her. "Well, you've lived all your life with money, so you don't know what it's like to be poor."

He went on. "My father lost everything he had in the depression of ninety-three. It killed my mother; she died of pneumonia that year. And Dad had to go out and grub in an office. He became a clerk, Corrie, after all those years of owning his company. It humiliated him, so much that a year later he killed himself.

"And I was a clerk, too, sitting on a high stool and working ten or twelve hours a day. Working until my eyes burned and my hands shook and I thought, sometimes, of doing the same thing that Dad had done. Then one day I went to my employer. I begged him to give me a loan. Begged! He finally consented—at an exorbitant interest rate, of course. So I labored at Harvard College, waiting tables in one of the boarding houses, doing the most menial work, being laughed at and humiliated by those whose fathers still had money . . . "

Again Avery had let go of her and was walking jerkily about the room, pausing once to wipe a fingertip across the polished surface of a table. "I'm not going to be poor, Corrie. I just won't permit my life to end up that way. I'll do anything to get myself out of it."

"Anything? Including marrying me?" Corrie did not know what suddenly prompted her to say this. She heard the words pop out of her mouth with horror.

"Oh, no! You're wrong if you think . . . I love you. You're like a dream to me. A lovely and perfect dream. I do love you, Corrie. And I want to marry you. I *will* marry you."

Later Corrie was never sure exactly how it had all begun. She heard Avery's words in a rush of gladness and pity. He was right, she thought. She *didn't* know how it was. She had never been poor, she had never worked in an office for twelve hours a day, her own Papa had not been humiliated but instead had bought her everything she had ever wanted.

And Avery did love her. Her instincts told her that he was telling her the truth. Perhaps he did need her money, but he also wanted to marry her because he loved her. And now, excitingly, he was putting his arms around her, pulling her so close that she could smell the starch from his high shirt collar, and the maleness of his body. Oh, she loved him! She did! She didn't care about Papa's will, or the threat of Donald Earle hanging over her.

"Oh, Avery . . . "

In answer she felt his arms tighten around her, and

heard his sharp, indrawn breath, as if he were deciding something.

"Corrie. Do you know I've never seen your hair down? I've always dreamed of seeing you so. With your hair loose and flowing over your shoulders."

Before she could protest, he had reached up and was pulling out the pins and tortoise-shell comb Li Hua used to anchor her heavy mass of hair in place. Corrie felt her hair slide down her head. Richly, sensuously. Avery's hand went up to the back of her neck. Gently he caressed her. His hands urged, persuaded . . .

Oh, she shouldn't be letting this happen, she thought wildly. His hands were stroking her, petting her as if she were a kitten. She could feel herself tingle and tremble.

There was the sudden rattle of another carriage veering up the street. It was as if the noise brought her to her senses. Corrie pulled away from Avery and went to stand at the window, trying to calm herself. Her eyes focused on the buggy. A man and a woman were riding in it, probably on their way home from the theater, she decided, directing her thoughts upon this rather than on Avery's nearness.

Then, as the buggy passed under the street lamp near the house, she saw the faces of its occupants more clearly. The man—she stared upward at him in shock. He had a wide, craggy face, boldly carved, stubborn in its strength. And, yes, wasn't the bridge of his nose slightly bumpy, as if it had been broken once?

He was Quade Hill, the same rude and forceful man who had virtually abducted her down by the wharfs this morning. She was sure of it. The woman he was with had turned her face to his, gazing up at his face possessively.

An irrational spurt of jealousy filled Corrie. Then the carriage rattled over a pot-hole, swept by the window and was gone.

"What's the matter, Corrie?"

"Oh—nothing!"

She turned away from the window. Hot blood pounded through her. At the sight of Quade Hill, her heart had started to thump like that of a little girl still in the schoolyard. What on earth had possessed her? Why, she disliked the man! Hated him!

"You look as if a cat had run over your grave," Avery said.

"I . . . that's hardly the case."

"Then come, Corrie, please move away from that window. The lights are dim enough, but I should have pulled the curtains. Let's pray that those people passing in that buggy were too much engrossed in each other to notice us standing here silhouetted against the lamp."

Too engrossed in each other. So Avery had seen that too.

Numbly Corrie waited while Avery pulled the somewhat frayed white curtains over the bay window. Then again he took her in his arms. She felt herself being urged toward a low horsehair couch that took up nearly one entire wall of the small sitting room. A blue afghan was tossed over it.

"Corrie, what's the matter? Didn't you want me to pull the curtains? You must see that we can't have everyone on the street looking in at us. That wouldn't be safe."

"I . . . yes . . . " Surprised, she heard her own breathing, deep and excited. And now, she wasn't sure how she had got there, she was sitting on the couch beside Avery and his arms were locked about her.

"Avery." She tried to push him away but her muscles seemed to have lost their strength.

"Corrie . . . Oh, Corrie, do you know how often I've thought of you, dreamed of your being in my arms like this? And now you're here. I want you, Corrie."

She heard his words with a sense of disbelief. Was she really sitting here, in Avery Curran's apartment, alone with him after dark? Somehow, oddly, she couldn't stop thinking about Quade Hill. That big, vital, hateful man, smiling down at that woman . . .

"Avery, I can't. I really can't." But his lips had closed over hers, smothering her words. He was kissing her . . . God, the way he was kissing her now, her words might as well have been pipe smoke in the air. Avery didn't hear her protests, and now his tongue was boldly exploring her mouth, sending a piercing excitement through her.

She felt his hands at her bodice, pulling apart the mother-of-pearl buttons that fastened it, and then the warmth of his touch beneath her corset, the exciting feeling of his fingers on her nipples, so different from Rabbitfoot McGee's. Fire, sweet, melting fire spread through her.

I'm being seduced. The thought came into her mind like acid. I'm being seduced and I don't want it to stop. I want it to go on. God help me, I'm going to let it happen.

Somehow her clothes were off and she was stretched out on the couch, nude, and Avery's mouth was raining kisses all over her. First his lips fastened themselves at her nipples, drawing sweetness and heat from them. Then they moved downward, over the curve of her belly to the juncture of her thighs.

Involuntarily she cried out, both in pleasure and fear, and Avery soothed her with breathless words as if he, too, were unbearably excited by all that was taking place.

"Corrie— Oh, God, I won't hurt you, I promise . . . You're going to like it, I know you are. Just relax . . . "

A shred of sense came back to her. "Avery. No, I shouldn't—"

"You should, Corrie. You know you want to. You've wanted me ever since we met. And I've wanted you . . . "

Avery's lips continued to kiss her, rolling up great waves of pleasure. If she let him continue, there would be more pleasure, Corrie was sure. A kind of joy she had never dreamed of before.

It wasn't what she had expected at all. Avery's hands were demanding and aggressive. The afghan had fallen to the floor, and the fabric of the horsehair couch prickled roughly against her delicate skin.

And yet Corrie, trembling uncontrollably, was barely aware of that. She could not think of anything except the frantic pleasure of being so close to Avery, so intimately close that their bodies seemed to melt together in warm, sweet, burning pleasure.

There was pain—a pounding at her tissues as he forced penetration—but it was quickly over. It was Avery, she assured herself wildly, her own Avery to whom she was giving her virginity. A last thought of Quade Hill flitted through her mind; what would that arrogant man think of her now? And then she had forgotten everything except the ecstasy building in her like fireworks soaring toward release . . .

❦ Chapter 5 ❦

That night Corrie had a strange, distorted dream in which she was running, terror-filled, through the streets of some strange city, a make-shift, dirty, cluttered town filled with rough men, who turned to hoot and whistle as she fled past. For someone was pursuing her, a man who had made her his quarry, and who was intent on capturing his prey. A heavy-set man with glossy black hair.

In the dream she stumbled on, her heart slamming so hard that she thought it would burst through her chest. She had to run, or he would hunt her down as a wolf searches out a rabbit, and he would kill her.

He would murder her in cold blood as he had others, as he had—

She awoke. The dream faded from her mind like the soft fingers of fog on the Bay. Corrie opened her eyes to find her room gray-pearled with the first hint of dawn. She shook her head to clear it, to bring back normality.

What a strangely vivid dream it had been. She could almost *smell* that crude town, and taste the coppery bitterness of fear in her mouth.

She forced her body to relax, letting her eyes travel around the bedroom. The door to her own familiar dark-room stood half open, hung with prints she had made. Inside she could see the array of her developing equipment—the oil-burning darkroom lamp, the fiber trays for developing, the bottles of hypo and intensifier, the brushes and rollers, the heavy printing frame, all of the things she had used so often that they were a real part of her.

It had only been a dream, she thought with relief. A silly dream.

She got out of bed, noting with surprise that her knees were still shaky. The big double windows revealed nothing but the gray dawn air laced with fog. Corrie pulled on a silk dressing gown. Then she crept out of her room and down the hall to the big new bathroom that Papa called an extravagance but secretly enjoyed.

She closed the door and locked it; the hollow click of the bolt disturbed the night quiet of the house. Then she turned up the gas light and went to the gilt mirror that had been hung over the red granite washstand.

She stared intently at her face. Were her lips still swollen from Avery's kisses? Did she look different, more womanly now? Her cheeks, she saw, were flushed a hectic red, her tawny gold-brown eyes wide. Her hair, the color of smoky-gold autumn leaves, tumbled down her shoulders.

She turned on the cold water and scooped some into her hands, splashing it on her face. The chill of the water jolted her awake.

In her mind, she could still hear Avery's voice, apologizing for what he had done.

"Corrie, Corrie, what a cad you must think I am. I swear I didn't mean to go so far. It was just that I've had you on my mind for so long. And then when you came here, to my apartment, well . . . I couldn't control myself. It was as if all my desires had been dammed up until they exploded. Can you understand that, Corrie? I wanted to stop. Really I did. Will you ever forgive me? Will you accept my apology?"

Corrie would. She did. She pulled on her clothes and kissed him a hundred times, reassuring him over and over that it was all right, it didn't matter, no lasting harm had been done. They were being married, after all, weren't they? And Avery should not worry. She would follow his advice and talk to Papa tomorrow. She would get him to approve their match.

"And the will, Corrie? You'll convince him of that, too?"

"Of course. It was completely absurd and unfair of him to write such a clause. I know I can make him see that!"

Then she let Avery drive her back in his buggy, the two of them jouncing along the streets without speaking, each wrapped in thought. Yet Corrie could feel the reassuring closeness of Avery next to her, and she knew that everything would work out somehow. She had not had total joy from their lovemaking, but that, she told herself, was because of the circumstances, because of her fear and virginity, and Avery's impatience. Later, after they were married, it would be better.

As he dropped her off at the same corner where they had met earlier, he again pulled her to him. "Corrie, promise me I'm forgiven? Promise? I wish to God I hadn't been so hasty."

"What is there to forgive?" she asked him. "We love each other, Avery, that's all that matters." She kissed him and ran up the street, knowing that he was still sitting in the buggy staring after her, watching to be sure she was safe.

Now, as she dried her face on the towel, she thought about going back to bed. No, she decided. She felt too wide awake now. Every nerve in her body was jumping with tension.

She extinguished the bathroom light and went back to her own room, the silken folds of her dressing gown rustling about her. No, she would not go back to bed. She would go into her darkroom and work until breakfast.

Work and think and plan her strategy for convincing Papa that he must let her marry Avery as soon as possible.

But work though she did, few ideas came to her. In a few hours, Li Hua brought her breakfast on a tray, and announced that "Mr. Earle" was here to see her.

"What?" Corrie, who had started to reach for the tray, felt her heart start to slam.

"He said he knows it's early, but he wanted to see you anyway. I told him to wait in the front parlor." Li Hua's dark, tilted eyes were sparkling again; she loved intrigue and, Corrie thought crossly, had probably aided and abetted Donald in interrupting her meal.

"Well, it's too early. It isn't even nine o'clock. I haven't had my breakfast and I'm planning to spend the entire morning working. I certainly don't want to see him. You'd better go right back downstairs and tell him so, Li Hua."

The girl smiled. "He said it wouldn't take long, Corrie. He promised he wouldn't disturb your day."

"But he is disturbing it!" Corrie found that she was clenching her fists inside the pockets of her dressing gown. What if he asked her about the ring? she thought. What could she tell him? "I—I don't want to see him, Li Hua. You go down and tell him."

"All right." With a whisper of her black and white uniform the maid was gone, only to return three minutes later with the news that Mr. Earle did not intend to leave until he had spoken to Corrie.

"Oh, very well! Tell him I'll be down. But first I'm going to eat my breakfast. And then I'm going to get dressed. If he insists upon coming here so early, then he is just going to have to wait."

Angrily Corrie sat down to consume her breakfast, a Spanish omelette done in the style her father had taught her to enjoy, and a cup of strong black coffee. But she barely tasted the spicy egg and tomato mixture, and at last pushed it away half-eaten.

She went to her closet and put on a powder blue tailored walking suit, a color that suited the changeable gold-brown of her eyes. The double-breasted, pointed front emphasized the tininess of her waist and the soft flare of her breasts. The skirt had been stitched twelve times around its flared bottom.

Corrie sat impatiently while Li Hua combed her hair up into a soft pompadour. When the girl had finished, she inspected herself in the mirror. Soft little curls fringed her temples, giving her a fragile look. Her cheeks were flushed a deep apricot.

"Well," Corrie said. "It does look nice, and I suppose I'm ready. And you needn't look so smug, Li Hua. If I didn't know better, I'd swear you arranged all of this yourself, just to see what would happen!"

"Oh no, Corrie." Li Hua bit down on her lower lip.

"Well, it doesn't matter. You'd better go and see if Aunt needs you this morning. I'm going downstairs now."

Donald Earle was waiting for her in the front parlor, his muscular body occupying a Chippendale chair as if he owned it. The parlor contained a white and gold cabinet filled with filigree silver miniatures, carved ivory from China, a mother-of-pearl and lace fan, and a silver snuffbox. Donald, Corrie thought with a quick indrawn breath, did not seem to belong among objects of such delicacy.

He looked up at her as she entered. His dark eyes narrowed. Almost instantly Corrie could sense his desire for her, heavy and intense. She raised her chin and swept into the room, her silk petticoats rustling.

"Good morning, Corrie."

"Well, I see that you have no better manners than to call upon a lady so early in the morning that she has not even completed her breakfast!"

Donald rose, smiling lazily. His eyes inspected her with deliberate ease, lingering on the rich piled-up chestnut-gold mass of hair and the swell of her breasts.

"You're beautiful, Corrie. God, there is something about you—something I can't leave alone."

"How I wish you *would* leave me alone!"

"But I won't. I assume that by now your father has informed you of the terms of his will, has he not?"

"Yes . . . he told me," she admitted. The bravado was rapidly seeping from her.

"Then surely you accept the fact that you and I will be husband and wife? After all, Corrie, you did take my ring. Although," he added, "I see you are not wearing it."

Involuntarily she glanced down at her hands. "No, I'm not wearing it. I have no intention of accepting it. I . . ." Her voice trailed off uncomfortably. Now was the moment when she should fling the ring in his face. But she couldn't. She had lost it.

"I plan to talk to Papa today and persuade him just how unfair he was to write such a clause into his will," she heard herself go on. She licked her lips to rid them of their dryness, wishing that his stare was not so intense. It was as if somehow he could see through the layers of cambric, silk and wool she wore to her very nakedness. "I'll make him see just how wrong he is. So you might as well resign yourself to the fact."

"Oh, I don't think you'll persuade him all that easily."

"Why, I certainly will. Why shouldn't I? After all, *I* am my father's daughter, and you are only a—a man who is *employed* by Papa, and nothing more!"

Donald's face reddened. His hard, black eyes glittered. "You do have a shrewish temper, don't you? Well, I'll tame it fast enough after we're married."

He got up from his chair and approached her, extending his hand to put it over hers. His flesh felt curiously repellent. The back of his right hand, she saw, was reddened and puckered by some old scar shaped, curiously, in a crescent. But she did not dare to jerk her own hand away.

" . . . and, Corrie," she heard him continue. "I want you to go and get that ring and put it on your finger. The next time I see you I expect you to be wearing it as a proper fiancée should. Because you *are* going to be my wife; you'll come to see that it is inevitable."

She did not know what excuses she made, or how she finally got him to leave. But at last he was gone, and Corrie leaned against the heavy oak of the front door, wishing she could throw the bolt, lock Donald out and never allow him in the house again. Touching him made her shudder, as if she had encountered something rotting and unclean. Why, *why*, had Papa ever decided to alter his will this way? Did he really expect her to fall into Donald's arms?

"Corrie! I declare, but you're acting oddly this morning. What has got into you? You'd think that a bogy man was pounding at that door trying to get inside."

Corrie jumped guiltily away from the door. It was Aunt Susan, descending the stairs in a figured lawn wrapper which emphasized the smallness of her waist. She was smiling, and in the varicolored light which filtered in through the stained glass set above the doorway, the fine, dry wrinkles on her aunt's face were plainly visible.

"I . . . oh, it's nothing, Aunt Susan. It's just that Donald Earle came here to see me. So early . . . "

"And you don't like Mr. Earle, is that it?"

"No, I don't. Oh, Aunt, has Papa told you about his will? He plans to force me into marrying Donald! He thinks I'll do it in order to inherit his estate! But he's wrong. I won't. He—"

Gently Susan touched Corrie's arm. "So he's told you, then." She frowned. "I told him he was being impossible, but of course he refused to listen to me. My brother really thinks that he can use his money to control people. I told him you wouldn't be taken in by such tactics. I told him you'd rebel." She smiled sadly. "He rears you to be a strong-minded girl and then he expects to manipulate you like any pliant little ninny without an intelligent thought in her head. Men! It won't work, I told him. Oh, men are impossible creatures, don't you agree, Corrie? Well, do you want to come shopping with me this morning?" she continued, in exactly the same tone of voice. "*He's* incommunicado today; he's conducting business in his room and won't be disturbed."

"Shopping? Go shopping with you?"

"Why not? Since you're going to be throwing away the bulk of your father's inheritance, you might as well spend his money while you've got the chance."

Bewildered, Corrie nodded, and followed her aunt upstairs to her sitting room, where she waited while Susan changed. She decided that she would talk to Papa on the way back from the theater tonight, when he would be sure to be in a mellow, expansive mood.

But as she waited for Susan, she found that she was swallowing hard, trying to quell the nervousness in her belly. What if she couldn't persuade Papa? What if she failed?

It was as if Aunt Susan's words had provoked some imp in Corrie, for the shopping trip turned into a reckless buying spree. Corrie bought lace-trimmed dressing sacques and two cambric and lace corset covers set with the most delicate pale blue ribbons. She picked out frilly bridal nightgowns adorned with rows of *point de Paris* lace and herringbone braid. She purchased four extravagant hats, and yards of taffeta and silk and serge, of English Torchon lace and white cambric embroidery. Finally, she chose a white china silk fan and a fancy ladies' stock collar with a large bow.

All of this would be part of her trousseau when she married Avery, she told herself defiantly. She ignored Aunt Susan's questioning looks and kept on buying, ordering all of the packages sent home. Let Papa try to control her life with his ridiculous will! She would show him!

Later, as the carriage, driven by Jim Price, Papa's driver, turned toward home, Corrie's reckless mood subsided. She sat quietly, depression creeping over her like congealing lard. What if Papa *wouldn't* change his mind? But of course he would. She tried to put her misgivings out of her mind.

The rest of the day seemed to pass very slowly. The sky had turned dull gray like old metal; there was rain in the air. Corrie read a book, rearranged the bottles of chemicals in her darkroom, and then took a long, restless nap. When she awakened in late afternoon, her body was damp with perspiration, for she had dreamed of frightening things. *Take off your clothes,* Donald Earle had been saying in her dream. *Rip off your dress, you little vixen . . .*

She was glad when it was finally time to leave for the theater. Jim Price had been given permission to go and visit his sister, who was ill with "female trouble," so Papa decided to drive the buggy himself. As they rode through the streets, Cordell Stewart kept muttering under his breath at the hordes of bicyclists who pedaled up and down the streets, seemingly oblivious to traffic. Then, growing more jovial, he began to reminisce about the time he had seen Mrs. Leslie Carter in *Zaza,* and the entire cast had gotten drunk. The police had raided the first act and taken all the actors to jail.

Corrie began to relax as she saw that her father's mood was rapidly mellowing. He appeared to have rested during the day; he looked stronger tonight, his breath faintly touched with the odor of whiskey and laudanum. But Corrie did not mind that. Surely after the play was over, she would convince him.

The Tivoli Opera House had been built in 1879 to replace the Tivoli Gardens which had burned down. Guests sat at tables under circles of gaslights that hung from the ceiling. A great chandelier of those lights was suspended from the center of the stage. There were statues in niches on either side of the stage, and garlands and festoons of flowers draped about. Circulating among the tables were waiters serving beer and cheese sandwiches.

At intermission, Corrie and her father strolled out to the lobby and stood amid other members of the audience. Corrie looked about her eagerly. What an elegant crowd it was! Men clad in fashionably cut evening garb relaxed, at ease, their smiles confident. There were beautiful women, their skin delicately flushed, wearing jewels and flowers, with feathers in their hair. Corrie drank in the arrogant glitter of diamonds and sapphires and pearls. And the gowns, tulle and *moiré* and *broché* satin . . .

Cordell Stewart, she noted, was not missing any of the beauties either. His slow, long gaze passed over each of the women.

She looked down at her own evening gown with satisfaction. It was another extravagance of Papa's. Made by Worth, it was a creation of very light *ciel*-blue satin bordered with black fur and embellished with bead embroidery in a design of irises. It clung sensuously to her figure —as, of course, it was meant to do. She too, the girl noted with delight, was attracting her own share of shares . . .

Indeed, someone was staring at her now.

She turned. A man was bowing to her, direct blue eyes focused on her with amused admiration.

"You look lovely tonight, Miss Stewart. Most fashionable. And I see you've left your camera at home this time."

"You! You again!"

It was Quade Hill, that maddening man who had rescued her from Rabbit-foot McGee, who had mocked and frightened her with terrible stories. A flush, beginning at Corrie's chest, rose hotly to her cheeks and lingered there.

"Yes, I'm like a bad penny; I keep turning up, don't I?" He was wearing an impeccably cut evening suit. He grinned boldly at her, his face creased with laugh lines, his eyes disturbing, for they seemed to see everything about her, good and bad, to miss nothing.

But before Corrie could formulate a reply—what was

it about this man that made her heart pump so irritatingly fast?—Quade Hill bowed to her again. He nodded to Cordell Stewart, then melted into the crowd which thronged the small lobby.

"Who was that?" her father demanded.

"Oh, no one. Just a man who helped me with my camera the other day. That's all. He certainly is rude!"

"Indeed?" Cordell Stewart eyed her sharply, but said nothing else. The warning call sounded, and they went back to their table.

The star tonight was Denis O'Sullivan; he was doing a repeat engagement, milking the audience of its laughter. Corrie barely heard any of the second act, although her father was laughing heartily. Dimly she realized that Cordell Stewart was relaxing even further, that he had consumed two cheese sandwiches and as many quarts of beer, and was thoroughly enjoying himself. No, she thought with relief, someday Papa would die as he had said—but not soon. A man who could laugh as loudly as her father was not yet ready for the grave.

When they left the theater it had started to rain, and the streets were aglitter with lights reflected in the water. The wetness seemed to magnify the sound of the horses' hooves, their jingling bridles, clattering iron wheels and the laughter from homeward bound theater-goers.

"Papa," she began as they started to climb upward, the horses struggling to maintain their footing on the rain-slick pavement. She had pushed Quade Hill entirely out of her mind.

"Yes, Cordelia?" Cordell Stewart was still laughing over a joke that he had been telling her; he wiped his eyes and flicked the reins carelessly with his left hand. Corrie saw that he was slightly drunk, his muscles relaxed and loose.

"Oh, Papa, I want to tell you what a terrible mistake you're making with your will. Forcing Donald and me together—I hate him, Papa! I could never live with him, and I certainly don't want him to 'take care of me' as you planned. I can take care of myself!"

"Oh, my bleeding foot!" Cordell Stewart roared this so loudly that a man walking huddled against the steadily driving rain turned to stare at them, his face a white blur.

"Now, Papa." Swallowing hard, Corrie remembered what Aunt Susan had said. "Papa, you brought me up to be independent, to make my own decisions and to think for myself instead of letting someone else do it for me. Well, you are negating all of that with your will. You are trying to mold my entire life for me! To make the most important decision in my life for me as if—as if I were stupid!"

"Aw, no . . . " Roughly he put his arm about her and for a fleeting instant Corrie could imagine what he might have been like as a young man, full of energy and confidence and good spirits.

"Now, Princess," Cordell Stewart went on, his voice a bit slurred. "You're not stupid. Dammit, I didn't raise you to be some little chit of a female with corn meal mush where her brains ought to be."

"Then change your will, Papa. Don't do this terrible thing and chain me to Donald Earle. Let me think for myself."

"Aw, awright, daughter. If that's the way you want it, that's th' way it'll be. Ain't going to die anyway. Not for a long time yet. Maybe I'll live forever, eh? Would you like that? Your old Papa a hundred and eight years old and still putting away his whiskey with the best of 'em?"

"Yes, yes, Papa." Her voice caught. "Then you'll change your will? You'll go to Mr. Bardley's office and fix it so that there's nothing about my marrying Donald?"

"I said I would, didn't I? Said I would! Cordell Stewart's a man of his word, Cordelia. Want you to know that."

Corrie looked in alarm at her father as he swayed on the black buggy seat. The rain had started to drive at an angle now, and it swept into the open seat, drenching their faces and clothes. The satin gown, she knew, would be ruined. Ahead of them the street stretched upward, each house slightly higher than its neighbor. Rain swirled down the pavement in gushing streams toward the bay.

"Papa, this rain," she said. "We'd better get home soon or you'll catch your death from a chill."

"Won't catch my death from anything," he protested.

But he urged the horses on a bit faster. Corrie felt

touched with some mad nighttime joy. Even the rainy street, streaked with shadows and reflected light, looked beautiful to her. Papa was going to change his will! She had convinced him! Once Donald knew this, she was sure he would lose his determination to marry her. It was only the ring . . .

The ring. She had not yet mentioned it to Papa. Whether she wanted his money or not, just this once she did have to have Papa's help. If he would give her the money, she could replace the diamond ring and return it to Donald. Then the whole unpleasant incident would be finished.

"Papa, there's one more thing I must ask you. Donald has given me a ring, a diamond engagement ring. But I . . . I was so angry with him that after he left I took the ring and I . . . I threw it away. Into a trash heap," she went on miserably. "It's gone. I couldn't find it again."

"You did what?" He was roaring with laughter. "You threw a ring away? That sounds like something your mother would have done! A little spitfire she was; I never could tame her." He seemed proud of what Corrie had done. "You're like Marie Antoinette, is that it? Let them eat cake!" He doubled over with glee.

Corrie frowned. "Papa, why do you liken me to Marie Antoinette? I'm certainly not like her. I lost my temper, that's all. I plan to marry Avery Curran, not Donald. We're going to be wed very soon, and that's why I was so angry and upset—"

"Marry Avery Curran! Didn't I tell you that I wouldn't hear of such a thing?"

"Why, yes, Papa," she said boldly. "But I'm hoping that when you have time to consider it, you'll change your mind. You see, Avery and I . . . when I saw him last night he said—"

"You saw him *last night?*" Oddly the slur had gone from her father's voice and he stared at her as if the effects of the whiskey had left him, as if he were stone sober.

"Yes, Papa, I did. I . . . " Her voice was barely audible.

"You slut! You sneaked out of the house last night like any common turnip of a girl and then you met that man, didn't you? Did he pick you up on the street corner? Did he, Cordelia? Did he take you to his apartment? Did he seduce you?"

"Papa! Oh! Papa—" She could not contain her shock and horror. The carriage lurched wildly; she clutched at the side of her seat, barely aware that she was doing so. She could not believe that her father would call her such names.

But Cordell Stewart raved on as if he had not heard her protests. "Little red-haired whore! Did you know that I caught your mother taking a lover once? Yes! I caught them together and I beat 'em with a stick, both of them, until the blood ran. She never cheated me again after that, no, sir, she didn't!"

"*Papa*, please, let me . . ."

But he did not hear. "And now my own daughter—it's her blood you've got in you, *her* blood! You let yourself be seduced by that pale, pewling ne'er-do-well . . . God! How could you do it to me, Cordelia? How could you?"

He was weeping now, his body shaking in huge, terrible movements that frightened Corrie more than anything ever had before. It was with a sense of unreality that she saw the bicyclist turning out of a side street, a small, sodden man pedaling grimly home at this late hour, water streaming in rivulets off his hat

Instinctively she screamed a warning to her father. But Cordell Stewart, still sobbing, had dropped the reins. He did not see the cyclist.

It all seemed to happen very slowly, each part played out in time like beads moving one by one on a string. First the right horse, a tall, frisky roan, skidded on the slippery pavement, shying up as it tried to avoid the man on the bicycle. Then the other animal lunged, jerking the buggy to the left.

They were falling.

Oh God oh God, the thought ripped through Corrie's mind like tearing silk. She felt herself being lurched half out of the carriage, and frantically grabbed for the solid support of wood, metal and leather that would protect her.

But it was too late. The buggy was tilting over, and as she fell she caught a wild glimpse of horses' bodies, the empty black beside her and her father's protesting arms.

Washed over all of it was the wet, shining patina of rain.

Then she hit the pavement and yellow light burst in her head, exploded like gas, upward and outward until it filled everything.

🌹 Chapter 6 🌹

Aunt Susan walked down the corridor and stopped at the closed door of Corrie's bedroom. She stood there, very erect, drawing courage for the moment when she must go inside.

Tiny dust motes floated in the air; at the end of the hallway the late afternoon sun fell through a stained glass window to the carpeting in a narrow rectangle of color. An hour ago Dr. Willodene had walked through that multihued shaft of light after examining Corrie. He was frowning and rubbing his palms together as if they were cold.

Involuntarily, without knowing that she did it, Susan rubbed her own hands together. Five days, she thought. In five days so much had happened; nothing, nothing was the same as it had been. Cordell Stewart was dead of a broken neck in the carriage accident. Corrie had a dangerous head injury, was still unconscious, and no one knew if she would survive. And lastly, a bicyclist of forty-two, on his way home after playing chess with a friend, had suffered two broken legs.

How? How could it all have happened?

Dr. Willodene, who examined Cordell's body after the accident, stroked his mustache and told her that Cordell had been drinking heavily and taking substantial doses of laudanum as well. It was this which had undoubtedly slowed his reflexes. But the street, he said, had also probably been slippery with horse droppings. A new rain after days of dryness could do that. There had been two other buggy accidents in the city that rainy night.

Cordell's funeral had taken place two days ago, a large, solemn affair attended by numerous members of the "Five Hundred," various saloon cronies and old mining friends, the shipyard workers and Cordell's own household staff. Li Hua, sitting at the rear with the rest of the servants, had wept audibly throughout the entire ceremony, but Donald Earle's face had held no expression.

Sitting there listening to the minister's droning eulogy, Susan had had time to wonder just what Donald Earle was thinking. He was one of Cordell's principal heirs. If Corrie were to die, he would inherit nearly everything— sixty percent of the estate. If Corrie lived and he married her within eighteen months, they would share one hundred percent. But, watching Donald's firm, tanned, masklike face, Susan could not guess his thoughts.

In deference to Corrie's illness, they had not read the will yet. But Susan was sure this could not be put off much longer. And if Corrie herself were to die—

No, Susan thought. A dry feeling, like a wad of cloth, stuck in her throat. Her brother's death she could accept. But Corrie was not going to die. She was not!

There had been dozens of inquiries throughout the past five days into Corrie's condition. Many came from girls Corrie had known in school, or through Lunt's Dancing School, where Corrie had gone to learn ballroom dancing. There had been, the day after the accident, an inquiry from young Avery Curran, but he had not called again. Donald Earle, however, visited two and sometimes three times a day.

"She's just the same," Susan had to tell them all. "Unconscious. Just lying there like a beautiful doll. The doctor says there's a chance she'll come out of it and be all right. If we pray."

Not a very good chance, however, Dr. Willodene told her privately this afternoon, stroking his peppery mustache in a habitual gesture. She could tell that he disliked being the bearer of bad news and so made himself fluttery and ineffectual.

"Do you notice," he asked, "the way she is starting to draw her arms and legs up into the fetal position? And her muscles are beginning to atrophy. In cases of this sort, some patients wake up spontaneously. Others . . . well, some have breathing difficulties. And, of course, they can't eat. There is little we can do for them then. They die fast enough."

"Oh, God."

Susan heard herself gasp and knew that she was close to weeping—not in a ladylike way, but loudly, furious that God should do this thing to a vibrant young creature like Corrie.

"There's no use upsetting yourself over it. What will happen, will happen. That's what I tell the families of all my patients. We do what we can. Then we have to trust in God."

The man's lower jaw wobbled like a big St. Bernard's, and Susan felt a stab of pure anger. He was just throwing religion at her like a sop, she thought.

"Indeed," she said coldly.

"Yes. Ah . . . well, I shall come back tomorrow at this time. Do continue the ice rubs. I am not sure what good they are doing, but at least we cannot say that we are not doing anything, can we? And, of course, as a last resort we can always trephine her skull."

"Think again, Dr. Willodene," Susan thought to herself. "I'll never permit such butchery to be performed on my niece!"

Shaking with anger, Susan showed him to the door. Trephine Corrie's skull! She sent a telegram to a famous specialist in Chicago; he was due to arrive soon by train. Surely he would be better than fumbling, mealy-mouthed Dr. Willodene.

Now she stood outside Corrie's door, trying to stop herself from shivering. Li Hua was sitting with the girl. In a few minutes it would be time to go to the kitchen to get more ice and bring it upstairs in a white enamel pan. Between them, she and Li Hua had followed the doctor's complicated list of instructions. Hourly they waved smelling salts, slapped Corrie's hands and face, gave ice rubs and medicinal suppositories, and then put more medicine under Corrie's tongue with an eye dropper. At Li Hua's suggestion, they had also lifted the flaccid arms and legs and massaged the muscles, moving the limbs up and down. This, said Li Hua, would keep Corrie from losing strength in her muscles when she finally did awake.

Susan paused briefly before the door and then opened it. The room was tidy. Corrie's photographic prints, tacked to the door of her darkroom, seemed to mock her. In the bed lay Corrie; the chestnut hair spread out loosely on her pillow had been washed by Li Hua until it shone with gold highlights.

But Corrie's face was the color of laundry soap. Only a small spot of red stained the center of her cheeks, and it was only the barely visible rise and fall of her chest that showed that she was alive at all. Dominating her right temple was a purplish-yellow bruise, which was already beginning to fade. It certainly did not look as if it could have caused such massive, long-lasting unconsciousness.

"Li Hua, it's nearly six o'clock. You go down to the kitchen and have Mrs. Parsons give you your supper. I'll sit here with her."

The Chinese girl looked up. Her oval porcelain face was drawn from lack of sleep.

"I'm not hungry yet," she protested. "I'll stay here. I want to." Mistress and servant girl exchanged a long look. Then Susan, with a rustle of petticoats, took the other chair near the bed.

"We'll both stay with her," she said. "There is nowhere else I'd rather be anyway."

The late afternoon sun faded imperceptibly to darkness. Susan rose to light the gas, to smooth back Corrie's hair, to accept the supper trays which Mrs. Parsons herself brought to them.

"How is the poor little thing tonight?" the woman asked. "Seems like just yesterday she was wolfin' down my raisin muffins and askin' me why didn't I pose for her by my new cookstove." The cook, her body as plump and doughy as the pastries she baked, sniffed audibly.

"She's about the same," Susan said. "I thought I heard her moan, but I'm too tired to be sure. Lord, but I'm tired."

"You've had it rough," Mrs. Parsons sympathized. "Remember now, I want to do what I can."

"I know," Susan said. "And I'm glad for your support. Perhaps later . . ."

"Yes'm." Mrs. Parsons left, leaving behind her, like a signature, the faint odor of rising bread dough.

Li Hua was dozing in her chair, and Susan did not have the heart to wake her. The flighty girl had proved herself surprisingly able at nursing, and for five days had quelled her high spirits to sit with Corrie. Perhaps in time, when she matured, Li Hua would make a reliable servant . . .

Susan, too, dozed. She slumped forward in her chair to dream of Corrie as a child of thirteen with eager gold-brown eyes and flying chestnut hair, clad in a soiled white dress, running wildly up and down the street with Biggie, her dog. Behind her, shouting with laughter and equally harum-scarum, raced Li Hua. And leaning from an upper window of the house, shouting encouragement to both, had been Cordell Stewart. Wild, cheerful man and hoydenish girls. That was what she had found when she had come to live here five years ago . . .

She was awakened by a noise. She jerked upright and realized that someone was knocking at the bedroom door.

"Yes? Yes?" she muttered, still half immersed in her dream.

"Ma'am? Are you awake?" It was Mrs. Parsons again; out of breath from climbing the stairs, she looked cross. "It's that Donald Earle again. The third time he's been here today. He says he wants to see Miss Cordelia for himself. Wants to see is she all right."

"But I've told him her condition hasn't changed," Susan said wearily.

"I told him that, too, but he don't care. Once that man gets a thought in his head, don't nothing going to make it leave. I declare I never saw a one like that. He wants that girl alive, and if knocking on our door could make it happen, she'd be up dancing a jig right now."

"Very well, then. I guess it can't hurt. Show him up and let him see for himself."

Donald Earle burst into the room, then stopped short when he saw the girl in the bed. For an instant Susan saw shock on his face.

He strode over to the bed. "Why are you keeping her flat down like this?' he snapped. "She should be propped up, so that the blood can circulate to her head properly.

No wonder she isn't waking! And I suppose you've called a specialist. I certainly hope that you have."

"Yes, he's coming tomorrow or the next day." Susan did not try to hold back her anger at the man. "How dare you walk in here and imply that I'm not taking care of Corrie properly?" But Donald ignored her. He bent over the bed and lifted Corrie's right hand and gave it a sharp slap.

"Corrie! Corrie, you're just faking this, aren't you? I know you can hear me. I want you to wake up. I want you to hear me and wake." His voice was loud and harrying. Again he slapped Corrie's hand, leaving a red mark on her skin.

"She can't hear you," Susan snapped. "And you're going to injure her if you keep on hitting her like that."

"A little slap won't hurt! She deserves it. Scaring us all like this, keeping us waiting . . . "

"Why, I'm very sorry for you," Susan said, rising to her full height. *"Inconvenienced* as you are, and kept waiting. For what, may I ask? For Cordelia to wake, or for you to inherit my brother's estate?"

Donald's dark eyes flashed at her. Then, deliberately, he lowered them until he was staring at her high, corseted breasts and the indentation of her still slim waistline. Susan caught her breath angrily. If she was not mistaken—and she knew she was not—he was looking at her with lust. She, Susan Raleigh, a woman nearly fifty! And here in Corrie's room, by her pathetic, half-alive body.

His eyes met hers. "I am waiting for my *future wife* to wake up," he said. "And when she does . . . "

Susan stalked toward him. She shooed at him as if he had been a rabbit nibbling at the flowers in her garden.

"Out! she cried. "Out! Right this instant! And I wouldn't make my plans any too solid concerning Corrie. She just might have something to say about them herself."

Donald's face darkened, a curiously childish expression crossing over it. He allowed himself to be backed toward the door, but his lower lip hung sullenly.

"Don't concern yourself with it, bitch," he whispered. "No one treats me this way. No one! And you'd just better make damned sure she does wake up. Or I'll fix you."

Susan stood shocked and speechless. Before she could

respond, he was gone. She stood listening to his heavy steps as they faded down the hallway and descended the stairs.

Bitch. He had dared to call her, Corrie's aunt, a bitch. A flicker of fright ran through Susan. Donald was dangerous, she thought. As dangerous as the half-starved stray dogs which occasionally roamed Nob Hill, overturning garbage cans and attacking small children.

Corrie Stewart lay at the bottom of a black, very deep well. Cradling her body was a pool of lukewarm water as dark as the well itself. Above her, far away at the top, people were gathered. Distantly Corrie could hear their voices, buzzing in a hum of meaningless syllables and phrases.

Sometimes there would be long pauses, spaces in which Corrie drifted on the odd dreams, threaded with streaks of color, which took her and rolled her about as if she had been a bit of dust caught in a windstorm, or a piece of foam tossed on the waves in the Bay.

Dreams. It was as if all her life had turned into fragments of colored glass, each shard a segment of memory. Avery, stripping the clothes from her body and kissing her naked belly. Quade Hill, staring boldly at her across the theater lobby, his eyes a direct, piercing, disturbing blue. Papa, his chest shaking with sobs, calling her *slut* and *whore*. His arms flailing in the air, protesting death . . .

Fragments. Brightly tinted, shiny fragments, meaning nothing.

She slept on, only faintly aware of the voices at the top of the well. Their tones were as meaningless as bird calls. Gradually her dreams became more restless, and once she thought she felt her legs moving. She was trying to run, that was it . . . to run away from someone who was pursuing her through a strange, ramshackle town . . .

She moaned.

Then, slowly drifting, her pursuer was gone and Avery was there, his face slivered like broken glass. His handsome, dear, beloved face now split apart with jagged cracks . . .

At times the voices at the top of the well became more

distinct. It was as if they tugged at her, pulled her upward out of the warm pool and toward them. But Corrie struggled to remain where she was. It was comfortable here in her pool of water, comfortable and safe. She did not want to follow the voices. Did not want to do anything but sleep.

Why are you keeping her flat down like this, broke through. Loudly, deeply, and full of trembling anger. When Corrie heard the angry voice she struggled even harder to stay safe in her pool.

Instead she began to rise up from the well. The voices were—yes—a rope, pulling her. Once she scraped the rough, mossy stones that lined the sides of the well, lacerating the skin on the back of her hand. She felt like crying out in pain. But she didn't; she was frozen, paralyzed, a marble statue. A statue which could not scream.

You're just faking this, aren't you.

Again the voice harried her brutally. The pain seared at her hands. Odd, that the rocks should hurt her so. Corrie felt a fuzzy panic. That voice. Where had she heard it before? What was it saying? It was that voice which was pulling her, by the very force of its anger, higher and higher up the well.

She didn't want to go.

No. She wanted to stay here where she was, among the rounded, aged, moss-grown pleasant stones.

I want you to wake up. I want you to hear me and wake.

No, she would not go any further up the stone sides of the well. She would remain where she was, suspended halfway between the warm water and the surface. She would never wake up.

The dreams changed. They were softer, a quiet, soothing murmur like high branches rustling in one of the big redwoods Papa had once taken her to see. She was a little girl. Papa held her on his lap, and she could smell the odor of whiskey and sweat and machine oil and tobacco. And now she was standing on tiptoe beside Mama's dressing table, looking over Mama's soft white shoulder into the mirror which reflected Mama herself, warm and beautiful.

Dreams. Fragments.

Without quite realizing it, Corrie had progressed further up the sides of the well. It was only with the greatest of effort that she managed to stay where she was. The voices became louder, pricking at her mind like the blunted points of tapestry needles, stirring her into further awareness. Unwillingly, she began to hear bits and scraps of their talk.

. . . thought I heard her move . . .

There. She did it again.

Do you want some luncheon, Li Hua? You've worked so hard . . .

No, I'll stay. Think she's . . .

. . . should really brush her hair again . . .

Did she moan? Did she moan, Li Hua?

She heard the words, but not their meanings. The voices spoke sounds. Strange sounds which meant nothing. But meaningless or not, the voices and their words were still a rope, pulling her, pulling.

I think she's starting to wake up, Li Hua!

Oh, ma'am, do you think—

Yes. She is. I heard her moan again. And her eyelids fluttered. Oh, God, Li Hua—

She was at the top. Somehow, soundlessly, she had floated directly to the top. Light assailed her, blinding and intense and white and real. Light beating at her, slapping her.

With enormous effort, as if she had come a very long way, Corrie opened her eyes.

❧ Chapter 7 ❧

Yellow sun poured through Corrie's bedroom window and cast pale rectangles on the cushioned window seat, and on the pink hothouse roses that Donald had sent. She was sitting up in bed, pillows bunched behind her, toying with the remains of a luncheon tray.

A week earlier she had come into the world quite unwillingly, screwing her eyes shut against the glare of the gas lights, tears sliding out. Papa was dead. They had not had to tell her that; somehow, even in the clouded dreams, she had realized it, had seen his flailing, protesting arms, and known.

She had regained full consciousness, calling often for Avery. The specialist from Chicago had arrived the next day, quite annoyed with her for recovering before he got there. She was one of the lucky ones, he informed her; very little was known about the working of the human brain and perhaps little ever would be. He told Aunt Susan to give her soups and fruit and custards and ordered complete bed rest. Then, grumpily, he accepted a sizeable payment from Aunt Susan and left to take the next train back to Chicago.

But Corrie was not doing a very good job of eating. Somehow she couldn't. Papa's death was not supposed to happen. He couldn't die, not her father, so alive and vital and laughing. With a sick rising of her gorge, she remembered the last words he had said to her. *Slut. Whore.* And the shocking thing he had said about Mama.

I beat 'em with a stick, both of them, until the blood ran . . .

Oh, she had to stop thinking of it! She loved Papa, and he had loved her. Nothing could change that.

But there was another reason why she could not eat. Avery. He had not come, nor had she heard from him. Donald, of course, had been outside her bedroom door several times since her recovery, but Aunt Susan had managed to fob him off with excuses. Corrie supposed she would have to see him eventually, but she would face that later.

But it was Avery who worried her. Why hadn't he at least written her a letter? Where *was* he? According to Aunt Susan, he had only inquired about her once, right after the accident, and hadn't been heard from since.

Now worry squirmed like a fish in Corrie's belly. She sighed and pushed the tray back. She couldn't possibly eat chicken soup; the very thought made her nauseous. There was typhoid going around the city; what if Avery had caught it—or influenza. Or worse. This was a seaport; Papa had talked about sailors bringing back strange foreign diseases. Avery's house had been in an area where sailors might take lodgings. Could he have possibly caught such a sickness?

Was Avery lying somewhere in a bed, too weak to call anyone? Did he need her?

Corrie reached up and yanked on the needlepoint bell-pull so that she could call Li Hua. She had to know! She couldn't just lie here helplessly waiting for him to contact her. What if he couldn't? What if he was already dead and she didn't even know it?

A few minutes later Li Hua rushed into the room, her eyes sparkling and her creamy skin flushed. Corrie was certain that the girl had run upstairs instead of sedately walking. In spite of her anxiety, Corrie felt a twinge of envy. Li Hua could run. She could chatter with Mrs. Parsons in the kitchen and beg for fresh doughnuts; she could come and go as she pleased.

While she, Corrie, was stuck here in bed, weak, shaky, and cold with fear for Avery.

"Li Hua, would you please find me some writing paper? I want to write a letter. And you can wait here for it; I'll want you to deliver it personally."

Li Hua's eyes lit up. She began rummaging through Corrie's writing desk, pulling open drawers and reaching into pigeonholes. The desk bulged with papers; Corrie hated to clean out drawers and very seldom did so.

"No, in the lower right drawer," Corrie instructed. "I think."

"Here?" Li Hua held up a rather smudged piece of paper.

"No, that's too untidy. Oh, I guess it will have to do." Forgetting her invalid state, Corrie began to get out of bed to reach for the paper. Instantly a wave of dizziness overtook her, small black dots crowding in front of her eyes, making her feel that she was in the middle of a strange blizzard. She felt her knees wobble. The black dots merged in front of her eyes to form a solid curtain.

She found that she was lying very comfortably on the floor; Li Hua's frightened face was bent over hers.

"Corrie! Corrie! Are you all right? You fell."

"I'm fine," Corrie said, feeling calm. "I saw a lot of black dots, that's all."

"You fainted! You shouldn't have been out of bed. The doctor said—oh, your aunt will be furious when she finds out. She'll be so angry." Desperately Li Hua began to drag at Corrie's arm, trying to lift her. But the Chinese girl was smaller and slighter than Corrie, and her efforts were not very successful.

"I'll have to call Mrs. Raleigh," Li Hua said at last.

"No! Not yet! I've got to do this by myself." This was ridiculous, Corrie told herself. She was as helpless here on the floor as a beached whale. How could she possibly have gotten so weak?

"But she said you couldn't get out of bed for six weeks. The doctor said you need absolute bed rest!"

"I don't care."

Corrie was trying to shove herself up from the floor now. Her arms felt shaky, gelatinelike, and the perspiration sprang out cold on her forehead.

"I think the doctor is wrong," she added. "The more I stay in bed, the worse I feel. No!" she exclaimed as Li

Hua started to fly in the direction of the door. "Don't fetch my Aunt!"

Li Hua paused.

"Now, just stay here and watch me," Corrie ordered. "If I start to fall, you can catch me, but otherwise I'm going to do this by myself. I'm *not* going to be an invalid! And you're not to tell Aunt Susan about this; I don't want her to be worried."

Minutes later, feeling as pale and limp and damp as a waterlogged linen towel, Corrie was back in bed.

"There," she said, hoping that she sounded stronger than she really felt. "I did get up and I did walk to my bed, and tonight I'm going to try it again. And tomorrow, too. And right now I'm going to write a letter."

It did not take her long to compose the letter to Avery. Ordinarily she would have taken great pains with it, but tonight she was filled with apprehension. Where was he? Was he all right? Why hadn't he contacted her? Was he ill? She loved him. Did he love her?

The questions poured out of her pen—along with a large, black blot; quickly she waved the letter dry and thrust it into the envelope Li Hua found. She scribbled his address on it.

"All right, you can take it now," she told the other girl. "And . . . please, if he's not there, try to find out where he is and if he's all right." Her voice had begun to shake. "All I want to know is that he's all right, that he isn't hurt, or sick, or—"

"All right," Li Hua said. With a look of sympathy and a swirl of her serviceable black skirts, she was gone.

Corrie reached for the discarded tray, pulled it toward her, and grimly, tasting none of it, began to eat.

Li Hua found Avery Curran's street without much difficulty. She walked quickly downhill, the wind toying at the ruffles of the hateful white lace-trimmed apron Aunt Susan made her wear. She didn't mind working for the Stewarts—not exactly. After all she had to work somewhere, they were kind to her, and she did love Corrie.

Still . . .

She pulled her plain black cape tighter about her

shoulders against the Bay wind. Still, she wasn't going to be a servant all of her life. If she lived in China, her mother had told her long ago, she might have had her feet bound. She might have been kept like a fragile porcelain doll, for her beauty.

She wasn't fragile, though, Li Hua thought defiantly, even if she was slight and small. And she didn't have her feet bound and she was an American. In 1877 her grandfather had been beaten and killed right here in San Francisco because he was Chinese. Her grandmother, with small children underfoot, had been driven out of her home. They had spoken only Chinese. Times were different now. Such a thing wasn't going to happen to her; she wouldn't let it.

She spotted the house where Avery lived. At a side door a large quantity of garbage and trash was piled up. Li Hua walked up to the front door of the cream and white frame house and nodded to the iron griffins, who seemed to disapprove of a servant going to the front door.

Boldly, she knocked.

After what seemed a very long time, she saw a hand pull apart the lace curtains of the center bay window. Then she heard footsteps. After a further wait, the door swung open.

"Yes?"

The woman at the door was middle-aged. A flowered chintz housecoat was wrapped loosely around a narrow body that exuded a stale, fusty odor. The woman's gray hair was coiled into two braids at the crown of her head, with wiry stray hairs sticking out in all directions. Li Hua looked at the braids with distaste. She could have fixed that hair into a decent pompadour or even a Eugenia wave. Why would any woman, even an old one, make herself look so ugly?

"I came here to deliver a letter to Mr. Avery Curran," she explained. "He lives here, doesn't he?"

"He did."

"He did live here? Do you mean that he doesn't any more?"

"Yes, he's gone. Last week, it was. On one of them steamers."

Li Hua frowned. She thought of the way Corrie's hands had shaken when she gave her the letter. "Did you say he's gone? But I have a letter for him."

"Who from?" the woman asked. Again Li Hua caught a whiff of sour body odor, and she wrinkled her nose in distaste.

"From Miss Cordelia Stewart. She asked that I find out where he is and deliver it to him. I'm to make sure that he's all right, and not ill."

"Oh, he's fine enough. Healthy as a dray horse. But you can't see him, because he ain't here, and he ain't likely to be back for some time to come, not where he's going. He did leave a letter, though. Said I was to mail it. I ain't got around to doing it, though, so I suppose you can have it and save me the price. If you're sure you're from this Cordelia Stewart woman."

"Yes, I am."

"Then wait a minute while I see if I can find it. I've got it with my knitting somewhere . . . "

There was another long wait. Li Hua was left to stand on the doorstep with the wind flapping at her skirts; the occupants of a passing surrey stared curiously at her. But at last the woman was back, and thrust a soiled, unsealed envelope into Li Hua's hand.

"Here."

Li Hua took it, forced a smile, and said thank you.

The woman's lips parted sourly. "Oh, that's all right. The rogue left still owing me five dollars. Said he'd send it to me when he had it. Ha. Likely chance of that. Handsome he is, but she'll find that's all."

As Li Hua turned, she felt the faded eyes on her, and sensed an old woman's amusement in them. Of course, she thought. The letter was unsealed, and the woman had read it.

Frowning, she started for the nearest cable car line.

Corrie put the letter down with a hand that suddenly had no strength. Nausea welled up in her throat and she had to swallow hard to push back the hot, metallic-tasting bile.

Avery had left for the Yukon.

He had joined the gold seekers, or the stampeders as

they were also called. He did not plan to return until he was rich. He intended, he informed her in his precise, rather beautiful script, to come back and shower her with a rain of gold nuggets.

Gold nuggets!

Corrie sank back onto her bed. She could scarcely believe what she had read. That Avery would think she could prefer a lapful of gold to him. That he should think wealth that important . . .

Her hand moved mechanically to pick up the letter again. Its elegant calligraphy seemed to dance in front of her eyes. *Dearest Corrie. I feel like a cad for leaving you like this, but I gathered from my talk with your aunt that your recovery is expected, and a chance came for me to get passage on the* Alaska Queen, *and I had to take it. I am asking my landlady to mail this for me, and I hope it finds you happily recovered and your own lovely self again. I was grieved to learn of your father's death, and I realize now that our marriage needs more than fine hopes—or the lack of them—to sustain it . . .*

The letter went on, explaining that Avery had made contact with some others going north, particularly a person named Mason Edwards who had arrived in San Francisco from Ann Arbor, Michigan. They were going to pool their resources.

I'm going to be rich, Corrie. I have the feeling that it is really going to happen to me. And when it does, I'll come back with a sackful of solid gold nuggets, and I'll fill your lap with them. My darling, I'll rain gold on you, and then we can be married properly. I won't have to feel like your poor relation, but can buy you the things you need and should have.

There was more, but Corrie could not read it. She thought of Avery's mouth, pressed against her own. Of his body, which had been so intimate with hers.

She felt her fingers begin to squeeze the fine paper of the letter. Then suddenly she crammed the letter into a ball. She crushed it together with the palms of her hands until the graceful handwriting was smeared beyond recognition by her perspiration and tears.

She was never to remember how she got through the rest of that day. Somehow she forced herself to eat a bit of luncheon, to get out of bed and totter around the room. Her legs were growing stronger with each step she took. And, she told herself defiantly, Avery or no Avery, she couldn't lie in bed forever.

But there was no triumph in being able to walk two times down the corridor and back. Without Avery, there was nothing to walk for. Why, she wondered with aching misery, hadn't he taken her with him? It might be years before he came back. It undoubtedly would be.

That night Aunt Susan came into her room and told her that on the following day they would read her father's will.

"The will?" A sudden, sick fear stabbed through Corrie. She had forgotten. Papa had promised her that he would change what he had written, but he had died before he could do so.

"Yes, dear. You knew that Mr. Bardley was holding off because of your illness, which I thought most considerate of him. But he can't put it off forever, and since you're growing better every day—" Aunt Susan frowned. "Corrie, have you been crying?"

"It's just—Papa . . . " Corrie heard herself reply, and was ashamed when Susan put her arms around her and gave her a swift hug.

"I know, Corrie, it's been so very hard. But I'm sure it will be a relief to have the reading of the will over with. Mr. Bardley is planning to come here so that you won't have to leave the house. Isn't that kind of him?"

"Yes, of course."

They met to read the will in Cordell Stewart's library. It was a big room, panelled in dark oak and smelling of old leather, cigar smoke and book bindings. Corrie had always loved this room, its shelves piled with books, papers, periodicals and small oddities her father had picked up on his travels. Some libraries, she knew, were merely for show. But Cordell Stewart had read all of his books, and she had read many. This room had been a friend to her. It hurt immeasurably to sit in one of the leather chairs and to know that her father would never come here again.

Donald, who had to come from the shipyard, was late, and they sat waiting for him.

"Well, Miss Cordelia, you certainly have grown into a

lovely young lady," Amos Bardley said, politely ignoring the fact that Corrie was pale and thin, the bruise on her temple not yet faded.

Corrie managed a smile. Amos Bardley had been her father's attorney for fifteen years, and said the same thing whenever he saw her.

At last Donald arrived, banging the door of the library and bringing a rush of outdoor air into the room. He wore a well-tailored dark suit which fit him tightly and made him look wider and shorter, like a bold, thrusting bull, Corrie noted uneasily. The red, puckered scar on the back of his right hand was uglier than ever. His shiny black hair caught the light.

"Well, Mr. Earle, now that you're here—" Amos Bardley began.

Donald stopped inside the door, ignoring the attorney and fixing his eyes on Corrie.

"So you're up and about now."

"Yes, I'm doing very well."

She was shaken by the look he gave her in front of the other two. It was as if she were a coveted, enormously expensive emerald, and he a man who would kill and steal to obtain it. She swallowed tightly. How strange that she should have such a thought. But she could not get it out of her mind as Donald sat down and the reading of the will began.

I, Cordell Starr Stewart, being of sound mind and judgment at this time, and desiring to dispose of my worldly goods, chattels and possessions . . ..

Corrie did not listen. Why should she? she thought with a stab of temper. The will was a monstrosity, drawn up without consulting her in the slightest. Now the deed was done. Papa had died before he could change what, in his foolishness, he had written.

Amos Bardley's voice droned on. Aunt Susan sat very still, head cocked to one side, eyes glistening. Donald's face was impassive.

"Well, that's it," Bardley said at last. "I'll see to it that the servants are given their bequests as soon as possible, of course. Funds were set aside specifically for that purpose . . ."

He went on with more talk of this nature. The servants

—Li Hua, Mrs. Parsons, Jim Price, Bea Ellen and the others—were called in to receive the news of their bequests. Their faces, Corrie saw, were both solemn and eager.

Corrie stood up, unable to bear it any longer. Papa was dead, but his will, unfair and autocratic, lived on. Now everyone would be forced to abide by it. She lifted her skirts and ran from the room, her forehead beaded with cold moisture. She let the library door swing shut behind her.

She had reached the bend in the corridor near the kitchen and was about to run up the back staircase when she felt a hand on her arm.

"Corrie? Where are you going?"

It was Donald, his face flushed. She could hear faint voices coming from the library and realized that everyone was still in the room, discussing the will. All the servants, too, she thought in panic. She was alone with Donald.

"Please, Donald, I don't feel well . . . " Corrie said.

She heard her voice grow faint and knew that this, at least, was the truth. She had exhausted her meager strength in running out of the library, and there was a sick feeling in her belly. She had not eaten any breakfast. Now she was feeling both hungry and nauseated at the same time.

She started to sway. But before she could collapse, Donald picked her up in his arms.

"You are sick, aren't you? I told that aunt of yours that she had better take care of you, and what a job she's done of it. You're practically swooning. I'll carry you upstairs."

"But—that isn't necessary."

"It is necessary. I won't permit my wife to lie in a heap on the floor like a pile of rags."

"But I'm not your wife!"

She wanted to cry with the frustration of being so helpless. Her long inactivity had left her weak. Her arm muscles were flaccid, no match for the powerful strength of this man who lifted her and began to carry her up the stairs as if she weighed nothing at all.

She closed her eyes, forcing back another wave of sickness, and allowed him to carry her. What could she do

about it, anyway? She was too weak to fight him, and there
was no one near to hear her calls.

They were upstairs, in the polished, lemon-oiled cleanliness of her room. She felt Donald putting her on the bed.
But instead of releasing her, he remained where he was,
his big body pressed against her.

"There's no one about," he said musingly. "I could strip
that dress off you in one minute, do you know that? I
could—"

"Donald!" With her last vestige of strength she managed to shove at his chest, pushing him back a little way.
"Please, Donald, you mustn't talk to me that way. Leave
me alone. I'm ill. I don't want you in my bedroom. And
I certainly have no intentions of m—"

"You may not intend it, my dear, but I do. And when
the time comes, you won't resist me." He stood up, looking
big and totally alien in this airy bedroom of hers. He was
arrogant and ugly, she thought wildly. How she hated him.

"Your lover-boy has gone away, hasn't he?" she heard
him say.

"My l-lover?"

"That man Curran. He went off and left you, didn't
he?" Donald was grasping her hand, pulling it toward him,
squeezing at it. "Can't you get it through your head, Corrie? I've wanted you, I've needed you to be mine. And
now your father's will has given me my chance. Where is
my ring? Didn't I tell you to wear it?"

His face swam toward her through what seemed to be a
swirling white fog. How had he known about Avery? she
had time to wonder numbly. She had never been the type
of girl to have the "vapors"—she despised those who did
—but she was certainly feeling faint now. Donald's face
was wavering as if she were looking at it under water.

He squeezed at her fingers so tightly that they stung.

"Please, Donald. My hand; you're hurting me."

"Tell me about the ring, Corrie. I spent good money
for it and I'd like to know where it is."

"I don't know."

It was the will, Corrie was thinking frantically. The will
which made Donald think he could talk like this to her.
The will which bound them both together like some hideous glue.

Somehow he was back down on the bed beside her, his face close to hers, his body pressed against her. His weight was so heavy that she thought he would crush her. "But I gave you that ring," he told her. "I gave it to you!" He acted like a thwarted little boy.

"I threw it away," she said.

"What? You did what?"

"I threw it in the trash! And I'm glad I did it. Glad, do you hear? And I'd do it again!"

Then everything, even Donald's furious face, faded, and she was only aware of her nausea, bitter and choking. She turned her head aside and was humiliatingly and thoroughly sick.

❧ Chapter 8 ❧

It was Li Hua who finally came upstairs and cleaned the mess Corrie had made of her bed.

"Oh, Corrie, what happened? I didn't know you felt so sick!"

"I didn't know it either," Corrie said at last. "I'm sorry."

She lay very still while Li Hua removed the bedding and replaced it with clean linen. Her body still felt clammy with perspiration. Donald was gone—thank God for that. She should put her finger down her throat whenever he appeared, she thought, choking back a bitter laugh. Then she would drive him away forever.

"You'd better move to the other side of the bed now. I'll take away these dirty sheets," Li Hua said. She worked quickly, her delicate, cameolike face expressionless.

Obediently, Corrie moved. She didn't care what she did. She only wished Li Hua would finish so that she could put her face into the pillow and weep. How had her life turned out like this? Papa dead. Avery gone. And now, Donald, with his angry eyes, virtually ready to devour her. Sooner or later he would wear her down. And then Papa's will would become an ugly cement, bonding Donald and herself together for the rest of their lives . . .

"Do you want me to bring you up some supper?" Li Hua was asking. "You might feel better if you ate. My mother always used to keep a few dry biscuits with her."

"No. I'm not hungry. Oh, Li Hua, would you just please hurry and finish the bed so I can sleep? I don't want anything to eat. I just want to be left alone!"

"But don't you want to change? You'd be more comfortable if you did."

"No! I don't want to change! Oh, Li Hua, would you please just go?"

The girl lowered her eyes, her lashes making a semicircle against her cheeks. Abruptly Corrie remembered Donald's remark about Avery. How had he known Avery had left the city? Or of her love for Avery?

Li Hua, her fingers plucking at the black fabric of her skirt, had just turned to leave when Corrie called her back.

"Li Hua! Don't go yet. Would you please get me a nightgown? I've changed my mind. I don't want to lie here in my dress."

"But you said—"

"I want you to get me a nightgown!" Corrie knew that she was being unreasonable, and that she sounded like Papa at his most autocratic, but she couldn't seem to stop herself. There was something wrong here.

Her eyes traveled to the wastepaper basket where she had flung the crumpled letter from Avery. Of course, she thought. Li Hua had read it.

"Li Hua," she said sharply. The girl, opening Corrie's bureau drawer to get the nightgown, jerked upright. She turned to stare at Corrie, her dark eyes wide. For the first time Corrie noticed that there were circles under them.

"Yes?"

"Li Hua, did you read that letter?"

"I . . . no, of course not."

"I think you're lying. I think you did read it, and I also think that you told Mr. Donald Earle what was in it. How could you, Li Hua?"

"No, I—I didn't! I—" Li Hua dropped the frilly nightgown to the floor and bent immediately to pick it up. "I'll get you a clean gown, Corrie. This one is dirtied. I'll have Bea Ellen wash it. You don't want to wear a dirty gown to bed, not when you've been as sick as you have . . . "

The girl was babbling, Corrie thought. Chattering with guilt.

"Li Hua!" Perspiring, Corrie managed to push herself up on the pillows, her anger giving her strength. "I don't care whether the gown is clean or dirty; just bring it here so I can put it on. I know you sat with me all the

time that I was sick, and that you were very faithful. Aunt
Susan told me all about how hard you worked. But I
want to know why you told Donald about Avery."

"Tell me," she insisted, as the girl looked away, her
eyes evasive. "You aren't going to wriggle out of this. You
told him and I know that you did. We've been friends,
Li Hua . . . why did you do it?"

Li Hua let the nightgown drop on the bed. It fell in
a soft fluff of cambric. The girl's dark, tilted eyes were
glazed with tears. "I didn't mean to tell him. I—"

Corrie could not control her fury. "You knew that I
loved Avery. You knew how much he meant to me.
But you told Donald about him." She had a sudden, terrible thought. "Is that why Avery left so suddenly? Because *Donald* gave him the money to buy his passage?
Oh, God, Li Hua, how could you?"

Even Corrie was shocked by what she had said. The
two girls stared at each other, and now the servant's eyes
did spill tears. Li Hua had come to their house as an
irrepressible thirteen-year-old; she had been not only a
ladies' maid but also a friend. They had shared laughter and jokes; Li Hua had been there to help her forget
when her mother had died. Corrie had taken dozens of
photographs of Li Hua; they had both cried when Corrie's
old dog, Biggie, had died.

And now Li Hua had done this.

"Li Hua, I can't believe you would betray me like this!
To tell that horrid Donald about Avery, to reveal the contents of my letter, which was my own personal business!"

"I had reasons," Li Hua muttered.

"What reasons? You've worked here in our house,
you've been more than a servant. What reasons could you
have had? And the ring—you were the one who measured
my finger for that, too," Corrie remembered. "He said he
bribed you. Did he, Li Hua? Did he pay you to betray
me? Did he?"

"No!" Li Hua shouted at her, the delicate voice raised
in a way Corrie had never heard before. "No, it wasn't
like that at all; you don't understand. I never would have
done it except that I couldn't help it, I—"

"Couldn't help it?" Corrie drew herself up. She felt her
right hand reach out to gather up the folds of the soft,

cambric nightgown. With a convulsive movement she picked up the wad of material and threw it at Li Hua.

"Oh, get out of here! Get out, Li Hua! You're not a friend or a servant to me any more—you're a betrayer!"

As the white cloth flew through the air the other girl ducked. Then, in a swift motion, Li Hua bent over, grasped the nightgown and flung it back at Corrie.

The cloth landed with a light touch just above Corrie's ear. Lavender-scented, embroidered lace hit her cheek.

"Oh!" Savagely Corrie grabbed for the gown and hurled it back. This time her aim was better; she hit Li Hua in the chest.

"All right, Corrie! All right!" The Chinese girl's voice was shaking, her dark, almond-shaped eyes wild. "I'm sorry I told about your Avery Curran. I had a reason, but you'd never understand it, would you? Not you, the spoiled little rich girl who always had everything given to her. You never had to watch your mother die in childbirth, as I did. No, yours died with three fat doctors in attendance. You never had to earn every grain of rice you put into your mouth, either. Well, I can tell you something. You're no lady, not you. Throwing nightgowns like a spoiled rich brat! Well, I should think you might want to be more careful. On account of the baby you're carrying. That's all."

On account of the baby you're carrying.

Corrie's body suddenly felt suffused with blood. Her skin burned hot, then instantly was clammy again.

"Li Hua!" She stretched out her hand to the other girl. "Oh, please, Li—"

But Li Hua, her expression grim and furious, quite unservantlike, had marched out of the room in a swirl of dark uniform. She slammed the door behind her.

Corrie's supper came, fried abalone as only Mrs. Parsons could cook it, pounded thin until it was sweet and tender. She pushed at her food, but hunger finally prevailed, and she ate nearly half of the large portion of shell fish.

She was *not* pregnant, she told herself fiercely. The whole thing was a lie, made up by Li Hua out of anger and spite. Surely it was nothing more than that. A girl could not become pregnant after only one time with a man . . . could she?

At last she pushed aside her tray and reached for a novel, *The Damnation of Theron Ware,* which was much talked of these days. The pages had not yet been cut, and she performed this chore with fingers that were cold and trembling. At last she let the book slide out of her hands.

Pregnant. No, she couldn't possibly be!

But involuntarily she closed her eyes and began mental calculations. It was true that she had not yet experienced her "sick" time of the month—not that those days had ever troubled her much. But that was nothing to be worried about, she was sure. True, her flux was a few days late. But it was not very late, and probably her long unconsciousness had interfered with her natural cycle. Li Hua did not know what she was talking about!

Still, pressing her fingers to her temples, Corrie found that her head was pounding. At last, impulsively, she flung back the bedcovers and got out of bed. A brief wave of dizziness assailed her, but she stood very still until it went away. Then she grasped the folds of the cambric nightgown and pulled it off.

She moved in front of the beveled mirror of her dresser to stare at her own nakedness. She had lost weight, but the body that she saw in the glass was still a voluptuous one, with firm breasts tilted upward. Her waist was slim, curving downward to a flat belly, then outward to lush curve of hips.

For long moments Corrie stared at herself, seeing only the total impression—the expanse of fair skin marked off by darker nipples and a fuzz of body hair.

Then slowly she focused on the line of her belly. Flat. Smooth. She frowned, her eyes narrowing. Didn't a woman who was expecting . . . didn't her belly bulge out? Corrie had observed Bea Ellen, the fat laundress, in the last cumbersome weeks of her seventh pregnancy. If she herself were expecting, wouldn't her body show signs of it?

She heard footsteps in the corridor. Quickly she reached for the nightgown and slid it on again, feeling the lace and cambric settle like a puff of wind about her shoulders.

There was a knock at her door. "Corrie, are you sleeping? I'm not disturbing you, am I?"

It was Aunt Susan. Corrie leaped guiltily back into bed. By the time Susan had opened the door, she was sitting against the pillows, her back straight.

"Corrie? Are you quite all right?" Susan wore a white shirtwaist blouse, a lace bertha, and a black serge skirt whose lining rustled when she walked. "Li Hua told me that you were not well."

"I'm fine now. It's just that I was upset by the reading of the . . . the will."

Susan nodded. "That's understandable. I'm sure I would be upset myself. I really can't understand why my brother would do such a thing. But he did, and it's all over and done now, so we might as well make the best of it. Fortunately, he did allow the grace period, so things can go as they are for a while yet."

"The grace period?"

"Cordelia Stewart, you were present. Weren't you listening?"

"I— No, I guess I wasn't," Corrie admitted.

"Very well, then. Your father specified that for the period of eighteen months, the final disposition of his estate is to remain in abeyance. That is, you'll go on living in this house, with a generous allowance, and Donald will continue in his job as general manager of the shipyard. At the end of that time, if you are married to Donald, you and he will inherit fully. If you are not, then you will get your twenty percent. I believe the charity your father has chosen is the Seamen's Widows and the Old Seamen's Home." Susan paused significantly.

"Isn't it nice that they will benefit, then?" Corrie's voice was low. "Aunt, I don't need eighteen months to decide not to marry Donald Earle. I can make that decision right now, today."

Susan was silent. At last she said, "Oh, Corrie, I wish I knew what to tell you. While you were sick, the man was . . . very rude to me, quite ungentlemanly. He said things to me which just are not said in proper society. I can only wonder why my brother was so taken with him."

"I believe he said it was because Donald reminded him of himself as a young man."

"Yes. Perhaps. Cordell's own behavior during those days was not totally admirable." Susan spoke dryly. "Nevertheless, Corrie, I should tell you that the money *is* something to consider. You've never lived without money. You don't know what a buttress it can be against the ugly things, the wretched facts of living."

Susan went on in this vein for a few minutes, while Corrie seemed to hear Li Hua's voice in her ears. *You never had to watch your mother die in childbirth. You never had to earn every grain of rice you put into your mouth.* Wasn't this the same thing that Aunt Susan was telling her, in a nicer way, of course? That she was rich and spoiled and didn't know what it was like to be poor?

"Money!" she began. "I don't need—"

But Susan put up a hand. "Never disparage wealth, dear Corrie. A woman does need it to cushion herself and make life bearable. Much as I dislike Donald Earle, I do feel that you should take your father's wishes into consideration. And I would not have done my duty properly if I hadn't informed you of it."

"But—"

"Don't argue, Corrie. Just think." Susan turned and left the room.

Corrie waited until the door had closed, then she sank down among the pillows. She could feel a quivering within her, and knew that in a few minutes she was going to burst into hot, shameful, wretched tears.

Avery, she thought. If you were here, all of this would be so easy. But you aren't here. I'm alone. And nothing, nothing is simple.

Three weeks passed, long, slow, and full of a futility that ate away at Corrie's nerves. She received no more letters from Avery, although she waited impatiently each day for the mail to arrive. Even Aunt Susan remarked on her eagerness. Was she waiting for an invitation to a special ball, perhaps?

She and Li Hua were back on speaking terms again, warily. It was hard not to be when Li Hua worked such long hours helping her exercise her legs and arms, giving up her own free time to do so. It was almost as if, Corrie thought, she were trying to make up for something she had done . . .

Each day Corrie's physical strength increased, until she could be up and dressed for the entire day. Against Susan's objections, she went outdoors and played lawn tennis. She put on her bicycling costume and rode her cycle in the streets, walking it uphill when her strength flagged. She went for long walks with her camera.

She would not be an invalid, she told herself grimly. Although her muscles responded to this determination, her nausea did not. Each morning when she arose she was sick. The queasiness stayed with her the rest of the day, often resulting in more vomiting. She lost at least five pounds.

Donald, as if sensing that he had gone too far, was on his best behavior now. He called occasionally on Corrie and took her several times to the theater. To please her aunt, the girl was civil to him. She went with him to the Alhambra, the Tivoli and the Alcazar. She accompanied him to Marchand's Restaurant and—trying to ignore her queasy belly—picked at pompano *en papillote* and terrapin.

The Donald who sat with her in the luxurious dimness of the well-known restaurant was a new Donald, a suave, worldly man who lingered over the lighting of his after-dinner cigar to stare thoughtfully into its flames. The man who spoke casually of daily events at the shipyard, or discussed his theory that the age of sailing was over, never mentioned the ring, or even marriage. Yet she knew he could not have forgotten.

One night after he brought her home and was helping her out of his buggy, she happened to glance at him and saw that his intense black eyes were again heavy-lidded with desire.

"Corrie—" His voice was thick as he reached for her.

She managed to twist out of his grasp. "I really must go in the house; my aunt is waiting for me. Good night, Donald."

"Very well. Good night." He turned without looking at her and stalked a few paces away. Corrie rushed up the walk and flung open the front door, to stand inside, trembling.

Nothing had changed, she thought in growing panic. Donald still wanted her desperately.

Donald Earle adjusted the tilt of the mirror that was attached to his shaving cabinet, picked up the cake of shaving soap and stood staring at his own reflection.

He looked bad this morning, he decided. His dark eyes were puffy, with smudges under them, and his black, thick hair was rumpled and disheveled. As usual, his facial hair was growing in dark and coarse, save for the white hairs which grew in a line near his chin. If he ever grew a beard, he knew, it would come in streaked with white like a skunk's tail.

He smiled briefly, examined his teeth, and again changed the tilt of the mirror. Not that he needed to grow a beard, he thought. He had gained forty pounds, most of it hard muscle, since those days in Chicago. Even Ma wouldn't know him today.

Thinking of her, he scowled. She had been dead nearly thirty years, and she could still make a sick feeling twist in the pit of his belly. Drunken, filthy whore . . .

He clamped his lips together and, making an effort, turned his thoughts to last night and Li Hua. This was the second time he had had her, and it had been worth the risk of discovery. The little Chinese girl had a tense, hot body that excited him. Her face had twisted with fright when she had seen the—

Donald broke off his thoughts, scowling. Again he had made the girl swear, on her mother's grave and on the breathing body of the sister she still had living in Chinatown, that she would never divulge what had happened that night in his rooms. Ever. And that she would keep him fully informed of every movement Cordelia Stewart made.

Abjectly, those slanted eyes of hers wide with terror, she had promised. Then, to clinch it, he had added one more threat. That was when he could tell, by the trembling of her mouth, that she would do as she was told.

He finished working up the lather and began to brush it onto his cheeks, whistling to himself. Perhaps this would be a good day after all. Certainly he was beginning to make some progress with that cold little bitch, Cordelia Stewart.

Corrie. God, but there was something she did to him, some way she had of twisting his feelings deep in his gut. He couldn't explain it, but he had never thought he would ever want a woman as deeply and completely as he wanted her. What a wife she would make. She was as beautiful as a camelia and just as cold and haughty. She was . . . unreachable. Yes, perhaps that was it. She was perfect. . . .

There was a quality about her which *belonged* to society. With Corrie as his wife he, the son of Nellie Blower (Earle was a name he had chosen for himself), would be accepted in any of the mansions on Nob Hill. He could have his name added to those in the "Five Hundred," could send his children to Lunt's Dancing School and see his daughter make a fancy debut—all of it. Not to mention the fact that he could do as he pleased with the Stewart Shipyards. He itched to get his hands on it. Sailing! Steam was where the future was, not sailing; even a five-year-old child would have realized it by this time. Even in Alaska, it was machines and big-business syndicates which would make the real money, rather than individual miners. Cordell Stewart had been a blathering, out-of-date old fool.

Donald twisted his mouth to get the lather into the indentation of his chin, his mind going back to Corrie. He had worked a lot of years and taken a lot of risks to get close to that girl. She didn't like him, of course; at least she thought she didn't. But Donald knew better. If she chose, haughty Cordelia Stewart could melt for him and spread her legs as wide as any girl on the Barbary Coast. He was sure that she secretly enjoyed the little game they were playing. It was his theory that women—particularly the haughtiest ones—enjoyed the prospect of being overcome by a man. It overrode their guilt feelings and let them enjoy sex. Even as they railed at you angrily, their bodies were arching closer to yours. They wanted rough treatment. They loved it.

He picked up his razor, still thinking of Corrie, of the way she would look naked. But then—as often happened

—her image began to melt and merge into that of the other girl, five years ago. The girl who had stood paralyzed behind the leaping flames, her eyes riveted to his own as if the two of them were bound by a white-hot band of molten metal.

For what seemed hundreds of years they had looked at each other. She— Oh, Jesus, the fire, the flames, had been reflected in her eyes . . . *GodGodGod God GOD* . . .

Donald shook his head convulsively, remembering it all vividly. Her fear, her hate, his own rising, tumultuous feelings . . . But he had had to survive, of course. So he had left, but not before, half-staggering at the front door to the office, he had experienced an electric, searing, gigantic climax . . .

His hand was trembling now as he gripped the razor. Millicent, he thought jerkily. Millicent too. That day when he crept into the cramped, smelly little room with the mattress on the floor which his cousin Millie shared with four other sisters. He was only nine then, but he knew what he wanted, and Millicent, at thirteen, was more than willing to teach him everything. She got rid of her sisters, and lit the candle so that they would have some light.

Her red-chestnut hair hung down on either side of his face as she moved on top of him.

And then the candle caught fire on the hem of her rucked-up skirts—

Fire . . . *Jesus!*

Donald felt a searing pain. He stared in the mirror at the stream of red blood running down his chin from his jaw, where he had cut himself. God, he thought. His hand was shaking violently now, and the blood continued to flow. That cold bitch! Corrie and her kind, *all* of them. None of them could ever understand.

❦ Chapter 9 ❦

One sunny, late March morning, Corrie resolutely put on her bicycling costume, fighting the nausea which troubled her each morning. She peered sharply at herself in the mirror. The cycling costume—daring but smart, Aunt Susan maintained—was made of blue velveteen, and had a divided skirt which showed her shapely ankles and half of her calf. It had a snug matching jacket with wide lapels and a ruffled blouse.

She narrowed her eyes. Surely she looked paler. And wasn't the skirt rather tight about the waist? She took a deep breath and pushed the thought out of her mind. She didn't want to think of that now . . .

She left the house and wheeled the bicycle out of its stall in the carriage house, breathing in deeply the clear Bay air. Swinging onto the seat, she began to pedal the bicycle downhill where the going would be easiest.

At a corner, a shapeless old woman carrying a huge tray laden with yellow hothouse roses was deep in argument with a customer, a well-dressed gentleman. Corrie swung out into the street to avoid hitting the flower vendor.

It was then that her rear wheel skidded on a wet spot on the pavement.

She went flying over the handlebars and landed with a painful scrape almost under a carriage wheel. She heard a shout, and then felt strong arms scoop her up.

"Don't you watch where you're going?"

"Of course I do! I skidded, that's all."

"These steep streets can be dangerous, especially for someone hampered by all those heavy, foolish skirts. You got your skirt caught in the chain, or hadn't you realized that?"

The voice was familiar.

"You!" Corrie cried. "That Rabbit-foot McGee man!"

Quade Hill grinned. He looked bigger than ever, his wide shoulders seeming to take up all the room on the street. His intense blue eyes gleamed with amusement.

"That's one name for me. And you're the camera girl. Or should I call you the bicycle chain girl?"

Corrie glared downward and saw that he was right—a two-inch oily black rip marked the place where the velveteen outfit had been snagged in the chain.

The old flower vendor was smirking at them, she saw with annoyance.

"What are you doing here?" she demanded.

"Why, I'm buying roses for a lady. Bargaining for them as any sensible person should do." His smile was amused. "At least, I was trying to buy them—until you squashed them."

She looked at the roses he still held. They were indeed crumpled.

"*I* didn't squash them—not on purpose! You were the one who picked me up; at least you could have put them down first!"

"And let you get hit by that carriage?" Quade's voice was quiet. She felt his hand support her elbow. "You look rather white. Are you sure that fall didn't hurt you?"

"Of course I am. I'm fine!"

"I'm glad to hear it. Then perhaps you will accept a rose from me, as a token of my good wishes?"

Before she could stop him, he selected one long-stemmed golden rose from the bouquet, and extended it to her. "Of course," he added, his smile showing strong white teeth, "there are a few petals less on this posy, but even a squashed rose is better than no rose at all, right? Especially when one looks a bit rumpled oneself."

His eyes ranged with amusement up and down her figure. Was he admiring the stylish flared waist of the jacket, the way it revealed the curves of her bust and waist? Did he notice the trimness of her calves in their black silk hose? Or—she bit down on her lower lip—was he merely thinking about how disheveled she looked?

"The best apparel for you to wear to ride that machine would be a pair of good, stout pants," he told her, shrugging. "But vanity holds you in thrall as it does the rest of womankind, doesn't it, Cordelia Stewart? Or should I call you Corrie, your little-girl name?"

"Call me anything you wish," Corrie snapped, "I'm not vain. I'm not! Aunt Susan said this dress was daring enough as it is. What would people say if I were to wear—"

He laughed at her, his head thrown back, his throat working. "Do you always react so furiously when you are teased?"

"Yes! No, I—" she stopped, feeling caught.

"And are you always so pretty when you are upset?"

Confusion overwhelmed her. Angrily she snatched up her bicycle from where it lay and swung herself back onto its seat.

"I am leaving, Mr. Hill," she said as coolly as she could. "As for this, you may have it—I've no place to put it."

She tossed back the rose he had given her. It flew through the air, a little spot of pure yellow. Deftly he caught it.

"Ride safely, Corrie Stewart. He saluted her with the rose. "And watch that hem."

Corrie tossed her head and rode off without replying. As she pedaled down the street, she was conscious that he was watching her sardonically.

Two hours later she was home again, breathless from walking the bike uphill. Her costume was marked with dust and grease, the blue velveteen sticking uncomfortably to her warm skin.

Aunt Susan swept into the foyer to greet her.

"Corrie, would you come into my sitting room after you've changed? I can't think where you could have picked up so much dirt."

"I fell." Corrie thought of Quade Hill and felt herself turn scarlet. "I skidded on a section of—of wet pavement. And my skirt got caught in the chain."

"Bicycles are for the brave and the foolish," Susan said

dryly. "Do go and change, Corrie. At once. I would like to speak to you."

Corrie did as she was asked. Fifteen minutes later she appeared in Susan's sitting room, dressed in a plain white shirtwaist with an ascot scarf and a dark blue broadcloth skirt, her face freshly scrubbed.

"Yes, Aunt?" Corrie looked about her. The sitting room was decorated in shades of gold and turkey red, filled with *bibelots* and plants which both hung and grew in pots.

Susan put aside her needlework and motioned for Corrie to sit down on the Morris rocker, the seat cushion of which she had needlepointed.

"Corrie . . . I must talk to you."

"Yes?"

There was an uncomfortable silence. "Corrie, are you ill?" Susan asked finally.

"Ill?" Corrie looked at her aunt, feeling her heart give a thump. Surely—oh, surely her aunt could not *know*. Yet Susan's lips were pressed tightly together, her blue eyes scouring in their directness.

"I've been talking with Bea Ellen and she let slip some interesting facts about your laundry. You have managed to soil more than your share of linens and towels, and— and there are certain other items which you have *not* been using recently . . . " Susan paused, flushing.

"Aunt!" Corrie pictured Susan and the hugely fat Bea Ellen talking about her. Anger flooded through her. "Why, Aunt Susan! I can't believe you would question the servants about me! With—with Bea Ellen of all people! Oh! It's disgusting—" Her voice caught.

"I know, dear. It *is* disgusting. I admit that, and I'm ashamed. But you do understand, Corrie, that I had to do it. I'm responsible for you. You have no mother, and now your father is dead too. If I don't take an interest in your affairs, who will? Oh, Corrie, you have your reputation to think of, and don't think people won't talk if they even *suspect*. Society can be so savage, sometimes, to those who flout it . . . "

As her aunt continued, Corrie bent forward, her eyes focused on the blue of her skirt and on her own fingers, stained with photographic chemicals, which twisted and turned themselves together.

"Well?" Susan asked at last. "Is it true?"

To Corrie's surprise, her aunt's eyes were wet with tears. "Oh, God, Corrie, I kept telling myself it couldn't be true. But I'm so afraid that it is. You've all the signs, and heaven knows I remember them well enough from when I had my own stillbirths . . . "

Corrie sat very still for a long time. "Yes. I'm pregnant." The girl's voice sounded strange, not like her own at all. "Oh, Aunt, it was Avery, and now he's gone, gone to Alaska, and I feel so sick. I just wish I could die!"

Half an hour later, Corrie had told Susan everything. She had talked and wept and talked some more, until it seemed there was nothing more left to say.

At last Susan reached for her needle, threaded it with light blue embroidery thread, and picked up her cut-work. Methodically she began taking stitch after tiny stitch, each one so precise that it looked as if it could have been done by a machine.

"Well, and what are you going to do, Corrie? You certainly can't sit here in this house much longer. Even with a tight corset, you'll soon start to show."

"I don't know. I was going to marry Avery, of course. In his letter he told me that he was going to come home and fill my lap with gold nuggets." Corrie gave a choking laugh.

"By the time he manages to get here, you won't *have* any lap," Susan said tartly.

Again they sat in silence, the only noise the faint rustle of the linen as Susan pulled her needle through it.

"Donald Earle wants to marry you," Susan said, drawing a thread tight.

"Yes, I know, but— Oh, Aunt, I couldn't possibly. Not even to give my baby a name."

"It won't be the first time a woman has married a man she didn't love."

"Yes, but, oh, not Donald! Aunt Susan, I love Avery. He's intelligent and ambitious and— We had our lives planned, everything. If only he would write me a letter, or come home, we could have our wedding right away . . . "

Corrie stopped. Sudden, startling thoughts had begun to whirl in her head. She thought of the wharf, of the day she had photographed the steamers moored there. The men scurrying like ants to get aboard. Avery had been part of such a crowd. And hadn't she seen a few women among them that day? Yes, she had.

"Aunt!" Corrie jumped up. "Why can't I go to Alaska and meet Avery? I could find him and marry him *there!* Oh, I could get on a steamer as he did, and surely it would not be so hard to find him. And I'm positive he wouldn't mind if we simply moved our wedding up a bit under the circumstances. After all, it is his child I'm carrying, and Avery has proposed to me, he does love me—"

Susan's needle stopped moving. "Corrie. How can you think such a thing? The man left you without a thought, and with barely an inquiry as to your welfare. *He left you,* Corrie. As for the Yukon, that fall from your bicycle must have addled your brain if you're thinking of doing such a foolhardy thing. Alaska is thousands of miles away; it's wild and desolate country. How many times did my brother speak of it thus? Such a trip would be dangerous enough for a man. But for a woman, and a pregnant one at that—"

Corrie could feel a hectic red begin to glow in her cheeks. "It can't be as bad as all that! There *were* women going aboard those boats for the Yukon—I saw them myself! And Avery does love me; he told me so! He can't wait to come home and take care of me; he said it in his letter . . . "

Susan tossed her needlework to the floor. "That may be true, Corrie, but you've a child to think about now, a baby who will be born fatherless unless you do something, and do it quickly."

Corrie jumped to her feet. "Marry Donald Earle? Is that your solution to this problem, Aunt Susan? Well, I won't do it. I'll never marry Donald Earle! I refuse!"

In the early morning light, a hundred questions raced through Corrie's mind, "Am I ready? Do I have everything? Am I doing the right thing?"

"If you don't have everything now, then you'll have to get along without it," Li Hua said with finality. Yet the oriental girl's eyes were sparkling with the excitement of the adventure, and once Corrie caught her casting an envious look at Corrie's packed trunk.

It was dawn, three days later. A thin, watery light filtered through Corrie's bedroom window, giving her furniture a lemon-washed look. Corrie stood in front of the mirror, smoothing down the seams of her blue serge traveling suit. It was constructed of a heavy fabric guaranteed not to show dirt, and had been pressed carefully by Li Hua into crisp freshness.

She paused for a moment in buttoning the smart Eton jacket to stare at herself in the glass.

She saw a girl who was perhaps too pale, save for cheeks stained with pink. Her hair, thick and lustrous, was puffed into a soft pompadour. Under her small straw hat, gold highlights caught the early sun. Her gold-brown eyes were darkened with emotion.

Quickly Corrie inspected the rest of herself—the smart cut of the suit accenting the soft curve of her breasts, the waist which still nipped in narrowly, the sensuous flare of hips.

No, she decided. She certainly did not look pregnant yet. No one would ever guess. And—perhaps because her worry had abated—she was no longer suffering from nausea. In only a few weeks, she would be married to Avery. They would both return to San Francisco, of course, since she could not rear a child in the wild North. And surely Aunt Susan would forgive her then for running away— she had to!

Corrie gave herself one last look, then her eyes moved to the open closet door where Li Hua had hung her pressed riding costume on a hook.

She had promised Donald she would go riding with him this afternoon on Ocean Beach. How angry he would be when he came to pick her up and discovered she was not here . . .

Well, she told herself, it can't be helped. From today on, Donald was out of her life. He could rant and rave as much as he pleased; it no longer mattered to her. In ten minutes—no, eight—she would be gone.

She went to her dressing table and propped up the envelope she had left. It was addressed to Donald, and contained the estimated price of the diamond ring she had thrown away, together with a brief note apologizing for her fit of temper. She was sorry, she told him. So terribly sorry . . .

Nervously, Corrie paced, opening and closing her pocketbook, stopping to inspect the big trunk. She touched the wooden crate into which she had packed her photographic equipment, and made sure its ropes were secure. Then she checked it again.

She had spent nearly all night packing and repacking the necessities which she and Li Hua had spent a hectic two days buying, carefully smuggling everything into the house. Heavy woolen ladies' underwear. A full layette for the baby, in case it should be born in Alaska, although she prayed it wouldn't be. Books. More underwear, in lisle and cotton, some of it lace trimmed.

Serviceable clothing. Extra blankets. Mosquito netting. Dried fruit and tinned delicacies, in case the steamer fare should prove to be less than appetizing. A heavy seal plush cape, muff and gloves. And last—this packed at Li Hua's insistence—a man's Norway sealskin coat and some men's woolen trousers, both small enough to fit Corrie.

"A man's coat!" Corrie had exclaimed.

Li Hua was adamant. "Yes, Corrie. My cousin is already in the Yukon and he's written me all about it. It can be thirty to forty degrees below zero in that place. It's a lot better to wear men's attire than it is to freeze to death!"

Corrie thought of Quade Hill, and his remark about a sensible bicycling costume.

"But it's nearly April!"

"It's still cold there, my cousin says. Things can happen. So you'd better take it." Firmly Li Hua packed the men's clothing into Corrie's trunk.

Corrie gave in. She had also decided to take nearly five thousand dollars in cash with her. Most of these funds came from the sale of the pieces of jewelry which Cordell Stewart had bought over the years for his "lovely Miss Princess Cordelia," and a tiara which had belonged to Corrie's mother, Gwen.

Forcing back tears, Corrie gave the jewels to Li Hua to sell, and stuffed the proceeds from their sale into a chamois money belt. She must carry her money on her person, hidden next to her skin, the servant insisted realistically. Then no one could steal it.

Corrie laughed. "But what if I want to pay a shopkeeper? Am I expected to hoist my skirts and dig down under my petticoats? What on earth would he think of me?"

"He'll think you prudent. Oh, laugh all you wish, Corrie. You can always keep a sum in your pocketbook so such a display won't be necessary. But—" Was there envy in Li Hua's eyes? "Even if you do have to turn aside and dig under your skirts, that's still better than being robbed and left penniless."

"I guess you're right."

Now Corrie continued to pace about the room, excitement skittering through her. In five minutes Jim Price, bribed and sworn to secrecy, would come to drive her to the wharfs. One hour from now she would be safely on the *Alki*, steaming north. Along the coast of Washington State they would find the "inner passage" and, sheltered from the sea winds by island after island, would make their way north to Dyea, Alaska. From there Corrie had been told she could get to the gold fields.

She glanced at the ornate little carved Swiss clock which Papa had given her for her birthday one year ago. Four minutes now, then three, and her new life would begin.

There was a knock at the door.

"Miss Cordelia? Are you ready? We'd best be goin'."

Corrie froze. She stared at her maidservant. Li Hua, too, looked solemn.

"Li Hua? It's time for me to go."

"Yes."

Suddenly the two girls embraced.

"Oh, Li Hua," Corrie cried, tears running down her cheeks. "I'll miss you! Take care of Aunt Susan for me. Tell her I *had* to do this; she's got to understand. I love Avery so much, I have to be with him. Make her see that, Li Hua."

Part 2

🌹 🌹 🌹

Chapter 10

The morning fog lay in fluffs of sheep's wool on the waters of the Bay. The scene at the wharfs was one of confusion, making Corrie think of another day, when she had been bothered by that lecherous man and rescued by another disturbing man . . . Dark-clad men and women rushed about, pushing to get near the four steamers moored at the quay. Buggies and drays, pulled by horses made skittish by the crowd, plunged through the throngs.

Corrie sat tensely in the jostling carriage, trying not to think of what Aunt Susan would say when she discovered she was missing. Would her aunt be angry? Or hurt? Oh, she loved Susan; she surely didn't wish to hurt her.

And yet Corrie felt that Aunt Susan would have done the same thing if she had been Corrie's age, and in her position. Her aunt had a wild streak in her like Cordell Stewart's. And like Corrie's own, the girl thought, biting down on her lower lip.

The manservant maneuvered the carriage among the throngs of hurrying people. "My sister says they got gold rush cars on them trains headin' east to New York," he chattered. "Got glass jars filled with nuggets and gold dust and gold bricks, too. Can you picture riding in a car like that? With a bar of gold? Now, my sister says—"

But Corrie wasn't interested in what Jim Price's sister thought, She was craning her neck to the left, toward a sign that said *"Ticket Office."* More people were jammed around the office, their faces angry as they shoved at each other.

But she would not have to jostle for her passage. Li Hua had already bought her ticket, and she would travel as "Mrs. Price." She had been promised a private stateroom, this managed with the help of a considerable sum placed in the hands of the ticket official.

"Well, I wonder how much closer we can get," Jim said. He flicked the reins and abruptly turned left to avoid colliding with a wagon laden with wooden cages containing pigs and chickens. Another cart, piled high with hay and spilling quantities of it onto the wharf, crowded up behind them.

"Get as close as you can, and then I guess we'll have to carry these things," Corrie said uncertainly. She caught a glimpse of a man in the crowd who looked somewhat like Donald.

But of course it couldn't be Donald, she asssured herself, clutching her sturdy pocketbook to her breast. Donald was at the Stewart Shipyards at this very moment, making plans to take her riding in the late afternoon. What a surprise he would get when he called!

The thought of Donald's consternation, however, was not a pleasant one; it only made Corrie more uneasy. Meanwhile, by dint of some very aggressive driving, Jim Price had managed to wedge the carriage very close to the last steamer in line, the *Alki*, for which Corrie held her ticket.

"This here is as far as we're goin' to get, Miss Cordelia. Now you got to get down there and battle that crowd of men."

"I'll be all right."

"It ain't no place here for a lady, none at all."

She struggled to inject confidence into her voice. "Oh, Jim, I'm sure it'll be all right. Please, do hurry! I don't want the ship to leave without me!"

Thirty breathless minutes later, Corrie was aboard the *Alki*.

"Mrs. . . . ah . . . "

It was a boy of about twenty, dressed in steward's uniform and looking harassed. He consulted a list scrawled with many names, some crossed out.

"Mrs. Price," Corrie supplied. She watched nervously as the crewman ran his finger down the list. Everything was going to be all right; she was sure of it. She had not yet managed to find her way to her cabin—the decks were too crowded for that, with all of the passengers milling about.

But of one thing she was expecially sure. This voyage was not going to be one of luxury. The ship was too heavily laden with humanity for that. Everywhere people packed the deck—men of all kinds and a few women, too, some dressed luxuriously, others plainly clad. One woman, weighing over two hundred pounds, sported an enormous hat bristling with long ostrich plumes, which blew ridiculously in the sea wind.

Extra bunks, bare of bedding, had been set up along the deck. Horses, mules and sheep jammed the forward deck, sending forth a barnyard stench that permeated the ship. Hay and feed for them was pyramided near the pilot house, and that too gave off its own fusty odor.

Corrie, gazing over the rail at the muted colors of the city, tried to breathe through her mouth. Dear heavens, she thought. They were not even out of the Bay yet, and already she was queasy. How could she ever last the trip?

Now she stared at the crewman in dismay. What was taking so long? What had gone wrong? The youth looked harassed.

"Ma'am, I see you're down for a private cabin."

"Yes."

"Well, I got to cut you out of it. See, there's so many on board, and the captain, he needs that there room. So you'll have to go in with the other women. We got a whole cabin for 'em 'tween decks, nice bunks and all. You'll be plenty comfortable there."

"But I paid for passage in a private cabin! It was part of my ticket!"

"It ain't no more," the youth said firmly. Then noting the dismay on Corrie's face, he added, "Listen, ma'am, we got two hundred beds on deck for men that don't get to go in any cabin. You want to give up your ticket, we got a hundred others that'll take it. But this here ship is crowded and you got to take the accommodations you're given, or you don't go."

"But—please, I need . . . " Corrie fumbled in her purse for the small amount of money she was carrying there.

Perhaps a small bribe—but how did you offer one? Did you just come out and say it bluntly?

She was hesitating, wondering how to begin, when another man walked up to them. He was short and broadshouldered—rather good-looking, Corrie thought, except for his nearly total baldness. But there was an air of authority about him, and Corrie saw that he wore a blue uniform, immaculately pressed.

The captain! She could not resist giving him an appealing little smile. If only he would help—

"What's the trouble here, Wanger?"

The boy spoke nervously. "Nothing, sir. Just explaining to this lady that she can't have that private cabin she wanted. You need it, sir."

"*I* need it?" The captain was grinning at her; a gold front tooth flashed when he smiled. His eyes flicked downward over Corrie's traveling suit, noting her curved bodice and flaring hips.

Corrie flushed. "Sir, I paid for a private cabin, and that's what I think I should have. I haven't been well, and—"

The captain threw back his head and laughed. "And you don't want to get any sicker, is that it? Well, ma'am . . . Mrs. Price, is it? You sure picked the wrong ship to travel on if you want fancy comforts. They're sending nearly everything up North that'll float. And we—well, at least we float. But that's about all you can say for us."

Corrie managed another appealing smile. "Please, I would so appreciate . . . "

She saw the captain waver. He looked speculative. "Well, ma'am, I think a single cabin might be arranged, since you been sick and all. See to it, Wanger." His tone was suddenly so sharp that both Corrie and the boy jumped.

"Yessir."

"And see the lady's trunks get to her cabin right away."

"Yessir." The youth's assent was quick and fearful.

"I'll be seeing more of you later, Mrs. Price," the captain told her, leaning forward and again flashing the gold tooth. "I'm Captain Zebulun Carter," he added. "That's a good old-fashioned name. My ma was a real reader of the Bible."

"I'm sure she was." The smile had frozen on Corrie's face. She didn't like Zebulun Carter and she wished his eyes had not inspected her quite so closely.

She followed the steward to her cabin, circling about the groups of male passengers and the wooden bunks, ignoring the stares the men gave her. They would sleep in the open air, she told herself, while she got a cabin. And all because she had smiled at that horrid, gold-toothed captain.

Abruptly, she felt ashamed.

Her cabin was small and plain, but to Corrie's profound relief, it was clean. Two bunks, one set above the other, covered one wall, with a storage drawer underneath. There was a built-in bureau with a curious metal rail about its top, in order to hold objects when the steamer pitched, Corrie supposed. Upon it sat an enameled basin and ewer; on the floor was a tin chamber pot. One small porthole gave a glimpse of tumbling white-capped waves and gray early April sky.

Well, she thought, this is it. She sat down on the bunk and looked at the metal top of her trunk, which had been shoved into the few open feet of floor space and which, she supposed, she would stumble over for the rest of the trip.

Aunt Susan. Abruptly a wave of homesickness swept over her, so achingly strong that she had to blink back tears. How long would it be before she would see her aunt again? But Corrie drew in a deep, firm breath. Her baby had to have a father—even Aunt Susan had admitted that. And Avery *was* willing to marry her. In a few weeks she would be a married woman, and then she and Avery could return to San Francisco . . .

If all went well.

For the first time, doubt assailed her. Corrie sank back on the rough brown blanket of the bunk. It shook with the rhythm of the motor and the tossing of the ship. Timbers creaked, and above her head she could hear loud bangs and thumping footsteps. A man laughed, and somewhere a sheep let out a protesting baa.

Corrie screwed her eyes shut and tried to summon up a picture of Avery's face. Finely carved, patrician features. A full mouth and clefted chin. Gray eyes full of dreams and plans. Silky blond hair and a luxuriant, full mustache. . . .

Another timber creaked and protested as if it were breaking. Slowly Corrie forced her muscles to relax. The picture of Avery blurred, then faded. Somehow she slid into sleep, a restless, pitching nap which was the only escape from her surroundings that she could manage.

When she awoke in the late afternoon, she smoothed out her skirt, redid her hair and inspected her face in the small hand mirror she had wrapped in flannel and tucked into the trunk. She was still pale, Corrie decided, but she didn't look too terrible. And her nausea had not grown any worse, for which she was grateful.

Corrie found her way on deck and managed to locate the dining saloon. It was a large room fitted with a big, polished table (also railed with metal bars) and lit by a skylight. Because of the number of passengers aboard, there would be several sittings for each meal, a short, bow-legged crewman informed her; the men with on-deck accommodations would be served on deck. She would eat with the other women.

While she was standing at the rail, idly looking out at the white, foam-flecked wake given off by the steamer, Captain Zebulun Carter again approached her.

"Well," he said. "How do you find your cabin?"

"It's very nice. Very clean."

He grinned, evidently pleased. "We do our best, but no ship carrying livestock can expect to be really clean. Seems like I can't get the stink of manure out of my clothes no matter what I do."

Corrie nodded, uncertain of what to say.

"Know what we're going to do with all them animal pens and bunks when we get to Dyea? We're going to make 'em into lumber and sell 'em. Got three hundred dollars per thousand foot for 'em last time." Captain Carter chuckled. He again gazed at Corrie's breasts, then looked away. "Don't know if you saw 'em, but we got two outhouses built on the deck for all them extra men. We're going to sell them, too, when we get to Dyea. Make somebody a nice, fragrant pile of boards!"

Corrie had never before met a man who spoke of such

things so openly. "I don't think that's a subject fit to discuss in front of a lady," she said faintly, moving away from him.

The captain's mouth twisted. "Oh, and it's a fine lady, is it? So sorry! I wouldn't want to offend your delicacy!"

Corrie stared at him. Of course, she thought. The captain did not really think her a lady at all. She was traveling by herself, without the protection of a man, going to a wild frontier area. A deep, painful blush burned its way up from her neck.

Fortunately for her composure, the squat little crewman blew a whistle sharply, and the captain gave her a nudge.

"It's your dinner time, Mrs. Price. I give the ladies first sitting—it's the gentlemen on the deck that have got to scrape the sides of the pot!"

Dining in the cabin crammed full of women proved to be an unforgettable experience. The barnyard smell was muted, and Corrie decided that either she was getting used to it or the wind was blowing it away. But the cabin was full of other smells. There was the heavy, lingering odor of eau de cologne; evidently most of the women present wore it. Or bathed in it, Corrie decided, wrinkling her nose.

The food—a thick beef stew accompanied by hot, raised biscuits and strong coffee diluted with condensed milk—sent up its own rich, meaty smell, to mingle oddly with the scent of perfume and animals and women.

The female passengers eyed the stew and each other. Never had Corrie seen such a varied mixture of women. There were a number of young girls. Some wore lace-trimmed shirtwaists and dark skirts, while others were clad in garish finery—bright tulles and silks—topped with flat sailor hats or headpieces covered with feathers, flowers and plumes. One girl, clothed in a deep violet gown with exaggerated wide shoulders, could not have been more than fifteen.

The big woman in the flamboyant ostrich-plume hat was here, too, poking at the stew with her fork and laughing with her neighbor. Who were these women? Corrie wondered. Some had pretty faces while others looked bold, sharp. She was unable to take her eyes from them.

Almost immediately she got the answer to her question as the person sitting next to her, a tall, rake-thin woman, wearing a black serge dress, spoke.

"Well, I never!" Her companion pressed her fingers into Corrie's upper arm. "A respectable woman tries to travel, and what does she find but a lot of fancy women. You're not one of them, are you?" She stared at Corrie suspiciously.

"What? Me? Oh, no, I'm Corrie . . . Price. I'm going to meet my husband at the gold fields," she lied.

The other woman nodded, her gray hair bobbing. "Well, I can see *we* respectable women are going to have to stick together. There's plenty fewer of us than that other kind. I'm Eulalie Benrush and I'm going up to meet my husband, too, at Circle City. He's been sick; got the typhoid dysentery, he wrote me. I brought along a full outfit, though, and I'm going to do some mining. Seems like somebody's got to make some money for us."

As Eulalie rattled on, Corrie looked about her. The women in the cabin did indeed seem to belong to two groups. The "respectable" ones were mostly dressed in dark, serviceable traveling clothes, while the "fancy" girls were garishly clad, and giggled among themselves as they ate like a flock of careless, gaudy birds.

But it was the big, brown-haired woman with the ostrich plumes who caught Corrie's attention. She had a laugh so merry and infectious that it was almost impossible not to smile with her.

"That hussy," Eulalie Benrush informed Corrie with another jab in the ribs, "that's Mattie Shea, I heard 'em say. She's the madam for half of these females—taking them up to work in the dance halls and to prostitute themselves to wicked men."

"Oh." Corrie eyed the notorious Mattie with curiosity. "She certainly does know how to laugh," something made her add.

Eulalie gave her a sharp look. "Laugh! Oh, yes, she can laugh at all of us honest women being forced to associate with the likes of her. I've got a mind to tell the captain just what I think of these arrangements of his. I'll tell him a thing or two."

Thinking of Captain Carter's gold-toothed smile, Corrie grinned inwardly.

The meal was over quickly; there was no possibility of lingering here with the loud noises being made by the men who were crowded on the deck outside waiting for their turn to eat. As Corrie left the cabin she was accidentally bumped by the big madam, Mattie Shea.

"Oh! Do pardon! The damned ship lurched and just sent me heading every which way!" The big woman laughed jovially, but Corrie saw that she clutched her midsection with one hand, as if something pained her there. No doubt she was suffering from seasickness. Beads of perspiration shone on her forehead.

"That's quite all right," Corrie said.

Mattie Shea gave her another smile and assessed Corrie with a look that took her in from head to toe, missed nothing. Then she nodded so that the ostrich plumes bobbed.

"You'll do, honey. It's a pity you ain't with us. I could help you get along right nice in Dawson City."

This statement was made in such a friendly tone that Corrie could not take offense at it. Besides, she could not help liking the big, frank-speaking woman.

"I'm afraid—" she began.

"Afraid! Oh, yes, they all are. All those proper women, like the one you was sitting next to. You've just put your finger right on it. I got second sight, and I know."

Again Mattie Shea gave her infectious laugh. She was still chuckling as she stepped over the companionway and emerged onto the deck, where a chorus of wolf whistles and catcalls greeted her.

"Aw, now, enough of that stuff," Corrie heard her call genially. "We got a long voyage ahead, hear?"

When the small gold chatelaine watch her father had given her said eight o'clock, Corrie put down the novel she had been reading and decided to go for a walk on deck. The cabin was so tiny that it made her feel like a pet rabbit in a cage. If she didn't get some air, she would surely suffocate!

It was dark and windy, the moon half-obscured by scudding clouds. The air felt wet, and it looked as if it would probably rain either tonight or tomorrow. She felt sorry for the poor men forced to sleep on deck. They were going to have a very uncomfortable trip.

She made one turn around the cluttered deck, noting that many others were doing the same thing, when she heard angry voices coming from the storage area at the stern of the ship.

A crowd had already started to gather.

"A stowaway! Damn you, boy!" Captain Carter's voice was loud and it held a quivering, outraged anger. "What in the hell do you think you're doing? I could've got two hundred dollars for your ticket—or more, you thieving little fool! What'd you do, come aboard in a trunk? And didn't you think you were clever, blast your stinking hide!"

People were rushing closer. Corrie joined them, hearing a dangerous note in the captain's voice. Standing on tiptoe, she managed to peek over the shoulders of the man in front of her.

A lantern held by a crewman illuminated the scene. The stowaway had indeed made his entry in a trunk, which stood accusingly open in front of him, filled with a few odd bits of clothing. The boy—for surely he could not be very old—wore a mackinaw shirt and loose woolen pants; a soft felt hat was crammed onto his head.

Only a youth, Corrie told herself, could have stayed cramped up in a trunk for that long, or would have thought of trying such a stunt at all. How had he managed to breathe? And what was going to happen to him now?

"Well, you little bastard, if you think you're going to get free passage, you got another think coming." Zebulun Carter had grasped the boy's arm and was shaking him. "You'll work, and you'll work your butt off. And you'll sleep on the bare boards of the deck. Or maybe in the outhouse, eh? Because we ain't got a bunk for you. How do you like that, eh, kid?"

Carter guffawed as he reached out and gave the boy's face a slap with the flat of his hand. The boy's face, half in shadow from the wavering lamplight, jerked to the side. He let out a little cry.

The captain slapped him again, and his hat fell off. To Corrie's shock, hair tumbled down. Long blue-black hair which caught and reflected the shine of the lamp, blowing wildly in the night wind. The assembled men, joined now by some of the "fancy" girls, let out a combined gasp.

"Jesus, it's a girl!" Corrie heard the man in front of her say. His shoulders still partially blocked her view.

"Sure is; look at the boobies on her. You can see 'em plain through that shirt," a little bearded man said.

"A woman! A pretty little Chinee girl!" Captain Carter's voice held outrage. "What the hell—"

Corrie, impelled by some fear she couldn't name, strained to see over the bulk of the man in front of her. Then, ducking, she managed to twist under his arm.

She pushed her way to the front of the crowd. The stowaway, small and lost in the shirt which was far too big for her, faced the captain with wild, defiant eyes. Then her mouth tightened as the captain raised his hand to hit her again.

"Li Hua!" The words flew out of Corrie's mouth in a high, surprised scream. "Captain Carter, please leave that girl alone! That's my servant! That's Li Hua!"

🌹 Chapter 11 🌹

Li Hua, backed against the ship's rail, faced the captain with blazing eyes. Her black hair, flowing loose to her waist, blew in the night wind, giving her the look of some half-wild, defiant creature.

"I don't care whether her name is Carrie Nation, I want to know what in the hell that little slut is doing on my ship!"

Captain Carter gave Li Hua a shove, then strode toward Corrie. His uniform was crumpled, and the lamplight glittered on his bare skull and the gold of his front tooth. He gave forth an odor of whiskey.

"I don't know what she's doing here," Corrie stammered, although she remembered all the sidelong looks Li Hua had cast at her trunk, and the girl's air of suppressed excitement . . .

The risk! Corrie thought furiously. The girl could have smothered in that trunk. Or found that it had been placed at the bottom of a huge stack of goods so that she couldn't get the lid open at all.

"Well, somebody had better explain it or I'm going to put the wench to work, and she may not like the little chores she gets. She can damn well be my cabin boy and empty slops. Or—" an expression of lust crossed Carter's face, "or she could—"

Corrie gave him a cold look. Then, as the captain glared back at her, she realized that she had taken the wrong tack with him. She tried to soften her expression, to smile up at him.

"Captain," she said quickly. "It was really my fault that Li Hua smuggled herself on board. She was my maid at home. I told her that she couldn't come with me, and she disobeyed me."

"Well, she won't disobey *me*, not if she knows what's good for her, or I might tell Cookie to fix us up some Chinee meat, eh?"

Carter guffawed. Li Hua stared at him with loathing.

"Captain Carter, please, would it be possible for me to pay for Li Hua's passage? I have the money and I'd be glad to do it. Then she would be no trouble to you."

The man looked at her. "And cheat me out of my little Chinee cabin girl?"

He was enjoying this, Corrie realized. He was playing with Li Hua, savoring the way her eyes followed him about, the way she was swaying with exhaustion. He was probably looking forward to humiliating her. Or . . . worse.

"I'm sorry you won't have a cabin girl. But I do have the money, and it would be a personal favor to me if you would let me pay for her passage. She could share my cabin. I've two bunks in it." Corrie forced her face into the most appealing smile she would muster.

"A personal favor, eh?"

"Yes."

"Well, nobody ever said Zebulun Carter couldn't do a pretty woman a favor. Although I already done you one, didn't I, when I gave you my own special cabin? I keep that one for my friends. So now you owe me two favors."

He grinned at her suggestively, the gold tooth flashing. Corrie willed the smile to stay on her face.

"Thank you so much, Captain. I'll bring Li Hua's passage money to you first thing in the morning. And now . . . ." She marched forward and took the girl's arm, pulling her away from Captain Carter. Li Hua's slender body offered no resistance. "And now, Captain, I believe that I'll take her down to my cabin. It's late and it's time that all of us were in our bunks. Good night."

Head up and shoulders high, her bearing as proud as anything that Cordell Stewart at his angriest had ever achieved, Corrie pulled Li Hua after her. They pushed their way past the gawking men, past the giggling dance hall girls, down to the haven of her cabin.

As soon as the cabin door had closed behind them, Corrie turned to Li Hua.

"What in the world are you doing here?" she demanded. "I thought I would faint when I saw you! I can't imagine —oh! Are you all right? You're swaying."

Her tirade turned into an expression of concern as she saw that the other girl was indeed wobbling on her feet. Her face looked pinched, and Corrie realized that she had probably been short of air in the trunk. Her muscles were undoubtedly badly cramped, too.

"Lie down on that bunk," she ordered, pointing to the lower one. "For heaven's sake, Li Hua, what am I going to do with you?" She yanked the brown blanket off the bunk and pulled it up over the girl. "You foolish thing, it's a wonder you didn't kill yourself with that stunt of yours."

Li Hua suffered these attentions, her lips pressed together. Lying on the bunk she looked even smaller and younger than she really was. But her eyes flashed defiantly.

"I wouldn't have smothered," she said. "I drilled air holes. And I did have some food. But I ate it all this morning."

"Oh, good heavens," Corrie said. "Well, I'm glad that you're all right. But when I think of what could have happened to you! Do you realize that if they'd put that trunk on the bottom of the pile you could never have gotten the lid open? You'd have had to stay inside until we got to Dyea. That would have been days! You could have died in that trunk, Li Hua!"

"I did have air."

"Air! Not too much of it, to judge from the look of you." Corrie bit her lower lip. "Are you hungry? We've had our dinner—not that it was anything much. But I do have some cakes and tinned things. I'll get them out."

Her anger forgotten, Corrie rummaged in the trunk until she had found the cans and the opener. Careful not to let the blade slip, she opened the cans and spread out the repast on the blanket. There were cakes, fruit, a meat paste, and some roasted nuts.

"I don't suppose this looks very tasty," she apologized. "It will hold you until morning, though. I wouldn't dare go out and ask that horrid captain for any more food right now. We're just lucky he's allowing me to pay your passage at all."

Li Hua sat up and began to wolf down the food, picking up the bits of fruit and nuts with her fingers.

Corrie watched her eat. Even eating with her fingers, Li Hua's movements were graceful, and the bulky men's clothing she wore only served to make her look more fragile and feminine. Corrie shuddered to think of that small figure lying lifeless, smothered in the bottom of a locked trunk.

At last Li Hua was finished. She pushed aside the little pile of tins, and Corrie began to gather them up, wondering where to put them. She would dispose of them in the morning, she decided—probably overboard, where all ships routinely threw their garbage.

"All right," she said. "I think you owe me an explanation, Li Hua. Why did you do this? Why on earth would you take such risks?"

The girl looked at her. Her finely carved mouth was set in a straight line. "I wanted to get away from— I wanted to come."

"But why?"

Li Hua was defiant. "I've heard nothing but gold, gold, gold. It's all your papa could talk about, and Jim Price, too. Everyone was going, even my cousin; he's in Valdez." Li Hua moistened her lips. "And I was tired of being a servant. I've been at your house since I was thirteen. Your aunt was very good to me. Still . . . "

She faced Corrie, her eyes blazing. "Oh, you wouldn't understand, would you? *You've* never had to work. Never had to take orders from someone, to wear proper clothing and be spoken to because you went outside to look at the flowers and to breathe some fresh air."

Corrie frowned. Had it really been like that for Li Hua? Yet surely there was something more, some further reason which the other girl would not reveal. For she looked almost frightened as well . . .

"Well," Corrie added, "I've paid your passage, or I will pay it in the morning. What are you going to do in the North?"

"I don't know. Perhaps I'll be a miner."

"A miner!"

"Why, yes, Corrie. Women can prospect for gold, too. Women can do anything they wish!"

Corrie fell silent, startled by the idea, which sounded like something Cordell Stewart might have said. But of course it wasn't possible. The maidservant would have to travel to Dyea, for the ship could hardly turn back now. When they arrived at their destination, though, she would make Li Hua board another steamer and return home at once.

Still, the thought of a woman mining stayed in her head. Never had she thought that Li Hua would possess so much boldness of spirit . . .

"Well," she said. "I suppose we'd better get to bed. I'll loan you some of my clothes. Unless you prefer going about in those men's garments."

"No, I brought some skirts and waists," Li Hua replied. "They're in the trunk that I came in."

"Good, we'll get them in the morning. If Captain Carter hasn't had another fit of temper and thrown it overboard."

Li Hua looked alarmed. "Oh, I hope he hasn't. I never thought of that. I had some other supplies in it too." She hesitated. "Thank you for paying my passage, Corrie. I don't know what I would have done."

The girls hugged each other. "Become a cabin girl, I suppose." Corrie managed to smile. "Well, come on, choose a bunk. We'd both better get some sleep."

They were awakened in the night by a scrabbling noise at the door of their cabin. Corrie sat up in the lower bunk, her heart slamming. The scraping sound continued, almost as if someone were fumbling at the lock.

But she had shot the bolt, Corrie told herself, her mouth dry. Could it possibly be a rat? If so, it was a persistent one, for the noises continued, stealthy and slow. Corrie sat frozen, her hands and feet turning icy. She heard a creak in the bunk above her and knew that Li Hua was awake too.

"Li Hua!" she hissed. "Do you hear that?"

"Yes."

"What do you think—"

There was a loud, popping noise as the bolt slid.

Slowly, horribly, the cabin door creaked open, letting in the night noises of the ship—timbers creaking, a slapping bang, the rumble of the boilers, the muffled voice of an insomniac on deck. A dark shape loomed in the doorway.

Corrie gazed ahead with fascinated horror. It was exactly like some gut-weakening nightmare out of her childhood. A big, blurred monster, looming at her out of the dark—

"You don't have to scream, little ladies," a voice said. "It's only me."

Corrie did not have to guess to whom that sniggering, self-satisfied voice belonged. She had heard it only hours before, first raised in fury at Li Hua, then filled with lust. *So now you owe me two favors. She can damn well be my cabin boy.* Had he come to collect the "favors" he felt they both owed him?

"Captain Carter! What are you doing here? How did you get in? I bolted the door."

"Yes? Is that so? Well, I told you I use this cabin for my friends. And I done had that bolt fixed." Zebulun Carter's voice held the suggestion of a smile. Although it was pitch black in the cabin, Corrie felt sure that his gold tooth was gleaming. She suppressed another scream.

"Get out of here, please, at once! How dare you burst into our cabin like this?"

"*Your* cabin? I told you, this here is the place I save for my friends. And I done you a special favor by giving it to you. You could be sleeping on the deck, you know. Sleeping with a hundred men . . . " He laughed. "You wouldn't want that, now, would you, Mrs. Price? It ain't very ladylike to bed down on the deck, right out in the open. This here's a lot more comfy. Yes, ma'am."

Corrie slid out of her bunk, forgetting that she was clad only in a light cambric nightgown.

"Get out of here! And please do it this very instant. Or I'll scream."

"Go ahead, ma'am. Scream. But, see, the wind's come up, and the ship's pretty noisy tonight. They ain't going to hear you. And even if they do, they'll think you're just one of them floozies we got aboard, having theirselves a bit of fun. You, though, Mrs. Price, you're different. You're a good piece of clean stuff. And that nice little bit of Chinee meat you got with you . . . I'd sure like to savor that, I would."

He was advancing in her direction. Although she could only see him as a dark shape, she could almost smell his progress toward her, by the stench of whiskey, perspiration and hair pomade and mustache wax.

"I said . . . get away. Get away!"

"Aw, now, honey, you owe me, both of you. You don't think this here cabin comes for free, do you?"

His hands grabbed her, pulling at her nightgown, handling her as roughly as if she had been a pile of laundry. He was fumbling at the hem of her nightgown, trying to lift it. She felt his fingernails brush her thighs. *My God, he's going to rape me,* Corrie thought frantically. She had to do something . . .

She felt his touch on her naked hip. She shrieked with revulsion and managed to kick out at him with her bare foot. She squirmed backwards toward the built-in dresser. The corner of its metal rail banged into her shoulder blade, filling her with a stabbing pain. The tin ewer clattered, and Corrie scrambled frantically for it, missing it in the darkness.

Then, abruptly, Li Hua flew out of the upper bunk. She landed with the lithe spring of a cat on Captain Carter. Her weight and the surprise of her landing bore them to the floor. They were tangled up and struggling in the darkness. Fists hit Corrie; she didn't know whose. She heard a scrape as Li Hua grabbed for the metal basin. Then there was a thud as it hit bone and flesh.

"Jesus God, you little bitch! What the hell—"

He had managed to stagger to his feet again, and beat at Li Hua with his fists. She fought back with the basin. Corrie added her clawing fingernails to the melee.

"Captain!" she finally gasped. "Captain, you'd better leave this cabin right now!" Her voice was shaking with fury. "I'm not Mrs. Price, you fool! I'm Cordelia Stewart, daughter of Cordell Stewart. The Stewart Shipyards, you damn bastard! *I own it!* And I can wreck you in San Francisco and everywhere else if word of what you've done tonight ever gets out! Do you hear me? I can wreck you! If you ever touch me or Li Hua again, if you even look at us cross-eyed, I'll ruin you! Now I want you to leave this cabin this instant. *My* cabin, do you hear? And I don't owe you any favors for it, none whatsoever!"

"But— you bought passage as Mrs. Price . . . I thought—"

"I know what you thought. But I didn't want it known I was traveling. And I'll thank you not to tell a soul who I am. Is that perfectly clear to you?"

Corrie's voice was cold and gaining in confidence. She was amazed to realize that Captain Carter was backing away from her. She could hear the change in his voice from fury to stammering obedience. And she could hear his hands brushing at his uniform, at the water from the ewer which had spilled on him.

"Yes . . . yes, it's clear . . . "

"Then get out of here. And I don't ever want to see you near this cabin again!" She remembered something else. "And you can fix that bolt, too. By tomorrow noon it had better be repaired."

"Yes, Miss Stewart . . . er, Mrs. Price . . . ma'am . . . " He almost fell over himself in his haste to leave.

Corrie closed the door and sank against it, her heart slamming as if she had been running over railroad ties. She had evoked the power of her father's money, she thought numbly, and she had cursed like a dockworker. She was no lady at all, that was sure. But at least she had got rid of him. And he wouldn't bother them again.

"Let's move that trunk against the door," Li Hua suggested.

"All right. But I don't think he'll come back."

The two of them shoved the heavy trunk so it was flush with the door; then they lit the lamp and went about the job of cleaning up the cabin. They mopped up spilled water and picked up the scattered food tins. The basin was dented where Captain Carter's skull had struck it.

"He certainly has a hard head," Corrie said, looking at it thoughtfully.

"Yes, indeed."

Then the two of them were laughing, clinging to each other and howling in triumph and semihysteria, as if they could never stop.

Dear Aunt Susan, Corrie wrote after much deliberation. *I'm on my way to the Yukon to find Avery and marry him. Please, please don't worry about me. I'll be all right, and Li Hua is here to help me. We should be home in a few weeks . . .*

Their third night of sleep aboard the *Alki* was disturbed by the loud crashes, creaks, bangs and slaps of high winds and seas.

The ship began to heave and pitch. From the glimpse Corrie got of the heavy seas, she was sure that water would inundate the entire vessel at any minute. Heaven only knew what Captain Carter had done with the men who were sleeping on deck—certainly that would be impossible now, with wild spray washing over their bunks. She hoped that room had been made for them somewhere inside.

Many of the passengers were seasick, but Corrie, to her utter amazement, was not one of them. Perhaps she had already done her penance in that line, she told herself wryly. The one advantage of the storm was that it blew the barnyard smells away so that she wasn't bothered by them. Li Hua, however, was miserable, and spent most of that day and night lying in the upper bunk.

Thankfully, the next morning they reached the Strait of Juan de Fuca. Walking on the deck, Corrie encountered the crewman Wanger, who told her that they had suffered some damage, and would have to pull into a sheltered harbor to make repairs. This, together with the continuing storm, would delay them for several days.

It was while they were anchored here, at the base of the Olympic Mountains, which rose in snowy grandeur almost from the water's edge, that the madam, Mattie Shea, became ill.

Corrie did not learn of this until the noon meal that day, when she heard some of the girls talking.

"Screaming and howling she is, like a banshee," observed Jinnie. She was the girl with the gaudy violet dress. Her features were childish and petulant. "Clutching her belly and moaning, telling us she's dying and all. Jesus! Wonder if she's got something catching, like cholera."

"Aw, no, she ain't got cholera," someone else said, but dubiously.

"All the same, *I* ain't going near her. I ain't never nursed anyone, and I'd gag if I had to."

"Who is sick?" Corrie demanded at last, feeling sorry for the person being spoken of so unfeelingly.

"Why, Mattie Shea, that's who." Jinnie tossed her head. "God! I ain't never seen nothing like it and I don't want to again. Don't seem like she hardly knows where she is. She's delirious."

Corrie remembered the big, jolly woman she had seen, and had to swallow, she was so shocked. "You don't mean . . . the woman who was always laughing?" she managed to ask.

"Sure, her. She ain't laughing now, though."

Corrie was about to question the girl further when she felt Eulalie Benrush grasp her sleeve.

"What do you think you're doing, talking to the likes of them? They're fancy women. Hoors! No decent woman would say a word to women like that, no matter how sick they get. Besides," she leaned over and whispered in Corrie's ear, "maybe she's sick from *you know what.* Ever stop to think on it? Those women pick up a lot of dirty things . . . "

"Oh, but—" Corrie drew back, startled. "Surely she can't be allowed to suffer! Someone should look at her. A doctor—"

"No respectable doctor would treat a prostitute," Eulalie informed her. *"I* certainly wouldn't lift a finger to help a hussy like that. Let her die. That would serve her right, her and her filthy ways."

Corrie did not taste another bite of the meal. To her dismay, she saw that the conversation at the table had moved away from Mattie Shea and gone on to the topic of the latest fashion in women's bathing dresses. They don't care, Corrie thought angrily. They don't, not in the slightest.

She left the table as quickly as she could, carrying a handful of fruit and cold biscuits for Li Hua, who still did not feel well enough to leave her bunk. She pushed her way through the crowd of men waiting on the storm-tossed deck for their food, ignoring the bold looks they gave her. Since Li Hua's entrance aboard the ship in a trunk, both of them had been the object of many stares, whispers and nudgings.

After she left the food for Li Hua (who groaned when

she saw it), Corrie wandered about the maze of narrow
companionways until she found the room where the sick
woman lay. Mattie Shea's moans were plainly audible,
and served Corrie as a guide.

The "fancy" women had been berthed in a space between decks, a crude area lined with three-tiered bunks
built of rough lumber. Trunks, bags and boxes were scattered about everywhere, and served as seats and tables.
Soiled clothing, stockings, camisoles, and even a frayed
corset, were flung about the bunks and on the floor. Fruit
parings, bottles, jewelry and pots of cosmetics added to
the clutter. The room reeked with the smell of perspiration, vomit, unwashed clothes and perfume.

Ugh, Corrie thought. She had come very close to room-
ing here with these girls, or in another place like it. She
wondered if Eulalie Benrush bunked here as well. She
couldn't imagine it.

"Oh! Oh, God, God, God . . . "

The groaning came again, mingled with little cries,
sharp and piercing. Corrie looked about her.

Then she saw a bunk at the far corner, screened off
from the others with a crude arrangement of blankets
strung up on a piece of satin ribbon. To prevent her from
infecting the others, Corrie thought hotly. She marched
over to the blanket and ripped it away.

Mattie Shea stared up at her. The big woman was almost unrecognizable without her ostrich plumes and her
wide smile. She looked thin, her face actually wizened, as
if she had lost pounds of flesh in only two days. Her skin
was waxy and her brown hair was hopelessly snarled on
the pillow, as if no one had bothered to comb it in days.
In fact, Corrie noted, Mattie had had no attention whatsoever, of any kind. Her bunk actually smelled, a rank,
horrible odor that made Corrie want to run away in dis-
gust.

But she couldn't, not with Mattie Shea's eyes fixed on
her, wide and full of pain.

"Oh! Dear God, who are you?" Even the madam's
voice had changed. No longer rich and plumply full, it
was hoarse from groaning.

"I'm Cordelia Stewart," Corrie blurted, not even realizing that she had given her real name. Mattie's eyes wid-

ened abruptly, as if this meant something to her. Then her expression dulled.

"I'm the girl you met at the first supper in the dining saloon," Corrie prompted. "Do you remember bumping into me? You said—" She faltered.

"What? Oh. Yes, yes . . . Oh! Oh, God, oh, Jesus, oh, it hurts. God, my belly. Can't they do anything? Can't they help me? Those bitches left me alone in here . . . not that I blame 'em," Mattie added after a pause. "They think they'll get my troubles, I guess." She rolled around on the bunk, clutching at her abdomen. "God, I wish I knew what was wrong with me. It comes and it goes. My belly, that's what hurts. My damned belly."

"Is there anything I can do? I could find you a doctor."

"A doctor! God! Oh, God, yes, anything . . . " Mattie grimaced, and her eyes seemed to glaze over as if she no longer saw Corrie at all, but something else, something just behind Corrie's shoulder.

"No! Oh, Pa, don't put your hand on my—" As Corrie jumped and involuntarily looked behind her, Mattie's voice changed. It became higher, softer, like a little girl's. "No, I won't do it. No! Oh, Pa, please—"

On the bed Mattie Shea suddenly spread her knees wide and began writhing, moving her pelvis up and down.

Corrie drew back in horror.

"Pa, no, keep away from me. I don't want to do it. No, Pa. No, it hurts. *It hurts, it hurts, it hurts, it hurts . . . "*

Corrie choked back nausea. Surely Mattie could not be talking about— But she *was*. She was reliving something that happened to her long ago. Corrie felt sure of this, as sure as she had ever been about anything. She shuddered in revulsion. She had never heard anything so frightening and horrible. Perhaps this was why Mattie Shea had become a prostitute, she thought wildly. Yet Mattie had been able to laugh. She'd been able to spread cheerful gaiety to others.

"Oh, God!" Abruptly the woman's voice changed back to an adult's. "Oh, but my belly hurts. Are you here to help me, Cordelia? Can you do anything? Anything at all to ease me?"

"I'll get you a doctor. There must be one on board."

"Yes . . . a doctor . . . " Mattie said feebly but suddenly

reached out her hand and grabbed Corrie's. Her pudgy fingers gripped Corrie's in a hold that was bone-crushing in its strength. Corrie wanted to scream out with the pain of it, but she managed not to.

"Don't—don't go yet. Stay with me, Cordelia. Stay here."

"But you need a doctor. He'll have medicine, things to help you. Maybe he can do surgery or . . . or something."

"No doctor . . . treat me . . . nothing he can do . . . Jesus!" And now, in a moment of utter horror, Mattie Shea sat up in her bunk. Her waxy face was twisted into a grimace. Her snarled brown hair stuck out around her head like a witch's, and she stared straight ahead at Corrie, her eyes dilated.

"You!" She said it in a deep, hoarse voice and she pointed a finger. "You watch out! I can see it! I see . . . oh, God, I see fire, flames. Flames licking and burning— watch out! Watch it! They'll burn you! *They'll burn you alive!*"

"What?" Corrie involuntarily shrank back as far as she could get. She felt the blood rush within her as she stared at this apparition. "What do you mean?"

"I said fire! I said fire and burning and black charred flesh! I said watch out, Cordelia Stewart!"

With a motion as abrupt as her act of sitting up, Mattie Shea suddenly sank back down on the bunk. She seemed to have expended all of her strength. For an instant she lay still.

"I've got second sight, you know," she said conversationally. Then she closed her eyes and lapsed into unconsciousness.

🥀 Chapter 12 🥀

Corrie ran out on deck, wrapped in a feeling of utter unreality. The storm was passing on, the sky was brighter
and the sea calmer. Passengers fled their cramped, evil-
smelling cabins to roam about the decks. Men stood about
in small knots, talking or gambling. Two youths in their
twenties occupied a spot by the rail, doing sit-ups and
push-ups, their faces red with effort.

Corrie hesitated. She couldn't get it out of her mind—
the apparition of Mattie Shea sitting upright in the bunk,
her tangled hair sticking up, her voice croaking out the
terrible words. *Watch out! Watch it! They'll burn you.
They'll burn you alive.*

An irrational fright pounded through Corrie. The
woman had said she had second sight . . .

But it was ridiculous. This was 1898, and people didn't
make such fantastic statements. "Second sight" was a
myth dreamed up by gypsies and old women so they
could make some money bilking people. At least this was
what Papa would have said. Papa scoffed at the supernatural, at spells and premonitions.

But Mattie Shea hadn't asked for any money. And—
yes—hadn't her eyes widened the moment Corrie gave
her name, as if she knew her, and had already glimpsed
the future?

A convulsive shiver went through Corrie, and it was
only with the greatest effort that she brought herself under
control. Her prediction notwithstanding, Mattie Shea was
very sick, perhaps even dying. She needed help.

Corrie drew a deep breath and started toward the two
youths who were doing calisthenics.

"Sir—" She plucked at the shoulder of the one doing
the sit-ups. His broad face streamed with perspiration as,
grunting, he heaved himself to a sitting position and
looked at her.

"Um?"

"Do you know if there's a doctor aboard? There is a
very sick woman in one of the cabins. I think she's dying."

The young man looked puzzled. He wiped some of the
moisture from his forehead. "A doctor? Gee, I guess
there's every sort aboard. There's a preacher and a piano
tuner and at least two lawyers that I know of, not to mention a big-time gambler from New Orleans and some men
from England—they really had a long trip to get here—"

"I said a doctor!" Corrie cried impatiently. "A woman
is sick, and she's in pain!"

The youth looked at his companion, who had stopped
his push-ups to stare at Corrie. "You hear of a doctor on
board, Culverson?"

"Yeah, I think I saw one somewhere. Some chap from
Canada, I believe. Don't know what his name is, though.
You ought to ask the captain. He'll find him for you fast
enough."

Corrie blurted out her thanks and made her way further
down the deck toward the pilot house, which was over-
shadowed by the huge, blackened smokestack. The last
thing she wanted to do was to speak to the captain. After
the incident in the cabin, she had carefully avoided him.
But now she had no other choice. It would take her hours
to find the doctor by inquiring among the passengers;
Zebulun Carter would be able to locate him quickly.

She approached a crewman, who told her to wait where
she was. In a few minutes, Captain Carter came striding
toward her, once again attired in his uniform resplendent
with gold braid and buttons.

"Yes, Mrs. *Price?*" His eyes were fixed on her warily.
His gold tooth gleamed. She could see a bruised area on
his forehead, and a red scratch at the corner of his mouth
where she must have clawed him.

"Captain, there's a woman in one of the cabins who is
very ill. She needs a doctor."

"What's wrong with her?"

"Does it matter?" Corrie asked sharply. "She's in a great deal of pain, in the abdominal region. One of the passengers told me that there is a doctor aboard, from Canada, and I'd like you to help me find him. He's needed right away."

Zebulun Carter's eyes flicked downward, touching her breasts and hips with contempt. "His name's Will Sebastian. I can find him for you, I suppose."

She drew herself up. "What do you mean, you suppose? You had better do a better job than that, Captain Carter, or you might find the consequences not to your liking."

"Yes, *ma'am.*"

Corrie stared at the man, hard, until finally Captain Carter looked away. "He's in his bunk," he told her. "He's seasick. I'll send a man after him if you insist. I don't know how much good he'll do you, though."

"Thank you," Corrie said, although inwardly her heart was sinking. A seasick doctor! Was this all the assistance that poor Mattie Shea was to receive?

Dr. Sebastian, however, did make the effort to get down to the crude cabin where Mattie lay. He was a tall, slender man in his late twenties, with thick light brown hair, brown eyes and a kindly mouth. He would have been good-looking if his face had not been bleached of all color. But although his gait was tottery, he *was* walking, and Corrie had to admire him for getting out of his bunk at all.

She waited out in the companionway while he examined Mattie Shea. No sounds came from within the cabin; evidently Mattie was still unconscious.

At last Dr. Sebastian emerged. His pleasant-looking face was whiter than ever, coated now with a sheen of moisture.

"It's no use," he told her. "The woman's dead. I don't know why you people couldn't have called me sooner. It's a disgrace, the condition I found her in." He glared at Corrie. "She was lying in her own excretions and had been for at least two days."

"Dead?" She was stammering. "But I just learned about her today. I didn't know they'd left her like that. None of them wanted to get near her."

"I know, I know," he sighed. "They all want to hide from illness. Don't want to admit it exists, because it might get *them*."

"What was wrong with her?"

"How the dickens should I know? Do you think I have one of those new X-ray contraptions and can see into her belly? If I could do an autopsy . . . But at least it wasn't any contagious disease that I could discover. At any rate, she's dead, and that's all that matters now. To her, at least."

"Oh, I wish I'd known sooner that she was sick. What a terrible shame."

"I think I'll give the captain the news and then get back to my own bunk," he added, swallowing. "She may be a corpse, but I feel like one."

And he was gone, leaving Corrie to return to her own cabin, shaken. Mattie Shea, whose laugh had been so full and rich and infectious, was dead. Shivering, Corrie thought of the frightening words the woman had said: *They'll burn you alive.*

She couldn't get them out of her mind.

The temperature dropped and snow whirled onto the deck to make it dangerously slippery. Corrie wore her sealskin cape when she attempted to get some fresh air. She was glad that Li Hua had had the foresight to pack a warm coat of her own; by the sixth day of the voyage the other girl had recovered from the worst of her *mal de mer* and had joined Corrie on her walks.

Both of them spent a lot of time on deck, staring out at the water, mountains and sky, all of it blue-misted and incredibly lovely. April here was wild and splendid. They were in the fiords and inlets of the "inside passage" where they were boxed in by huge, rugged mountains and wild islands. Only once, briefly, did they break into open ocean. This is God's country, Corrie kept thinking. And surely He is still somewhere about, admiring what He has made.

She saw glaciers marked by hundreds of fissures and by dark, dotted streaks of rock deposits. The ice masses were dull white shaded with turquoise, and striped by eerie floating white fingers of mist. Corrie got out her camera and photographed them, wishing there was some

way she could capture the countless subtle variations of
ice and color.

Four days later they were in the Lynn Canal, the last
segment of their route before they reached Dyea. Ribbons
of clouds hung over the massive hulks of stone rising sheer
from the water and capped with fierce crags. And around
them, on all sides, were the glaciers, rivers of ice frozen
into spectacular patterns, catching the sun with their flashing spires.

Even the waters of the canal itself were beautiful,
rather milky, translucent green, the result of the glacial
run-off. Corrie photographed all of it frantically, wishing
Papa were with her to enjoy it too. How he would have
exulted in this wild land!

But the idyll ended abruptly.

Five days later than anticipated, they arrived in Dyea
Harbor just after sunrise one morning. The settlement lay
lined up at the foot of the mountains like a string of
shabby wooden beads. From here, Corrie knew, the gold
seekers would leave for the Yukon River itself.

"Well, you're here, Mrs. *Price*," Captain Carter said,
passing her as she leaned over the rail gazing out at the
harbor. "And I hope you like what you get. Ain't no docks
here, no wharves, nothing. Just a high tide and a lot of
sand and mud flats and junk. Piles of junk everywhere
and you're lucky if it ain't washed away by the tide."

He grinned at her as if he took pleasure in this thought.

"But . . . aren't there any tugboats or other boats to
transport our luggage?" she asked in bewilderment.

Carter gave a short laugh. "Tugboats! Ha! No, ma'am,
but we do got lighters, though. Lighters and carts. Oh,
you'll get ashore, all right. We don't drown many of them,
we don't. Not *too* many."

"But no one told us it would be like this! So . . . .
crude . . . "

"You didn't ask, did you?"

He grinned at her and moved away to attend to the
business of unloading, leaving Corrie to look out at the
settlement of Dyea with trepidation. Perhaps he had exaggerated, she told herself at last, to get his revenge for
the scratch which still marred his face.

But by the time the *Alki* had anchored, Corrie decided

that the captain had not exaggerated at all. In fact, if anything, he had underplayed the mass confusion as the steamers struggled to deposit thousands of stampeding passengers and their freight onto a beach with no docks or jetties or any orthodox way of disembarking.

Sheer, utter chaos. Horses and sheep were swung out over the water and dropped into the sea to swim ashore— if they made it. Lighters—flat, ugly boats—angled clumsily alongside the *Alki* and were loaded by the crewmen, who laughed if a sack of flour or rice accidentally fell into the water.

Many more tons of goods, Corrie saw, were piled in disorderly fashion on the beach. Everywhere she looked there were stacks of lumber, sleds, boats, cases of evaporated milk, picks, shovels, mining contraptions and crates. Dogs, goats and sheep ran about or were tethered to crates. Men roamed among the stacks of provisions, trying to carry them out of reach of the tide licking the shore. Some were too late; many sacks and bags were already soaked, and some floated in the water.

"Well, I saved you two ladies a ride on a lighter." Captain Carter was back, grinning wildly. It was clear that he felt great pleasure in seeing the dismay on Corrie's face. "A nice, glamorous lighter. Of course, you might get a bit wet, but you won't mind a little ice-cold water, will you? A little water never hurt no woman yet."

"Thank you for your efforts," Corrie said coldly.

"At your service, *ma'am*." He made her an insolent little bow, and Corrie had to suppress an angry retort. How dare he—

But it didn't matter, she reminded herself. Unpleasant as he was, Captain Carter was not important now, and they would probably never see him again. Staring at the chaotic beach scene, Corrie was uneasy, filled with questions. What were she and Li Hua going to do? Where would they stay? How was she to find Avery? And what would happen to her baby?

By the time they reached the shore, hard, dry flakes of snow had begun to fall. A horse and wagon—driven out into water up to the horses' bellies—unloaded their lighter. Then the driver began throwing sacks and trunks onto the sand.

By dint of frantic shouting and promises of money, Corrie was able to convince him to transport their trunks and her camera box to town. He was a burly blond man of twenty-five, who eyed both girls appreciatively.

"Do you know where you're going, miss?"

"Yes," Corrie replied bravely. "To town, of course."

"Well, you'll probably have to camp out, missie, because all the hotels are jam-packed full. Even the tents are full!" He grinned at her.

"Just get us to town. We'll find something!" Corrie told him desperately.

The city of Dyea was so raw and new that its lumber was still uncured. The settlement itself was about a mile square. Tents mushroomed everywhere, and more of them overflowed onto the beach itself. To Corrie's dazed mind, it all looked as if it had been thrown up only an hour ago by a carpenter in a hurry. Which was probably not far from the truth, she told herself, swallowing hard.

The cart rattled and jolted over the rough street. At last Corrie and Li Hua found themselves standing on a tipsy, half-rotten plank sidewalk in what had to be the ugliest town in the world. Raw frame buildings lined the streets, many with up-and-down board construction resembling farm sheds. Big signs on these structures vied for attention: "Klondike Lodging House, 25¢." "Bailey's Hotel." "Dance Hall." "Dyea Hotel."

The town was surging with humanity. Men in rough mackinaws and boots and fur hats crowded the walks and tramped in the mud. Some stood in knots, arguing or laughing loudly. Most, Corrie saw, were eyeing her and Li Hua; both looked vastly out of place in their smart traveling suits and sealskin capes.

There were, she observed further, more than two hundred men visible on the street, and she and Li Hua seemed to be the only two women. What had they gotten themselves into? she began to wonder with a sinking heart. This crude and ugly town, these men with their bold stares . . .

Corrie tried valiantly to hide her dismay from Li Hua. "Well," she said quickly. "The man said the hotels were full, but perhaps he was mistaken. At any rate, we've got to find out. We certainly can't camp out on the streets."

Li Hua looked at her luggage piled near the wide mud-rutted street. For the first time she seemed shaken. She clutched at Corrie. "I never thought it would be like this."

"Neither did I. But we'll figure something out. We've got to!"

They heard a silvery giggle behind them and turned to see five of the women from the ship riding past them, all jammed together in a crude cart. In their flowered and feathered hats, their silk finery, the girls were like gaudy, exotic birds. Among them was Jinnie, the girl who had said she would "gag" if she had to nurse Mattie Shea. A man sat amid them, laughing too.

Corrie watched them pass by.

"They don't have to worry about a roof over their heads tonight," Li Hua said in an odd tone.

"No, they don't." For some reason the remark irked Corrie. "But we do. I think we had better start looking for a hotel room until we can decide what to do next. We'll have to leave our luggage here, I guess, and hope nobody steals it. You take that side of the street. Go to the hotels and see if you can find lodgings for us. I'll take this side."

"But—"

"Li Hua, do you want to spend the night sleeping in a puddle of mud?"

"Of course I don't." Li Hua left, the ribbon-trimmed flounce of her navy serge skirt dragging in the clods of dirt which littered the planks.

Corrie hesitated, then turned and began walking toward her left, where a building, larger than the others and set closer to the street, had a sign that announced itself as Bailey's Hotel. Doggedly she tried to ignore the stares she received from male passersby.

"Hey, sweetheart, you come up to work in a dance hall? Lordy, but they need a beauty like you. Them girls got mighty ugly faces."

"Please let me pass. Please."

A group of men were squatted on the plank walk, blocking her passage. They were gambling, bent intently over three walnut shells while a professional gambler moved the shells about with a quick hand. She halted, realizing that she could not get past them without venturing into the thick ankle-deep mud of the street.

"Say, little lady, want to join our game? We let women play—if they got plenty of gold dust!" A big, bearded man in a red plaid "Monkey Ward" mackinaw grinned at her, showing spaces in his front teeth.

"No, I don't want to gamble, thank you. And could you please let me pass?"

"Oh, a lady, is it? You'd better stand up, Jim, and let her by. She don't want to get her pretty feet dirty."

Were they laughing at her, or were they trying, in a rough way, to be friendly? Corrie didn't know, and didn't dare to look at them to find out. She fled past them and toward what now appeared as a haven: Bailey's Hotel. Surely an establishment that big would have at least one room. She and Li Hua could share a bed if they had to. She'd be willing to pay anything.

Another big crowd of men was pushing out of a dance hall, laughing and shoving, and again Corrie had to stop. It was just at this moment that she saw a familiar face approaching her from the far side of the group of miners. No, it couldn't be. How could it be him?

Donald Earle!

Shock paralyzed Corrie. She stood frozen, staring at his wide shoulders pushing aside those who tried to jostle him.

Donald!

Corrie gave way to panic. Without another thought she whirled and began running back the way she had come. She tripped and skidded on clumps of mud scattered on the planks, nearly losing her balance. A gray-haired man reached out and caught her elbow just in time to prevent her from sprawling full-length.

"Miss? Are you all r—"

But she ran on, impelled by her unreasoning terror. She didn't know or care where she was going; she only knew that she had to get away. Somehow—how? How?— Donald had managed to follow her to Dyea.

She plunged along the planked walk, a stitching pain in her ribs.

❦ Chapter 13 ❦

"Oh! Damn!"

Corrie let out an involuntary cry as she skidded on another patch of mud and went flying. She twisted in the air, fought to catch her balance, and then came down, hard, on the planks. Pain shot through her spine.

"Well, it's the bicycle girl again, I see—temper and all," an amused male voice said at her elbow. She felt someone grasp her under both arms and lift her to her feet.

Corrie was dazed, and conscious only of her hurt and of the need to get away from Donald. "Please—let me go, I can't let him see me!"

"First it's your bicycle, then this." There was a chuckle, a familiar one.

Corrie whirled about to face her captor. "You!"

He grimaced. "Yes, I'm afraid it is me. Sorry I don't have a rose to hand you this time."

His blunt, bold face looked the same as ever, the blue eyes laughing. He was dressed in a red plaid mackinaw and fur hat, and seemed much bigger than she had remembered, his shoulders powerful under the woolen fabric. Yet he was smiling at her, laugh wrinkles crinkling his face and giving him a curiously boyish look.

"I didn't want your rose!" she retorted furiously. "And what are you doing *here*, of all places!"

His smile faded. "What am *I* doing here? What are *you* doing here? My God, girl, when you're taken home, you certainly don't stay put, do you?"

Corrie's tailbone still throbbed, and she felt jittery with fright at seeing Donald.

"Oh, do be still!" she snapped. "And do let go of me! I'm quite all right now, I assure you, and I've got to get away. I can't let him see me—"

"Can't let who see you?"

"Never mind! Oh, please let go of me!" She tugged at him desperately. "I don't want him to see me! He mustn't!"

"Why not? It appears to me that you're a mighty pleasant sight to look at, even if you are covered with mud at the moment."

Instead of releasing her, Quade Hill pulled her in the direction of a sign which proclaimed, "Bud's Road House, dinners $1.00."

"Please!" She shoved at him with her free hand, feeling like a child in the midst of a tantrum, but unable to stop herself. "I told you, I *can't* let him see me!"

"Well, whoever he is, he is undoubtedly going to do just that if you stay here," Quade said, hustling her along so fast that she thought her arm was going to be wrenched out of its socket. "This town may be crawling with people, but there's only one main street for them to crawl in, and this is it. Come on, I'll buy you a meal. You look starved, and that ought to get you out of sight for a minute or two. And besides, I'd favor the company of a pretty woman."

"But I don't—"

"This place will do," he said. "I ate here yesterday. Bud may not be a gourmet cook, but at least his coffee is civilized."

Despite her protests, he pushed her through the low doorway of the little establishment. She stood for a moment adjusting her eyes to the dimness.

The building—it was a cabin, really—was built entirely of logs, with a rough plank floor and six log slab tables. The small, dark, smoky room was full of men, but Quade Hill dragged her toward the corner, where there was space at one of the tables. The other four occupants —bearded men speaking a rapid-fire French—glanced at them, moved down a bit, and then went back to their own meal.

"Sit down," Quade ordered. "We don't stand on ceremony here in the North."

"But I'm not hungry."

"I am." Then, as Corrie gave a quick look toward the door, he added, "Who are you expecting to come in here, anyway? A ten-foot grizzly bear?"

"No, of course not. Don't be ridiculous."

Corrie sank limply onto the bench, wincing as her bottom touched the wood. Her heart was pounding and she felt sick. If Donald were to come in here . . . She felt sure he was right outside on the street, perhaps only a few hundred feet away. Had he seen her? She prayed that he hadn't.

She heard Quade say something to the tough-looking, raw-boned woman who came to take their orders. After she had left, he said, "Now, Cordelia Stewart, what's this all about? You won't stay home where you'll be safe, will you? No, you've got to roam. But this time you really took the bit into your teeth, didn't you? Alaska! How did you get here, of all places? And who is this mysterious man you want to get away from at all costs?"

Corrie shot another glance at the door, feeling like a rabbit who knows that a fox is crouched just outside its burrow.

"Mr. Hill, please. I—"

"Call me Quade. We're informal here. Now, go on and tell me. Just who is this formidable man?"

"His name is Donald Earle."

"Oh. Indeed."

Was she mistaken or did Quade's eyes narrow as she said Donald's name? She thought she saw an odd, mixed expression of anger and puzzlement cross his blunt, strong face. But she plunged on, explaining Papa's will and Donald's part in it as best she could.

"I don't want to marry him," she finished. "It's Avery I love, my fiancé. I know Donald is only interested in me because of Papa's horrid will. I'm sure he doesn't love me. And I don't love him!"

"Yes. Go on." Quade's blue eyes, the intense color of the Yukon sky, had darkened and his gentle mouth had hardened to a grim line.

Quickly she told him of Avery, and of her own plans to

find him here and marry him. The only part of the story that she omitted was her expected baby; surely her pregnancy didn't show yet, and it was none of his business anyway.

"So your fiancé doesn't know you're coming?"

"No. But I'm sure he'll welcome me. He does love me very much. He—" She faltered. She was barely aware of the fact that the woman had returned with steaming mugs of dark coffee.

Quade shoved one of the mugs toward her. "Here, drink this. It'll help steady you. You're shaking like an aspen."

"I don't need steadying! I'm fine. And I don't need coffee either. What I do need is to get somewhere Donald won't find me. I'm so afraid he'll try to make me go back with him. I don't want to marry the man; I won't!"

"Drink." Quade forced a mug into her hand. "And tell me, where do you intend to go to get away from this man, this Donald Earle? Out into the mountains? Up the Dyea Trail?"

"No, of course not. Don't be silly. How could I? I don't even have any camping things. All I have is my trunk and my camera supplies and chemicals. I'm planning to use public transportation and hotels here."

"What? You don't have any gear or provisions? No rice or flour or beans?"

"No."

"My God, girl. Don't you realize that they've been short of food in Dawson City? This is wild country here, raw wilderness! Food doesn't grow on trees here; it has to be shipped up from the States or shot on the hoof. The Mounties decreed that you have to have twelve hundred pounds of provisions before they'll let you cross the Chilkoot Pass. That's so people like you won't starve to death." Quade took a swallow of coffee. "Didn't anyone tell you that?"

"Yes," she stammered. Her heart was beginning to sink. "Of course I read the little books the merchants gave out at the dry goods stores. But I thought—I mean, I'm not planning to do any mining, and I won't be here very long. They said—they said there were lots of hotels here, places to stay—"

Quade slammed his coffee cup down onto the table, its contents splashing toward Corrie.

"Deliver me from *cheechakos,* greenhorns and fools," he said to no one in particular. "All right; you're here, without even the barest of provisions. And you say that you're here to marry someone. Just where is this lucky man? I presume that you at least know where he is."

"Of course I know where he is!" Corrie stated emphatically. A stab of doubt crossed her thoughts, but she was not about to betray her fears to Quade Hill. "He's here in Alaska. Mining for gold. On the Yukon River, I believe. I'll begin making inquiries right away. I feel confident it won't be hard to find him."

Quade hit his head with his palm. "Cordelia Stewart, do you realize just how big this country *is?* I was here before, five years ago, and I know. There are thousands of square miles of land here, with hundreds of rivers. And the towns—he could be in Dawson City, or Circle. Forty-Mile, Eagle, Valdez. My God, girl, there are tens of thousands of men swarming about all of these places. They wander here and there without anybody to keep track of them, and nobody to care, either, if one of them turns up missing. There's no telegraph yet, and damned few telephone lines—none of them in the gold fields. Mail service is rotten. And yet you think you're going to come up here, just like that, and find your Averill man and marry him!"

"His name is *Avery,*" she said carefully. "And I am going to find him."

"I wouldn't bet on it."

Corrie was close to tears. How patronizing this man was, how maddening! How dare he treat her as if she was completely ignorant; what had he called her, a *cheechako?* And yet she felt a twinge of fright at what he had said.

The big woman brought their food, two plates laden with fried whitefish and mashed potatoes, and Quade began to eat. Corrie looked down at her own plate and shuddered.

"Go ahead, enjoy it," he told her. "That's fresh Yukon fish. And you'll need something to give you energy. If I'd suffered the fall on my backside that you did, I'm sure I'd want something to pick my spirits up."

"I'm not hungry! And do please quit referring to my . . . backside."

He looked up from his food and grinned at her.

Corrie watched him eat, her mind in a panicky whirl. Provisions, gear, rice, beans. Twelve hundred pounds of it. No telegraph . . . good heavens! And there was Li Hua, she remembered with a sudden stab of dread. The girl was still on the street, canvassing the hotels. How could she have forgotten? If Donald were to see her . . .

"Excuse me, I have to go now." She struggled up from the rough bench.

He pushed her back down again. "And where are you going? I thought you said you didn't want this Donald Earle person to see where you are. He's certainly going to spot you if you go back on the street now, isn't he?"

"Well, I can't stay here in this miserable little eating hut forever!" she retorted furiously. "And I've got to find Li Hua! I forgot about her. She—"

"Li Hua?"

"Yes, she's my maid; she came with me. Donald knows her. If he sees her he may realize that I'm here too. Li Hua is looking for a hotel room for the two of us," she explained.

He was laughing. "Sweet heavens, do you mean that you don't even have a hotel room?"

"No." Corrie was seething with anger and fright. How dare he laugh at her? She *was* ignorant; she supposed that was true. But that wasn't her fault; she hadn't known Dyea or the Yukon would be like this. How could she have?

She could never find Avery by herself, she realized dully. She had come all these miles for nothing. If she were sensible, she would go back to the beach and engage steamer passage for San Francisco immediately.

No, she told herself defiantly. *I won't do that. I won't give up like a silly ninny and go home.*

Now Quade was telling her about the scarcity of hotel rooms, but Corrie barely heard him. Something Aunt Susan once had said suddenly came into her mind, as plainly as if her aunt herself were present. *You've never lived without money. You don't know what a buttress it can be against the ugly things.*

Money. Money, Corrie reminded herself, could buy not only goods, but also services . . .

She straightened her spine on the hard wooden bench and heard her own voice say airily, "Oh, I'll get a hotel room later. At the moment what I really need is a man who will take me up the Yukon River. Someone who will buy my provisions for me and get them upriver for me, and help me to find Avery. I can pay. I have a good deal of money with me, and I'll pay well."

Quade's eyes narrowed at her. "I hope you're not looking at me when you say that."

"I am looking at you. I'd like to hire you, Mr. Hill."

"Cordelia Stewart, I'm a journalist, and my business is writing newspaper and magazine articles. I roam, Miss Stewart, wherever my nose happens to take me. And at the moment it happens to have taken me to Alaska, where I have better things to do than to play nursemaid to young girls on wild goose chases."

"I'm not here on a wild goose chase. I'm here to marry the man I love."

"Very touching." He stood up, digging coins out of his pocket. "But I'm sorry, I can't oblige you. As I've told you, I have other business here. Go to one of the hotels; they might recommend someone to you. Or go home. That's even better. The thought of you trying to get to the Yukon is absurd. Why, you'd be like a newborn kitten among wolves."

"I would not! And I'm not going home! Wait! Where are you going?"

But Quade was already striding toward the door. Furiously Corrie ran after him. Was he just going to leave her here? He couldn't! Irritating as he was, she needed him. How could she possibly trust some stranger recommended by one of these ramshackle hotels? Quade was right. She was a babe in the woods here, she did need help, and she'd never be able to reach Avery without it.

"Please! Oh, please!" She pulled at the sleeve of his mackinaw. "I've got to locate my fiancé. And I don't trust these hotels. What if they recommend a rogue to me?"

Quade grinned. "Most of the men here are rogues, or they probably wouldn't have come. Come to think of it, I'm one myself." He gave her a mock bow. "Don't worry, little lady. You'll find yourself someone. I was here in ninety-three and I'll wager you'll find plenty of men for hire. Money will do a lot for you in a place like this."

"But what if—" God, he was infuriating!

She was really panicking now. She could sense his desire to be away from her. She knew she couldn't let him go out of that door. If she did, she'd never seen him again, and she'd be all alone here in Dyea, without gear or provisions, and small hope of finding Avery. Li Hua would be no help at all. She'd have to go home—she'd be forced to.

"But you can't leave," she pleaded. "There's Donald. If you go, he'll find me—"

"Let him. Perhaps *he'll* take you up the Yukon."

"Oh, no, you can't mean that. You don't know Donald. You don't know the kind of man he is. He—"

"Corrie, the meal has been pleasant, but now please get out of here and leave me alone." Quade lifted an arm and shook her off as if she had been a dry leaf stuck to his sleeve. "I haven't time for you and your foolishness."

"It's not foolishness!" They were outside on the plank walk. Corrie ran after him, shamelessly pulling at his clothing. "I'll pay you well, I swear it. I'll make it worth your while. You can't leave me here. You can't!" Corrie said angrily.

"What are you, a little leech?" He shook her away again, and she flung herself at him, heedless of the amused smiles of passersby, or Quade's increasing annoyance.

"Would you do this to your mother?" she demanded. "Would you leave her stranded in this awful city without help? Would you do that to her? Or to your sister?"

He stopped, so suddenly that she bumped into him. His eyes were so cold and bleak that she shivered.

"What did you say?"

"I said . . . would you do such a thing to your sister?" she faltered.

"All right. Damn your pretty little hide, Corrie, I told you that I have to follow my nose, and the last thing I need is a female hanging on me. If it weren't for—" Then he cut the words off savagely, as if he had said too much.

"Do you mean you'll do it? You'll help me?"

He took her arm and began yanking her around the side of the little log restaurant and toward the back, his face twisted with fury.

"Yes, damn you, I will. God knows why; I must be a fool to give in to an impulse like this. But why not? I followed one impulse to get here, so what difference will one more make?"

At the side of the roadhouse were more planks laid over the mud so that the owner could get to his trash pile. Corrie stumbled along them behind Quade, clutching at him for balance. She didn't understand all that he was saying, only that his intensity was somehow frightening.

"Where are you taking me?" she gasped.

"Around the back way and then to a hotel. Where else? You roped me in to take care of you, and I assume that you don't plan to sleep in the street. Where did you leave your trunk? Pitiful as it is, I suppose I had better collect it. And we'll have to find that friend of yours. Did you really travel all this way north with a ladies' maid, Cordelia Stewart?"

Money, Corrie learned, did indeed buy things. Within half an hour, she and Li Hua were inspecting a room in a place called the Gold Nugget Hotel, which was so new that parts of it were no more than a board framework. Their room still had sawdust on the floor. It was small, its walls crudely plastered. A lumpy mattress had been flung on the floor; a metal washbasin sat beside it. A wooden block with three upright nails hammered into it served as both candlestick and soap dish. There was one small, grimy window.

Corrie surveyed the room dubiously. "Is this all you could get?"

"Don't complain, Miss." Quade scowled at her. "Look, there's a plate glass window, a real luxury here. The manager probably threw out four good customers to put us in this room. Of course, if you wish something more luxurious, I'm sure I can get you a place in one of the local brothels. I understand they have fine brass beds there, with white-quilted coverlets. Of course, the work might be a bit demanding. The population here consists mostly of men, and they're a rather lusty sort—"

She slapped him. The smack echoed in the room, and she heard Li Hua's indrawn, shocked gasp.

"How dare you speak to me that way?" she whispered. "I'm not one of those women and I won't be insulted. I—"

He stared down at her, his face twisted. She could almost smell the anger emanating from him, sharp and musky.

"Slap me again, Corrie Stewart, and I'll toss you out onto that muddy street right on that pretty backside of yours, and be damned if you ever find your fiancé. Do you understand?"

He grasped her shoulders and shook her, not very gently. Then, suddenly, his grip relaxed. "You're right, Corrie, I shouldn't have spoken to you so boldly. And I'm sorry. But I am doing you a favor; can't you get it through that little head of yours? I don't need your money and I don't want to be saddled with you. And if you dare to hit me again, I'll dump you."

"Oh, go to hell!"

The words popped out before Corrie had time to think.

"What did you say?" Now he was grinning at her mockingly.

"I said . . . oh, never mind." She turned aside, her face flushed. She was beginning to regret hiring such a rude, impossible man. She'd made a huge mistake, she was sure.

But now Quade was striding across the room to where he and the hotel owner had unceremoniously dumped their trunks and the camera box.

"All right," he said, the tone of his voice more normal. "I see you're still no lady, and God knows I'm no gentleman, and I guess I've stopped trying. But we're stuck with each other, and we might as well make the best of it." He poked at Corrie's trunk with the toe of his boot. "Is this yours? Where's the key? I want to see just what you've brought along."

"You want to open my trunk! But whatever for?"

"Because you hired me to provision you. How can I

buy them if I don't know what you're already carrying? Come on, give me the key."

"But—" Corrie looked uneasily at Li Hua. "But I have personal things in it . . . undergarments and items of that sort."

"So? I don't care if you have an entire corset factory in there. Give me the key and let me see for myself."

Silently Corrie dug into her pocketbook and produced it. She and Li Hua watched as Quade knelt down, turned the key, and opened the lid of the trunk. He began to rummage through it.

"Well, at least I see you had the sense to bring some men's clothing. I confess I'm surprised. But for sweet heaven's sake, why would you bring these canned things? Dehydrated foods take up a lot less space and weigh less. Well, you can eat them up now and get rid of the cans . . . "

He poked deeper into the trunk. "Underwear! Lace! Do you think this is Nob Hill? How much good do you think these fancy things are going to do you here, unless you—" He grinned. "Well, you told me not to talk about that, so I won't. But I'll tell you this: the brothels and the dance halls are the only places around here that those ribbons and furbelows are going to do you any good at all."

Corrie flushed angrily and resisted the urge to lift her palm and smack him again. How rude he was! But she didn't dare to slap him, for she was sure he would carry out his threat to dump her. Then she'd really be in trouble. He said he had been in the Yukon before, and she needed his experienced help; she knew now that she'd never find Avery without him.

He was still pawing through the trunk, and Corrie stepped forward to catch a novel that had fallen out onto the floor.

"What's this?" Quade was holding up a square of flannel cloth. "A flannel washrag?"

The layette! Blood rushed to Corrie's face. She darted forward to grab the diaper, which she snatched from him.

"Oh, how dare you?" she cried. "Pawing and poking through my private things—oh, it isn't any of your business what I'm carrying here! Just—oh, just close the lid and mind your own business, will you?"

Quade stared at her. Then, deliberately, he reached in and drew out another object. It was a white cashmere infant's cloak, delicately embroidered in a fleur-de-lis pattern. Corrie had paid eight dollars for it. He held it up with an odd expression on his face and examined it as if it had been a blacksnake which had secreted itself in the trunk.

"No wonder you didn't want me in here," he said heavily. "So that's why you're so anxious to find that precious Avery of yours and marry yourself off to him."

Shame washed through Corrie and she felt tears prick at her eyes. Still she faced him, not allowing her eyes to drop.

"Well, what of it?" she said. "I've hired you to do a job for me, and I expect you to do that job. Nothing else about me is your concern!"

☙ Chapter 14 ☙

They were killing each other on the streets of Dyea.

They had to be, Corrie thought. Never had she heard such frightening night sounds. Voices shouted, cursed, yelled, guffawed and hooted. Pistol shots had rung out twice in the last fifteen minutes. A dog began to bark loudly, then yipped as someone—evidently—threw a stone at him, or kicked him. Footsteps echoed hollowly on the plank walks. Corrie heard a heavy, falling sound, and then more laughter. From the dance hall up the street a piano kept up a frantic, tuneless pounding.

Corrie lay rigidly on the mattress, staring upward into blackness. Beside her, Li Hua stirred in her sleep. And on the other side of her—Corrie could scarcely credit that this had really happened—Quade Hill lay wrapped in a blanket. He twitched, threw out an arm, muttered something, then resumed his regular breathing.

She was sleeping in the same room with a man.

Corrie bit her lower lip and sucked in her breath sharply. She could just picture Aunt Susan's horror at the very idea.

There had been absolutely nothing she could do about it. She had assumed, naturally enough, that the hotel room was for herself and Li Hua only, and that Quade would seek other quarters, if he did not already have them. Thus she had been totally shocked when Quade, after an hours-long, unexplained absence, had returned with a roll of blankets and proceeded to arrange them on the floor.

"And what do you think you're doing?" she demanded.

147

"I'm planning to get a good night's sleep, that's what. I would suggest that you do the same. There's a lot to do tomorrow and I want to get started early. I have to provision up, too. I came here without much notice."

"But surely you're not going to sleep *here*? In this room?"

"Where else?" In the light of the kerosene lamp Quade had managed to obtain from the hotel owner, his face had a savage look. "Listen, girl, hasn't it dawned on you yet that Dyea is crammed with people? This city is bursting at the seams. I was planning to use a tent, but now that you're here, things are different. I had to spend a good deal of money to get this room for us and I see no reason why I shouldn't use it too. We'll have a lot of time to spend in tents and I personally prefer a roof over my head."

"But . . . you're a man."

"I certainly am. That has nothing to do with it. You barged up here, little Cordelia Stewart, without knowing what it was all about, and now you're going to learn. Women are in the minority here. Yet incredible as it may seem, they are treated with respect—the decent ones anyway. That's the code up here, the miners' code, if you can picture such a thing."

"I really can't . . . "

"You can, and you're going to have to." He was grinning at her, laugh wrinkles crinkling at his eyes and mouth. His blue eyes gleamed at her wickedly. His big body seemed to fill up all the room as he arranged the blankets. "Don't worry, I won't rape you. Unless you want to be raped, that is."

That had been four hours ago. Somehow Corrie had managed to push back her anger, and she and Li Hua had settled themselves, lying down on the mattress in their clothes. Li Hua fell asleep almost immediately, but Corrie lay awake, seething.

She would put up with his arrangement for tonight, because she had to. Tomorrow morning she would fire him. He was impudent, impossible! Surely she could find someone—anyone—in Dyea who could get her to Avery and do it in a polite and proper way.

She lay there angrily, wishing he had not decided to put

his bedroll so close to her side of the mattress. She was uncomfortably aware of him. Another raucous laugh rose from the street below and Corrie turned on her other hip, stopping her ears with her fingers. Never, she thought, never had she imagined the trip north would be like this. First Captain Carter. Then Mattie Shea and her spooky prediction. Then Donald Earle. And now Quade . . .

Li Hua gave a delicate snore, and Corrie's eyes, which had started to droop, popped open. How could the girl sleep so soundly, as if she didn't even hear the street noises? And why on earth had she decided to remain here?

For Li Hua had resisted all of Corrie's efforts to buy her a return steamer ticket. She was going to go to the Klondike and stake a claim, she insisted.

"But Li Hua, how can you? A woman!"

"If that Mrs. Benrush we saw on the ship can do it, then I can too," Li Hua retorted. "But it doesn't matter. I don't want to go home, and I won't. If you don't want me to accompany you, of course I won't. But I *am* going to the Yukon and no one is going to stop me!"

Corrie stared at the other girl. How Li Hua had changed. Once she had been a servant girl, full of high spirits yet obedient. Corrie thought of her as a quick and capable maidservant, a gifted hairdresser, a girl who could giggle at secret jokes and participate in pranks played on the fat laundress Bea Ellen. She could never have imagined Li Hua would prove to be so stubborn and defiant.

She reached out and touched the Chinese girl's hand. "Are you sure, Li Hua? I would be glad to pay your passage back home, really I would. I have enough money. And I do feel responsible for you somehow."

"Responsible! Why should you? I'm a free person, Corrie, not your servant any more. I'll never be that again." The soft, delicate voice was disdainful.

"Well . . . " Finally Corrie smiled. "Well, all right. At least we can travel up the Yukon River together until I find Avery. We can be company for each other."

"Company. Yes." For an instant Li Hua's face softened, and she seemed the girl that Corrie had always known. Then her expression clouded, and she turned away.

Now Corrie lay stiffly, hearing the noises of Li Hua's breathing beside her. She *was* glad Li Hua was here, she admitted to herself. She had been shocked to see her aboard the *Alki,* but after that, she felt glad. She wouldn't have to be alone here. She would have a friend . . . She fell into a fitful sleep punctuated by oddly vivid dreams of Captain Carter and Mattie Shea.

Shortly before dawn Corrie stirred drowsily to realize that the poorly insulated room had grown bitterly cold. Something warm was pressed against her back. Unconsciously she snuggled closer to it, and the warmth remained, sensual and pleasant and safe. There was a weight across the curve of her hips, too. Corrie felt secure.

She drifted back to sleep again and this time her dreams were not of Mattie Shea but of Avery. She was lying with him on the sand at Ocean Beach while the sun baked down on them. Avery's blond hair shone in the sun like gold. He was murmuring in her ear. *My darling, I'll shower you with nuggets, and we can get married. . . .*

She opened her eyes to realize that it was light, and that she was lying with her back snuggled up to Quade Hill, and his arm flung across her hips. Somehow, during the night, he had moved toward her.

Or—she gave a horrified start—was it the other way around? For she herself was lying off the mattress and on the bare floor, brazenly close to Quade.

She jerked away from him, chagrined. But before she could get to her feet, Quade stirred. The hand that lay across her hip flexed. Slowly, lazily, his hand ran over the curve of her belly and breasts with a sensuality that was at once frightening and deeply stirring.

"Stop that!" Corrie gasped and shoved his hand away. "How dare you," she whispered, hoping that Li Hua wouldn't awaken to hear this.

She could feel Quade's warm breath on her neck as he laughed. "Well, what do you expect me to do, Cordelia Stewart? Or shall I call you Delia? That seems to suit you much more than Corrie. Anyway, I'm not a man of ice, you know, and when a beautiful girl crawls into my bed-roll with me . . . "

Corrie abruptly sat up. "I'm not in your bedroll! I—"

She stopped, horrified, as she realized that she was, in-deed, sitting on half of Quade's rumpled blanket.

"If you're not in my bed, then you're the next thing to it. And here I didn't think that you liked me all that well." Quade sat up, too. He stretched and yawned nois-ily. "I guess I was sorely mistaken."

"You were not mistaken! I don't like you! And I can't imagine how I got here. The room is so cold; that must be why I . . . "

Corrie's cheeks were burning. She scrambled to her feet and brushed off the folds of her traveling suit, in which she had slept. "Oh, I can't imagine how I could have hired a man so rude, so lacking in basic good manners. You—you're fired!"

"Fired?" Quade had stood up, too, and again she was conscious of just how big he was, how strong and power-ful. His blue eyes held an odd, soft look, as if he had not yet put on his mask for the day.

"You don't dare fire me, Corrie, because you know damned well that you're not likely to find any other man around Dyea who's half as good as I am. It may not seem that way to you, but I'm an honest man, and I really have no intention of making love to a woman who doesn't want me. So you can rest easy, my dear girl. Your virtue—what there is left of it—will be completely safe with me."

Your virtue, what there is left of it. Corrie felt herself go rigid with anger. She stumbled over the corner of the mattress, where Li Hua still slumbered, and went to the plate glass window. She stared blindly out at the street.

She hated him! To say such things—she felt sick with the shame of it. But worst of all was her knowledge that her body had betrayed her by seeking Quade Hill's warmth during the night.

Half an hour later the three of them had breakfast in what the hotel called its "dining room." A small room opened off the miniscule lobby and possessed the same raw newness as the rest of the building. Huge plank tables were filled with "stampeders," as they were called, doggedly shoveling food into their mouths. Corrie, gazing at them, could not believe that these were the same revelers who had kept her awake last night.

She sensed some of them staring at her, and was glad that she had managed to rub the worst of the mud spots off her skirt and to wash her face and hands in the frigid water in the china ewer. Her face, viewed in the tiny hand mirror, had regained its color, and her slanted, golden-brown eyes which papa called "wicked" were clear and sparkling. Li Hua, too, had washed, and now looked scrubbed and eager, her lush black hair pinned into a full pompadour.

Even Quade looked presentable. To his credit, he had left their room and made his ablutions elsewhere. Although many of the men here were bearded, he had shaved and changed to a clean flannel shirt which made his shoulders look as broad and as formidable as ever.

Breakfast seemed to be the big meal of the day; they were served bacon, coffee, flapjacks, syrup, and a huge mound of greasy fried potatoes. The bacon was limp and the pancakes filled with doughy lumps of flour, but Corrie ate hungrily.

Optimism was beginning to flow back into her. She was starting to feel that she had made the right decision about Quade after all. Obnoxious as he was, perhaps he did have some rough rudiments of good manners. He *was* competent. He *had* promised to get her to Avery. What more did she want of him? For a few weeks, surely she could put up with his rudeness.

While they ate, Quade talked casually of his work as if the incident of the previous night had never happened. He was a journalist and wrote articles and essays for the Chicago *Tribune* and the New York *Times*. His writing had taken him around most of the country and abroad. At present he was planning to write a guidebook to the Yukon.

"But don't you plan your travels in advance?" Corrie asked curiously. "You mentioned yesterday that you arrived here with very few provisions yourself."

For an instant he glowered at her, and she was sure he was going to say something rude. "My plans changed. I came north at the last minute," was all he said, however.

She was cheered to learn that Quade's absence last night had been because he was scouting about the town of Dyea, investigating Donald's whereabouts and intentions.

"Well?" Corrie breathed. "What did you find out?"

"He's staying at Bailey's. He's waiting here in town, rumor has it, for a big dredging machine to be shipped up from Seattle. He is looking for other investors and I gather that they are going to form a corporation," Quade explained.

"A corporation!" Corrie was thoughtful. "I heard Papa and Donald arguing about that. Donald wanted to take big business to the North, and Papa was angry."

Quade nodded, and again she fancied that she saw an odd, secretive look on his face.

"Did you learn how long he has been here?" Corrie asked.

"About three days."

"Then he could have been following me! Don't you see, our steamer, the *Alki*, was delayed because of the storm and engine trouble. So his boat could have passed ours."

Quade shrugged. "Well, whatever the man's reasons, he's certainly here now, and he's not lacking for female company, either. They said at the hotel that he had a woman in his room the other night—paid her quite a lot of money, too, from what she told the manager. He's a strange man with strange needs, I gathered."

"Oh." Corrie found that she was flushing.

"I performed another chore last night, too. I went down to the beach and found your friend Captain Carter in a tent saloon there. I had a little talk with him."

"You did?"

"As far as he knows, he was carrying some dance hall girls and a few wives and that's all. One of the women was named Mrs. Price. Period." Quade smiled briefly. "It's amazing what a roll of bills can do for a man's memory."

So that was where Quade had been last night—covering up her trail so that if Donald did decide to look for her, he would not be able to find her. Corrie felt a blush rising from her neck to cover her face. And she had loosed her anger at him—had even tried to fire him.

She stared down at her coffee cup, at the black, thick mixture that filled it. Well, she was not going to apologize to him, she thought with a touch of defiance. He *had* been rude. And wasn't she paying him to do those very jobs for her?

Now Quade turned his attention to Li Hua and began to quiz her on her plans. To Corrie's surprise, the girl told him she had nearly four hundred dollars with her; she had stowed away on the *Alki* in order to avoid spending it. She planned to buy her own provisions for the trip to the gold fields, she said.

Corrie stared at her. "But, Li Hua, I thought you didn't have any money. Four hundred dollars! Where did you get it?"

Li Hua gazed back, her dark, tilted eyes suddenly hard. "Some of it I saved. And there was my bequest from your father." She hesitated. "The rest of it I stole."

"Stole!"

"Yes. Your father used to keep a gold nugget as a paperweight. I took it to an assayer, along with another one I found among his things. No one missed them, and I needed the money a lot worse than anyone else did."

Corrie felt speechless. "But Li Hua, to steal—"

The other girl lifted her chin. Corrie sensed that Quade was amused by all of this.

"All right," Li Hua said. "Stealing is wrong, and I know that. But, Corrie, do you think that your father came by *his* money honestly? He didn't. Once he told me how he used to sell supplies to the miners on the Comstock at inflated prices—at prices dollars more than they would have to pay for them anywhere else. He made a fortune off them. If that isn't just another way of stealing—"

Corrie heard a deep, rich laugh and looked over to see Quade wiping tears of laughter from his eyes.

"A brilliant rationalization! We all have valid reasons for doing things, don't we?"

Both girls glared at him and Corrie, oddly, found herself siding with Li Hua. "Don't be so superior. Perhaps she did need the money," she snapped.

He inclined his head. "Maybe. Who am I to argue with two such determined women?"

Quade ordered more coffee for all of them and went on to explain his plans. Although he did not know Avery's exact whereabouts, he had decided to aim for Dawson City. This was one of the largest mining towns, and from there other cities along the river could be reached if necessary. Most miners eventually filed a claim, and Quade was hoping to contact Avery through the claims office in one of the river cities. Meanwhile, he told them, they would buy provisions here in Dyea from disillusioned miners going home from the Klondike.

"There are plenty of them about," he said. "Last night I met one poor devil who's spent two years trying to get here by the Edmonton route. That's overland, from Canada. He got lost dozens of times, came down with scurvy, and nearly starved to death. Now after two years, he's just arrived and he doesn't want to do any mining; he just wants to go home."

The two girls were silent, and Corrie felt a sensation of dread. What kind of a harsh land had she come to?

Quade began to explain the route they would take. The Yukon River, he said, was an enormous waterway almost two thousand miles long, sprawled across the whole of Alaska and part of Canada rather like an upside-down teacup. To reach it, they would first have to walk the Dyea Trail to the Chilkoot Pass, a formidable snow-covered defile over the coastal mountains into Canadian territory. They would then go to Lake Bennett at the head of the Yukon and wait for the ice to break on the river. Here thousands of men would be building their own boats to take them upriver once the ice was gone. Steamers ran too, and Quade had decided that they would take passage on one. It would then be about four hundred miles up the river to Dawson City and the gold-bearing creeks.

"Oh," Corrie said. "Well, that sounds simple enough."

"Simple!" Quade snorted. "Good God, girl, nothing here in the Yukon is simple. Will you ever get that through your head? I told you that each miner has to have twelve hundred pounds of provisions with him, or the Mounties won't let him travel. Most men pack it on their backs, or on sleds. That means dozens of trips forward and back, over the trail and then over the Pass. It's killing work, Corrie, and I mean that literally. Men are dying in order to get their provisions moved."

"So how can we—"

"Oh, you needn't worry about that happening to us. I gather you have sufficient funds, so I'm planning to hire Eskimo packers to carry our supplies. The trip will be rough enough as it is. I certainly can't ask a pregnant woman to pack provisions over a trail."

"Would you please lower your voice?" she asked furiously. "Do you have to tell it to the entire dining room?"

Quade grimaced. "Sorry. Listen, Corrie, I think you're a damned idiot to want to go on with this. This is no land for women and babies."

"I don't care! I have seen women here, and I'm as strong as any of them. I'll survive; don't worry about me."

"Indeed. You're a lovely little hothouse flower, Delia girl, as fragile as that rose I gave you in San Francisco. Your beautiful petals are going to wilt up here, did you know that? Wilt and blow away. Why, I'll wager you've never carried anything heavier than a camera in all your life."

"I'm not a—a hothouse rose!" Corrie cried. "As for my carrying things, didn't you just finish telling us that we were hiring packers? What difference does it make how I get over the Pass? I came here to find Avery. Nothing else matters to me."

The waiter came to their table with the bill, and Quade looked at Corrie. "Well, my dear, the gentleman has brought our check. Since you seem to be financing us on this venture, don't you think you'd better pay him?"

"I—oh—" She reached for her pocketbook, then stopped. She had forgotten to transfer the funds from her money belt. "I . . . I don't think I have that much. Three dollars, is it? The rest of my money is . . . elsewhere."

She was miserably conscious of the waiter's grin. Quade, too, was smiling. "I can imagine." His eyes raked deliberately over her. "Well, I hope that wherever you're keeping it, it's safe."

"Don't worry, it's extremely safe—especially from you! Now, if you won't mind advancing the money for this meal, I'll go up to the room and repay you. That is, if you wouldn't object too strongly?"

Quade made a face at her sarcasm and reached into his pocket for the money. As he pulled out his leather billfold, something fell out of it onto the floor.

It rolled near Corrie. Impulsively she bent over and picked it up. Then she opened her hand and stared at the object in surprise. It was a cameo brooch, bordered in filigreed gold and carved with the creamy, patrician profile of a lovely woman. But the woman's face was blackened and charred with carbon, and nearly half of the filigree had been melted into a shapeless blob of gold.

"You dropped this," Corrie said slowly. She felt repelled by some eerie quality of the brooch. What was it? She could almost see the flames which had burned it, searing the lovely face.

With a shudder she flung the cameo down on the table. Instantly Quade picked it up and thrust it back into his pocket. She was surprised to see his intensely blue eyes darkened and narrowed to slits, and his features twisted.

"Where would you ever get such a burned, horrible thing?" She heard herself ask. "And why are you carrying it about?"

"None of your business," Quade snapped. "You're entirely too nosy, Cordelia Stewart, especially for a young woman who's made it very plain that she expects others to keep clear of *her* affairs. Well, I ask the same of you. Ours is a business relationship, no more. Can you understand that?"

She eyed him. "Very well."

"Then go back up to the hotel room, both of you, and stay there. I'm going to go out and try to find us a couple of down-at-the-heel miners who are willing to part with their provisions."

Quade got up from the table, thrust some bills into the waiter's hand, and left without looking back at her.

🌹 Chapter 15 🌹

They would leave the next morning. Corrie stood in the hotel room, jammed now with supplies, and stared at everything in wonder. She couldn't believe that all of these things were really for only three people.

There were sweaters, mackinaw coats, heavy rubber boots, blankets, oiled clothing, blanket-lined mittens, snow goggles, fur hats. Huge sacks of beans, oatmeal, rice and flour. Desiccated vegetables, dried raisins, apricots and apples. The fruit was especially important to prevent scurvy, Quade said. Men actually died of it here.

He also insisted that she buy quantities of evaporated milk at exorbitant prices, even though it came in cans.

"You'll need it," he explained briefly, and changed the subject. Corrie blushed. How she wished he didn't know about her baby! But he did, and, she was convinced, despised her for it.

He also purchased two tents, some "Klondike stoves," and cooking gear. In vain she protested that she didn't need any of them, that she had no plans to do any mining.

"But I do assume that you like to stay warm and dry? We need those tents, Corrie. We can skip the mining supplies, but we do need food. As for clothes, plenty of women here wear men's gear when they have to, and you will, too, on the trail. When it hits forty below, you'll be very grateful for it."

Would she? It was mid-April now. She wouldn't still be here by the time cold weather came, she reminded herself. In only a few weeks, she'd find Avery. They would be married and go back to San Francisco. Her child would be born in civilization, with all the amenities.

Since Li Hua had gone to fetch hot water for a bath and Quade was still shopping, Corrie decided to write a last-minute letter to Aunt Susan. She could picture her sitting alone in the Stewart house, determinedly doing her needlework and worrying.

Briefly she wrote of the steamer trip and Dyea, trying to minimize their frightening aspects. Again she mentioned that Li Hua had stowed aboard, and assured her aunt that all had ended well and that she was looking forward to having female company on the trail. *So perhaps it is all for the best,* she wrote, blinking back sudden tears. *I have hired a reliable man to get me to Avery, and I will write you again as soon as I can (I understand mail service is rather uncertain here). My dear aunt, I am feeling fine and healthy, and you are not to worry about me . . .*

Quade's sudden entrance into the room caught her off guard. She turned away to conceal her still moist eyes.

"Oh! You startled me!"

He set down another heap of bundles onto the already crowded floor. "Well, I hope you're ready."

"Yes, of course I am."

"This is your last chance to back out. Go home, why don't you, little Delia? Go home! Then I won't have to waste my time watching out for you and I can get about my own business, which is what I'd much rather be doing anyway."

She stared at him, uncomfortably aware of his bigness. He always seemed to fill the entire room.

He took her hand and brought it around so that her palm was forced to touch her belly. "There," he said. "Think about that—your child. Don't go off on this wild goose chase; be sensible for a change. Go down to the steamer office and buy yourself passage home, you and that wild little Li Hua girl of yours. They'll eat you both alive here in the Yukon, and personally I don't want to see it happen."

"They won't 'eat me alive' as you put it," Corrie began hotly.

He cut her off with an impatient gesture. "Surely there's some man in San Francisco who would marry you?"

"No, there isn't," she snapped. "Not since Donald came north. And I'd die before I married him. Anyway, just why are you taking such an interest in me? Am I such an annoyance to you that you can hardly wait to see me leave?"

He frowned at her, beetling his dark brows together. "It's none of your concern."

"Isn't it? You act so proprietary where I'm concerned, Mr. Hill. You act as if you had some right to say these rude things to me. Well, you don't. You have no right at all."

He avoided her eyes. "You look like someone, that's all. Your hair, and your defiant spirit, the way you talk. Dammit, I can't leave you up here to be preyed on. I can't."

All she could do was to stare at him.

She did wear men's clothes on the trail, the ones Li Hua insisted she buy, what seemed so many weeks ago in San Francisco. A pair of woolen pants, cut for a slim boy, clung sensuously to Corrie's hips, so that Quade eyed her with an intent look that made her flush. She wore a white woolen shirt which somehow managed to accent the soft jut of her breasts, and a heavy mackinaw made for a small man, but looking rakishly charming on Corrie. In this garb, she had a reckless feeling of freedom. She didn't even mind the other stampeders staring at her and Li Hua who, also in pants and jacket, did look like a slim, pretty youth.

"Do you think they think we're young boys?" she asked her friend as they set out. "With our hair tucked up under our hats, I suppose we could pass for boys."

Li Hua laughed gaily. "Never! We're women, and the men know it. Still, I think they're much too tired to do anything about it just at present. I believe that their only thought right now is whether or not they are going to make it down the trail."

It was true that the Dyea Trail did look intimidating. It appeared at once extremely wild and quite civilized. The trail itself was a natural canyon or ravine carved out of rough crags and hills. But the signs of men and animals were everywhere.

Hundreds of stampeders—many of them boys no older than Corrie—pushed wheelbarrows or pulled sleds piled high with provisions. Some wore back packs. Others shouted at dog teams or drove horse carts. There were even ten-horse pack trains pulled by resigned animals.

The snow was dirty with tracks, animal excrement and objects thrown away by the stampeders: cigar butts, clocks, books, clothing, the last abandoned when it became too heavy. And everywhere were the stacks of bags and sacks that marked a "cache." Like a toiling ant, a man would lug forty or fifty pounds as far as he could carry them, then return for more of his load, only to repeat the process again and again.

Corrie felt sorry for these poor, struggling men. They passed one middle-aged stampeder slumped in the middle of the trail weeping bitterly because he had hurt his back and couldn't go on.

They, however, were luckier. In Dyea Quade had found two Eskimo men to transport their goods, round-faced youths named Tannaumirk and Natkusiak, who regarded Corrie and Li Hua with curiosity and chattered happily among themselves, standing very close to each other to talk. They had two sleds with dog teams.

Nine miles from Dyea, they set up their tents in the shelter of Dyea Canyon. This was a stopping point, and a tent city had sprung up here. Before them were acres of tents, piled provisions, milling men and tired horses. Quade went out to reconnoiter, and returned to inform Corrie and Li Hua that they were lucky they had hired packers in Dyea.

"It's costing one hundred dollars a day for pack trains, and the native packers are going on strike here, it's rumored. I hope ours don't get the same idea. If they do, it could cost us as much as six hundred dollars to get to Lake Bennett."

Corrie bit her lip, thinking of her dwindling money roll. "I suppose we'll have to pay it."

But Quade's eyes flashed. "Not if I can get it cheaper,

we won't. Transport is one thing, but highway robbery is quite another!"

Corrie was too weary to protest any of Quade's decisions. Perhaps because of her pregnancy, she was stumbling with tiredness from the long walk. After an hour or so on the trail, the snow had quickly lost all of its fascination for her. Now it was merely another obstacle, to be climbed over or trampled.

Worse, the snow was beginning to melt, sending streams of ice water down the hills to invade the trail. In places the road was a seemingly bottomless mire of mud. Mules, oxen and pack horses floundered along in it or lay where they fell.

Corrie had to avert her eyes from the animal corpses they passed, stiff, staring-eyed and horrible. One well-rotted corpse of what had once been a fine chestnut mare caused her to turn aside and gag.

Quade, too, looked upset. But he said, "Come, Corrie, you'll have to have a stronger belly than that! Be thankful you're not on the White Pass Trail. I've heard they have so many carcasses of dead horses there that it looks like a charnel house, and smells like one, too. In the summer the stench is incredible."

Corrie, who liked animals and loved to ride, was horrified. "Oh, the poor things! How could people treat them that way?"

"The Yukon is no place for a horse, my dear. There isn't much feed for them here. Most of them come up here to die, and that's the plain, hard fact of it."

Corrie did not reply. It was all she could do to keep going. Only the thought of Avery kept her struggling on. In a few weeks—oh, surely it would not be longer than that —she would be in his arms again. He would stroke her hair and kiss her and tell her how he had missed her, how glad he was to see her. She could forget all of this horror . . .

To Corrie's surprise, Li Hua turned out to possess a tenacious strength, and did not seem to grow tired. Several times she offered to carry Corrie's camera for her, and on the second day insisted on taking a photograph of Corrie and Quade together. Nothing, it seemed, would dissuade her.

They posed by a bald outcropping of rock, both of them staring grimly into the camera. "Well," Quade said, after Li Hua had squeezed the shutter bulb at Corrie's instructions and they could move again. "We're down for posterity now, you and I. I wonder what our grandchildren will think of us—your grandchildren and mine being separate, of course," he added with a grin.

"I'm sure I don't know," Corrie said.

"I hope I didn't overexpose the plate," Li Hua put in.

Corrie tried to smile at her. "I'm sure you didn't, Li Hua. We'll develop it in the tent tonight."

They spent two nights on the trail. On the second night, Corrie was awakened shortly after she had fallen asleep by a deep, ominous, rumbling sound. She sat bolt upright in her blankets and nudged Li Hua.

"Wake up! What was that? That noise?"

"Mmmmm," Li Hua mumbled.

In the morning Quade told her that she had heard a small snowslide. "It's nothing to be very concerned about, though," he explained. "It's spring, and this happens all of the time. Tons of snow rumble down wherever they happen to want to go. Most of the slides are pretty harmless. We'd just better hope that it doesn't happen at the Pass."

"Oh. I surely hope not." Corrie felt slightly weak. Snow that roared. Dear heavens, she thought. What next?

The following day they reached Sheep Camp. This was a wind-swept valley twelve miles away from Dyea where yet another tent city had sprung up. Here the scene was one of total disarray, with thousands of tents, a sea of them, each with its stovepipe sticking out of a hole in the top, and its white frosting of snow.

A bitter wind pushed at the tents, whirling hard, white flakes through the air and battering at the now-familiar piles of provisions. According to Quade, the miners' code decreed that men would leave others' caches alone. Corrie certainly hoped so. She couldn't imagine anything worse than to lug twelve hundred pounds of provisions all of this distance, only to have them disappear.

She watched tiredly while Quade and the two packers set up their tents and fed the dogs.

"Civilization!" Quade gloated, grinning at her. "Well,

of a sort. I hear they have a hospital here, and mail service, and tent saloons. You can even buy a dozen eggs, if you can afford the price. Would you like an omelette? I'm quite an omelette chef, they do tell me."

Corrie tried to smile, but she barely heard his light banter. All she knew was that by tomorrow morning they would be struggling up the formidably difficult Chilkoot Pass.

It was a frightening sight. Against a blinding white background, swept by wind and bathed in strange white fog, a black line of men, like toiling insects, wound up the mountain. They seemed tiny, dwarfed by the hugeness around them.

"But this—this isn't a pass!" Corrie gasped to Quade. "This is a mountain!"

He nodded.

"Why, it goes straight up and down!"

"Thirty-six hundred feet of hell, they said in Sheep Camp. It's so steep they had to cut steps in it."

"But how will we climb it?"

"We won't; not the steepest part, anyway. The dogs can't manage the steps, so we'll have to take the Petterson Trail to the right, there." Quade pointed to a flatter area, where more figures labored upward at a gentler angle. "It will take us a while longer, but we'll get there."

Corrie narrowed her eyes against the glare and stared at the dense line of men climbing single file to the summit of the pass. To their left, a tram line hauled up sleds. And beside the long queue of men were other black dots sitting alone. These, Quade explained to her, were men who had stopped to rest. They would have to wait hours to get back into the line, he added.

"Hours!"

"Yes, that's right. It doesn't pay to get tired here on the Chilkoot."

"I see. But—what's that? Over there." Corrie pointed to a trough to the right of the line where she could see something which looked like a ball of snow hurtling down.

"That's the chute. And that blur you see is a man sliding down. When a man gets one load to the top, he just sits down in the snow and toboggans back down again.

Look—they've worn a groove as deep as the walls of a room."

"Goodness," Corrie said, staring in wonder. "How Papa would have loved this." Then she remembered her camera. She had had a good rest the previous night, and new energy filled her. "I believe I'll just get a photograph of all this."

"A picture? Corrie, we've work to do! Even you and Li Hua are going to have to carry packs if we want to get up to the top. Put that thing away and come on."

"No, I've told you, I want to photograph this," she said stubbornly. "In a way, I promised Papa I'd—"

"Corrie, I'm telling you that we've got to hurry. There's a storm building at the summit, and the men want to get started. We'd better not cross them. Packers are worth their weight in gold nuggets here. Without them we'd have to carry everything on our own backs."

Quade was right; a storm was building. The wind dug unmercifully at Corrie's exposed cheeks. She pulled her hat closer about her ears and concentrated on manipulating the camera. She did manage to get two dramatic shots (at least she hoped they would be), one of the long line of men, and one of the huge, brooding majesty of the Chilkoot itself, which seemed to tolerate these small men on its gigantic back as a dog tolerates ticks.

"All right, dammit, come on!" Quade was pulling at her. "You've had your fun. Let's go, Corrie, or I'm warning you, we'll have to wait out the storm and our packers may decide to desert us."

The heavy pack cramped the back of her neck and caused her head to ache with throbbing intensity. Perspiration dampened the woolen underwear she wore. The blisters on her feet, rubbed raw by her heavy boots, were agonizing. Even though they were taking the less precipitous trail, Corrie thought, it seemed the climbing would never end.

To make matters worse, Quade kept pulling at her, urging her to go faster.

"Don't lag, Corrie! We've got to hurry on."

"But I'm climbing just as fast as I can," she panted angrily. How dare he act as if she were a drag on them? She wasn't! She could go just as fast as anyone.

The wind roared viciously at them, and Quade made both girls wrap scarves completely around their faces so that only their eyes showed. They passed several men who had dropped along the trail to rest, pitiful, defeated figures. One of them was a boy of no more than seventeen, his cheeks marred by two circles of grim white, the first signs of frostbite.

They had passed too many such men.

"Get up! Get up and go on!" Corrie screamed at him, unable to bear the sight. He was so very young, only a boy, really. She stumbled toward him to smack him hard on the shoulder with her mittened hand. "A storm is coming; you'll freeze if you stay here!"

He stared at her dully. "Going to freeze anyway. Never should have come . . . should have listened to Ma . . . "

"Get up, I said. Please! You have to move."

"No . . . I can't; my feet won't move . . . "

"Corrie." She felt Quade at her elbow, pushing her onward, away from the boy. "Come on, you can't stop here by the trail with every poor sod you find. We've got to go on ourselves, or we'll be the ones who freeze."

"But we can't just leave him—"

"Corrie, I tell you, come on. You've got your own survival to think about, and your baby's. We'll tell the Mounties about him when we get to the Customs House. They'll come back here and get him."

Corrie looked about her wildly, at the dim shapes of other men further away, sitting hopelessly in the snow.

"Will they? If they do, it's going to be too late for him." She went over to Li Hua. "Loosen my pack, will you? Throw off everything but my camera."

Her fingers stiff from the cold, the other girl did as Corrie asked.

"Corrie!" Quade shouted. "What in the hell are you doing? You can't toss away your gear—"

"Can't I? I paid for it, didn't I?" She went over to the boy and, slipping off her right mitten, gave him a stinging slap on the cheek. Then, weeping with the effort, she dragged him to his feet.

"Walk, will you?" she shouted at him. "Walk! Oh, come

on, please walk, or you'll die. Do you want to die? Do you?"

Somehow, hounded by Corrie, the boy managed to take a few steps. After she had yanked him a few yards further, Quade took the boy's other arm. Together they half-dragged him to the summit.

"There's one poor devil who'll never stake a claim," Quade said after they had left the youth—without ever knowing his name—at the Customs House in the charge of one of the Mounties. "Odds are he's going to lose some toes, if not a whole foot. You're an idiotic girl, did you know that, Cordelia Stewart? Throwing away good beans and rice." But he took her arm and was looking down at her with eyes oddly warm. A shiver melted its way through Corrie's middle.

"You're foolish, little Delia, but you're all right," Quade added.

"Thanks," she said dryly. She had to glance away from the intensity of his look.

They were on Canadian soil now. The Customs House, topped by a wildly flapping flag, was nearly invisible in a swirl of blowing snow. They waited in a long line to weigh their goods, pay duty, and register with the Mounties. Piled up beside them were the tons of goods so laboriously hauled upward, each cache marked by a long stick.

"The sticks are so the snow won't come and bury them," Quade told her cheerfully. "Did you know that the snow is probably sixty feet deep here?"

"Sixty feet?" Corrie's voice shook. A terrible thought had just struck her. Had Avery come over this pass, too? If so, had he survived the crossing? Or had he been like the boy they had helped, one of the pitiful ones to sink exhausted and frozen by the wayside? There was no way she could know.

❧ Chapter 16 ❧

Li Hua lay on her back, wrapped in blankets, staring upward at the blackness that was the roof of the tent. Beneath her the snow-covered ground was hard. There had been no time to lay spruce boughs for a mattress. Beside her Corrie breathed slowly and regularly, deep in a dream.

The storm had been a bad one, full of knife-sharp ice crystals spraying past the tent to fill the air with eerie white objects, so that visibility was only a few feet, and even nearby objects were obscured.

"I don't like this one bit," Quade told them. "And neither do the packers. It's April, and the snow is unstable underneath the surface. We'll be moving our tents out of here at the first light."

They couldn't move quite yet, for the snow had only abated in the last hour. Besides, it was still dark and both girls were exhausted from the climb. Even the sled dogs needed food and rest.

Li Hua shifted about in her nest of blankets and wondered why, for the first time, it was she who couldn't sleep. Unwillingly, her mind went back, memories forcing themselves upon her.

He jerked her into his buggy, that first time, and refused to let her get out, smothering her screams with a gloved hand. She was taken to a strange street, to a big gray house bristling with Victorian gingerbread. Later, in a large upstairs room, on a brass bed, he pressed his body over hers and whispered strange things to her.

You're a hot little thing, a hot little body, aren't you? And no virgin, either, I'll wager. Tell me about her. Tell me everything you know about her, or you'll regret it. I can make things happen to you. Do you believe me?

Yes, she believed him. Especially after she saw the——

But Li Hua twisted about in her blankets again, blanking out the terrifying scene, the—— No, she couldn't think of that; the sex itself had been frightening enough, but that . . .

When she learned that Donald Earle was actually in Dyea, she thought she would vomit. It had been all she could do to hide her fear from Corrie. What if he came for her again? Oh, God, what if he did?

She managed to assure herself that he wouldn't want her. Besides, she told herself, why should she worry? It was Cordelia Stewart he really lusted for, Corrie he had come north for, not herself. She, Li Hua, was only a means to an end.

Above her the wind bellied out the folds of canvas, then pushed them inward. A chilly current of air whistled in through a crack. In spite of the stove, it was cold. Corrie stirred in her sleep, moaning slightly and turning on her side.

Shivering, Li Hua finally slept too, her slumber filled with uneasy dreams in which she was trapped in a steamer trunk, trying desperately to open the lid. Still dreaming, she heard an odd, deep-throated rumbling, as if all of the ballast in the hold of the ship was shifting from one side to the other.

Strange . . . She held her breath. That rumbling. Where had she heard something like it before? It was sand, that was it. Tons and tons of beach sand, heavier than anything she had ever imagined . . .

Suddenly pain seared up her right leg. Sharp, agonizing, liquid pain brought Li Hua awake instantly. At the same time a crushing weight slammed over her. She opened her mouth to scream and realized that the canvas was crumpled up in huge folds against her mouth. The tent had collapsed over them. The weight pressed against her, on her legs and thighs and chest and face. The pressure increased inexorably, as if she were a stone pushed into the earth, beyond hope of moving.

"God— Oh, dear God . . ."

Panicking, Li Hua screamed with pain. Suddenly she knew that the heaviness she felt was not beach sand or ship's ballast at all, but snow.

It was a snowslide, an avalanche.

She and Corrie were buried in snow.

Corrie felt a slamming blow, punctuated by Li Hua's scream. Instantly she snapped awake, only to realize that she was being held down by some monstrous force so that she couldn't move. Her right arm was pressed over her face.

"We're buried, we're buried, we're buried," Li Hua was babbling. "My leg—it hurts! I knew I— Oh, I'm sorry for what I did, Corrie, I didn't mean to, I had to, *I had to*, don't you understand . . . "

Buried.

The other girl's voice babbled on hysterically, and Corrie, trying to reach out toward it, found that her left arm could only move a few inches. She was pinned under the tent. An avalanche, Corrie thought dully. The roaring snow. It had rumbled over them and buried them.

"I had to, I had to, don't you see, I had to. He made me!"

Corrie's mind was very clear. They were trapped under the snow, she knew. Her brain began to work, emotionless as a clock. Air. There was a small air space formed by the tent and the crook of her arm. Li Hua also must have access to a small amount of oxygen, or she wouldn't be able to scream as she was doing. But how long would they be able to breathe under these conditions? Not long, surely. And Li Hua was hurt.

Corrie struggled to move, perspiration suddenly moistening her skin beneath her heavy woolen clothing. A worm of fear wriggled in her. Quade and the two Eskimos had pitched tents nearby. What had happened to them? Were they buried too?

Li Hua's screams grew fainter.

"Li Hua? Are you all right?" Corrie called. She could

hear a dim crackle as millions of ice crystals shifted and reformed.

Someone would come, Corrie assured herself. She raised her voice and began to call out for Quade, her voice beginning to crack from fear. Already it seemed warm in the pinched space of the collapsed tent. Corrie's head ached from lack of air. Her chest was burning.

"Quade! Quade!"

Their air was nearly gone, she knew. In a few seconds more, she and Li Hua were going to suffocate to death as surely as if they had been marched to a scaffold and had a rope knotted about their necks. Yet she had committed no crime at all, other than being pregnant with Avery's baby.

The baby. It would die with her, of course. Die without ever seeing its father, without ever feeling the sun on its shoulders . . .

Her mind was fogging. Dimly she was aware of Li Hua's ragged, desperate screams. Or was that her own voice, fading in and out . . .

"Corrie! For God's sake, is that you? Keep screaming and I'll find you . . ."

Did she dream Quade's voice? Dream the sensation of weight sliding off her body, miraculously freeing her?

The canvas moved aside. Hands reached for her. Hands that brushed away layers of snow and yanked at her, pulled at her legs, extracted her from cold, wet snow and lifted her up into a night scattered with cold, bright stars.

Air. Sweet and cold. Corrie gasped and wept.

"Delia! Oh, my darling, are you all right? I thought I'd never dig you out of that damned tent." He was hugging her to him, grasping her in his arms, slapping snow away from her face and breasts and hair. She clung to him, to his strength.

But almost instantly she felt herself being handed to someone else, to one of the round-faced Eskimo men who reeked of fish. She stood swaying, hanging on to him, her head whirling with dizziness.

"He go get other woman," the Eskimo said in her ear. It was Tannaumirk. "You strong woman, you be all right, you not get too much snow. Others die, you live."

* * *

"All right, I'm Dr. Will Sebastian. Where's the man with the broken leg?" The voice was rushed and business-like, weary from long hours of work. But the grayish light showed a familiar face: humorous mouth, steady brown eyes, a forelock of light brown hair. The young doctor wore a sealskin parka and a fur hat with ear flaps carefully in place.

Corrie stared at him. "Dr. Sebastian? From Canada?"

"Yes, I'm from Windsor. Now show me where he is, will you? I've another patient to look at when I'm done with him."

"You mean her," Corrie said. "She's a woman. And she's in that tent right over there. It's her leg. She's been in quite a lot of pain."

"A woman! Well, she's lucky she's still alive, anyway. A good many of them aren't."

He bent over and crawled into Quade's hastily re-erected tent. Corrie felt herself sway from weariness. Dr. Sebastian had been the doctor on the *Alki,* she told her-self with tired astonishment—the seasick physician who had dragged himself out of his bunk to attend Mattie Shea. Surely Li Hua was in good hands.

She hesitated, wondering whether to go and ask if he needed her assistance. Nearly two long days had passed, punctuated by the cries of those trapped and the shouts of those digging. Every available man had turned out to help with the rescue work—even Corrie had worked along with them, shuddering as they pulled out body after body. Sixty bodies had been wrapped in blankets and put on sleds, ready for transport back to Dyea, where they would be buried or shipped home.

It was only a miracle, Corrie knew, that she and Li Hua were not members of that grim procession. Even her camera, because of its sturdy box, had come through in-tact. They had been at the very edge of the flow of snow, Quade had informed her, and thus had not received the full brunt of it.

Now she stared at the tent, wondering what was hap-pening inside it. She could hear the murmur of voices, punctuated by an occasional groan from Li Hua. She thought about what this injury would mean for the girl. Of course she would not be able to continue on the trail now; that would be impossible. She would have to return to Dyea and take a steamer home.

Leaving you alone with Quade Hill, a little voice in her brain said tartly.

Oh, be still! she told it.

"Miss, come in here, would you?" It was Dr. Sebastian, thrusting his head out of the tent flap.

"Me?"

"You're the only miss I see around here just at this moment." A brief smile softened the words.

"All right." Corrie crawled into the tent. Li Hua lay on a pile of blankets near the stove, her face white and twisted from her long ordeal. For all of her pain, the girl's features were fine-drawn, beautiful. Dark hair tumbled around her shoulders, and her skin seemed translucent and pale. She had a fragile appearance. Dr. Sebastian had slit the seams of the men's trousers Li Hua wore, rolling them to her thigh. The long underwear, too, had been cut, and Li Hua's bare leg looked somehow forlorn and vulnerable.

The doctor was again bent over his work, but he glanced up when Corrie came into the tent. "I want another woman present," he told her. "You look familiar," he added. "Haven't I seen you somewhere before?"

"Yes, I was on the *Alki*. I called you about Mattie Shea, remember? You were . . . " She suppressed a wild giggle. "You were seasick."

"Ah, yes, *mal de mer.*" He grimaced. He was rummaging in a black leather bag for a vial of medicine. "Here," he said to Li Hua. "Have some of this. It's laudanum, a tincture of opium. It'll help you with the pain. What in the dickens are you two girls doing here at Chilkoot? Don't tell me that you're going to go and get a job in one of those dance halls in Dawson?"

"We're certainly not!" Corrie glared at him. "Of course we're not. I'm going to meet my fiancé and marry him, and Li Hua is planning to be a miner."

"Really?" Tossing a mane of brown hair out of his eyes, Dr. Sebastian glanced down at Li Hua. "This girl's about as delicate as a parakeet; she has bones like a bird. Why would she want to be a miner?"

Li Hua, choking back a cry as he manipulated her

leg, tossed her head angrily. "My name is Li Hua. I'm very strong. And you needn't talk about me as if I wasn't here."

"Excuse me, I didn't mean to. We doctors seem to have a habit of doing that." Will Sebastian's mouth curved in the beginnings of a smile. "Li Hua," he added. He said the name slowly, as if savoring it on his tongue.

"I have every intention of becoming a miner," Li Hua went on. "Why shouldn't I? Just because I'm a woman . . . " She gasped as Dr. Sebastian's fingers probed the break. "There were other women on the steamer who were planning to stake their claims—"

"So the gold bug's bitten you, has it?" Then, as she winced again, the doctor added, "That's all right, Li Hua. Cry out if you want to. Your friend here is going to help me. I'll give you as much opium as I can, but even so this is going to hurt, and you'll have to bear it. I'll make a splint for you until we can get you back to Sheep Camp."

"Sheep Camp?"

"Yes, there's a hospital there. We're taking all of the wounded back there. After that, you can go back to Dyea and take a steamer home, of course."

The girl's liquid, dark eyes flashed. "I will not go back to San Francisco!"

"And what exactly *are* you planning to do, then? Stake your claim on the Eldorado? If we're lucky, they'll have some plaster at Sheep Camp to make a leg cast for you. But even so, I don't think you'll be able to do any mining while you're wearing it. Or afterwards, either. You're likely to have a limp for a good, long time. You won't be in any condition to mine."

Li Hua seemed to sag all over. But she said nothing more, and lay very still while Will Sebastian's slender, capable hands finished their work.

❧ Chapter 17 ❧

A watery April sun had risen. Li Hua and the other wounded had been loaded on sleds ready to be transported back to the small hospital at Sheep Camp. Quade and the two Eskimo men were among the volunteers to take them there. Corrie had wanted to go too, but Quade had flatly vetoed this.

"The trip back is going to be too rough for you, Corrie. Are you that anxious to try the chute? That's how you'd have to get down."

"But Li Hua and I—"

"For once will you follow my orders? I said you're not coming; you can wait here for me and that's final."

"Oh, very well!" Corrie snapped angrily.

At least she could say good-bye to Li Hua. She found the girl wrapped in brown wool blankets, lying on a sled, at the rear of what was evidently to be a dog-sled caravan. Most of the sleds held bodies. Nearby a man with broken ribs was moaning, and two boys, burned and bruised when their stove fell on them, were lying on their litters, wrapped in bandages.

Li Hua lay asleep, the pale sun giving her skin a wan cast. She looked, Corrie thought, like a porcelain princess, her rich black hair streaming out loosely beside her face, framing its delicacy.

"Li Hua? Are you awake? Can you hear me?"

The girl's eyes fluttered open. Her pupils were large and black. "Corrie," she whispered.

"I suppose I'd better say good-bye now, since Quade

won't let me go with you." Corrie fumbled in the pocket of her sealskin coat, into which she had thrust some bills taken from her money belt. "I'd like to give you the money for your passage home, Li Hua, since you've spent yours."

Li Hua's lips pressed together; her eyes were vacant. "If you wish, you may buy my provisions. I won't need them now."

"Very well." Corrie pulled out some bills and gave them to Li Hua.

"Thank you, Corrie."

"It's nothing. I have enough money. And—and somehow I feel that this is all my fault. That you came here, I mean—"

"Your fault?" Li Hua managed a small groggy laugh. "How? *I* was the one who stowed away in the trunk, remember? Besides . . . " she hesitated. "Besides, I can't forget what I did."

Corrie stared at her, suddenly remembering Li Hua's wild ravings in the tent. "What are you talking about, Li Hua? What did you do?"

There was a long pause, while the other girl's eyes seemed focused on the white slopes of a distant mist-veiled peak, remote in its beauty.

"It—it was Donald Earle," Li Hua whispered at last. "I told him you were coming north. I did that, Corrie."

"What?" Corrie felt the blood pound in her face. She felt slapped, hurt, betrayed. "Oh, Li Hua, how could you? And to think that I paid your passage here! And let you travel with me! Oh, Li Hua, I thought we were friends!"

Li Hua's eyes filled with slow tears. "You don't understand—"

"No, I don't. What possible reason could you have for doing such a thing? There wasn't any reason, was there? Except money. That was it, wasn't it? You betrayed me for a bribe!"

"No! I—"

"You stole my father's nuggets. You measured my ring finger for money. Why shouldn't you have taken other bribes?" Corrie had never been so furious. She could feel adrenaline surging through her veins. She wanted to pick up something and throw it, as her father used to do. Once she had seen him smash a valuable Chinese figurine against the wall of his library; it had burst into a thousand green shards. Now she felt exactly the same way.

Furiously, out of control, she ripped off her blanket-lined mittens and threw them at Li Hua. They smacked against the girl's blanket and slid to the snow where they lay, mute and accusing. Corrie was instantly sorry she had thrown them, which only made her angrier.

"Oh!" she cried. "How dare you, Li Hua! Betraying me to a man like Donald. Do you know what sort of a person he is? Do you?"

Li Hua's face seemed to freeze into a pale mask. "Yes."

"Well, I'm glad you have to go home, do you hear me? I'm *glad!* I don't want you on the trail with us. I don't want you anywhere near me, ever!"

Li Hua inclined her head very slightly. She said nothing, although her black eyes brimmed with tears.

With a hollow feeling, Corrie pulled on her mittens again. She watched as the long caravan of sleds moved up the white slope. Walking beside Li Hua's sled was Quade, his movements light and loping, as if he had not spent the past days digging out avalanche survivors and provisions, and getting very little sleep.

Corrie stared for a long time until they were small dots in the distance. Then she stumbled toward the tent which Quade had left set up for her. All about her were men digging out the last of their supplies, or carting them further downslope to Crater Lake, which lay like a sheet of white below them, marred by men, tents and provisions.

Blindly she pushed her way past a group of men gathered about an outdoor cookfire, ignoring their inquisitive looks. She crawled into her tent and threw some more wood—brought in Sheep Camp at exorbitant prices—into the stove. She flung herself onto her blankets.

She must have napped; she awoke to find that it was several hours later. The sun was low in the sky and bleached to the color of a water-logged lemon. Her stomach gave a loud, complaining growl, and Corrie realized that she was hungry.

Not bothering to pull on her hat and coat, she crept outdoors to paw uncertainly among the stacks of provisions which Quade and the two packers had left piled up near the tent.

What should she prepare? Flour? Rice? Beans? Beans had to be soaked for a long time, she was sure. As for flour, that meant baking bread, and she wasn't sure how to do that. All of these homely processes had been something that Quade did, because he was paid to do them. While he was at the stove, she had spent her time with her camera, or in the crude canvas-draped darkroom she had devised, developing the camera plates.

Her head was beginning to ache. Corrie sat down on a bulging sack and put her face in her hands. The scene with Li Hua had been ugly and disturbing, and she could not forget the way the other girl had looked, dark eyes glittering with unshed tears as if somehow she, Corrie, had done something to hurt her. When clearly it had been the other way around!

Avery suddenly came into her thoughts. Where was he now? Was he all right? Would he even want her when she arrived?

But of course he would, Corrie assured herself. Hadn't he told her in his letter that he loved her and wanted to marry her?

Still, Corrie sat for long minutes more before finally getting to her feet to see about her meal. She would open a can of condensed milk, she decided. And she would cook herself some oatmeal and dried raisins. Odious as that sounded, she was reasonably sure she could manage it.

It was while she was rummaging in the sack looking for the raisins that the man came walking uphill from a group of tents pitched below. He was young, tall, wore a red mackinaw, and, like so many of the *cheechakos* who didn't know that a beard could be dangerous in severe cold, had a full set of bushy, carrot-colored whiskers.

"Hey," he said. "You're the little lady with the temper."

She looked up, stung. "I am not! I do not have a temper!"

He laughed. "Oh, yes, you do, and I know because I seen you yellin' at that little Chinese girl with the broken leg. Why are you so mad, anyway? Is it because you got left all alone here? I saw that man of yours going back to Sheep Camp."

Above the flaring bush of beard, she saw a thin, avid face. "Please," she murmured. "I have work to do."

She was uncomfortably conscious of the way her men's trousers clung to her figure, revealing the still-slim curves of her hips and thighs. Her white woolen shirt showed the push of her breasts against the loose fabric. Then, too, she had let down her hair to comb it, and it streamed about her shoulders in a cascade of chestnut-brown.

"What work?" he asked. "Cooking?" He was grinning at her. "You know what? I'd like to see you in some real women's clothes, instead of that men's stuff you got on. Not that it ain't purty." He leered at her. "Still, you'd look awful nice in one of them fancy dresses with plenty of ruffles and a low neck, like they wear in them dance halls . . . "

He thought that she was a dance hall girl. Even Dr. Sebastian had thought that. Corrie thought she would cry with vexation.

"I'm not one of those women, thank you. And would you please just go away and leave me alone? I don't mean to be rude, but I have work to do." She thrust her hand into a gunnysack and pulled out a package at random. It was labeled dried apricots. She snatched it up and got to her feet, preparing to go back into the tent.

"Hey," he protested. "Where you going?"

But she was already inside the tent, dropping the flap pointedly shut behind her. She tossed the oil-cloth-wrapped package of apricots onto the blanket and sat down, her heart hammering. If Quade had been here, she thought furiously, that man would not have dared to approach her. She dashed away angry tears. Anyway, what about Quade's famous remark on the miners' code of ethics? She had probably just met the one miner who had never heard of it.

She tore open the wrapper and began eating the apricots raw, savoring their tart, sharp flavor, when the man pushed open the flap of the tent and crawled in.

"W-What are you doing in my tent?"

"Listen here, little girl. You're giving it away to one man already, aren't you? Why not two? It wouldn't hurt you none, and you're going to be selling plenty of it when you hit the Yukon, anyways."

She turned quickly, and hurled the package of apricots at him.

He caught it and tossed it aside, giving her a wide, eager smile. "Say, that's no way to treat a fellow, is it? All I want to do is see you don't get lonesome while your man is away, that's all."

"He's not my man! And I'm not lonesome!" She was backing away from him but there wasn't much room to maneuver in the cramped quarters of the tent, especially with the stove, red-hot with the wood she had piled into it, blocking the rear of the tent.

"Aw, come on, will you? I won't hurt you none. Surely you got enough for just one extra . . . "

He was like a wheedling dog, crawling after her ludicrously on hands and knees. A big, avid, hairy red setter, she told herself hysterically.

"Get away from me, please! I'm not a dance hall girl, for God's sake; I'm an honest woman. Can't you get that through your head?"

He crawled toward her. His breath smelled foul. Sickeningly, his hands reached out and fumbled at her clothes.

"No," he insisted. "I don't believe it. You're too pretty. You got to be one."

"Well, I have news for you; I'm not!" She struggled to push him away. "And—and if you don't get out of here this very moment, I'm going to tell Quade about you when he gets back. Do you hear me?"

To her surprise, the intruder seemed to falter, and Corrie pressed her advantage. "And do you know what he's going to do to you when he finds out?" something made her add.

"What?"

Corrie allowed her eyes to narrow menacingly. "He's going to find your cache and he's going to take a big knife and slit all of your food sacks! And then, when he's finished with that, he's going to take a knife to *you*."

With each word, her would-be attacker grew visibly more troubled. As the man shrank back, Corrie felt a wild confidence flow into her. In some horrid way, she was even beginning to enjoy this. She let her inventive powers flow.

"You see, Quade kills people who take his women,

didn't you know that?. He slits their throats and then he tosses them onto the snow to feed the wolves."

"He—he—oh, my God—" The youth looked stricken. Still on his hands and knees, with a last exhalation of foul breath, he backed out of the tent.

He was gone.

Corrie released a high, shaky laugh at the ridiculousness of what she had done. Then, abruptly, she was sobered. Fool or not, the red-bearded young man could have raped her. He had come perilously close to it, and there would have been nothing she could have done to stop him. If it had not been for the mention of Quade . . .

Corrie sank back on the blankets and held her arms tightly as she found herself shivering.

The sun hung on the horizon like a flat red pancake for what seemed a very long time. Finally it went down, allowing the long Arctic night to settle about the camp. Hours later Quade returned from Sheep Camp, his mackinaw covered with snow, to tell her that Li Hua was safely settled in the tent hospital. The two burned youths had been treated with salve and bandaged again, and the man with the broken ribs had decided to return home.

"As for me, I wrote an article about the avalanche and sent it off to the *Tribune*—they even have mail service in Sheep Camp, praise be. I promised them a whole series on the Yukon; it's big news these days. Everyone, it seems, harbors a secret dream about gold."

They were inside the tent, a candle sending wavery shadows leaping up the sides of the canvas as they moved about. Corrie told him of the red-bearded man who had crawled into her tent, and tried to make light of the incident so that Quade would not worry. She laughed gaily as she compared the intruder to a dog.

Quade was not amused. His blue eyes blazed at her and his gentle mouth was set in a hard line.

"My God, Corrie, why are you laughing? Don't you realize what could have happened to you?"

"Of course I do. But I'm laughing because it *was* rather humorous, now that I look back on it," she told him defiantly. "Don't you see, that funny man, creeping after me like a red setter—"

"Red setter be damned!" He gripped her shoulders. "Haven't you *any* sense, Cordelia Stewart? You're a woman up here virtually alone among all of these men. Sweet heaven only knows where some of them came from, or how they earned their living before they came here."

"I thought you said there was a miners' code! I thought you told me they *respected* women. That they—"

Quade looked uncomfortable. "That was the code five years ago when I was here last, and it still is. Men have to leave other men's caches alone, and if they use someone's empty cabin, they must replenish the firewood and food. But as to women—"

"Women don't come under the same code of honesty, is that it?" Corrie's gold-brown eyes flashed angrily.

"Corrie, you don't understand. You—"

"Oh, I understand, all right. The men have a code about the polite treatment of women, but it may or may not apply, depending on whether the miner in question has ever heard of the code or not. And on whether he thinks the woman is decent. If he doesn't, if he thinks she's headed for a dance hall or a brothel, why then, anything goes! Isn't that right?"

Quade was gripping her shoulders, pulling her so close she could see the dark anger in his eyes.

"You do have a fiery temper, don't you?"

She struggled to twist away from him. "Yes, I suppose so, and I'm not altogether proud of it. What if I do? Why should it matter to you? *You're* not the one who's going to marry me; Avery is!"

The words popped out of her mouth totally without thought. For an instant they seemed to float about the interior of the tent while Corrie listened to them with horror.

Quade dropped his hands from her shoulders. "No, I'm not going to marry you, Corrie," he said quietly. "But I'll tell you this. You have hired me, against my better judgment, to get you to this fiancé of yours, and I intend to see to it that you do get there. In good health and unmolested. For your own good, you're going to travel under the protection of a man, so that this sort of incident won't happen to you again."

"But I am under the protection . . . you . . . " she stammered.

Quade's eyes flashed. "No, I mean really under my protection. I can see that it won't work for us to have separate tents; it gives men the idea that you're free and available. You're going to travel as my woman, in my tent. That'll keep their hands off you. They all know that I'll kill them if they touch you. And it won't be a lie. Because I will."

He spoke with such sudden savagery that Corrie drew back from him.

"But . . . in your tent!" she gasped. "You can't mean that we'd be sharing the same . . . " The thought filled her with a horrified fascination. To sleep so close to Quade that she could reach out and touch him . . . Oh, God, what was she thinking?

She faced him. "I think I know what you're talking about, and I won't have any part of it. I *am* decent, no matter what you may think; I have no intention of being your mistress. We'll go on just as we have been. I'm sure that will be protection enough."

"Will it?" His teeth were gleaming at her. "You told me yourself that the reason the man left your tent is because you told him I would kill him. You need protection, Corrie. You don't realize what an impression you make out here. My God, you've got a face that's all peaches and milk, and a body that can't be hidden even under men's clothes. And your hair, like chestnut gold, flying out from under your hat—"

Quade lifted his hand toward her face, and for one frozen moment Corrie thought he was going to touch her. But then he dropped his hand and moved away from her, busying himself by lighting a second candle from the first one.

"You may be an honest woman," he went on, "but the man was right: you don't look it. You look like a fancy woman, the very best, the top stuff, headed for the finest dance hall or theater in Dawson City. If you were on the stage there, they'd be throwing gold nuggets at you, Corrie. You'd be knee deep in them."

She stared at him. Unconsciously he had brought out an object from his pocket and was staring down at it. She noticed, with a little thrilled shock, that it was the burned cameo.

"I *won't* sleep in the same tent with you."

"Yes, you will. That way the men will think you're my woman and they won't dare touch you. Oh, don't worry, I won't touch you either. I'll keep you pristine and pure for your Avery. We'll be like brother and sister." He gave the cameo a long look and then thrust it back into his pocket. "That's how it's going to be."

"Brother and sister," Corrie repeated. "Very well," she told him coldly. "You've made the decision, haven't you? And I guess I'm not in a position to argue. Now, if you would please leave me alone, I think I would like to read."

"Fine. Read, then. I have some writing to do."

She reached for one of the novels she had brought. With shaking hands she removed the embroidered linen bookmark that kept her place. She focused her eyes on the page, uncomfortably aware of Quade rustling nearby as he got out a box of writing paper, an inkwell and pen.

Avery, she thought. She tried to summon up a picture of her fiancé's handsome face, his perfectly carved profile, his burnished golden hair and mustache. But somehow the image was blurred and unsatisfactory. Instead she only saw Quade. Quade's rough-carved features, bold and strong . . .

☙ Chapter 18 ☙

Lake Bennett was a long finger of ice lying squeezed between formidable, timber-covered hills, overlooked by stark mountains. The lonely, empty wilderness was as wild and harsh as anything Aunt Susan could ever have predicted. Along the way, they had seen moose and elk, and twice black bears had lumbered past their tent. At night wolves howled eerily, their cries hollow and lonely.

From this ice-bound lake would begin the long waterway journey to Dawson City.

To Corrie's dismay, Bennett City turned out to be yet another bare tent settlement, stretched out for miles along the frozen lake and swarming with thousands of stampeders. Stove-piped tents were jumbled everywhere, among piles of raw lumber and skeletons of half-finished boats. The clear air was filled with the scraping of saws, the tapping of calking irons and the smell of new wood.

It was, Corrie thought in discouragement, as if ten thousand men had decided to set up camp in the midst of a lumber yard.

The wind from the glacier-capped mountains blew constantly, uncompromising in its grim chill. The snow had nearly melted from the ground, revealing the exposed ugliness of bare earth and mud, and the untidy debris of human habitation. Trash, lumber scraps, tin cans and old bottles were everywhere. One joker had even constructed a complete tiny house made of nothing but empty beer bottles, with a pole, sod and canvas roof.

The chief occupation in Bennett City was boat building, Quade told her. "Steamer passage is expensive, so
most of the men are making their own boats—scows,
dories, even hollowed-out logs—anything they can rig up.
I've even seen one with a paddlewheel. I just hope all of
these contraptions will float."

"But the lake is frozen! How can anyone get through?"
She stared out at the expanse of white ice roughened into
hummocks by the wind and snow.

"The ice will break up soon. Then the Yukon will be
open and you and I can take passage on one of the river
steamers." Quade gave her a self-mocking bow. "I may
be a many-talented man, but my abilities do not extend
to boat building, I'm afraid. So we've nothing to do for
two or three weeks but wait. You can take all the
photographs you want. And you'll enjoy watching the ice
break up; it's an exciting experience."

The days passed slowly, punctuated by Corrie's rising
concern about Avery. Was he all right? Most worrisome
of all, where was he? Quade's inquiries at the lake had
thus far been fruitless. No one, it seemed, had heard of
the Curran party, and Quade speculated that Avery
might have been among the few who had attempted to
make the trip with dog teams along the frozen river. Or
perhaps he had taken the White Pass route, or crossed
over the glaciers near Valdez.

"Anyway," Quade told her, shrugging, "there's no
sense in fretting over it, Corrie. If he's here, we'll find
him. If he isn't, if he's dead, well . . . "

She did not need to have the sentence completed for
her. By now she knew how uncertain life was in this
country. Avery could be dead somewhere, frozen to
death, and she might never learn of it.

Quade was a puzzling man to live with, Corrie learned.
He adhered scrupulously to his promise to treat her as a
sister. Often he was cheerful and light-hearted, so that
she found she enjoyed being with him. Yet at other times
he was moody and silent.

One day at supper he was especially quiet, his expression forbidding. Suddenly he asked, "Do you consider me
a rational man, Corrie?"

"What?" She stared at him, puzzled. "Why, of course I do. Why on earth would you ask me such a thing?"

He looked away from her. "Perhaps you wouldn't think I was so rational if you knew more about me. Have you ever had . . . strange feelings? Odd, unexplainable feelings that keep after you and won't let you alone until you obey them?"

"No. I don't think so."

"Of course you wouldn't. Most people don't have any urges more distressing to them than the impulse to take another piece of chocolate cake, or to make love to their neighbor's wife . . . " Quade was frowning. "Have you ever gone somewhere, Corrie, because a feeling told you to go there?"

She couldn't help laughing. "Of course! I have a feeling that I need a new shirtwaist, and so I go shopping. I have a feeling that I'm hungry, and so I—"

He scowled at her, his expression savage. "Stop making fun of me. No, I'm not talking about those kinds of urges. But suppose . . . suppose you saw a man in the street one day. A man who looked vaguely familiar, rather like someone you had a—a grudge against, but he looked heavier and older. So you ask around. You manage to find out his name, and you learn that he isn't the man you used to know, but a completely different person, with a different name and background and occupation."

Quade hesitated, then went on. "Yet there's something about him, Corrie. Something that won't let you alone, that nags at you and gives you no peace. Until finally, you," Quade paused, "have to follow him."

She saw that Quade's hand had gone unconsciously to his pocket where he kept the burned brooch. "It isn't even rational," he muttered. "It makes no sense, and I always considered myself sensible above all things. Sensible and reasonable."

She stared at him. "No," she said slowly. "That's never happened to me. Who was the man? And why would it be that important to—"

He made a swift gesture of dismissal. "Look, let's just drop the topic, all right? It's my own private nightmare, and I never should have mentioned it."

He would say nothing more.

* * *

Corrie thought often of her baby these days. If it was a boy, he might have his father's features and coloring, and inherit Avery's aristocratic good looks. If it's a girl, she might look like me, Corrie thought with amused delight. Either way, Corrie was happy just knowing the baby would be a child of her own and Avery's joining . . .

Imperceptibly, so that she barely noticed it happening, her belly began to thicken. Finally she was forced to loosen the waist of the men's pants she wore.

"It's more practical for you to wear men's gear here," Quade insisted. "A skirt hem would only drag perpetually in the mud. Take my word for it, you're lovely enough no matter what costume you wear. And I do think a flannel shirt rather becomes you." In one of his more cheerful moods, he chucked her under the chin, grinning at her; angrily she pushed him away.

To pass the time, Quade had been teaching her to cook. She could now bake a reasonably light loaf of sourdough bread on the oven that came with Quade's Yukon stove. She had also learned to make griddle cakes filled with bits of dried apple or raisins for flavoring. Quade had bought syrup, and amused himself inventing new desserts he could cook with their limited supplies. "You need fattening up," he would tell Corrie, laughing at her irritation.

Thinking of Papa, she took plate after plate of photographs, developing them laboriously in the crude, canvas-draped darkroom Quade had helped her rig up in their tent. She captured the untidy squalor of the tents, and the sodden shacks on the main street of Bennett City. She spent an hour one morning photographing the extraordinary sight of men perched on head-high scaffolding to whip-saw lumber.

One day, after standing in line at the post office for five hours, she received a letter from Aunt Susan.

Corrie, darling, are you all right? I've been so worried about you and about Li Hua. That man you hired to take you to Avery—is he trustworthy? You know I disapproved of your decision to go north, but now that you are there, I can only wish you the best of luck. I love you, Corrie, dear. If there is anything, anything at all, that I can do to help you . . .

According to her aunt, there was war fever in San Francisco. The Stewart Shipyards, now being run by an assistant in Donald's absence, were working at a hectic pace, turning out battleships for the Spanish-American War. Donald was directing their operations with letters from Dyea. Had Corrie seen him there? Was she eating properly? Was she wearing warm clothing? Did she need money? When was she coming home?

Corrie read the letter, alternately laughing and sighing. She immediately wrote a reply, deliberately vague about her life at Lake Bennett with Quade, and not mentioning the avalanche at all. Why worry her aunt unnecessarily? Li Hua could give her all of the details when she arrived back in the city, and the news would be more reassuring when given in person.

On the day after the mail came, Corrie took a walk down to the lakeshore to look at the progress being made on the boats. There a voice hailed her.

"You! Mrs. Price! Is that you?"

She turned to see Eulalie Benrush trotting after her, clad in a rusty black skirt which had been dragged through the mud until its hem was crusted with dirt. Over this garb the long-nosed little woman wore a men's mackinaw far too big for her; its sleeves extended nearly over her finger tips.

"Mrs. Benrush! From the *Alki!*" Corrie could not conceal her surprise.

"Yes, I came over the Pass and as soon as the ice breaks, I aim to get me passage on a steamer and go up to Circle City to find that husband of mine. I'll be glad to get out of this dirty, crowded place, I will. Why, half of these filthy men don't even care where they go to *relieve themselves.*" This last she whispered loudly.

Then Eulalie's eyes fastened on Corrie. "Wearing men's clothes, are you? *I* wouldn't be caught in my coffin with a pair of breeches on me. A lady's got to have her standards, that's all. Say, you aren't traveling alone, are you? On the *Alki* I told myself you were much too pretty to be coming up here."

"I . . . no . . . " Corrie said faintly.

"You got another woman with you, then?"

"No, not exactly. I . . . I've hired someone to take me up the river."

Eulalie Benrush's lips straightened to a thin line. "A man. I thought so. I thought I seen you the other day goin' into a tent with a man. Only I told myself it couldn't be you because you was a lady, or at least you *seemed* like one!" With a twist of her features, Eulalie managed to convey the impression that she believed Corrie no longer fit into that category.

"That was Mr. Hill, the man I hired," Corrie began to explain quickly. "He—"

"Men is men up here, young woman. Foot-loose they are, too, and most of 'em left their morals at home. As for the *whores*, well, they never had no morals to start with, did they?"

With these words, Mrs. Benrush lifted the muddy hem of her skirt and marched off, leaving Corrie, flushed scarlet, to stare after her.

The middle of May passed, bringing with its warmer temperatures what Quade assured her was the North's most vicious wildlife, the mosquito. Soon they would have to start using the mosquito netting they had brought, and the patent insect repellant.

It was getting more and more difficult to share the tent with Quade. True, he kept his word: he treated her with brotherly courtesy, allowing her privacy to wash and dress. Four times he had spoken sharply to men who showed too much interest in Corrie. On one of these occasions, he had actually had to bring out his pistol and handle it significantly. After that, the men kept their distance.

If living at close quarters with her cost Quade any effort, he did not reveal it. But when he was near, Corrie was all too aware of him; the bigness of his body, his rough vitality, his rugged good looks so very different from those of Avery, so much more manly. She learned his moods, the things that would make him laugh, the times when he seemed edgy and distracted and barely aware of her presence. She knew the way he slept on his back with one arm flung behind his head. She knew, too,

the nightmares that sometimes consumed him, so that he
would call out in his sleep, giving odd, strangled cries.

Mostly the cries were garbled, but once she heard him
say very clearly, *"Oh, God, no! The fire! The fire!"* He
jerked upright in his blanket roll, punching at the canvas
of the tent with such ferocity that she was worried he was
going to turn on her.

"Quade!" She prodded him in the shoulder. "Quade,
wake up. It's only a nightmare, a bad dream."

"What?" In the smoldering light of the stove she could
see that his deep blue eyes were wide and blank. His fists
were clenched into knots.

"It's me—Corrie," she told him hastily. "You were
having a nightmare. Go back to sleep, Quade."

He still looked blank.

"Quade, I've told you, the nightmare is *over*. It's all
right."

At last, obediently, he had turned over and slept. In
the morning she mentioned the incident.

"What are you talking about?" He glanced at her irri-
tably, reaching for the tin bowl he used to mix up pancake batter. "Nightmares are for little boys who see bogey
men in the dark."

"Then you're afraid of the bogey man, too," she told
him softly. "Because you did have a nightmare; I heard
you. You were shouting out something about fire. 'Oh,
God,' you said. 'The fire, the fire.' "

Quade was silent for a moment. He stopped stirring the
thick batter. Then, "Shall I add chopped-up apricot to
this?" he asked her. "It'll be good for you; keep you
from getting scurvy."

"I'm not planning to get scurvy. And you're evading
my question. This isn't your first nightmare like this, you
know. And each time you rise up with your fists clenched
as if you'd like to kill someone. Is it—" She hesitated.
"Does it have something to do with that burned-up
brooch you carry about with you?"

"Corrie, I thought we agreed that I was to keep out of
your affairs and you would keep out of mine."

"I think it is my affair when you yell in the night and

start bunching up your fists and thrashing about. Perhaps one night you'll lash out at me."

Quade set down the bowl of batter. Slowly his fingers went toward his pocket. He pulled out the cameo and let it lie in the palm of his hand. Evil and fear seemed somehow embedded in its charred gold.

"Look at her," Quade said softly. "The cameo girl. Look at that face of hers, so serene, so quiet. She's almost rigid, isn't she, as if she were waiting." He stared down at the brooch.

"Who was she, Quade? The woman who owned the brooch?"

"She wasn't a woman—at least, not yet. She was a girl, almost eighteen. She would have had her birthday in another week, if she'd lived. I gave her this brooch."

"Was she—"

"She was lovely, Corrie. True, she—she seemed to be very angry sometimes; she wasn't happy with the life she was forced to lead. She wanted more freedom, wanted to be a writer like me. Instead she was stuck at home, had to be a debutante, and she hated that."

There was a long silence, and then he went on. "I remember her best as a little girl, though. She had chestnut-honey hair like yours, with highlights that caught the sun. And it was very thick and heavy, too, as yours is. She was a very lively child, always running or skipping or rolling her hoop, ceaselessly busy—"

"Who was she?" Corrie whispered.

"My sister, Ila. She was burned to death in my father's office by an arsonist. We believe he was my father's office clerk, trying to cover up evidence of the money he had embezzled from the books. It was a Saturday morning; he must have thought the office would be empty. Ila was found in a back room. She and my mother had quarreled that day; Ila'd been typing on the new typewriter my father stored back there—"

Quade's eyes were glittering.

"I'm so sorry," Corrie whispered. "I didn't know."

"Have you ever thought, Corrie, really *thought* about what it would feel like to be burned to death? The horror of being burned alive? I have; I think of it almost every day. Because they said her skirts must have caught fire— the flames caught at her hem and then ignited the rest of her like a torch. She must have screamed. God, how she must have screamed . . . "

Quade's face had turned as white as rice paper; beads of moisture shone on his forehead.

Burned alive, Corrie thought, swallowing. She reached out to touch his arm. "Quade, you mustn't think about it any more. Horrible as it was, it's over now. It happened a long time ago."

Quade disagreed. "No, Corrie, it isn't over, and it won't be until I've found him and killed him."

"Quade, no," Corrie whispered, frightened.

He was staring down at the brooch, turning it over and over in his hands. "Sometimes I look at this cameo, and it's as if *she's* in it somehow, staring out at me. There are days when I can feel her fear, her terror and hatred, her desire to live. I can hear her screaming, silent screams, Corrie. They are the worst kind."

Corrie watched, shaken, as Quade slowly put the cameo back in his pocket. He looked at her.

"I'm going to carry this brooch with me until I find the man who killed Ila—whoever he is. After he's dead, she'll find peace. That's all I want for her."

As May progressed, the man-made sounds of axes, saws and hammers were augmented by the deep rumble of snowslides as they let go and came rushing down the sides of the mountains. The slides came often, occurring as frequently as every ten minutes. Everything was starting to thaw and melt, Quade said. If Corrie went into the woods, she was to be careful not to get too close to any overhanging snow, for it might tumble down on her. She didn't need any such warnings. Corrie told him with a grimace, One avalanche was enough for her.

One morning she awoke after having had an uneasy dream filled with images of Mattie Shea. She dressed quickly behind the blanket Quade had hung in the tent for her, then crawled out.

The rising sun tinged the sky with pink and yellow; she could tell the day was going to be clear. She stood daydreaming a moment, her thoughts turning to Avery, wondering where he was, and if he was thinking of her. And Li Hua, she mused, was she all right? Surely she was back in San Francisco by now, recuperating from her broken leg. Had she found another job? Or had she gone back to work for Aunt Susan?

The sun nudged upward like a glowing coin. Then suddenly, blindingly, its light hit the glaciers. Diamonds, rubies, amethysts, a thousand glittering jewels caught the rising sun.

Corrie stood entranced. After a moment she realized that something was missing. She could not stand there alone in the presence of such beauty.

"Quade!" She ran back into the tent. "Quade, oh, do come out here and see this! It's incredible! I've never seen anything like it!"

Quade came out and watched with her. For long moments they stood silently, aware that others, too, had stopped their work and paused to look. At last the sun rose higher and the sparkling accident of nature was gone, leaving the mountains blank, white against the blue sky.

Quade spoke in a low, wondering voice. "I don't know how many times I've looked at those mountains, but I've never seen anything like that before. There are a lot of things a person gets to see just one time. I think that was one of them."

They went back into the tent to eat their breakfast. Never had Corrie felt closer to him.

Lake Bennett had gradually been changing. In protected areas along the shore, frail purple crocuses had pushed up. Corrie had seen skeins of Canadian geese veering across the sky, making wild, honking cries. There was now some open water on the lake, and the remaining ice was soft, and honeycombed with little tunnels, as if fairy worms had been boring in it.

On May 29, the ice broke up. It began suddenly, in midday, under a sky as deep blue as a California grape. Quade came running to find her, but she was already making her way close to the shore. She stared in wonderment.

It was as if God Himself had chosen to play a gigantic, capricious, thundering game. For the lake, which had seemed an almost unbroken sheet of watery ice, suddenly began to move, to shatter like glass, ton upon ton of screaming, cracking, exploding crystal.

"Quade! Good heavens, I can't believe this." She clutched his arm. The sounds exploded like colliding freight trains. Gigantic floes of ice crashed into each other, pounded each other to bits, hurtling and groaning.

"Fantastic, isn't it?" He was grinning at her, his strong face alight, as if he had planned the entire spectacle expressly for her pleasure. She could barely hear him above the thundering roar of thousands of tons of ice.

"They say the sound of this can be heard fifteen miles away," he shouted to her above the din. "And you should see what happens on the Yukon itself. These floes are five and six feet thick, and they push down the river like monsters, gashing away tree trunks, gouging out earth, doing just as they damned well please. Sometimes a caribou or a moose gets carried away with them."

"It's incredible—so powerful!" she shouted.

"Yes, and you should see it when all of that power dams up. Ice chunks heap and pile up on themselves, blocking the water flow. Then there'll be floods everywhere, maybe for hours, maybe for days, until something breaks them . . . "

They watched until most of the ice was gone. Some of it was heaped on the shore, pushing aside tents and uprooting boats. There were small crystal shards of ice like millions of smashed chandeliers littering the shore.

"This is another thing I'll probably only see once," Corrie commented at last.

"No, this is a spectacle that happens every year. You could watch it every year for the next fifty if you were to stay around here that long." Quade was smiling and Corrie, walking toward the tent with him, felt curiously contented.

It happened naturally that night, unplanned and somehow tacitly accepted by both of them. By the light of two candles they ate their supper, a duck Quade had shot and stuffed with rice. Corrie was about to begin washing the dishes when she looked up to see that Quade was watching her. Suddenly self-conscious, Corrie tugged at the blue woolen sweater she wore, which clung to her body, accenting its curves. The deep blue brought out the richness of her hair and the creamy delicacy of her skin.

"No wonder that man crawled into the tent with you," Quade observed. "Cold air and ice and my cooking seem to agree with you, Corrie. You look like a ripe apricot, ready to fall into someone's basket."

She stared at him, surprised by the husky urgency in his voice. He had not acted like this before.

"Little Delia, don't look at me like that, or I might do something I'll regret. I don't know how I've stood it this long, occupying this tent with you like some ridiculous plaster saint. I'm not a saint, girl, and I guess it's time you knew it."

"Quade?" The tin plate she was holding dropped from her fingers.

His eyes held hers, so intensely blue that she could not look away from him, nor did she wish to.

"Don't talk, Delia. Just kiss me. God knows I've wanted to do it for weeks."

His arms went around her. She felt the warmth, the bigness and maleness of him, the clean smell of his body. His mouth was warm on hers, his lips soft, gentle, exploratory. Slowly his embrace changed, grew more intense. His hands caressed her back as if she were precious to him, as if she were the very world to him. . . .

She clung to him. His kiss grew harder, more demanding. Her breath quickened as he caressed her with growing urgency. She had never imagined anything like this wrenching excitement as her body responded to his. She didn't want him to stop; she wanted him to go on and on. She wanted to open herself to him, to give herself to him utterly. . . .

"Darling—darling, I've got to be close to you, I've needed you for so long. . . ."

"Yes, Quade—" Corrie murmured.

Their voices were husky whispers. She didn't know what they said to each other, only that Quade was undressing her, slowly, luxuriously. He pulled her sweater away, her camisole, her pants and underdrawers, kissing the bare flesh that each garment covered. The urgent warmth of his breath was unbearably exciting. . . . Magically, Quade shed his clothes, after carrying Corrie to a blanket.

"Your breasts are lovely, Delia. So full and beautiful—I've got to kiss them, to love them . . . "

He began by kissing her cleavage, then the soft undersides of her breasts. His mouth worshipped the rounded globes of her flesh until she trembled with desire. He tongued her nipples, at first softly and then with mounting passion, until an electric quiver raced through Corrie's body to her groin, and she could not help moaning in deep pleasure.

She arched her back, pressing closer to him. She loved the warm, living feel of his body, his powerful chest and belly, the swollen maleness of him. It was as if, she thought feverishly, she belonged here. As if she had lived her entire life waiting for this moment in Quade's arms.

His kisses moved down her belly, exploring the rounded curve of her tummy, lingering over her navel, worshipping her hipbones with growing desire. Then his mouth moved to the soft fluff of her venus mound, and he kissed her there with sweet urgency.

"Delia . . . oh, God, darling . . . "

Again, she arched and moaned with a wild, bursting pleasure as he kissed her, exploring her fully with his flicking tongue, drawing her to heights of excitement she had not dreamed possible.

Then, gasping for breath, she reached for him, for the hard, urgent column of his maleness. She guided it into herself. Slowly, deliciously, he began to thrust. An aching sweetness swelled in Corrie's groin and bloomed there like a trembling rosebud about to open.

She joined him, matching his grinding, potent hips with her own. She dropped all inhibitions and without thinking, gave of herself all there was to give, and more. . . .

Was what they were doing right? Was it moral or proper? She didn't know or care. She only knew that she and Quade were joined together, that his body was a part of her as she was part of him. Both of them belonged somehow to the elemental forces of ice, and the grinding, smashing Yukon river.

His movements became faster and more intense. She could feel him swelling as he thrust deep within her.

The aching pleasure grew in her. It swelled, grew stronger, sweeter, until at last it burst in an explosion of the purest, most ineffable gold. She soared with Quade, she arched and cried out and clung to him and rocketed with him in the pure release of their bodies and minds. Full of joy, they rose together like two golden stars. . . .

Later they fell asleep, wrapped in the same blanket, by the dull red glow of the stove. Their bodies, still moist from lovemaking, curved against each other like spoons. Corrie savored the moment, feeling that she was as much a part of Quade as his fingers or his hand or his ribs. With Avery she had not felt like this, or dreamed that such perfect, lazy contentment could occur. She could spend the rest of her life in Quade's arms. She could never ask for more happiness than this.

"I told you I wasn't a saint," he murmured to her just before sleep overtook them. "Forgive me?"

She only sighed and kissed him and snuggled closer. There was nothing to forgive.

❧ Chapter 19 ❧

Li Hua was not in San Francisco, as Corrie imagined. She was still in Dyea, at the Klondike Hotel, recovering from a bout of dysentery which had left her weak.

Will Sebastian, the doctor, had paid two Eskimo packers to take her back to Dyea, refusing to accept payment. In the hospital tent at Sheep Camp, he had brushed off Li Hua's thanks.

"But—" Li Hua had stared at him. "But I couldn't allow you to do that for me! I'll manage to pay—"

The young doctor gazed at her with warm brown eyes, and it was as if, for a moment, something hung between them, something as fragile as a spider web, as easily swept aside.

"No," Will Sebastian said at last. "I don't want payment. You've got to be moved out of here; there's no other choice, and I won't have you on my conscience. And you certainly can't do any walking in your condition—"

"But I'm strong, I can—"

The doctor's mouth curved in a smile. "I'm sure you are strong. But it's clear you've never tried walking in a cast. I certainly wouldn't let my wife stay here alone, and I can't permit you to do it either."

"Your wife?"

Something in Li Hua froze. She hadn't thought of him as having a wife. Especially not now, when he was looking down at her in an oddly soft yet angry way.

"I did have a wife, once. It seemed she didn't care for a doctor's long hours, nor did she wish a husband who was more interested in helping people than in making money."

199

"Oh, so you mean she—"

"No," he added, "It's Dyea for you. I'll give you a letter to the owner of the Klondike Hotel there. I fixed him up when he was choking to death on a piece of caribou steak. He'll remember that; I certainly do."

She had been helpless to resist his suggestion. Dully she had done as she was told, arriving back in Dyea to find that, sure enough, at the Klondike Hotel the note from Will Sebastian was as good as gold dust. Her room would be fifty cents a day, with meals extra, a special rate just for Dr. Sebastian's sake.

The dysentery had begun while she was still along the Dyea Trail. She had been forced to the ignominy of asking the Eskimo guides to frequently stop and carry her into the trees so that she could relieve herself.

They performed this task with stolid faces that did not reveal how they felt about it, but Li Hua had been mortified. When at last she reached the small, bare room with its narrow brass bed, its utilitarian dressing table and its nails on the wall for her clothing, she had crept to the bed and cried with relief.

At the hospital she bought a pair of crutches, and, she began to teach herself to get about. Herman Knolte, the hotel owner, carried up her meals twice a day from the German restaurant next door: greasy trays of potatoes and sauerkraut and sausages. Li Hua, weakened as she was, could not touch any of it. Kindly Mr. Knolte made inquiries for her at the steamship offices. There was no shortage of berths for the trip home.

Li Hua had not left her room since her arrival in Dyea, and thus did not know if Donald Earle was still in town. Herman Knolte told her that no one of that name was staying at the Bailey Hotel. Good riddance, she thought grimly.

Once she awakened with nightmares about the man, to find that her body was running with cold perspiration. She had to heave herself out of the bed and, with the aid of her crutches, stump weakly to the plate glass window. There, eyes fixed, she stared blindly down at the miner who had paused just outside the hotel to relieve himself against a post.

Slowly her terror subsided.

She had not meant to do such a thing to Corrie, really she hadn't. But she had no other choice. She had tried to explain this to Corrie, to tell her that she was sorry, and to warn her. But Corrie had not given her the chance . . .

On the fourth day of her confinement in the hotel, Li Hua's appetite started to return. By the sixth day, after trying to choke down more of the greasy sauerkraut that Herman Knolte brought her, she decided that she was well enough to go down on the street and look for a decent restaurant. Then she would purchase her steamship ticket.

The next day, Li Hua dressed in black serge skirt and white shirtwaist, its Swiss embroidery and delicate tucks showing off her figure charmingly. She combed out her long, black hair until it gleamed, then pinned it up. Lastly she pulled on a plain straw bonnet and her warm woolen coat.

Carefully she made her way on crutches into the corridor, hopping over the bare, uneven floorboards that creaked under her weight. The stairwell angled steeply downward to her left, its walls smeared with grease and scribbling. *J.P.S. Ithaca, New York. Gold or bust, J. Beane was here. Try Flo, Nugget House.*

After thinking a moment, she went down the steep steps sitting down, her right leg extended stiffly in front of her. At last she was outside on the boardwalk, leaning heavily for support on her crutches.

The sun was low, and it threw long shadows across the street. Even the mud ruts cast shadows. Knots of men lounged about or hurried on errands; a few hundred feet away three men cursed as they tried to extricate a horse and cart stuck in mud up to the hubcaps of the wheels.

Li Hua drew a deep breath. Wasn't the New York Kitchen just a few doors away? She would go there. Beef, she thought. Perhaps some vegetables and rice, or chicken. She was still dehydrated and shaky from the dysentery, and she knew she simply could not stomach another bite of sausage.

Inside the little restaurant, a hubbub of voices greeted her. Li Hua paused in the doorway, trying to adjust her eyes to the noisy, smoky warmth. The tables were all full, she noted in dismay. But the air smelled deliciously of roasting meat, and she saw a platter of it being carried to a table.

"Hey, little girl! Come over here, why don't you?"

A heavy-set man with plump, ruddy cheeks was motioning her. "Hey, we got plenty of room here, and the caribou is damned good!"

Caribou. Li Hua eyed the man; he looked jolly, friendly, a hearty burgher or patriarch of a family. And even if the meat was caribou instead of beef, it did smell good, and she was suddenly starving. Besides, she told herself, surely no harm could come to her in this crowded, noisy, cheerful place. Even if she wished to, she could not eat alone, as there were no empty tables.

She hobbled over to the table.

"Say, what happened to you? Trip over a piano leg?" The group of men at the table guffawed uproariously.

"No, I was caught in the avalanche on the Chilkoot Pass," she told them. Did they think she came from a dance hall? Well, let them. It was warm here, it was safe, and she was going to get a good meal. Her stomach rumbled. Let them laugh!

The ruddy man ordered for her, and the food came, caribou and potatoes and beer and a dried apple pie with a lopsided crust. Li Hua ate hungrily, bantering back and forth with the men, and allowed the ruddy man to pour shots of whiskey into her mug from a bottle he carried in his mackinaw pocket.

The others were from Ohio, they told her, heaping more slices of meat upon her plate. The big, red-faced man was from New York.

"Which place you work at?" they were asking her, shouting uproariously among themselves as Cordell Stewart had done with his drinking cronies in his library. "Ma Tracey's? Gee, but that woman has an ugly face. Looks like she got it pounded in with a horse shoe."

"I'm not with any—"

"Or is it with Flossie's, then? Old Fat Flossie can pick 'em!"

In vain she protested that she did not work in any crib or dance hall, but they did not believe her. She realized that they had probably been drinking for some time.

At last she fished out a bill from the small purse she

carried and pushed herself up from the table, supporting herself awkwardly with the crutches.

"Hey! Where you goin'?"

"I have to get back to my hotel room."

"Aw, not yet. The night's just begun. Got to have our fun yet, we do."

Before she could stop them, they paid her check. Then she found herself being helped out of the restaurant, a pair of strong hands under each elbow. Someone else carried her crutches for her, stumbling and weaving ahead so that she could not reach them. The room, the noisy, laughing faces, whirled.

"Please—my crutches! Give them back!"

"Aw, you don't need 'em now, do you? You got plenty of help to walk. We're just havin' a bit of fun, is all. Didn't we buy your dinner for you and treat you nice?"

The red-faced man from New York was one of those who grasped her arms. As they emerged onto the street, Li Hua gave a little gasp, for while they were eating, the sun had gone down. Gas lamps gleamed from windows across the street, and the hills at the end of the town seemed bigger than she remembered them, and much darker, as if they were about to fall down on the buildings and crush them.

Li Hua shivered in the cold. "Please . . . my crutches. I've got to get back to my hotel." She could feel the liquor she had drunk whirling in her head.

"You got a hotel room? All we got is tents. Want to see our tents?"

"No, I don't want—"

But they didn't seem to hear her. They were laughing among themselves, and the ruddy-faced man told her to keep her cast lifted high or she was going to get mud on it.

"Please. Please put me down," Li Hua pleaded.

"Aw, come on. Pretty thing like you doesn't want to be all lonesome tonight, does she? Not when she's got a bunch of us nice folks to be friendly-like and buy her dinner and all."

Li Hua hesitated. The whiskey had gone to her head, confusing her thoughts. Surely these men couldn't really mean any harm. They were just teasing, that was all, playing a sort of game with her. In a few minutes they would give her back her crutches and take her to the hotel.

"All right," she said.

They had a tent on the beach. Or, rather, three tents, pitched near each other in a circle near enormous mounds of gunnysacks and mining equipment. A group of sled dogs were tied nearby, asleep. At a distance the water lapped, making the coldest sound that Li Hua had ever heard. Above, the moon had appeared from behind a screen of silver clouds. Its face was roughened and molten yellow, like a nugget.

Roughly they pushed her inside one of the tents. She stumbled forward, catching herself with her hands. She found that she was sprawled on a nest of tumbled blankets that smelled of perspiration and dog.

"Hey, you going to give it to us for free, little pretty? We bought your dinner, after all." The ruddy man was behind her, breathing on her in great, sour gusts of liquor. "We're gonna be nice and polite, ain't we, boys? One at a time it'll be, and nothing to it. So hurry up and get your drawers off."

"What?"

She thought she hadn't heard him right, for the liquor seemed to be spinning in her head, making their voices sound fuzzy. She tried to twist herself about so that she could face him, but the cast encumbered her; she couldn't move properly. Then somehow he had her pinned down by the shoulders, with her nose shoved into rough wool.

"Listen here, pretty. You whores're all alike. Think you got something special between your legs. Well, I got news for you. Me and my friends here, we got a game we play down in the red light district. We go down there and we get it for free. We take 'em and we pull 'em into our carriage and we stick it to 'em. They got to give it to us for nothing, see, because they sure can't holler rape. Now, can they?"

He laughed, a loud, cheerful, well-fed guffaw.

Then he was yanking at her skirts, pulling them over her head. She felt the smothering, rough fabric jerk over her nose and mouth, and another yank as something was twisted about to secure it. She flailed her arms desperately;

they were trapped in the binding cloth as if she were restrained in a sheet.

She tried to kick. Fingernails scratched at her thigh as her stockings came off. Strong arms grasped her midsection, rolling her on her back.

She heard crawling movements, felt a blast of cold air as the tent flap opened. "All right, Joe, she's ready. God, if she ain't kickin' and carryin' on like a little mule, and with that there broken leg, too. Well, we got to teach her something, right? Teach her she can't be uppity, that's all. She's got to be generous with her favors, or they're going to get took from her.

"What you screaming for, little pretty? Ain't you got a relish for a good, strong cock? Like that, eh? How you like that? That's a good one, ain't it? Yes, sir."

She did not know how much later it was. They left her lying on the beach, face down in the yielding sand, with her skirts still tied above her head.

Her bare legs and buttocks were unbearably cold, and ached in a fierce, bone-hurting way that seemed to come from the wet ground itself. Her crotch burned. How many of them had there been? She had lost count. Some must have had her twice. But their laughter and their rapid thrusting movements and their juices had all merged into one nightmare.

How they must hate women, the thought had come to her in the midst of it. How they must despise them.

She hated the men, too. If the heavily lined serge skirt had not been pulled over her head, she would have clawed them, bitten their faces and tasted their blood. As it was, she could barely breathe, and by the end of the ordeal she had nearly lost consciousness.

The air on the beach revived her. She had felt them dump her, felt the shock of the sand, smelled its coldness. Someone laughed.

"What'll we do with her, anyways?"

"Oh, just leave her there. Someone'll find her. No sense letting good stuff go to waste, eh, Joe?" Laughter. "We got her broken in good, anyway. She'd ought to be grateful for that."

More guffaws. Then they were gone. Li Hua lay in the

sand, consumed with hate. She lay quietly until the voices were gone. Minutes passed. Then she began struggling at the cloth that held her.

"My God Jesus Christ in Heaven, what's this?"

Another voice. Li Hua sat up, her head still covered with the dark serge of her skirt. In the gloom she knew she must look like an apparition.

"Don't move, whoever you are. Don't move, dammit, or I'll let you have it. I got a pistol, and I can use it. I've got a . . . Oh, Jesus."

Hands pulled, tugged, drew down the fabric from her face. Air rushed in at her. She saw a young face, open-mouthed, staring at her with wide eyes.

"A woman! A naked woman! What are you doing here?"

"What— what do you think I'm doing? I— They—"

She began to sob. But instinctively she grasped at her skirts and pulled them down over her body. As she did so, her hand brushed her naked hips where the money belt should have been. It was gone, and with it her passage money. They had robbed her.

"Oh, no . . . no . . . " she mumbled incoherently. She bent forward and began to retch into the sand.

"Oh, hey. Hey, you don't have to do that. I won't hurt you. I won't touch you. I promise I won't. Say, what's the matter with you, anyway?"

His name was Martin Javenall, he was nineteen years old, the son of a wealthy banker in Seattle. He picked her up in his arms and he took her to his tent, a half-mile further up the beach. She clung to him, weeping helplessly. She was barely aware when he knelt down at last, laying her on the sand. Then, pulling her by the armpits, he dragged her into his tent.

He fed sticks of firewood into the stove until it glowed red and sent little gusts of heat to warm the tent. He dragged out a black wool blanket—this one didn't smell of dog—and tucked it around her, lifting up her cast and arranging the blanket so that she was encased in a cocoon of wool. When he had finished, Li Hua rolled onto her hip so that she faced the canvas wall of the tent. She would not look at him.

"Hey, what happened to you, anyway? Are you one of those—" He hesitated. She could hear how young his voice was, how full of curiosity and fear. And, yes, hadn't his hands lingered a long time as he pushed the blanket in around her? My God, she thought. Him, too. All of them.

"No!" She half sat up and spat the words out at him, almost screaming them. "No, I'm not one of *them!* Why should I be? Just because you found me on the beach, just because I was . . . " She started to cry again.

"All right, all right, I just thought—" He hesitated. "Do you want some food or something? I got a pan of cold biscuits here; I only ate half of them. I'm not used to cooking for one. You see, my partner, Jed, got the typhoid fever and I had to take him into town. There's a hospital there. I think Jed's going to die."

She was still facing the canvas, and didn't answer him. But his voice went on, low and reflective. "You don't have to cry because of anything I said. I wasn't trying to insult you. All I thought was— I mean, you were— Your legs and all showing . . . How was I to know what kind of girl you were?"

She heard him rummaging around, and then the biscuits were thrust in front of her, still in their pan. "Do you want these? I burned them a bit, but they're not bad. I ate six of them myself."

"No."

"You sure?"

"Yes! Yes, I'm sure! What's the matter with you?" She was screaming at him again, her voice high and thin. "I've been raped, and here you are offering me biscuits! I've been raped, I tell you! Don't you even know what that means?"

"Sure." He pulled the pan away, surprise in his voice. "Of course I know what it means. I'm not stupid. But you should have known— I mean, you came here, didn't you? You've got to expect some—"

"I've got to expect a little rape. Is that it?"

"Well, I guess I shouldn't have said it like that. But it's true, I guess. What made you come here, anyway?

"I suppose you came for the gold," he went on. "That's what they all came for in one way or another. Men to mine the gold, and women to mine gold dust from the men." He laughed dryly, suddenly sounding much older than he was.

"I'm not planning to mine anything from the men!" She was starting to perspire under the blanket; her skin felt sticky and unclean.

"Well, if you aren't, you should." He grinned at her. She saw that he was tall and gangly, with a round face still padded with baby fat. He had a sizeable mustache; he must be very proud of it, she thought irrelevantly.

She was strong, the slow realization was coming to her. Very strong indeed. She had survived this rape with little more than some itching and burning, and a dirty skin. She was alive and full of hate and she was not going to cry any more.

"What's your name?" she asked directly.

"Martin Javenall. My friends, they call me Marty. My father, he calls me a darn fool for coming up here in the first place. Say, the coffee's almost hot enough," he added. "I could warm it up. And I'll give you a lot of sugar in yours. You probably could use it."

"Yes." She hesitated. "Marty, do you have some water you could heat? I feel terrible this way. I'm dirty. I . . . I need a bath."

He turned his head sharply and he gave her a long look. The big-knuckled hand reaching for the coffee pot trembled.

"A bath. Yes. I could get one for you."

You too, she was thinking. You too.

"All right," she said. "Why don't you heat up the water, then?"

✿ Chapter 20 ✿

They were to take a steamer called the *Nora*. It had two decks, and was squat, flat-bottomed and completely unglamorous. The lower deck was heavily laden with fresh logs for stoking the engine. There was also a movable cargo boom with pulleys and cables which would be used, Quade said, to free the boat from sandbars.

Their fare to Dawson would be seventy-five dollars with meals a dollar each. The trip would take them four and a half days, provided they did not encounter any complications.

"Complications?" Corrie asked.

Quade grinned at her. "You'll soon learn, my dear, that the river provides plenty of excitement. Rapids, sandbars, snags, ice, current—you name it. But don't worry, we'll miss the worst of it when we have to change steamers later on, at the Ramparts. It'll be a nice trip, you'll see. The scenery here is like nothing else on earth."

There were thirty passengers on the *Nora*, many of them going upriver to sell merchandise. A short, cheerful man named Mr. Pappos confided to Corrie that he was bringing a shipment of fresh fruit and vegetables, as well as twenty crates of Scotch whiskey. Four women were aboard: Corrie, Eulalie Benrush and a little blonde woman named Ellin Hardacre, who had brought her small daughter, Annie, along. She was meeting her husband in Dawson. He ran a hotel there and needed her as cook.

They left on a clear, sunny June day; the mountains which loomed over Lake Bennett seemed laundered into freshness. Even the litter of Bennett City was somehow softened, but as they boarded the steamer, Eulalie Benrush nodded curtly to Corrie, gave Quade a stony stare and drew Ellin Hardacre aside. The two of them whispered together, then glanced significantly at Corrie.

Corrie flushed and turned aside.

"What's wrong?" Quade asked. He had come to stand at her side, staring at the clutter of boats at the lake edge. His face was reflective, his mouth gentle. His dark hair blew in the cool wind.

"Oh, nothing."

"Nothing? You're scowling as if you'd found a viper curled up among your bedclothes."

"Really, Quade, nothing's wrong. Nothing at all."

He eyed her sharply, but said no more.

The rumbling vibrations of the engine started, and the river journey began. Caribou Crossing was the shallow stream which was the outlet for Lake Bennett. It was crammed with small boats, most of them equipped with a single mast and one crude rectangular sail, which gave them the look of a child's bathtub toy. Would these strange little craft really make it all the way up the Yukon? Corrie wondered. Many had two sets of oarlocks, and their occupants were already rowing frantically in an effort to gain distance over the others. Ahead, she could see more of the boats, their sails white dots against green shoreline.

The *Nora* herself contributed a considerable amount of wood smoke to the air, and Corrie and Quade found themselves a spot at the bow where sparks and soot were less likely to fall on them.

Corrie leaned over the rail, gazing down at the motley river traffic, feeling breathless and caught up in the excitement of it all. A man waved to her and gaily she waved back.

"Look! Oh, Quade, look! There's a boat that looks exactly like a horse trough. Why, I think they've made it out of a log!"

"No doubt," Quade agreed dryly. "When a man doesn't know what he's doing, he gets some very interesting ideas."

The following morning, the *Nora* entered the Windy

Arm of Lake Tagish, a narrow, lovely trough of water
wedged in by plunging mountains. Here the wind did
indeed blow forcing the sailors in small boats to tack
back and forth in order to make any progress. Some of
the small craft were already falling behind, or smashing
into the big cakes of ice which still floated in the water.
One unhappy boater spilled into the water, letting out
a high, shocked squeal. Corrie shuddered in sympathy.
She was relieved when the man's companions pulled him
out, blue-lipped, sodden and cursing.

Tagish Post was a customs house, and Corrie got out
her camera and photographed the nearly four-mile-long
line of boats along the riverbank, waiting to have their
papers cleared.

Hours later they approached what Quade told her
was Miles Canyon. This was one of the most dangerous
stretches of the river, bordered by high, granite walls
and with a current so fast and vicious that it actually hog-
backed in the middle. However, Quade explained, they
would not traverse Miles Canyon or the equally dangerous White Horse rapids two miles downstream, but
would stop instead just at the head of the gorge and transfer their goods to a horse-drawn tramway which had
been built to circumvent the dangerous water. Their tickets would then admit them to another steamer.

At the tramway was a roadhouse, and they stopped
and ate while their goods were being unloaded from the
Nora. Quade said he wanted to question the roadhouse
owner, so Corrie, who was feeling restless, excused herself and said that she would wander around and meet
him later.

The sun had already set, leaving a pale afterglow which
would soon fade into total darkness. Corrie walked
about, looking at the tram horses and wishing there was
enough light so that she could take a photograph of
them. They looked so starved and weary, she fancied she
saw a melancholy, pleading look in their soft eyes.

As she was approaching one particularly sad-looking
animal, Eulalie Benrush and Ellin Hardacre walked past.
Both women ostentatiously held their skirts aside, as if
afraid Corrie might contaminate them. Behind them
trailed little Annie Hardacre, dressed like her mother in

serviceable black serge. Her eyes were fixed curiously on
Corrie.

Corrie straightened her spine, blood burning her cheeks.
How dare they look at her that way! As if she was a bad
woman, a prostitute. And even the child . . .

Jerkily Corrie turned and began walking toward the
roadhouse, her mind going back unwillingly to the night
the ice had gone out, the night when her body had willingly embraced Quade's . . .

They slept that night in each other's arms, and even
in her sleep Corrie felt a warm, burgeoning happiness.
Delia, he had called her. *My lovely little Delia.* She
awakened in the morning to find him gone. She stretched
lazily in the warm blankets which still held the faint,
musky odor of his body, feeling satiated, content, and
lazy with pleasure.

Then she felt it, the soft stirring in her belly as if a
butterfly fluttered there, trying to free itself.

At first Corrie did not know what it was. She lay very
still, thinking that it felt like tiny wings. Or perhaps
minute bubbles of porridge, popping one by one. Then
slowly, piercingly, she realized. It was the baby. She had
felt life for the first time; her child was moving within her.

Her son and Avery's. Or was it their daughter? She put
her hand to her belly and pressed it there, feeling her
fingers tremble against her skin. She had forgotten, she
thought, appalled. She had forgotten her baby.

She flung the blankets aside and sat up, a tight feeling
pressing at her chest.

Her baby.

And foolishly she had slept with Quade, glorying in the
strength of him, and feeling as if she belonged to him.
But she didn't at all. In actuality, she belonged to Avery
Curran, to the man who had fathered her child. She had
traveled hundreds of miles to be with Avery, to marry
him so that he could be a husband to her and a father to
her unborn child.

How could she possibly have forgotten?

No, she told herself, she couldn't allow herself to fall in
love with Quade Hill; she must have been mad even to
consider such a thing.

Quade came back into the tent whistling, carrying a pail

of cold lake water. His blunt, boldly carved face looked
relaxed and at peace. His mouth had softened, and his
blue eyes were soft, as if the tragedy eating away at his
soul had—for now—been put aside. When he saw the
look on Corrie's face, he put down the bucket.

"So." He said it slowly. "Second thoughts, Delia? I
didn't mean for it to happen last night, you know. Or
perhaps I did. But whatever happened between us, you
should know that I'm sorry. It won't occur again."

Please, let it happen. I want it to happen. I love you! A
thousand words of protest whirled through her mind, but
she said none of them. Instead she blinked her eyes
rapidly, for they felt moist. Corrie found she could not
look at Quade.

"You're right, of course. It can't happen again, ever."
Corrie swallowed. "Because I felt life," she said in a low
voice. "I felt my baby move. Avery's baby."

Quade looked stricken, exactly as if she had slapped
him. Then he turned and left the tent. He was gone for
several hours.

Now Corrie, watching the retreating backs of Eulalie
Benrush and Ellin Hardacre, took a deep breath and tried
to push back the memory of Quade's sweet caresses. For
one night, for one stolen night, she and Quade had loved
each other. And now—

"Corrie, where have you been? It's getting pitch dark
out here. It's time to get on the tram. I've been looking all
over for you."

Quade's face seemed oddly closed and grim, and his
walk was stiff and angry.

"I haven't been far," she told him. "Quade? Is anything wrong?"

"No," he said shortly.

"But you seem—"

"I said nothing is wrong, Corrie. I had something to
discuss with the roadhouse owner, that was all. Now let's
go along to the tram, all right?"

At the other end of the portage they transferred to a
sister steamer, the *Ora,* and slept aboard.

That night Corrie tossed restlessly on the hard board
bunk in the cabin allotted to the women, and listened to

the sounds of young Annie whimpering in her sleep. At
dawn the boat made a wood stop; Corrie could hear the
thump of the logs as they were loaded on board. The
smell of wood smoke filled the air.

The passengers rose and breakfasted. Corrie and Quade
paced the deck. One passenger, a Mr. Truffo, amused
himself trying to shoot birds from the boiler deck with a
repeating rifle; the explosions seemed to echo and re-
verberate against the river banks. Corrie was privately
glad that his aim was poor.

The four long days passed in a blur of rocks, bluffs,
sand bars and rushing water. The river's face changed
with each new bend, from Hootalinqua to Big Salmon,
Little Salmon, Five Finger Rapids and Rink Rapids.
Corrie clutched Quade's arm as they went through Five
Fingers, where big, rocky islands stood up like the col-
umns of a wrecked bridge. The current there was murder-
ously swift.

Below Rink Rapids were many small islands, and wide,
high banks where sand martins flew in and out of their
nests on the face of the cliffs. At first Corrie thought she
was seeing snow on the riverbanks, but Quade told her
that this was a layer of old volcanic ash.

Corrie shivered. How violent this country was, she
thought. Nothing ever happened quietly, but always with
a thunder or a roar.

Hellsgate was a narrow opening which the river had
carved through rock. Then came Fort Selkirk and a miles-
long wall of rock, solid and high. Every sound echoed as
the boat went through. Below that were more steep banks,
sand bars and islands. There were other rivers: the
Stewart, the White, the Sixty-Mile and the Indian. They
emptied violently into the Yukon, hurtling and washing at
its banks until trees toppled into the water and the river
was the color of sand.

At two o'clock on the fifth day, an afternoon drenched
with sun, they came to Dawson.

Dawson City. It stretched along the curve of river like
some exotic oriental seaport, its shoreline bristling with the
masts of thousands of boats, all jammed tightly together
and moored three, four and five deep. Many had canvas

spread over them and, Corrie noted with shock, were lived in.

She stared, open-mouthed. Dawson was like some mad combination of every town and tent city they had seen so far. Men were crowded everywhere. They paced about the waterfront, climbed on boats, lugged supplies, or loitered in the streets. Dogs sniffed at piles of provisions, trotted about, fought, barked and slept. Somewhere a goat baaed.

"Well, this is it, the place you've come all these miles for," Quade said. His face was grim. "I'll wager your Avery is here somewhere. I hope you're satisfied, Corrie."

"Oh, yes, I . . . I am," she said weakly. A painful lump filled her throat. She felt an onrush of the same panic that had struck her in Dyea. Dawson was so disorganized, so sprawling and confused. What would she do here? Where would she go? How was she to find Avery now? What if he wasn't here at all?

"They'll send lighters out to unload the steamer," Quade went on. "And then we'll have to get you lodgings. You can't stay in a hotel or you'll spend all your money. I imagine there'll be someplace where you can live respectably, though."

"But—what about you?"

The lump seemed massive now, a huge wad of cloth filling her entire chest. *Quade—oh, God, Quade—* She wanted to cry out to him, to fling herself weeping into his arms. Instead, she stood still, staring at the raw town of Dawson.

Crude, ugly, it was as desolate as her thoughts at this moment. From here she could see part of the main street which faced the river: ungainly buildings made of logs or planks, many with pilings sunk into the water itself. The buildings were silhouetted against a backdrop of swooping Yukon hills. Throngs of men roamed about, and by now she knew what they would be like—rough, boisterous, excited.

"I told you I'd help you to find your fiancé, and I will, Corrie. As soon as we dock I'll go to the claims office and to the post office. They may know where he is. I'm sure this is the likeliest spot for him to be. I'll find out where his claim is—if he's filed one yet—and I'll help you to dispatch your letter to him. But beyond that you can't expect me to go. I have business here in the Yukon, Corrie, as I've told you. There is a man I must contact here. When we were in Canyon City at the roadhouse I learned he'd been seen only a day ahead of us. He was coming up-river with a load of heavy equipment. I'd like to interview him." As he said this, Quade did not look at her.

"Do you mean you're not going to stay here with me until Avery comes?" Corrie's voice rose.

"No, I'm not. I can't, Corrie."

"But you promised! I'm paying you to stay with me, Quade—I'm paying you well!"

"I don't care about your money. I won't take any of it, Corrie. I did this as a personal favor to you, no more. You'll be all right here; I wouldn't leave you if I didn't think you would be. I'll find you a good place to stay. If all goes well, you'll be with your fiancé in a few days and then you'll be a married woman and he can take care of you."

"But you *have* to take my money!" Corrie cried wildly. "I can't allow you to bring me all this distance for no pay. I won't take your charity!"

"Be still, Corrie," He said it roughly, turning away from her so that all she could see was his profile, his bumpy nose, the firm lips and well-shaped chin. "I'm rich, Corrie, rich enough. I don't need your money, and I don't want it."

He could hardly wait to discharge himself of his obligation to her, she thought angrily.

"Then if you don't want my money, why did you bring me here?" she heard herself demand.

Quade turned and stood staring down at her so savagely that she took an involuntary step backwards. "Does it matter? What does it matter any more?" Quade turned back to the view of Dawson. "Now I'd suggest that we see about unloading our provisions. Your precious Avery is going to be very glad indeed to see all those bags of flour and sacks of corn meal that you've carted up here for him."

"You don't like Avery, do you? You've never liked him. You've always called him by those superior names—"

"Whether I approve of your fiancé or not hardly matters, does it?" Quade said angrily. "I did a job for you, and now that job is nearly finished. Oh, don't look at me that way, Cordelia Stewart. You're a grown girl now, aren't you? You came here of your own free will. No one forced you."

His right hand had thrust itself into his pocket, and Corrie knew that once again he was touching the charred brooch. His blue eyes were very cold and distant.

He found her lodgings with a woman named Millie Mussen, a widow who owned a laundry and boarding house situated on a side road at the distant end of Front Street. Millie's crude log cabin was embellished with a huge, beautifully lettered sign proclaiming, "M. Mussen's Laundry, Mending Free of Charge. Fortunes Told $1. Boarders Reasonable."

Behind the cabin were strung ten clotheslines, each one sagging with the weight of long underwear, wool pants, socks and shirts. One line at the back held a row of flannel diapers.

Millie herself turned out to be a plain woman of thirty, tall and windburned, with a matronly figure and soft, brown eyes. She came to the door to meet them, a year-old baby slung across one hip. Her hands, Corrie saw, were reddened and covered with sores from constant scrubbing with lye soap.

Quade explained what they had come for.

"Yes, I have a room. She isn't a dance hall girl or a whore, is she? If she is, she can just go to Paradise Street. I won't have her."

"No, she's perfectly respectable. She's going to wait here in town until her fiancé can come in and marry her. And you needn't worry, she has enough money to pay for her room in advance."

"Oh." Millie's eyes traveled over the sealskin cape Corrie had put on for the occasion, over her smart blue broadcloth skirt with its flared bottom flounce stitched and trimmed with matching cording. "You wouldn't drink, would you?" Millie asked.

Corrie shifted uneasily, wondering if Millie had noted her condition. But of course not, she assured herself; the full cape was concealing.

"No," she replied. "I don't drink."

"And you're clean in your habits?"

"Yes, of course I am." By this time Corrie was flushing.

"Well," Millie Mussen said. "I suppose it'll be all right. I only take one boarder at a time as I only have the one extra room, and I'd rather have a woman than a man, God knows. It's five dollars a week and I cook plain; nothing fancy, do you understand? And you'll have to help with the washing up and keep your room straight. With all I've got to do, I haven't time for it, and I'll charge you less if you help out. You can store your goods in my lean-to if you want. Is that all right?"

The baby had started to crow; she was a chubby, round-faced little thing with brown ringlets and a dimple in her chin. With a pang Corrie wondered if her own baby would be as adorable.

"Oh, yes," she said quickly. "That would be fine."

"Then it's settled," Quade said. "Give her two weeks' rent," he told Corrie. "I'm going down to the claims office and see what I can find out."

"When will you—" Under the stare of Millie Mussen, Corrie could hardly clutch at Quade's arm as she longed to do.

"I'll unload your things before I leave," he told her shortly. "It should take me a while; you've got enough provisions here to feed a regiment."

He started toward the cart they had hired. Corrie, feeling frozen, watched him.

"Well," Millie Mussen said. "No sense us standing here watching him work, is there? Come in and I'll show you your room. It's plain, God knows; there's no way of getting anything pretty up here. It doesn't even have a real window, just moose hide. But I've got some magazine pictures I can tack on the wall for you, and the place is clean."

"That sounds nice," Corrie mumbled.

She stood on the rough planks that had been flung over the mud and watched Quade for a moment longer. She felt suddenly bleak and bereft and very much alone.

✿ Chapter 21 ✿

"One whiskey, coming up."

The young bartender grinned at Donald Earle. He shoved the glass of whiskey across the polished surface of the bar, managing at the same time to give a twirl to the end of his handlebar mustache.

"How much?"

"Fifty cents a shot, the best stuff in the city of Dawson."

"Sure it is," Donald grumbled.

Donald Earle paid anyway, and then sat nursing his drink, watching idly as the barkeep, wearing a starched shirt, white apron and diamond stickpin, waited on another customer. Carefully he weighed gold dust on a small scale, catching the spills with a little square of carpet. Again he stroked his mustache and Donald wondered if he were secreting gold dust in it, to be shaken out later, after the saloon had closed. Instinctively he thought of his own money belt, safely about his middle and crammed with bills. He had worn the belt for years and now it was softened with long use, so comfortable that he barely felt it.

He sat staring at the pale liquid in his glass. The fierce burn of the whiskey going down mellowed him, numbing his physical tensions so that they became bearable.

Cordelia Stewart was here in Dawson. He had seen her twice, once emerging from that little log hut that called itself a boarding house, and two days later buying an apple from Apple Jimmie, the little pockmarked Greek

219

greengrocer who sold apples at a dollar each. She hadn't noticed him; each time he had pressed back so as to melt into the crowd. He did not want her to see him yet; he needed time to think and plan.

The little fool; she had tried to run away from him in Dyea. He twirled the glass of whiskey around, warming it with his hands and laughing dryly to himself. He could still remember his own shock when, coming out of the smithies, he had seen her, chestnut-yellow hair massed under a fur hat, gold-brown eyes wide. He had thought she hadn't come north after all, for her name had not been on the *Alki*'s passenger list. So for a moment his own surprise had been as great as hers, as powerful as an elbow punch to the pit of the belly.

Before he could react, she had whirled about and run off. He gave another snorting laugh. Where, in a city as small and as crowded as Dyea, did she think she could run from him? In five minutes she would be off the boardwalk and into the mud.

Involuntarily Donald's fingers pressed tighter on the glass as he thought of the way she had tried to cover her tracks. Bribing Captain Carter to tell him she hadn't come! Did she suppose he could not make a man like Carter tell what he knew? Did she really imagine that hotel owners and waiters would not remember her?

He frowned, staring at the beveled glass inserts which ran along the top of the mahogany bar and reflected distorted images of the whiskey ads and the two small, dark, nude paintings which graced the opposite wall. The paintings, along with the rest of the bar fixtures, had been shipped upriver from Seattle or San Francisco. Only the sawdust and mud on the floor were local.

He had guessed that she was traveling to Dawson City: it seemed logical enough. His hunch had been confirmed by that Benrush woman, with whom he had had several conversations since he had sought her out in Dyea. From other sources he learned that the man she had hired to escort her was named Quade Hill, a newspaperman who seemed to drift about from city to city, wherever he could find a story. *Hill* . . . That bastard. Donald also learned that Corrie and the journalist were sharing the same tent. Savagely he downed the whiskey in one burning gulp.

Well, let her, the little whore. And let *him* see what happens. There was no evidence, not a shred of it. Donald was not even the same man of six years ago. . . .

"Give me another. And this time make it your good stuff; I don't want any rot-gut."

"Yes, *sir*."

Donald waited while the man poured another shot and slid it across the bar to him.

Let her, he was thinking. Let her do anything she pleased. Let her run from him halfway up to the Arctic Circle if she wanted. Let her think she was going to marry that money-hunting fool Avery Curran, that milksop amateur. She'd learn. Oh, yes, she would learn that it didn't pay to snub Donald Earle, to throw his ring away.

He tilted the glass and drained its contents, his eyes watering against the sting of it. He thought fleetingly of the way Corrie Stewart would look naked, her body all golden and soft. Tight and curved and ripe. And virgin or not, it didn't matter, he told himself. Perhaps it was even better this way, more exciting. Because she would be sorry enough for what she had done. She would beg him to forgive her, beg him to allow her to make it up to him . . .

He stood up, feeling the hardness in himself, the tension again, unassuaged this time by the whiskey. Nothing would stop it for long, he knew; not a drink, not a whore, not anything. Only Corrie Stewart.

Today, he thought. Today he would talk to her.

Millie Mussen braced the wooden tub with one strong, bare arm, and cranked a set of long underwear through her wringer. The smell of wet wool and soap was strong in the air.

Corrie paced restlessly about the lean-to. The cabin had three rooms. The main room, the largest, contained Millie's and baby Alberta's bunks, a stove, a small barrel-stave-top trunk where Millie kept personal things, two slab chairs and a table. The second room was Corrie's, just barely large enough for a single bunk. The last room, at the back, was heated by another stove. Here Millie did her laundry in a series of tubs.

"Goo!" said Alberta. "Da!" She crawled happily on

the plank floor amid the piles of muddy overalls and shirts.

"Would you like me to take her out for some fresh air?" Corrie asked. She went to the back door of the lean-to and cracked it open to squint out at the bright day. "The sun is warm enough for her. And I could go to town and check the mail. It's been more than two weeks, and there must be a letter from Avery by this time. I can't understand what is taking him so long to write me."

To her vast relief, the day after they arrived in Dawson, they had finally received some word of Avery's whereabouts. "Well, my brave and foolish Corrie, it seems that we are in luck," Quade told her. His eyes were the dark blue of the evening Yukon sky. His face, rugged and tanned from the Yukon sun, looked oddly gentle. "Your fiancé filed a claim on Little Skookum, evidently only a few days before we got here. He came over the White Pass Route."

Corrie stared at him. "How do you know all that?"

"I bribed the clerk at the claims office." Quade shrugged. "You're a very lucky girl to have found him so quickly. If he hadn't filed a claim, it might have taken months to locate him. This country is big. It sucks up people and spits them out again. Men drift about here; they're like seeds blowing in the wind. And it looks as if your precious Avery isn't in any hurry to blow in your direction, Corrie."

She was angry. "That isn't true! Avery loves me; he said so in his letter! That's the reason he wants to find gold—so he can buy me the things he thinks I should have."

Quade looked quizzical. "Do you mean fancy carriages and purebred horseflesh and diamond tiaras and a big house on Nob Hill?"

"Yes, I suppose. Not that I want any of those things."

Again Corrie had to push back that odd, hurting lump at the back of her throat. Quade was looking at her intently, as if he could see right into her soul.

But when he spoke, his voice was tender, and a little sad crease twitched at the side of his mouth.

"You may not want them, darling, but he does. And he

wants them damned badly. It's plain he desires them a
hell of a lot more than he wants you."

"That's not true!"

"Isn't it? I hope to God you're right."

That had been two weeks ago, two weeks of impatient
waiting. Now Millie looked up from her wringer.

"Might be a lot of reasons he hasn't written yet," she
said. "Men get all wrapped up in gold; they go kinda
crazy over it. If he's hit a good vein, nothing will make
him leave it." She nodded. "Oh, all right, you can take
Alberta out if you want. But be careful of the dogs."

"Of course," Corrie said. Millie was deathly afraid of
the dogs which roamed the city, many of them half-wild
and hungry.

Five minutes later Corrie and Alberta—as plump and
rosy-cheeked as if she lived in California, and dressed in
a blanket-cape Millie had made her—made their way
down the crude boardwalk into town.

It had been a dull two weeks, with little but the distraction of baby Alberta for entertainment. Corrie occupied her time by doing some shopping for Millie and by
getting the mail. Once she bought an apple for the little
girl from Apple Jimmie, but felt so guilty at its exorbitant
cost that she had not dared to buy one for herself or Millie.
She hung blankets in her tiny room to make an improvised
darkroom, and took several photographs of Dawson's
turbulent streets and waterfront.

Millie Mussen, true to her word, hung three pictures
from *Cosmopolitan* and *Strand* on the wall above Corrie's
bunk. At night, by the kerosene lamp, she tried teaching
Corrie to knit.

The plain-faced woman proved to be surprisingly nice,
and she had not said an unkind word about the increasingly obvious thickening of Corrie's waistline.

"I'm sorry," Corrie told Millie one night as the two of
them sat together knitting baby comforters. "I told you
I was respectable. I don't know what you must think of
me!"

"I don't think anything at all," Millie replied cheerfully, reaching for a new skein of the precious yarn. "Babies come, and there's little we can do about it. This is
the North, you know, and things are easier here, more

free. When your Avery contacts you, you'll be married, won't you? So it will be all right."

"Yes."

Corrie had bent over the wool, not wanting Millie to see the stricken expression on her face.

Now, with the child wriggling companionably in her arms, Corrie picked her way along the boardwalk. She wore high-topped boots; Millie said that everyone in Dawson City wore them, because of the mud. Carefully she balanced on one plank of the tippy walk, then hopped on to the next. Walking here was a succession of ups and downs, with boards missing here or smashed there. In some places the sidewalk tilted perilously, the result, Millie said, of the permafrost as it melted and refroze. In places a rough log corduroy had been laid down, and in other areas sawdust from the town's three or four sawmills had been spread out to carpet the mud.

She passed by cabins much like Millie's, sod-roofed, some with windows made of green moose-hide, or even old pickle jars.

Nothing, she thought, not even a pickle jar, could ease the rawness of this place, or make it anything other than what it was, a hastily built boom town which existed only for gold and would decay as soon as the bonanza was gone.

Front Street was a hubbub of men, carts, horses, mules and dog teams. On the river side leaned a continuous row of frame buildings, booths and shacks. In crude lean-tos, you could buy a dozen eggs for eighteen dollars, four loaves of bread for a dollar, or even, to Corrie's astonishment, a "mammoth's molar" for one hundred dollars.

The walks were jammed with men in muddy boots and mackinaws. Corrie pushed past them toward the side of a hotel, where more than twenty letters had been tacked to its bare boards, and were fluttering in the wind. This rather haphazard way of receiving letters was common here, she had found, for it took a day or more of standing in line if one wanted to get mail at the post office.

While Alberta crowed and grabbed at the fastening of her cape, Corrie's eyes rapidly scanned over the posted letters. It was not a heartening sight; some had obviously been here for weeks, and the ink, smudged with moisture, was nearly illegible.

Then, as she spotted two new letters, her heart began to pound.

But the letters, one of them addressed to *R. Tripodi, City of Dawson,* and the other in an elaborate copperplate hand, were not for her. Corrie bit her lip and turned away, disappointed. Perhaps, as Millie said, it was still too early to expect to hear from Avery. She should have patience, Millie counseled. Quade, too, before he left, had reminded her that mail service was not dependable here. There were so many thousands of men and only one small, beleaguered post office.

Again her mind ranged back to the moment two weeks ago when Quade had left her. He had seemed in a hurry, his big body moving restlessly, as if he would like nothing better than to be on his way.

"There's a man going up the Bonanza," he told her. "I gave your letter to him and it should reach your fiance in a day or two. I advise you to wait here in Dawson City for him to come in and get you. Then he can arrange for a marriage service, transport of your provisions, or a steamer ticket, whichever you decide to do. Meanwhile you'll be comfortable here. Mrs. Mussen looks a respectable woman, and she'll see to it that you're all right."

"But Quade—" She clung to him. Millie was in the back of the cabin taking down her laundry, and would not see them.

"Corrie, for God's sake, will you stop acting like a clinging child?" His voice was harsh. He removed her hands and looked down at her with an odd expression. "You would think that you didn't want to be married to this Avery Curran of yours. That *is* why you came here, isn't it? To provide a father for your child? To marry, as you put it, the man you love?"

She saw that Quade's mouth was twisted into bitter mockery. She pulled away from him to stare blindly at the crude frame buildings of the main street, dwarfed by the knobbed hills behind them.

She heard his voice go on implacably. "In a matter of days your fiancé will be here to claim you. And as I told you, Mrs. Mussen will see to it that you are fine here.

She knows her way around, and I've slipped her twenty dollars, just to be certain she'll watch out for you."

"Slipped her twenty dollars! That rids you of your onerous obligation to me, does it?"

"What obligation?" Quade's smile was a bitter slash across his features. "You hired me to take you to Dawson City and to find Avery Curran for you. Well, I've done both, and what's more, I've saved your money for you. I'll send you a letter in care of Mrs. Mussen when I get myself located. Or at the Canadian Bank of Commerce, if she's not here."

"But," she said desperately, "where are you going? What are you going to do?"

"I'm going to write some stories for the *Tribune*. And I'm going to write a guidebook to the Yukon; it's desperately needed. And there is some other business—" For an instant Quade's features looked hollow, haunted.

"Well, never mind that, Corrie. Good-bye, and I hope you're happy. I'm sure you will be. Girls like you are like cats: you always land on both feet, don't you?"

With that he was gone, striding down the plank walk with rapid, loping grace.

"Quade! Oh, please wait—"

Corrie picked up her skirts and ran after him. But he didn't stop or even look back, and then he climbed into the cart he had hired to transport their luggage and was gone.

She brushed one hand across her eyes, blotting away the hot tears which filled them. Crying! she thought furiously. She was *not* crying over the likes of Quade Hill!

Two weeks later, again feeling traitorously like sobbing, she stumbled along the main street of Dawson City, her neck beginning to ache from the burden of carrying Alberta, her heart full of leaden despair.

"Caw! Caw!" The little girl was trying to say her name. Corrie buried her face in the wispy brown curls that protruded from the woolen hood which Millie had sewn for the baby. "Caw!"

The most imposing side of Front Street was that facing the river. Here the buildings were larger, and a few, such as the depot of the North American Trading and Transportation Company, were constructed of corrugated iron.

Signs strung on banners across the street caught her eye. *The Criterion, Geo. Noble, Manager. The Mascot Theater, Go Once, Go Often.* From a dance hall drifted a ribbon of high-pitched female laughter.

Corrie headed toward another building, a few doors down, where more letters were tacked outside.

"Ma'am? Ma'am? Want a paper? The *Yukon Sun,* only fifty cents a copy! Best paper in town! You get all the Spanish-American War news and all the gold news too! Also ads from our local merchants—"

"What?"

"I said a paper, lady!" The newsboy was about fourteen, thin-faced and grimy, and he stood rudely in the center of the walk in order to hustle passersby.

"Oh, all right." Corrie fished into her handbag and extracted a coin. The boy took it without comment and shoved the paper into her hand. "Tell all your friends about the *Yukon Midnight Sun,*" he ordered her. "Best paper in town."

She continued down the street, glancing at the paper, with its ads for jewelers, theaters, embalmers, dry goods stores.

An hour later, disappointed, downcast and still with no letter, she was headed back toward Millie's cabin. She did not notice the man pacing impatiently back and forth on the planks in front of the cabin until she was nearly there.

"Donald!" She felt all the blood leave her face, and she nearly dropped Alberta in her shock. The little girl let out an indignant squeal and clung to the fur of Corrie's cape.

"I see you bought a paper. Did you have a nice journey upriver?"

There was sarcasm in Donald's tone. He wore a well-cut calfskin coat and a soft hat, and with his glossy black hair and white teeth he looked jaunty and arrogant. His eyes were black and intense. And, she noted with revulsion, the scar on his hand was as ugly as ever, crescent-shaped, reddened and puckered.

Involuntarily, she stepped backwards, closer to the security of Millie's cabin. Her heart was pounding. Yet this was a public street, she scolded herself. What could Donald do to her here? She didn't have anything to be afraid of.

His eyes seemed to take in every aspect of her appearance, from dark-fringed, gold-brown eyes, to the trim, smart skirt she wore.

"A pretty woman like you should be careful on these streets, Corrie," he told her. "These Klondike men can be ruffians."

"Can they?" She let her eyes meet his.

"Who was that man you were traveling with?" he demanded.

"That was Mr. Hill. I . . . hired him to take me upriver." Corrie barely knew what she said. She kept glancing toward Millie's cabin. Little Alberta was squirming to get out of her arms. Where was Millie, anyway? If only she would come out of the cabin and rescue her!

Corrie's mind began to work rapidly. Somehow Donald had managed to follow her here. He was implacable; she knew that he would never give up. He wanted her and he meant to have her. Her thoughts raced.

She realized that Donald was still talking to her, and had been for some time.

" . . . and so you nearly fooled me. I almost concluded that you had decided not to travel north after all. Imagine my surprise when I saw you in Dyea, racing down the walk like a frightened little girl."

He smiled at her, his heavy, willful lips curled with amusement. He was enjoying her discomfort, she knew; he was somehow stimulated by her fear.

"Yes, I did run from you." She managed to say it steadily. "But that doesn't matter now. I'm engaged to marry Avery Curran, I've located his claim, and he'll be coming here to get me any day now. Any relationship you and I might have had is over now. I hope you can understand that. I'm sorry if I brought you any inconvenience . . . " She thought of his ring she'd thrown away, and flushed. "I didn't mean to do anything to hurt you."

"My, what a pretty little speech that is! Do you give it to all of your rejected suitors? Can't you get it through your head, Miss Cordelia Stewart, that I intend to marry you? That I've come all this distance to do that, and I won't be satisfied with anything less?"

Corrie stared at him. Two men were clattering along the boardwalk only a few hundred feet away; she took courage from their nearness. Surely there was little that Donald could do to her here, at the end of Dawson's string of cabins and buildings, within a half mile of throngs of people.

"I'm sorry, but I am planning to marry Avery and nothing can alter my decision. I'm sorry if that hurts you, but—"

Faced with the hard black of his eyes, she was floundering. He moved closer to her, one hand reaching out to grasp hers and with a panicky feeling she remembered the day they had read the will, when he had carried her up to her room.

"Corrie, you don't understand." His voice was low, choked. "I came here to make money—I won't deny it. I've made contacts here, investors willing to take a chance on my ideas. But the other reason was you. I've got to have you; I need you, and I want you to come to me. Not only because of your father's estate—although you can't deny both of our lives would be better if we had full control over his holdings. But also . . . "

Donald's fingers tightened convulsively on hers, the scar visible and ugly.

" . . . but also," he went on, "because I've got you in my blood. You were thirteen when I first saw you. Just thirteen and already a woman—I could see it in your eyes, and in the way you carried your body . . . "

"Donald—" Panicking, she tried to pull her hand away from his. "I've told you that what you want is impossible. Please let go of me. I understand how you must feel, but—"

"*Do* you? Do you understand the nights when I've lain awake, planning for the time when you'd come to me? When I think of the money I spent on that ring you threw in the streets as if it had been garbage, as if *I* were garbage . . . "

Corrie took a frightened step backwards. *Why* didn't Millie come out of the cabin?

"Donald," she told him, "don't you see that my papa should never have encouraged you as he did? His money doesn't mean anything to me; I don't care whether I get twenty per cent of it or none of it at all. And Avery doesn't care, either. We're going to be married and we're going to be happy. Nothing else matters; not my father's estate and not you!"

Donald's eyes flared with anger and Corrie continued hastily, "As for you, if you try one thing to stop me—just one thing—I'll write a letter to Amos Bardley, my father's executor, and I'll tell him exactly what you've been doing, harassing me and following me about. He—he'll negate the will!"

She was on shaky ground, for she had no idea whether this was possible, but she didn't care. All she knew was that Donald had stepped back, and was eyeing her with shocked disbelief.

She plunged on. "Yes, he'll charge you with wrongdoing, and he'll remove you from the list of my father's heirs! And he *will* do it, too, don't think he won't. Mr. Bardley has known me since I was a child and is an old family friend."

"Very well." Donald's lips were compressed into a sullen line. "I'll see about that. I'll consult a solicitor here and I'll just see."

"Do that!" Corrie cried, her control slipping. "Go ahead and try, if you wish. But it won't do you any good. I don't ever wish to see you again."

"All right, Corrie." Donald's complexion had turned a mottled shade of gray-red. "You've made yourself very clear, haven't you? But you're making a mistake. Today I bought a claim at Number Eight Bonanza, from a man who got sick. My partners and I are going out there tomorrow to start installing our equipment. If you want to tell me you've changed your mind—"

"I'll never change my mind!"

"I think you will. I'm a patient man, Corrie. By the terms of your father's will, I have fifteen months left in which to persuade you to change your mind; I can wait. And I do have ways of getting what I want."

🐿 Chapter 22 🐿

Corrie tossed and turned on the narrow bunk in Millie
cabin, trying to sleep. It was the Fourth of July, a time
for much celebration in Dawson City, judging from the
number of exploding firecrackers, shouts, squeals and
whinnies which came from the center of town, blown on
the warm, bright air.

For three days now, hordes of men had been streaming
into town for the festivities. A platform had been built
for the celebrations, although, as Millie dryly said, the
city needed outhouses much more desperately than it
needed reviewing stands. Earlier today had been the pa-
rade, followed by speeches and contests, held under the
big, garish streamers which the merchants had strung on
poles across the mud. Men had even perched on roofs in
order to see everything clearly. Now probably right at this
very minute, Corrie thought dully, Cad Wilson, a well-
known "danseuse" at the saloon, was probably dancing
wearing a belt of gold nuggets. Men had talked of little
else for days.

Corrie turned on her stomach and buried her face in
the rough ticking of her pillow, stopping her ears against
the bang of the firecrackers.

If only it were dark! Then perhaps she could sleep.
But it wasn't dark; incredibly, unnaturally, it was light
for virtually twenty-four hours now; June twenty-first had
been the longest day of the year. And, as if they had
gone berserk in the constant sunlight, plants, flowers and
grasses were growing to double the size that could be ex-

pected in San Francisco. Millie had planted a lettuce garden on the sod roof of her cabin; she and Corrie had already picked huge onions and radishes. Everything here seemed to thrive on the steady sun.

Even the mosquitoes, she thought, slapping at one. They, too, seemed to relish the sunlight, as well as the blood of any human, horse, mule or dog they could find. Little Alberta was covered with bites. Corrie and Millie were, too, although Millie had told her that the mosquitoes of Dawson were "civilized" compared with those around the creeks and gold beds.

Corrie tossed and turned, trying to achieve a comfortable position on the narrow pine bunk. She was about five months along now, she calculated. In only four more months, her child would be born. By then, she must have found Avery, so that her baby would have a name and a father. . . .

But that might not be easy. She tried to be patient, as Millie had counseled. She had waited long weeks now, with no word from Avery. Desperately, she had sent him another letter, paying a miner five dollars to deliver it personally. Two of the men for whom Millie did laundry asserted they had seen him at his claim on Little Skookum. They said he was in fine health.

But still he sent no word.

Mingled with her fear and humiliation was anger. She wanted to storm out to the claim to find him and, in fact, had been about to do so when Millie stopped her.

"Don't do it, Corrie," the other woman had advised. "In the first place, travel out there would be rough for a woman unescorted. But there's also your condition. Why, the other men would laugh at him, and he would hate you for it. Besides, you would have to come back to town anyway to find a preacher to marry you. No, you'd best wait here for him. I tell you, some of these men go half-crazy when they hit a good vein of color. They don't sleep or eat, they don't want to do anything but sluice for gold. My husband, Bill, was like that. When he was panning a hundred dollars a day, he barely knew I was alive."

Was that the reason Avery didn't come? Or was there something more? Corrie moved restlessly about on the bunk, trying to push aside her misgivings. She could almost hear Avery's voice: *I'm not going to be poor, Corrie.* And Quade's: *It looks as if your precious Avery isn't in any hurry to blow in your direction.*

"Corrie? Oh, Corrie, are you awake?" Millie's voice interrupted her jumbled thoughts.

"Yes." She sat up. Millie, clad in a shapeless cotton nightgown, came into her room, holding a basin of water. She looked very tired.

"Corrie, it's Alberta. I told you she had the summer diarrhea—"

"Yes?" In spite of herself, Corrie felt a prick of panic. For the past three days the baby had been listless with what Millie called a "summer complaint." It was caused, Millie maintained, by the crowding here, and by the fact that it was so hard to get condensed milk. They had already used all of the milk that Corrie had brought with her.

"Well," Millie rushed on, "it's worse than I thought. She's hot, she's burning up with fever now. And she looks terrible. Corrie, would you get a doctor for me? I'm sorry to wake you up, but I don't think I should wait until morning."

"All right." Corrie got out of bed and began pulling on her clothes, grabbing the first garments she saw on the nail. During these weeks she had grown fond of little one-year-old Alberta, with her chirpy voice and unflagging energy. She had even prayed that her own baby would be as healthy and appealing as Millie's. Now this had happened.

"Go right to Front Street and ask for Dr. Bourke," Millie ordered her. In spite of her calm voice she managed to convey desperation. "He has a log building right on the street; I pass it every day. I hope he's available; oh, Corrie, he's got to be!"

"Dr. Bourke, Front Street," Corrie repeated.

"That's right. Wear a cloak, Corrie, against the mosquitoes. And do be careful; it's the Fourth of July. Oh, I wish you didn't have to go! I wouldn't ask you if Alberta didn't need a doctor so badly."

Corrie pushed her way among the throngs of celebrating men, trying not to look at the ones who staggered in and out of the saloons or at the youth who leaned against

the post of a hotel and vomited copiously onto the boardwalk.

Twice hands plucked at her sleeve and slurred voices
tried to detain her. Each time, with a frightened little
cry, Corrie twisted away and hurried on. Some of the
men carried bottles hidden in their coats, out of view of
the red-coated Mounties who patrolled the town. The
Mounties would run out of space in their stockade tonight, Corrie thought, stifling a nervous laugh.

She raced on until there was a stitch in her side and
she had to slow down to a walk. It was nearly midnight,
and all respectable women at this hour were safely behind cabin or hotel doors.

She found Dr. Bourke's office, a log structure with a
canvas awning and a painted sign which thrust out over
the boardwalk. Six men were sprawled on the boards in
front of it, playing cards. They barely looked up as she
stumbled up to the stout wooden door and began pounding on it.

"He ain't there," one of them finally informed her. He
was in his mid-twenties, untidy and muddy. But he was
clean-shaven and seemed sober.

"Do you know where he is, then? A child is sick!"

"He took off from here about two hours ago. Said
there was a cabin fire somewhere—some damned fool
got careless with his stove and two of 'em were burned
bad. Pardon my language, ma'am."

"Oh, but I need—

The men turned back to their game. Corrie stood there
helplessly. What was she to do now?

"Please—" She plucked at the sleeve of the man who
had first spoken to her. "Please, do you know of any
other doctors here in town? I've got to have one right
away! Alberta is terribly sick, and she's only a year old.
She—"

"Go on over to the hospital, then. The beds are all
taken and I heard that you have to wait for a man to die
to get one. But there might be doctors there." The man
lay down his cards, his expression softening. "And good
luck."

"Thank you."

She hurried on toward the hospital—St. Mary's, it was
called, run by the sisters of St. Anne. A big street banner,

she remembered now, had advertised "tickets" which the miners could buy for fifty dollars to insure a year's worth of health care.

But at the hospital the superintendant, Father Judge, came hurrying out to tell her that all of the doctors were out on calls. "It's the Fourth of July and we've had a lot of accidents. Both Dr. Barrett and Dr. Thompson are doing what they can; it's been hectic. As it is, I don't know where we're going to put any new patients. We're full up with typhoid here."

"But a baby is ill! You can't tell me there aren't any more doctors!"

"Well, perhaps . . . There is one doctor who is new in town. I heard that he injured his leg in a boat accident and had to give up mining. You'll find him in a log cabin near the bank." Father Judge gave a vague wave of his hand. "Sebastian's his name, yes, that's it. I feel sorry for the man. He had to give up his claim."

Corrie brought Will Sebastian back with her, the slender young doctor supporting himself awkwardly with two hand-carved pine canes. He had injured his knee when his boat overturned on the Yukon below Whitehorse Rapids, he told them with a wry twist of his humorous mouth. Fine light brown hair tumbled half into his eyes, and brown eyes smiled at them both.

He went on anyway, and looked for a claim to stake, but a second, painful fall brought a recurrence of the knee injury. He had been forced to return to Dawson City.

"Have you been letting this child drink out of the common drinking cups?" he asked Millie sharply.

"What? Do you mean the cups in the town? Of course not!" Millie's eyes filled with indignant tears.

"Each person should have his own drinking cup, and you should boil your water first. People buy door-to-door water here, and they've no conception of what they're getting. Also, folks build outhouses anywhere it takes their fancy, and all of it drains back into the river. I keep telling people these things. Why won't they listen?"

"Is it my fault that Alberta's so sick?" Wetness shone on Millie's cheeks. "I didn't know, doctor. I never would have . . . if I'd known."

"Of course you didn't know." Abruptly Will Sebastian's voice softened. He gave Millie a pat on the shoulder. "Just remember to boil your water next time, all right?"

He examined the baby, then reached into his scuffed black leather bag which looked as if it had fallen into the river with him, and extracted a vial full of a whitish powder.

"Here," he said. "Get me a spoon and add some boiled water to this. We've got to get fluids into her as fast as we can, and we've got to keep sponging her until the fever breaks. I don't think this is typhoid, just a bad case of fever and diarrhea. She's pretty dehydrated, but I think we can help her."

"Oh, thank God," Millie breathed.

Will Sebastian grimaced. "Let's not send up any prayers of thanks just yet. We have a long night ahead of us."

The doctor himself took charge of sponging the baby, his slim, strong hands wiping Alberta's body with the dampened rag with surprising gentleness.

"I had a little daughter of my own," he mused at one point when Millie was nearly swaying with her exhaustion and Corrie, holding the basin, trembled with fatigue. "She died in infancy. That was before my wife left me."

"Oh," Corrie said. "I'm sorry."

"Don't be. It happened, and it's over now. I saw that friend of yours here in Dawson yesterday," he added abruptly.

"What?"

"Your friend. The little girl with the broken leg. Li Hua, was that her name?" Will Sebastian's voice seemed to linger over the syllables of the Chinese girl's name, as if his tongue savored them.

Corrie jerked upright in the homemade pine chair. "Did you say *Li Hua?*"

He nodded.

"But she's not in Dawson; she can't be! She's gone home to San Francisco."

"Oh, she's here, all right, with a nice pair of whittled canes to get about on." He looked ruefully down at his own knee. "She and I make quite a pair, we do."

Li Hua, here in Dawson! Corrie struggled with her

shock and dismay. "But why? Why would she come here? I don't understand!"

"I don't know. Nonetheless, she is here." Something in Will's voice told Corrie that the subject was closed. She saw that there was a dulled red flush along his cheekbones. Why, he likes her, she thought numbly.

"Boil some more water, will you, please?" he ordered her. "And then strain it through muslin and cool it."

The hours passed slowly. Finally Millie, her face gray and puffy, slumped down on the other bunk and fell heavily asleep.

"You'd better go and get some sleep, too," Will Sebastian told Corrie, brushing a strand of soft hair out of his eyes.

"No, I'm all right."

"You're tired. Please go and sleep. I can handle this; I've done it often enough before, God knows."

By morning Alberta's fever had broken. She drank three cupfuls of cooled water and, to Corrie's delight, was sucking on a hard biscuit. Better still, her bowels were no longer running.

Millie was ecstatic. After she pressed money into Will Sebastian's hands, she continued to grip his fingers with her own, her eyes filled with tears. "I don't know what we would have done without you! You saved her, Dr. Sebastian, I know you did. It's a miracle."

He managed to look both embarrassed and slightly quizzical. "Miracle? Children are tough little animals, and your daughter is no exception. I'll wager that in a day she'll be creeping all over the floor and getting into mischief again."

"I can't wait," gloated Millie.

"All I ask is that you boil your water and keep your outhouse away from the cabin. Kill all the flies you find, too," he went on in a sterner voice. "You women *must* do this if you expect to remain well this summer. Typhoid— the real thing—is rampant here, and a lot of men are going to die from it. They won't keep themselves clean, and they will persist in sharing drinking cups. I've seen cups in saloons that hundreds have drunk from, one right after the other, and sixty percent of them turn the cup toward the handle, thinking it'll be cleaner there."

He limped toward the door. "Well, I'm going to be practicing here for a time, I guess. We may see each other again—in pleasanter circumstances, I hope."

For the rest of the day, Corrie and Millie took turns sleeping while one sat with Alberta. In the late afternoon, Corrie awakened after her nap and found that Millie had washed all of Alberta's diapers and had hung some on the line and some by the stove to dry them faster. Smiling, Millie informed Corrie that she was going to go down to Front Street to buy some champagne. Twenty minutes later, she had returned with two bottles.

"Oh, I suppose it's very foolish and unladylike for the two of us women to drink such stuff all by ourselves," she said gaily. "But I just have to celebrate. Alberta is all I have left now, Corrie. And the way I look, over thirty, and plump and plain as I am, I may never get another husband, so she may be my last baby. And she's saved, she's well. I feel as if I want to celebrate. Will you have some champagne with me, Corrie?" Millie brandished the bottle. "I didn't know which kind to buy; I just had to take what they gave me. I hope this is all right."

"Yes, of course. But, Millie, you're not plain at all!" Corrie said vehemently. "Of course a man will want to marry you, as nice and generous as you are."

"I doubt it." However, Millie's face had lit up, and gaily she began rummaging about for something with which to remove the cork.

"I've never opened wine before, have you, Corrie? I'm sure I'll be all thumbs at it. But we have to do something. Oh, I can't just sit here as if everything were very ordinary!"

While Alberta slept—a peaceful, relaxed slumber this time—Corrie and Millie managed, with a knife, to get the champagne opened without losing more than one-fourth of the contents, which sprayed all over the floor in an extravagant whoosh. They laughed, poured the remaining clear, golden fluid into cups, and tasted it.

"Bubbles!" Millie said in wonderment. "It bubbles and prickles my tongue."

Corrie had never seen Millie like this, so young and

light-hearted, almost as effervescent as the wine she poured. Was this what Millie had been like when she was younger, before she had been married and widowed, before her hands had gotten so raw? Had Millie once been pretty?

Alberta continued to sleep. Huddled on her tummy, she made snuffly noises, her small hindquarters thrust up just as usual. Although they hadn't intended to do so, Corrie and Millie finished the first bottle and opened the second one.

She was getting drunk, Corrie told herself, accepting another glass of the golden liquid. The cabin was actually whirling about her, and the diapers draped by the stove seemed to tilt and glow fuzzily.

Corrie's muscles were relaxed, her brain giddy. She felt more optimistic than she had since she arrived here. Surely her wait was almost over. Avery would send for her soon, perhaps even tomorrow. In a few months she would have her own husband, her own baby to hold.

Then, like a shadow of a cloud moving across the big Yukon sun, Corrie's thoughts darkened. It was Quade, she thought dully, who should be coming for her, Quade Hill in whose arms she wanted to be . . .

Grimly she swallowed more of the bubbly liquid. She heard herself talk to Millie, but what she said, she didn't know. They prepared a light supper, paced about the cabin, poured out the last drop of champagne. At last they said good-night to each other and went to bed.

At midnight, disturbed by a gust of wind coming through the open window, one of Alberta's diapers, hung too near the stove, began to smolder. Shortly afterward, it ignited into flames.

Corrie was dreaming that she was back on the *Alki* and that somehow Quade was aboard with her, both of them standing at the steamer's rail and gazing out at the daunting, mist-draped beauty of the Lynn Canal.

It's my sister, you see, Quade was saying. *Ila. She's in the brooch. Her spirit, or ghost, or whatever you want to call it. She's there. When I take it out I can see her in that cameo face. She looks up at me, Corrie, and sometimes I can hear her screaming. Silent screams, Corrie. They are the worst kind. . . .*

Gritting her teeth as she slept, Corrie tossed about, attempting to wrench herself away from Quade's impossible, disturbing words. No, it was not possible for a girl to haunt a brooch—for her spirit to be embedded in stone and metal. What nonsense!

She fell deeper into sleep. As she tossed and turned, Quade came once more to her dream. This time they were in the tent again, and Quade held her close, both of them aching with desire for one another.

Darling, he whispered. *My darling Delia.*

A big, tall, powerful man, his hands were nonetheless incredibly gentle. They caressed her with a deep, abiding love, as if she were the most precious woman on earth. And joyfully she pressed herself against him, lost herself in his embrace . . .

Then, frustratingly, it all slipped away. Corrie stirred again, climbing rapidly to consciousness. Something was wrong. Something was very wrong.

She forced open her eyes; drew a deep, troubled breath. Smoke. She smelled smoke. The realization jolted her.

"Millie! Millie!" She was groggy with sleep and champagne, but somehow she managed to throw aside the blanket and stagger toward the main room of the cabin where Millie and the baby slept.

She froze in the doorway. In the half-light which streamed in through the window she could see the red puff of flames which had enveloped the sheet-metal stove and was already reaching up to take the last of the diapers that Millie had hung there. One burning square of flannel had fallen upon the small, round-backed trunk where Millie kept letters, magazines and important personal papers.

"Millie!" Corrie screamed. "Wake up!"

"What?" The other woman sat up groggily in her bunk and began to cough.

"The cabin's on fire! Oh, God, Millie!" Corrie rushed to her and, not knowing what else to do, gave the woman a sharp slap on the cheek. Then she grasped Millie's arm and dragged the heavy, inert body onto the floor. Millie, however, did not get up, but lay where she had fallen, coughing.

"Millie, wake up, I tell you! There's a fire!" Desperately, past all kindness, Corrie slapped her again.

This time, to Corrie's immense relief, Millie got to her hands and knees and began to stagger to her feet. "Bertie . . . "

Corrie did not know she could move so quickly. She dashed over to Alberta's bunk, scooped up the sleeping baby, and then, choking with smoke, pulled the stumbling Millie out of the cabin.

"Thank God you got Bertie, oh, thank God," Millie was babbling. "But, Corrie, oh, your money! In the trunk—oh, my God, our money."

Ten minutes later, with the help of four men who lived in a nearby tent, and for whom Millie did washing, the fire was out. Shaken and weak, Corrie and Millie counted up the damage. The log structure, although smoke-blackened, was basically undamaged. Millie had been lucky in that respect. With a few repairs and some scrubbing, the cabin would be as good as new. Even the laundry, soaking in water-filled tubs, was untouched.

But their money was gone. Corrie, whose rounded belly had grown too large for the money belt, had stored her funds in Millie's trunk. Now the chamois, together with the paper bills it contained, was blackened and charred, worthless.

Corrie was penniless.

❧ Chapter 23 ❧

"Don't worry, Corrie," Millie assured her. "You can stay here rent free. I can get along without the money, and besides, I owe you for saving Alberta's and my life. No matter what I do, I can never repay you for that."

Corrie suddenly realized just how much she had depended on her money now that she was without it. It had always been there, a cushion against disaster, a protection as real as if Cordell Stewart himself were there to guard her. Now that it was gone, she felt curiously naked. Li Hua had once called her a spoiled little rich brat. Perhaps, Corrie thought, to some extent she had been right.

Still, she would not be poor for long, she reminded herself. She immediately wrote to Aunt Susan for more money and she hoped to hear from her within a month or so, before the river closed to boat traffic. Avery, she assured her aunt in the letter, had been delayed in the gold fields but would soon come to town for her. Everything was going to be fine.

What a liar I am, she thought bleakly as she sealed the envelope. For days she clung to hope, trying to push back her growing despair. Avery would come; he had to! Several times it occurred to her that Donald Earle might be at the root of Avery's nonappearance. Was he somehow paying Avery not to come? Rapidly she shoved aside this thought. Whatever Avery's faults, surely he would never countenance such a dishonorable action. Surely the delay, whatever it was, was legitimate.

Millie, however, seemed undaunted by the fire, and Corrie tried to keep her own worries to herself. She worked with Millie to extract the bits of melted gold from the trunk; Millie's own savings had not been much damaged. She helped to scrub the cabin and to finish the laundry that was piled up. As she cranked the wringer and lugged heavy tubs of clothes outdoors, she began to develop a respect for Millie's courage in doing these things day after day without complaining.

In increasing desperation, Corrie continued to check for a letter from Avery. She would give him one more week, she decided. Then she would go out to his claim and find him, whether the miners laughed at her or not, and whatever the hardships might be. Perhaps, she told herself, she had made a mistake in not telling Avery of her pregnancy in the letters she had sent him. She dreaded appearing before him with her rounded belly and surprising him with the fact of his impending fatherhood. Surely breaking the news to him would be easier if he himself came to town and she could see him within the comfort of Millie's cabin, with Millie herself nearby.

But if he did not come soon, she would have to summon all of her boldness and courage and seek him out herself.

Three days after the fire, after she was returning from a fruitless trip to the post office, she noticed that a new sign had been erected in front of a small log house which had previously housed a small iron goods store. The sign, handsomely lettered in big curlicues by one of the professional sign painters in town, read "Pear Blossom Salon, Hair Care for Ladies. Palms Read, $1."

Corrie paused. Pear Blossom. Why did that name cause her heart to beat faster?

As she stood staring at the sign, two fashionably dressed women emerged from the salon, the scent of attar of roses drifting with them. Both were beautiful. One, auburn-haired, wore a dress of light green silk elaborately trimmed with darker bands of green satin at the puffed shoulders, breast and hem. The lines of the gown flowed lushly to reveal a large-breasted figure with a tiny waist.

The other girl, slimmer and younger, wore buff-colored brocaded satin. Her blonde hair was puffed and arranged in a confection of tight curls and switches, into which silk roses had been artfully woven.

Both had soft skin, pink, avid lips, insouciant walks. . . .

Corrie caught her breath as she realized who these women were. They were Klondike dancers, of course—the gorgeously plumaged, high-spirited and notorious women who performed on the makeshift stages of the dance halls . . . for money or the gold nuggets which the enthusiastic miners tossed at their feet.

And the auburn-haired one—Corrie heard the other girl call her Cad—must be Cad Wilson, the famous girl who danced wearing the gold nugget belt, which was reputed to have been given her by a group of the richest "Eldorado Kings." Rumor had it that the belt went around her waist one and a half times.

The dancer named Cad had sultry gray eyes and a pouting mouth. She nodded to Corrie who plucked up her courage. "Please, could you tell me who owns that salon?"

"Why, it's a Chinese woman. They call her Li Hua."

"Did you say Li Hua?" Corrie stared at Cad Wilson. Her heart slammed inside her chest. Pear Blossom, of course, was the English meaning of Li Hua's name. So the oriental girl was here, just as Will Sebastian had said! Yet all these weeks, Corrie had avoided looking for her, remembering how her former friend and servant had betrayed her.

Cad Wilson eyed Corrie curiously. "Yes, do you know her?"

"Once, a long time ago—"

"Well, she's a tough one, she is. She's very good with hair, though, and she can make anyone look beautiful—if it pleases her to do it."

Dazedly Corrie murmured something, then she turned and stumbled into the Pear Blossom Salon. Li Hua was a traitor. Still, something urged her through that door, something inside her wanted to see what Li Hua had become.

The salon was a small single room furnished with a sheet-iron stove, a bunk, and a table and chairs fashioned out of log slabs. Some attempts had been made to beautify these surroundings; the bunk held a gaily striped woolen blanket, and the rough table had been spread with an embroidered cloth. On the table, in even precision, were

arranged combs, brushes, bottles of pomade, a curling
iron, an assortment of China and steel beads, jet and
paste-jewelled combs and hair lock retainers.

Two women were in the cabin; one, wearing a plain
shirtwaist and skirt, was seated at the table with her back
to Corrie. Her blue-black hair was dressed in a plain, soft
pompadour.

The other, a plump girl with a discontented face, was
obviously a customer. She was saying, "No, I don't want it
smooth, I want plenty of curls, and I want it sort of pulled
back and up—like this—and then breaking into a sort of
puff, like. Do you know what I mean? I want to look
pretty, dammit!"

As Corrie stood frozen, the dark-haired woman inclined her head, the gesture almost mockingly servile. Yet
the customer did not seem to notice, and went on with
her orders, preening in a small hand mirror which the
other held up for her.

"I want you to make me look like Cad Wilson! You
made her look good—well, I want to look good, too. I'll
take that jet thing, and the one with all the sparkles. How
much you charging? Whatever it is, I can pay it. I got
plenty of gold dust."

"All right. That will be ten dollars for the comb and
another ten for the jet circlet."

"Ten dollars!"

But Corrie barely heard the prostitute's outrage.

"Li Hua!" she was gasping. "Li Hua, is it really you?"

The oriental woman turned, dropping the beaded comb
onto the floor. Corrie saw a lovely, pale oval face,
widened dark eyes, a mouth open in dismay. Li Hua's
eyes, she noted, looked weary, infinitely tired.

"Corrie!"

Absurdly, Corrie's eyes were moist, and she dashed at
them with her fist.

"Say, what is this?" demanded the plump prostitute. "*I*
was here first! You got to wait your turn, honey," she said
to Corrie, eyeing her distended belly.

Corrie ignored her. "Li Hua, you were supposed to go
on to Dyea and take passage for home!"

The other's face twisted. "Well, I didn't, did I?"

"Say, just a minute here, Pear Blossom or whatever

your name is," put in the customer. "You got to do me, not her, or I'm not going to pay you. Hear that, you little slanty-eyed bitch? I ain't got time to sit here and listen to the two of you jabber. I got a busy night tonight; I got to go back and rest up."

"Very well." Li Hua gave Corrie a quick look from under her lashes and bent to pick up the comb. She turned to the plump girl. "Choose the jewels you'd like, Miss," she said coldly.

"All right, I will. I'd like that one. No, not that, the one with all the jet things—"

Corrie picked up her skirts, adjusted the light wool shawl she wore, and moved to the door. In an instant she was back out on Front Street, with its pedestrians, its newsboy hawking papers, a woman selling fresh-baked loaves of bread.

But still she did not move away from the cabin. Something held her, and she waited on the walk. Li Hua's face had looked so . . . so changed, her loveliness hardened, yet more fragile now, as if something had hurt her very badly.

A few minutes later, the fat prostitute had emerged from the cabin, a flat sailor hat pinned insecurely to a great mound of bejewelled hair. She swept past Corrie in a rustle of petticoats and a swirl of cheap perfume.

Corrie pushed open the cabin door and reentered. "Your sign says that you read palms," she said quickly to Li Hua, adjusting the knitted shawl she wore so that it concealed her figure. "I'd like you to read mine. I'd like to know just what the future holds for me."

Li Hua rose from her chair and stood by the stove, leaning on a cane and rubbing her left hand tiredly over her face. She looked smaller and more fragile than Corrie remembered. When she took a step, Corrie heard the thump of her plaster cast against the plank flooring.

"I don't want to read your future, Corrie. You and I both know what it's going to be. As is plain to see, you're expecting a baby, and, as far as I can tell, there is no wedding ring on your finger yet."

"Avery is coming for me! He has received my letter but he's been delayed because of work on a good vein, that's all!"

"Oh, really?"

Corrie felt anger tremble through her body. "I thought you weren't going to be a servant, Li Hua. And here you are, doing the hair of these—these women. At least when you worked for us, you worked in a decent house for respectable people. Now look at you. Doing hairdos for prostitutes! Whatever has happened to you, Li Hua?"

The other girl sat down in a crude chair so suddenly that it rocked under her weight. "I'd rather not tell you. Please go away, Corrie. I don't want to see you."

"But your sign says you read palms. I want mine read," Corrie demanded.

"All right." Li Hua sighed. "I'll read your palm and then you'll have to go. I have more customers coming. I've been doing a very good business here," she added dully.

Corrie thrust out her palm and Li Hua took it in her own small, smooth, cool hand. She held it a moment and Corrie could feel her shaking. Then, abruptly, she let Corrie's hand drop.

"I don't know any more about reading palms than you do."

"But your sign says—"

"So it does. And I make up something pleasant: I tell them they have a long life line and that there is a good-looking man in their future. I try to vary it so that if they compare notes later they won't feel they've been cheated."

"Oh. Yes, that's what Millie does, too, with the miners. Only she tells them that there is gold in their futures."

Li Hua smiled faintly. "People will believe anything good. To them, Dawson City is a place of hope. They think that they're going to strike it rich, to find a mother lode of pure gold or the world's richest man, or whatever. But they don't know. For every nugget of gold, there is something dirty here. Something ugly and frightening."

"Li Hua? What are you talking about?"

There was a long silence, broken only by the sound of a group of miners passing in front of the cabin, laughing loudly.

"I was raped." Li Hua's voice was tight and strange. "Or 'broken in,' as they put it. I don't even know how many times they had me. I lost count. I was helpless with my cast, and I couldn't run, and they took away my crutches. They shoved me into a tent and they tied my skirts up over my head and they—"

Li Hua swallowed convulsively. "I was picked up afterward by a boy named Marty Javenall. A good boy, a banker's son, from Seattle, who thought it would be rather pleasant and exciting to have his own woman with him. He brought me here. Got me over the Pass and past the Mounties and upriver on his boat. Of course, I paid him to . . ."

"Li Hua!"

"That's right, I became a whore." Li Hua rose from the chair and hobbled to the rear of the cabin where the bunk was neatly covered with the striped blanket. She stood staring down at the bed, her hand rigid on the cane. "Marty wanted what I had, and I gave it to him for a price. What did it matter? So what if that makes me a whore? It also makes it quite all right if I become a hairdresser for dancers and those creatures that you saw. I'm not any better than they are."

"But . . ." Corrie struggled to contain her shock, to make sense of all this. "But what about the man who brought you here? What happened to him?"

"Marty's dead." Li Hua spoke in a monotone. "He's been dead nearly a week, from typhoid. I took him over to the hospital and they finally gave him a bed, but it was too late. He died. Crying and suffering and calling out for his mother; he didn't even know I was there. I went back to his tent and took all of his money and bought myself this cabin."

She lifted her chin defiantly. "I didn't have any right to it; I should have sent it all home to his parents. But I couldn't. I have to live, I have to have something, don't I, for all I've gone through?"

Corrie did not know what to say.

"I was the one who told Donald Earle where you were, too. He—he pulled me into his buggy and he took me to his house and he . . . he forced me. . . ." Again she swallowed. "He made me tell him everything. I never knew there were men like that. He threatened to sell me to a brothel in Chinatown, a place where they keep the girls locked up and never let them out, where they do terrible things to them. I didn't want to go there. I was frightened, and I hated it, but I told him about you, just as he demanded. So you see, Corrie, I really am a whore, and whores have no morals. Didn't you know that?"

Corrie stared at the girl who had once been her servant and friend. Rabbit-foot McGee, she thought suddenly. It was as if she could almost see him again, feel his stubby fingers grabbing at her, hear Quade's voice, crisp with anger. *He could have thrown you down a stairwell somewhere and locked you in a room.*

A deep shudder went through her body. If the situation had been reversed, if it had been she herself instead of Li Hua—would she have held out against such terrifying threats? *Could* she have?

Sudden tears burned at the backs of her eyes. She stumbled toward the girl she had known since they were thirteen.

"Li Hua— Oh, God, Li Hua—"

Somehow they were in each other's arms, holding each other tightly. Li Hua sobbed into the front of Corrie's shirtwaist, and Corrie cried too.

"I'm sorry, Corrie, so damned sorry," Li Hua wept. "I felt terrible, I wanted to tell you so badly, and I was ashamed. I was weak, Corrie. Weak! I shouldn't have betrayed you, I should have been braver—"

"Braver!" Corrie choked, thinking of Rabbit-foot Mc-Gee, of Donald's brutal strength. "Oh, Li Hua, don't feel bad. Please don't. I might have done the same thing you did, I'll never know for sure. . . ."

They cried together for a few more moments, then Li Hua pulled back and, forcing a shaky smile, produced two lawn handkerchiefs, their scalloped edges embroidered in the finest and most intricate pattern of fleur de lis.

"Here." She gave one to Corrie and used the other herself. "I sell these things, too, did you know?" Her mouth gave a brief, bitter twist. "So that Dawson whores can make believe they are real ladies . . . "

She poured tea, and the two exchanged stories on what had happened to them since they had seen each other last. An hour later, still feeling shaken, Corrie was back out on Front Street.

Li Hua had told her everything—everything about Donald. Corrie quickened her pace but was unable to forget Li Hua's story.

"He is enraptured by fire and flames. He is obsessed by them in a terrible, terrible way . . . "

I never knew there were men like that. He did such unspeakable things . . . Oh, poor Li Hua! How horrible for her. How he used her . . .

Corrie felt filled with a perspiring horror. And to think that Donald had been able to secure Papa's trust! How could her father have been taken in like that? Did he want a son so very badly that he was able to blind himself to a man like Donald?

Li Hua assured Corrie that she was not to worry about her. "I'll be fine here. I have a little business now, and a bit of gold dust left, too. And I'm planning to make more. There's money to be made here by people who are smart enough to take what they can."

"Money? Plans? But Li Hua—"

The other girl had turned stubbornly away, her narrow back held straight. "I'd rather not talk about it yet, Corrie. I tried to contact my cousin; he was supposed to be in Valdez. I haven't heard from him, and for all I know he could be dead by now. So there is no one here to tell me what to do."

"But I wouldn't—"

"Wouldn't you? I'm a whore now, remember?" Li Hua's shoulders were rigid. "Whether it pleases you or not, Corrie, that's what I am."

Corrie stumbled blindly toward Millie's, barely aware of the uneven, half-rotted boards that jutted up to trip her. Donald. Li Hua. How long ago it seemed since she and Li Hua had romped together on the street with Corrie's dog, Biggie . . .

She passed the claims office, noting that, as usual, there was a long line of men spilling out onto the walk, waiting to file their claims. Most of them, directly in from the creeks, were muddy, their faces welted with mosquito bites. A few had squatted down to gamble as they waited, as if their excitement about gold did not leave them even for one minute.

Corrie hurried past them, hearing snatches of their talk —phrases like "placer gold" and "skunks" and "pups" and "color." As she was nearly past the long line, she looked up and saw a man squeezed into line between two bearded *cheechakos*. Something about him attracted her attention. He was wearing a yellow flannel shirt open at the throat and was gazing at the hills that loomed over Dawson, his eyes dreamy as if focused on some private dream of gold.

Corrie stopped. Shock pounded through her in throbbing waves until she thought she would faint from weakness. It was Avery Curran, standing in line with all the others. Avery, who had gone all these weeks without contacting her.

"Avery!" she heard her voice cry out. She swallowed hard and yelled again.

He whirled about. "Corrie, is it really you? My God, is it really you?" An odd mixture of gladness, surprise and dismay crossed his features, but he did not leave his place in line.

She rushed up to him. Something prevented her from throwing herself into his arms. Instead, she looked up at the face which had been in her thoughts so often.

How handsome he was, even more so than she had remembered. Like a young Greek statue, she thought dazedly. Or a painting by Da Vinci. His eyes were gray and still dreamy, and his golden hair and mustache were burnished by the sun. The aristocratic cheekbones, the cleft chin, the full, sensuous lips, belonged to the same face which so many women, including herself, had admired. His shirt, though faded, was tidy, and by now she was well aware of how much effort was required to keep clean here when all water had to be heated on a stove.

"Yes, it's me." She was amazed to hear her own voice sound so self-assured. She didn't feel assured at all, or even very joyful. She felt shocked and nervous, ready to sob or laugh or scream. "I've been waiting all these weeks for you!" she heard herself add. "Didn't you get my letters? I sent you a half-dozen!"

He flushed. "I did get your letters, of course. But we were so busy, Corrie, you've no idea. You see, we thought we'd found a rich vein of color, but it didn't pan out the way we expected." He shifted his feet as if her presence made him uneasy.

"I guess I didn't really think you would come here, Corrie, so boldly. It never occurred to me that you would. The Yukon is no place for a woman."

"Then you haven't been very observant, Avery. There are plenty of women here," she told him tartly.

"Perhaps, but they certainly aren't the kind of females that you . . . I mean . . ." He stopped, his face reddening again. "How are you, Corrie? You look good."

She tugged uneasily at the partially concealing shawl. Had he noticed her condition? Had he really looked at her at all?

"Oh, I'm fine," she told him, lifting her chin.

"Good, I'm glad to hear that. I've come in to stake another claim, as you can see. I was able to get one on French Hill with some other men. We're moving everything." He lowered his voice. "We think this one might pay better—at least we're hoping it will. There are claims on the Eldorado where a man can get a thousand dollars in four pans. That's what I call gold, Corrie! Real gold!"

People were staring at them.

"Avery, I . . . I must talk to you. Can't we go somewhere less public?"

"Of course, Corrie, but in an hour or so. I've told you; I have to file this claim and I certainly can't leave my place in line now. I've been standing here for three hours already."

"But we have to . . . I've been waiting—" she floundered.

"Corrie." For the first time he reached out to touch her. His fingers felt very cool. She was uncomfortably aware of the stare of the man in line behind Avery. Did he think she was some prostitute Avery knew? she wondered furiously.

"Corrie, I made this trip into town at a very inconvenient time," she heard Avery continue. "And I must get my claim filed as quickly as I can. Sometimes there is crooked business going on in the claims office—well, I won't bother you with that. But surely you can wait an hour or so to talk to me, can't you? I'll buy you a meal when I'm finished here. We can talk about old times."

He was smiling at her, the old, charming smile that she knew so well. He was so handsome, so arrogant and patrician! His teeth were white and even, and his skin had turned very brown in the sun. Once she had adored

Avery's features, had devotedly photographed him from every angle.

Now . . . Involuntarily she pushed aside the thought of Quade's rugged face, the blue eyes which could hold hers with such disturbing intensity.

"Wait for you!" she cried furiously. "I've been waiting here in town for weeks! I was about to travel out to your claim and find you!"

Avery shifted his booted feet again, his smile a bit fixed now. "You were going to do that? I suppose I treated you unforgivably, didn't I? But I meant to write you. We were so busy, Corrie. If you'd ever been out there on the creeks, you'd understand—"

"Would I?" Cold fury pushed through her. She could hardly believe that she had once laid in this man's arms, had moaned with pleasure as he kissed her, and was even now carrying his child. It was as if, like a trick played in a carnival mirror, she was now seeing a new image of Avery. His mustache was too long, she told herself angrily. And his chin was weak.

"Aw, lady, leave the man alone, will you? Didn't you hear him telling you?" The man behind them was grinning; he scratched at his beard and then spat out a brown stream of tobacco juice toward Corrie. It landed within an inch of her hem. It was, she thought with rising fury, as if they were two males allied against her, the intruder, a woman.

"Oh, do be still!" she snapped at the man. "Avery," she pleaded. "Avery, I must talk to you. Surely you can see that it's an embarrassment to me to talk to you here."

"You haven't lost one whit of your loveliness, Corrie, did you know that? You're just as pretty as you ever were, and just as bold and stubborn," Avery smirked.

Was his laugh slightly forced?

"Avery, I won't wait, and I won't be put off any more. I should have come storming out to the claims when I first arrived here, I can see that now. I should have forced you to— But you'll listen to me now. And I won't wait. If I let you get back to that claim of yours, you won't answer my letters again and I'll be left here in Dawson."

"Now, Corrie—"

"Don't 'now Corrie' me! I have rights, Avery! You seduced me, after all, or had you conveniently forgotten that? *I'm pregnant, Avery. Pregnant!*"

She could not believe that she was really saying these things in public, in front of a long line of men, all of them listening avidly. Tears of humiliation pricked at her eyelids. If only she could slap Avery across that handsome face of his and walk away! If only she never had to see him again!

But there was the baby. She could not forget her child.

"Avery, you must talk to me and I'm going to stay right here in line with you until you do, no matter how long it takes. I'll stay here until midnight if I have to."

"But Corrie—"

Then Avery's mouth twisted and she could see him swallowing back whatever reply he had been going to make. "Oh, very well." He gave her a sort of frozen smile. "Wait here with me, then, if that's what you really want to do."

Part 3

🌹 Chapter 24 🌹

"Do you, Avery Curran, take this woman, Cordelia Stewart . . . "

The minister, a man named Fardon Potts, was twenty-five years old, tall and thin, with a prominent Adam's apple. He was delighted with the little poke of gold dust which Avery had given him as a contribution for his struggling new church in Dawson City. And he was equally delighted with the idea of Corrie traveling all these miles north to find her fiancé. Fardon Potts, it appeared, was a romantic.

Millie gave Corrie a long, blue woolen shawl which she could pull about her shoulders to make her pregnancy less obvious. Under it Corrie wore a blue serge walking skirt with a taffeta underskirt and a lacy white shirtwaist with a bertha collar. On her head she wore a plain flat sailor hat, her masses of chestnut-gold hair dressed in a loose pompadour. Glimpsing herself in Millie's small mirror, she saw a pale, set face, with lips that trembled.

Holding Alberta in her arms, Millie served as Corrie's matron of honor. A miner pulled off the street was the other witness.

Fardon Potts' voice, filled with surging highs and lows, went on with the brief ceremony, held in the half-finished church amid scraps of lumber and heaps of sawdust. Corrie stood rigidly, trying to convince herself that this was real and not some half-waking fever dream.

But she had to do it for her baby's sake, she reminded

herself firmly. Her child would be special. Wanted and loved and cherished, as she herself had been.

She felt a ring slide on her finger. It was thick and ungraceful, made from a nugget and purchased hastily from Jos. Mayer and Bros., who specialized in "souvenir" jewelry. Corrie was not even sure if the ring had been made for a woman or for a man. Fleetingly she thought of Aunt Susan. How grieved her aunt would be at the haste, the poverty of this wedding. And Quade, what would he say? Would those blue eyes of his be filled with a piercing anger at her for marrying a man she no longer loved? A thick, agonized pain seemed to expand in her throat. With effort, she pushed Quade out of her mind. If she thought of him now, she would surely weep. . . .

"Well, now you're married," Fardon Potts said. "Wouldn't you like to kiss your bride, Mr. Curran? I believe that's what's done now." He beamed at them.

"Oh, yes." Avery kissed her, his lips dry, the feel of his mustache soft and silky. Involuntarily she thought of Quade, of the kisses he had given her, and drew back.

"Well," Millie said, sighing happily. "That's that, and you're married now, for better or for worse. I hope it's better. Would you like to come back to my house and have some champagne? While you were dressing I sent out for some, and I've some salmon steaks, too. We should have a good wedding supper."

"Sorry, we'd like to, but we don't have time," Avery said. "I have to get back to my claim. The others are waiting, and I really hadn't intended to get married today."

"Well, you certainly had a fine day for it," Fardon Potts put in, beaming at all of them until Corrie felt an irrational urge to slap him. "We've had a marvelous month so far, don't you agree? It's been so balmy, hardly any rain to speak of."

"Yes, yes," Avery said impatiently. "Come on, Corrie. I told you, I'm in a hurry."

They walked outside to the mule cart which Avery had hired to take Corrie and her luggage back to the claim. The miner who served as best man tipped his hat to Corrie and Millie and sidled off toward a saloon down the street.

"We'll go back for your things, Corrie, and then we're leaving," Avery said. "You can give Mrs. Mussen a ride on the cart if you wish."

"Very well."

It was as if they were strangers being polite to one another.

They rode back in silence to Millie's. Corrie sat rigidly in the cart, her eyes seeing nothing of the littered streets or the blue Yukon sky which arched above them, washed clean to an incredible purity. On another day, she might have found that sky beautiful; the hills bulked behind the city, lovely in their mingled shades of muted greens and blue-greens.

But today she could take no joy in her surroundings. She was married to Avery at last. This was the moment for which she had dreamed and planned, for which she had endured the long journey, the hardships and despair. Yet now she could find no happiness in her accomplishment. Instead, her mind boiled with conflicting emotions: anger, frustration, relief, despair.

Quade, she thought numbly. *Oh, Quade.*

Back at Millie's, Avery went to the lean-to to begin loading Corrie's provisions. Millie embraced her.

"Oh, Corrie, I'm so happy for you, so glad that things finally worked out. I hadn't wanted to say so, but I *was* worried about you. And now you're safely married, I feel so much better. Avery might get rich, you know. At least it's possible. Some of the bench claims are good, they say."

Corrie tried to smile. "Take care of Alberta for me. And be sure you boil her water properly—"

"Oh, yes!" Millie made a face. "And you, too, Corrie. You boil yours, too. And—and come back to visit me, do you hear?"

"Of course I will." Again they embraced and Corrie blinked back tears. "Millie," she whispered. "If you should see Quade Hill again, would you tell him that I've married, and everything is going to be fine for me. And—that I'm very happy."

"Yes."

"*Very* happy, don't forget that. And—and tell Li Hua

—she's at the Pear Blossom Salon—tell her that I've married too. She'll want to know."

"I'll do that, and you take care, Corrie, hear? Eat the proper foods so you won't get scurvy, and drink milk, and—"

Millie's good wishes were still ringing in Corrie's ears as they left. The pair of mules, scrawny and ill-fed, plodded on, the cart wheels screeching over hardened ruts of mud. Dust roiled up about them in choking clouds. The provisions, hastily loaded, slid around on the bed of the wagon.

"Well, at least you came well supplied," Avery said. "It will save us some reprovisioning later, and take care of the extra mouth to feed."

He spoke almost warmly, and Corrie was unaccountably angered. He denied accepting any money from Donald, flaring up at her so savagely when she had asked him about it that she had to drop the subject. Still, she could not repress the idea that it had been Donald who had kept Avery from her so long, hoping to prevent the marriage.

Well, she *was* married now, and Donald Earle no longer held any power over her. For that, at least, she could be grateful.

The outskirts of Dawson City were a welter of tents and cabins. There was a crude ferry to take them to the other side of the river. Here the terrain, with its knobbed hills, grew steeper, so that the mules picked their way with weary care. She and Avery talked little. As they rode, she turned the gold ring over and over on her finger. It was not really a proper wedding band at all, she thought. Nothing about her wedding had been as she once dreamed it.

And nothing, she decided, seemed completely real today. Not the sun, hanging like an orange in the cloudless blue sky, or the somber hills, scarred where men had been stripping them for lumber. Or the disarray they were beginning to see, cabins, scattered lumber, machinery. In places the valley, blotched with heaps of gravel, looked like a field of tiny, ugly volcanoes.

They passed more cabins, more conical piles of gravel, big mechanical dredges, signs announcing claims with the odd names of Sourdough, Gulch Claim or 48 Below. The air was heavy with wood smoke.

At the junction of Eldorado and Bonanza creeks was the settlement of Grand Forks. It consisted of two rows of cabins, shacks and tents strung out along a crooked mud street which was littered with cordwood, carts, lumber, garbage, men, dogs and horses. Corrie saw a sign labeled "Viennese Confectionery," and wondered what sort of confection they could possibly produce here. There was the Gold Hill Hotel and a place called the Dance Hall and Card Room. It all looked unutterably shabby and makeshift, and the sight of the little settlement only drove Corrie's spirits further downward.

They stopped at a roadhouse for supper, a place predictably named "The Nugget." The two-story log building had a crude board portico, plate glass windows, and signs advertising "spring beds," whiskey and ale.

Corrie ate her meal without tasting any of it. The owner, a fortyish woman named Miss Gilhooley who wore a soiled white apron tied about her buxom figure, seemed to know Avery. As she served them, she bantered with him about people they both seemed to know—Caribou Bill, Nels, Peterson—and Corrie sat at the slab table feeling silent and awkward.

She didn't know any of these people. And, it was becoming increasingly obvious, Avery didn't want her here.

At the end of a long day they finally arrived at Avery's new claim. Corrie was too exhausted to observe many details other than that the sloping claim, located on a "bench" hillside, looked incredibly desolate and littered. Halfway down the slope was a dwarfed, squashed-looking cabin; surely it could not be as small as it looked?

Avery introduced her to three men. These were co-owners of the claim, she gathered; she had an impression of bearded, muddy, tired-looking faces welted with mosquito bites. One of them, a youth named Mason Edwards, was clean shaven, however, and looked no older than Corrie. He, at least, seemed friendly.

The men did not conceal their surprise at seeing her, and Corrie was sure they had also observed her bulging abdomen. Flushing, she pulled the blue shawl closer about her.

"Corrie has journeyed all the way from San Francisco to be with me," she heard Avery tell them. "We'll have to change all of our arrangments, of course, but it can't be helped. You three will have to move out of the cabin and pitch tents tonight. Tomorrow you can start building yourselves another place. It's extra work, but I don't see any alternative."

"Aw, you din't say nothin' about no—" began one, a short, dark-haired man named Bill Houtaling.

"Unfortunately, my wife is a lady and not used to living under conditions like these," Avery said coldly. "Go on, down to the cabin with you. Get your bedrolls gathered up."

As the men obeyed, Corrie said to Avery, "I didn't mean that they should be inconvenienced."

"Well, you are inconveniencing them anyway. You certainly can't share a cabin with four men. What did you expect, Corrie? They've never even heard of you, and you can't blame them for being a bit surprised."

"I see," Corrie said. Her face felt as stiff as a mask. He was very angry at her, she realized. She was merely an annoyance for these men, none of whom wanted her.

To cover her embarrassment and dismay, she began to look about her. The low light showed the hills were an odd, flat-topped shape broken up by an occasional peak. They were timbered with spruce, some of which was blackened and charred, as if burned by a fire. To Corrie's right was a running creek squeezed by hills on either side.

To her left, a steeper hill rose about two hundred feet high and then leveled out. This, she gathered, was the "bench" which marked an earlier level of the gold-bearing stream. In the distance she could see other cabins and tents, and men walking about amid heaps of dirt and tailings.

"Why are the trees blackened?" she asked at last, dully.

"We burned them for dry timber," Avery said. "When we cut firewood the soot gets all over our hands and it's harder than glue to get out." He shrugged. "As I told you at the claims office, this is no life for a woman—at least not one like you."

Corrie did not know what to reply.

Again Avery shrugged. "Well, at any rate, you can

make yourself useful while you're here, can't you? I assume you can cook. If not, you're going to have to learn. Then all four of us can be working at once, instead of having to detail one to do the cooking."

"Yes. I can cook."

She turned away from him and walked blindly downhill, toward the cabin. From a distance it had looked small enough. But now, as she drew closer to it, she drew a quick breath, dismayed.

The little structure was more like a hovel or a coop than anything else. Its walls were lower than a man's head, so that Avery, who was tall, would have to stoop when he was inside. The logs were crudely chinked with moss, and the nearly flat roof was covered with a blanket of sod. Dead weeds had been laid over this surface, giving the cabin an eldritch look, as if some fairy-tale hag or troll lived there. From the weeds, a metal stove-pipe protruded upward like a long snout.

"We found this cabin partly built and we just finished the job today," Mason Edwards said, coming up to Corrie. His light blue eyes admired her. He was about nineteen, with a big, rangy farm boy's body which still had not quite filled out to a man's bulk. His cheekbones were broad, his face wide and humorous, and scattered with freckles. His straight blond hair hung boyishly in his eyes as he offered her an apologetic smile.

"People live in places lots worse than this," he added. "You can count yourself lucky that the roof is solid. But don't worry, there's a stove, and we'll fix it up nice. We'll get some oil paper to line it. And some slabs from the lumber yard for flooring."

He grinned at her like a puppy trying to please. "You're going to like it here, Mrs. Curran—at least as much as any woman could like a place like this, which isn't much."

Corrie looked at him and tried to smile, thinking that it was Avery who should have been telling her these things. But Avery was up the slope talking to Bill Houtaling, and was not even looking at her.

She stifled a cry of shock as she entered the cabin. Never had she seen any permanent human living place this primitive. Even Millie's three-room cabin in Dawson had been luxurious compared with this.

There was one room, its ceiling scarcely high enough for anyone to stand upright. The floor, though swept clean, was made of dirt. There were two windows, one on each side of the door, covered with washed cotton flour bags stretched over frames. These, of course, blocked any view of the outside but did let in a little light.

On two of the walls, rough slab bunks had been built in double tiers. There was a big Klondike stove and some very crude shelves made of saplings and slabs. The furniture—what few pieces there were—was constructed of halved logs. In one corner was a small plank trough filled with water. This, Avery told her, was where they tested dirt taken from the shaft for its gold content.

The cabin was neat, and as clean as it could be under the circumstances. Still . . .

Corrie looked about her silently, willing herself not to cry. She wouldn't cry; she just wouldn't! She would let Avery think she didn't mind all of this squalor, that she expected it. She would rather die than give way to despair in front of him.

She undressed for bed, shivering as she put on the fine embroidered cambric nightgown which she had bought so many months ago on her shopping spree with Aunt Susan. The gown, part of a bridal set, was sewn in Empire style and trimmed with point de Paris insertion and a ruffle of four-inch lace. She had bought it while dreaming of Avery, and saved it all of this time. As she pulled it over her head, it smelled stale, as if it had been shut up too long.

Now, hearing male laughter outside the cabin, she buttoned the nightgown at the throat and fumbled for the small mirror that she had tucked into her pocketbook. She held it up and peered at herself. She looked soft and pretty and romantic, with her chestnut-gold hair flowing richly over her shoulders, and the delicate lace at her throat. Her eyes were wide, fringed with dark lashes, arched over by graceful wings of brows. Her mouth trembled. She was a beautiful bride, she supposed; she looked as she had always hoped that she might look on her wedding night. But it didn't matter. It didn't mean anything at all.

She put the mirror away and sat down on a lower bunk, swallowing hard to rid herself of the lump that was caught in her throat like a piece of dry lint.

Just then Avery came into the cabin with a clatter of boots. He slammed the door and latched it with a leather thong. She saw that he was carrying a bundle of canvas tenting. An odor of whiskey came from him.

"I may have brought you to humble surroundings, but you certainly shouldn't have to walk about on a dirt floor," he said, not looking at her. He tossed the cloth to the floor and began to unwrap it and spread it out. "This will be some kind of flooring, at least. It will act as a ground pad."

She watched as he meticulously spread the canvas everywhere, leaving bare only a circle near the stove.

"There," he said at last. "That's better."

"It's very kind of you to think of it. I'm so tired tonight that my brain is foggy. But I do thank you, and it will be good to walk on canvas rather than on dirt."

"I didn't think of it, Mason did."

"Then I'll have to thank Mason, won't I?"

Avery stood up, surveyed the canvas, and began to unbutton his shirt, rumpled and soiled from a day of traveling. Corrie watched, her heart beginning to thump, as he pulled it off, revealing an undershirt frayed but clean. His arms, she observed, were smooth, nearly hairless. She remembered the last time she had seen Avery's naked body. How long ago that seemed now. Was it really possible that once she had lain with him, had joined her body with his and received his seed?

He continued to disrobe, hanging each garment neatly on the cabin's one nail hook. Soon he was nude, his form thinner than she remembered it, but compact and beautiful. If, she told herself shakily, a man's physique could be thought of in those terms. Yet the sight of him did not affect her at all.

"Do I bother you, Corrie? Why are you flinching?"

"I'm not flinching."

"You certainly are." He was coming toward her, a curiously intent expression on his face. Corrie averted her eyes, but found that there was nowhere for her to look save at the moss-chinked logs.

"Look at me," Avery ordered. "Look at what you've married. Do you like it? You'd better: you've traveled far enough to get it."

"Of course . . . "

She felt like a small, frightened bird which has been grasped, fluttering, out of its cage by a huge human hand. This was her wedding night. This was the night she had struggled all these miles for, for which she had endured the steamer and Captain Carter and the Dyea Trail and the awesome Chilkoot Pass.

And this, she told herself with growing panic, was Avery, the man she had been determined to marry, whatever the cost. Now she knew how foolish she had been to come here, how headstrong and reckless. Hadn't Quade told her so? But she had refused to listen to him.

Well, it was too late. She had come, and she was here, Quade was far away, she had no idea where, and it was unlikely that she would ever see him again.

"Why don't you take your nightgown off, Corrie?" Avery's voice was suddenly soft, reminding her of that night months ago, in his basement room, on the horsehair sofa.

"Oh, Avery . . . " Her hands fluttered. "I'm pregnant now, I'm ugly, I couldn't—you wouldn't want to look at me under these conditions . . . "

"Probably not. At any rate, you're a woman, aren't you? God knows I've lived long enough without one."

She fumbled at the neck of her gown, her chest and face washed by a hideous, hot flow of embarrassment.

"I can't, Avery."

"Why can't you? I saw you before, didn't I? I kissed you everywhere and you didn't have any scruples about baring your body to me. What's so different now? I'm your husband, with all the rights of one. And if I've got the name, by God I'm going to have the advantages."

The advantages. In ten thousand years she never could have pictured a wedding night exactly like this.

"No, Avery, I can't! Not like this, not so coldly, as if we were strangers, or as if I was one of those women in one of those little cribs on Paradise Alley. I'm not. I'm your wife, Avery. . . . "

She straightened her spine and smoothed the fragile cambric over her knees, trying to speak with dignity, although she knew that her voice was trembling, as were her hands.

"Yes, you are my wife, aren't you? You could hardly wait for that privilege, could you, Corrie? You refused to stay at home and wait until I could come back rich and marry you properly and buy you a buggy and a house and take care of you as a gentleman should. No, instead you had to pursue me up here like a—a *detective,* and force yourself on me—"

"But I'm pregnant, Avery! You know that changes things. I had to come!"

"Then you should have done something. Douched, or aborted it, or whatever it is that female adventurers do. I've heard of those things, and surely you could have done something. Whores, after all, can take care of themselves, can't they?"

"But I'm not a whore!" She spat out the words. "I wasn't brought up to know of such things. You seduced me, Avery. Part of this was your fault, too, you know!"

"Yes. Well, that doesn't matter any more, does it? You're here and I'm here and by God we're married, and we might as well get the good out of it, hadn't we? Especially as the damage has already been done."

He glanced significantly at her belly. Again she smelled the stench of whiskey.

"Get under the blanket, then, Corrie, if you're so timid. I don't want to look at you anyway. Just get underneath and undress. Hurry up, will you? I'm tired of waiting."

The anger seeped out of Corrie like water out of a cracked ewer. Obediently, numbed of all feeling, she climbed under the rough, mustard-colored wool blanket and pulled it up to her chin.

With cold fingers she unfastened the buttons of the nightgown and inched it above her head. The wool of the blanket pricked at her bare skin. She could feel her feet hitting the bottom of the bunk. She wanted to weep. She wanted to leap out of the bunk and go and visit the privy. She wanted to—

He was in the bed with her. She could feel his skin against hers, its smooth surface muscular and taut. His hands were exploring the warm swell of her breast, the mound of her belly, the triangle of hair further below.

Her last thought, as Avery lowered himself onto her, was of Quade Hill. *Darling,* her thought was choked. *Oh, God, Quade, where are you? Please help me . . .*

🕸 Chapter 25 🕸

July, August. The brief Yukon summer passed in floods of rich sunlight which doused plants and flowers with hour upon hour of light. The sun rose, moved about the sky, dipped toward the horizon and then rose again. Fireweed, a brilliant pink, blanketed the grass. Deep purple basque flowers and lupines bloomed everywhere.

During the day, Avery usually left her to her own devices. In spite of her dissatisfaction with their marriage, Corrie found that in an odd way she was enjoying herself. There were long, long days when the air was a balmy eighty degrees and the sky a glazed bowl of brilliant blue. Mosquitoes, flies and no-see-ums were thick, and Corrie, in exasperation, had to wrap her entire head in netting. She wished she could have five minutes alone with the dry goods store owner, who had sworn to them that the insect repellent he sold them was effective.

Corrie wandered along the stream and discovered rare flowers, monkshood and Northern ladies' slippers. She picked huckleberries and currants and crowberries and learned to cook them all. She found a kind of dock-weed, and, on the gravel bars, wild onions. These had a strong, concentrated flavor, but were delicious when tossed into a moose stew or used to flavor a pot pie made with duck or squirrel.

Her cooking skill improved with each week. Her first bread had been too brown and filled with air bubbles.

She thought back to the way Quade had done it, and her next effort was better. Mason Edwards found her a fresh supply of sourdough starter. Recalling with a catch of the heart Quade's experiments with sweets, she taught herself to make simple desserts from fruit, flour and syrup.

Avery said little about her cooking, but she noticed he had grown plumper. It was Mason Edwards, with the ravenous appetite of a young man, who complimented her on new dishes.

She took photographs: of the mine shafts, of their own cabin, of the huge dredges and ugly piles of tailings which scarred the landscape. She pitched a tent inside the cabin to use as her darkroom and several times was asked to take photographs of miners passing through.

One of them, a grizzled man of sixty who told her he had once mined in Leadville, Colorado, paid her a twenty-dollar nugget for her efforts.

"If you ask me, you beat out that Mr. Hegg with his studio in Dawson," he told her. "Leastwise, you're every bit as good as he is, woman or not."

She blushed with astonished pleasure more for the compliment than for the nugget, although it was the first money she had ever earned.

Several times she begged to help with the mining operation itself, to have something to occupy her time, but Avery refused. This was no work for a pregnant woman, he told her flatly. It was much too dangerous. And Mason Edwards, his face earnest, had agreed with him.

So stifling her resentment, she had gone back to her cooking and her wandering and her photographs, and the laundry she did in the big pot Mason had found for her.

Time. You could measure its passing with the growth of an unborn child. Each week her belly grew firmer and more rounded, the baby's thumps stronger, and she herself more breathless as she clambered about the hills. There were times when she wished fiercely for her old, slim waist. She felt that she must look ugly and ponderous.

But at least, she told herself, Avery was too busy to look at her. His initial anger subsided into a sort of absent-minded possessiveness. She was his—when it occurred to him to want her.

The men began a second mine shaft, and spent hours feverishly hauling dirt and gravel upward in the crude windlass they built. They were trying, Mason told her, to determine the twistings of the meager vein of gold.

The only time she and Avery were alone together was at night, when Avery closed the cabin door behind him and locked it with the thong of leather. Even then it seemed as if they were still strangers. She still undressed beneath the blanket, sensing that he found her belly grotesque. He would roll on top of her, and in a few minutes she would feel his shudder and it would be over.

Waiting for the mail became a way to relieve the tedium of the days and the stifled misery of her nights. The men took turns going into Dawson City to collect their letters. Bill Houtaling had a wife in Denver and Basil Heming, the other partner, a large family in Detroit. Mason got regular mail from his parents, who owned a farm near Ann Arbor, Michigan.

No letter came from Susan, though, and in late July they learned that one of the Yukon-bound steamers had sunk in the channel near Ketchikan. Had Susan's letter —with money for Corrie—been aboard?

Worried and disappointed, Corrie wrote her aunt another letter, urging her to hurry her response before the Yukon closed to river traffic. Once the river froze, Avery said, there would be no more mail from outside until spring.

She wrote glowingly of the fact that the men were now panning a hundred dollars a day. *Oh, aunt,* she added impulsively. *I do love and miss you so much. My baby is due in early December. I wish you could be here when he comes, and could hold him in your arms. . . .*

A week later, a letter came from Millie Mussen, hand-delivered by Miss Gilhooley at the Nugget, with whom it had been left. In painful script Millie wrote that she had met a young miner when he came to have his laundry done, and was marrying him and going home to Seattle.

He doesn't think I'm plain, either, she wrote joyously. *He likes me just the way I am; he says I'm a real lapful of woman! Ha, ha, but you know I could not resist, and*

*even though he never did find a claim up here that was
worth anything, I think he can make me happy, Corrie.
He is a journeyman carpenter and Alberta loves him, especially when he carries her about on his shoulders. . . .*

Corrie squeezed the letter in hands that suddenly
shook. By now, she thought, Millie would be on a steamer
headed for Dyea or Skagway, well on her journey. She
would probably never see her or Alberta again.

She found that she was blinking back tears, and angrily
dashed them away. What sort of monster was she, to cry
at the news of Millie's good fortune? She should be happy
for her. Millie had met a good man, Alberta was going to
have a new father, and Millie's hands wouldn't have to be
covered with sores and chilblains any more. Perhaps she
and her new husband would buy the millinery shop she
had dreamed of.

Still, Corrie felt oddly bereft. Without Millie, Dawson
City would not be the same. And until now Corrie had
not realized just how much she had been counting on seeing Millie when she returned there.

More long weeks passed. Then one day in mid-August,
while roaming the hills in search of berries, Corrie
stopped, drawn by a small patch of wild roses blanketing
a sunny hillside. The blooms were small and pale, but
their scent seemed to her to be unutterably fragrant, and
she sat down among the blooms, momentarily at peace
with herself and the world.

The roses were delicate in the full-flushed yellow of
their blossoming, hummed over by fat bees. Overhead the
sky stretched, clean blue. A crisp breeze blew from the
hilltops, picking up the tang of wild grasses and the scent
of wildflowers.

Impulsively Corrie's hand reached out to pluck a bouquet—they would brighten the cabin. Then something
made her pause. Why not let these lovely, rare blooms
stay where they were, underneath the sky? In the cabin
they would wilt quickly. And weren't men already dese-
crating these Yukon hillsides with their mines and piles of
tailings and brush fires and lumber cutting? Surely one
small patch of golden roses could be allowed to survive.

She sat, arms clasped about her knees, dreaming.

The sudden crash of footsteps behind her interrupted her reverie.

"I don't know which is lovelier, you or those posies among which you sit. I might even offer you one, as I did before, but I'm afraid you'd fling it right back in my face." A familiar chuckle.

Corrie whirled about as fast as her heavy figure would allow. "Quade! Quade Hill, what are you doing here?"

He stood silhouetted against the blue sky and moss-covered rock, tall and bulky, his shoulders straining against the cotton jacket he wore. Corrie struggled to her feet and ran toward him.

They were in each other's arms. For long moments he held her tightly, his hands squeezing her and caressing her feverishly, as if he could not let her go. She burrowed gladly into the warmth of him, savoring the tallness of his body, the power in the muscular arms which held her.

At last Quade drew away. For the first time she was able to get a close look at him. He had lost weight, she saw, and there were new hollows beneath his cheekbones, a grimness to the line of his jaw which she found worrisome.

"Quade, is anything wrong? Are you all right?" she questioned him anxiously.

He brushed her concern aside. "The important question is, Corrie, are *you* all right? That's the reason I stopped here. Millie told me you were married, and Miss Gilhooley at the roadhouse told me where to find you. Did you get what you wanted, Cordelia Stewart? Or should I call you Cordelia Curran now?"

Corrie looked at him dully. "I'm Cordelia Curran."

"And are you happy, my Delia?"

"Y—yes. Of course I am." She could not look at him.

"You're lying, Delia."

Corrie was silent.

"I say you're lying, you little fool. Do you think that I don't know you well enough to recognize when you're not telling the truth? You made a mistake. When will you admit it?"

Blue and intense, his eyes fastened upon hers, holding her in their depths as if she were a mouse trapped by a cobra.

"My baby needed its father," she murmured.

"I see."

"Well?" She was abruptly defiant. "What is wrong with that? Isn't that why I came to the Yukon? To find Avery and marry him? Isn't that why I hired you?"

Quade looked away, his eyes focused on the furthest range of hills capped with a fringe of pines. The mountains shaded in the distance into a hundred hues of green-gray.

"Yes, Corrie." He said it heavily. "That's why you hired me. And I performed the job as specified." He paused, then told her abruptly, "I think you should go back to San Francisco to have your baby. I want you to leave before the freeze sets in."

She stared at him. "That depends on Avery's wishes. After all, he is my husband."

"He is a goddamned fool! Do you think that I don't know what is going on with you? Avery Curran is no more a real husband to you than—than a grizzly bear might be! Even that female at the roadhouse remarked on Avery's obsession with his mine. He's gone crazed thinking about gold."

"That's the way men are when there is gold in the ground."

"Do you really think so? Oh, God, little Delia, do you think *I* would be that way where you are concerned?"

In one savage motion, Quade reached for her and enfolded her in his arms. He pressed her against him so fiercely that Corrie could barely breathe. And yet, wildly, she reveled in the discomfort. This was Quade who held her, Quade whose hands stroked and kneaded her back, as if they spoke things which his lips could never tell her.

They clung together breathlessly. The scent of the wild roses blew about them like sweet perfume. For Corrie it would be a fragrance forever associated with Quade, with the fierce strength of his arms about her, the hardness of his body against her own. It was as if they were suspended, adrift in this sleepy blue summer afternoon, as if time had stopped in this moment of wild roses.

"Well." At last, heavily, Quade put her aside. "I must go now, Delia. There is something I must do—" He broke off, as if he had said too much. "Millie Mussen has left town, so if you want to reach me, I will be stopping periodically at the Canadian Bank of Commerce. They'll get any message to me."

The pain that stabbed through her was not physical, but mental, so full of anguish that she thought she could not bear it.

"Quade, must you leave so soon?"

"Yes. God help me, I must. And right now, no doubt that fine husband of yours will wonder where you have gone to. You belong to him, Delia, not to me. You made that decision the day you married him."

He reached out and ran his fingers gently along her face. Slowly he drew her closer. Corrie closed her eyes. She could sense the nearness of his lips. Her heart beat wildly in anticipation of his tender kiss.

Suddenly he dropped his hand. Corrie opened her eyes and saw him turn and march resolutely down the hill. She blinked and tried to hold back tears of shock and surprise, then found herself sobbing uncontrollably.

Back in the cabin, Corrie paced back and forth, fighting the tears that spilled from her eyes and flowed down her cheeks. She was alone, for the men were all working at the mine shaft and barely noticed her return, save for Mason, who waved her a cheery greeting.

Never had she done anything harder than to let Quade go. As he walked back over the hills the way he had come, his figure receded into the distance, growing smaller until at last he disappeared into the heavy shadow cast by one of the hillsides.

Quade! she wanted to scream after him. *Quade, please don't go. Take me with you. . . .*

Yet something in her could not utter the words. Perhaps it was too many years of being reared by Aunt Susan in the prim and proper rectitude of the 1890s, when a woman was expected to be virtuous and cling to her husband. Corrie had taken marriage vows with Avery. She had lain with him, and was carrying his child. Like it or not, she had committed herself to him. Well, hadn't she?

Cheeks wet with tears, she fumbled among her trunks until she found the box of photographic prints which included the one Li Hua had taken of herself and Quade on the Dyea Trail.

She stared at the two solemn people posed stiffly by a boulder. She looked slim in her men's gear, next to Quade's formidable size, his vital energy plain even in the photograph. She touched the photo with her finger. How dear his face was to her, every inch and line of it, from the blue eyes set under their ridge of bone, to the small dimple at the corner of Quade's mouth which sometimes showed when he smiled.

Then carefully she tucked the photograph away underneath the others, for Avery must not see it.

September arrived, marked by the season's first frost, which, to Corrie's vast relief, killed off the swarms of mosquitoes and made the hillsides habitable again. The hills were ablaze with the colors of autumn. The fireweed was brilliantly red, and the scattered cottonwoods and birch trees suffused with yellow, as if the sunlight were caught in them. Even the creeks seemed to turn a deeper, richer color. Corrie thought that she had never seen the country look more beautiful.

On the fourth of September, Avery told her that a company based in San Francisco had installed another big dredge not far from them, and was expecting to take out a lot of gold. Corrie was horrified to learn that this was the Earle Mining Company. She could hardly conceal her agitation. But later, as she went about her daily chores, she told herself that she was being foolish to allow her heart to thump so wildly. She was safe married to Avery, wasn't she? Donald would have to accept his twenty percent share of Papa's estate and be thankful for it.

The first week in September Corrie saw her first display of the northern lights. The aurora borealis was nothing but an electromagnetic phenomenon, Mason told her, leaving his work at the mine shafts at the end of the day to come and stand with her.

"Some say it means we're going to get cold weather," he said. "I prefer to think that it's just God up there, showing off His power."

She smiled. "Well, whatever it is, it's certainly beautiful."

For long minutes they stood entranced, gazing upward at the triple and quadruple arches that swept the night sky from horizon to horizon in a shimmering, flickering spray of green. The display seemed mysterious, almost supernatural, and all of it was accomplished without the slightest sound. And, as if to add to the eeriness of it, there was a chilly wind. Corrie could feel it lifting her hair and nudging at the folds of her skirt.

Down the slope she could hear shouts as Avery, Bill and Basil winched up buckets from their second mine shaft. Intent on their work (did they ever stop?), they had barely glanced up at the display, and Corrie knew that it meant little to them. The only color they were interested in was yellow, and that could be found at the bottom of a bucket, glinting among stones and gravel.

"I love the aurora," Mason told her. "I'd heard so much about it, and now here it is. When I finally go back to college I'll think about it when I'm working with my books, and I'll remember the times we've had up here. And I'll remember you, too, Corrie. You're very beautiful."

Corrie shivered. Again she felt the chill wind, like a premonition of winter, blowing against her cheek. And, oddly, she could almost fancy that it came from the aurora itself, borne somehow on that gigantic, silent display of waves, rays and bands.

"Mason. You won't remember me, not for long, anyway," she said quickly. "After all, I am married to Avery and I'm about to have his child. Anyway, you can't really find me attractive like this," she added with a small, nervous laugh. "I look like an elephant right now."

"But I do think you're attractive; you're the most beautiful woman I've ever known! I love you, Corrie!"

"Oh, Mason, no."

"But it's true. I do love you." He tossed his long blond hair out of his eyes. She had cut it for him, but still it was shaggy and blunt, and he looked for all the world like a sun-bleached farm boy. He seemed even younger than his nineteen years, still awkward and unsure.

Impulsively she took his hand. The men downslope at the mine shaft were not looking in their direction.

"Mason, I really can't let you say such things to me. I'm a woman, a married woman expecting a child. You should go back to Ann Arbor and find some girl to share your life with you. It can't be me." She tried to lighten her voice. "Although I must say I couldn't have gotten on without your plant lore and your help with the sourdough starter."

"Yes, the bread." Mason laughed softly, his profile silhouetted against the errie, misty, spraying arcs of the aurora. Corrie was conscious that he was squeezing her fingers tightly. "Corrie, why did you marry him, anyway? I mean Avery. You don't love him, I know you don't. And he doesn't love you."

"Mason!" She pulled back.

"Well, you know it's true. When I saw the way he looked at you that first night he brought you here, I wanted to hit him. I still want to. To take a beautiful girl like you and marry her and then to treat her as if she doesn't even exist, as if she's a—a servant, or a machine, or . . . good for only one thing . . . " He nearly choked in his indignation.

"Mason, you're overstepping yourself. This really isn't your business. Avery and I are very happy; of course we are. Why shouldn't we be?" She was dismayed to hear her own voice rising. "So, please, I have to ask you not to interfere any more."

"Interfere! But I'm not! You just want me to leave you alone, is that it?"

"Yes. I think you'd better. Mason, I am sorry."

"Well, I am too." Then, before she could step back or react, Mason reached for her and kissed her, a huge, rather wet kiss that covered all of her mouth and part of her chin. It was as if he were an overanxious puppy. But the body that pressed itself against hers was anything but puppylike. It was young, hard and strong.

"Mason!" She struggled backwards and managed to take in some air. "Mason, you mustn't—"

"I don't care."

He buried his face in her neck with fierce passion and then kissed her again. This time his kiss was not unfocused, but hard and yearning. She could feel his heart pounding against her. He was young, she thought; he was virile, he wanted her, said he loved her—why couldn't she feel anything but this horrified, numb despair?

Desperately she shoved at him again.

"Mason! For God's sake, what if Avery looks up here and sees us? He hates you already. What do you think he'd do if— he'd make you sell your share of the claim! He'd put you off the claim and you'd have to go home. Oh, Mason, you're much too young for me!"

Slowly, reluctantly, Mason released her. She could see the skin of his face tinted faintly green by the aurora. His hair hung down into his face.

"All right. I'll stop because you ask me to. But I won't stop loving you, Corrie. I'm not too young for you. I'm older than you are. And I'd make a better husband for you than that gold-hungry Avery any day of the week!"

Angrily Mason turned away and stalked downhill. Corrie stumbled into her own cabin and closed the door, fastening it with the thong. She lit the lamp and then sank down on a log bench.

If only Avery could kiss her like that, she began to think disjointedly. If only—how different their lives might have been.

The second week of September they had a heavy rain, cold and chillingly miserable. Corrie and Avery sat in the cramped space of the cabin nearly all day. Avery would not play cribbage, and he did not want to read any of the novels Corrie had brought. He spent most of his time pacing about, opening the door to peer into the gray mist a dozen or more times a day.

The cabin leaked. Water and mud seeped through the sod roof in at least eight places, so Corrie finally gave up putting pans underneath to catch the drips. It was only in the winter, Avery told her sourly, that a sod roof was efficient. You could pour water over an air leak and it would freeze immediately, sealing off the hole. But now, with the rain . . . He shrugged.

Corrie's nerves were stretched tight from listening to the constant noise of the water splashing on the sod of the roof, dripping through to the canvas flooring.

"When are we going back to San Francisco, Avery?" she asked at last.

"Not until I strike it rich, I've told you."

"But when will that be? You're getting gold right now. Every night there's more gold dust, and you've a whole poke full of nuggets. What more do you want, Avery?"

"I want to be rich. Filthy, stinking, wallowing rich, like the Eldorado Kings. I want to be rich beyond all imagining, so that I can go into town and buy a one-hundred-dollar bottle of wine and think nothing of it. I want to be able to buy myself a big mansion in San Francisco—six mansions if I want—and just shrug my shoulders at the cost."

"But Millie said that all the best claims along Discovery and the Eldorado were taken. She said—"

"Damn Millie! What does she know? There's gold under this hill, Corrie, there's got to be. A whole, solid mother lode of it, and I intend to find it. If it isn't here, then it'll be somewhere else. Men are taking out plenty of gold, and I want some too. I deserve it as much as they do, and I'm not going to quit until I get it."

Corrie stared at him, at the intense look on his face. "But what about our baby, Avery? I don't want it to be born here in the north. I want it to be born at home, in my own bedroom, with Aunt Susan to help me, and Mrs. Parsons nearby, and Bea Ellen . . . " She almost choked with homesickness.

Avery made an irritated gesture. "Look, Corrie, I didn't ask you to come up here, did I? It was a bold, unfeminine thing to do, and you did it without asking my advice on the matter. And now you dare to complain. Well, I married you, didn't I, as a gentleman should? I gave your baby a name. What's wrong with him being born up here? We can name the mine after him—when I hit good color."

"Avery, I don't care if a mine is named after my baby. I don't care about gold at all. I just want to go home."

"Fine, then. Go home."

"But I don't have the passage money. Aunt Susan hasn't sent it yet. Avery, I—"

"Oh, damnation!" he said explosively, and for the first time Corrie began to realize the full extent of Avery's frustration, toiling away here on his mediocre claim in the midst of fabulous rumors of other men's discoveries.

"I can't afford it," he went on. "Oh, don't look at me that way. I've made a bit of gold, it's true, but I must save it. I might have to buy into another claim or get more provisions. Do you know what the cost of food is here? It's robbery! Even paper, for God's sake, is six sheets for a dollar. No, Corrie, I have to keep my poke intact in case I should need it."

"And if your wife and child require it?"

"You don't. You're well taken care of here. If you'll just be patient, I'll give you your steamer ticket. You can have a hundred of them. I told you I'd shower you with gold, didn't I? Well, I will, if you'll only give me half a chance."

"But I don't want to have my baby here," she repeated stubbornly.

In answer he grabbed the oilskin slicker which hung on a nail near the door and went outside into the rain.

It was the next day that he had an accident. The rain had cleared, but it was cold and the sky was a metallic gray. When Corrie peered out of the cabin door, the hills looked desolate, as if they hated the human beings who were scarring them. She was on her way back from the outdoor privy when she heard shouts coming from the mine shafts.

She ran downhill as quickly as her awkward belly would allow her.

Mason, Basil Heming and Bill Houtaling were gathered about the windlass, staring downward into the number two shaft, which was crudely lined with halved logs.

"He's down there!" Mason cried. "He rode a bucket down, and the rope must have broken on him. I guess he's all right, though. I can hear him yelling." The smile he gave Corrie was meant to be reassuring.

"You ask me, there's a jinx on this here claim," said Bill Houtaling. "Caused by a woman."

Corrie flushed. "Oh, what nonsense!" she snapped. "Why isn't someone getting another rope? We can't just stand about staring. Well? Surely you must have more rope."

Bill Houtaling gave her a furious look, then ran to do her bidding.

"Avery!" she called, peering downward into the blackness of the shaft.

"I'm all right, for heaven's sake! Just rig up another rope and haul me out, will you? We're wasting time!"

"Bill is getting one now." The shafts, one of them now sunk twenty-two feet to bedrock, were relatively dangerous, Corrie knew, especially now that they had begun digging a "drift," or tunnel, through to the first one. This time, it appeared, they had been lucky, for Avery was brought up dirt-covered, sputtering, and clutching at his left ankle.

"Avery, are you all right?"

"Yes, but I can't understand why this rope broke. It's almost as if someone was tampering with it. Dammit, it was almost new when I bought it in Dawson two weeks ago."

He was limping and wincing, but when she tried to help him, he waved her away angrily. "Leave me alone! I'm not hurt, I just twisted my ankle. It won't stop me from working. I can go back in the hole and handle the dirt and Mason will work the windlass for a while, that's all. I just can't understand why this happened. It shouldn't have."

He was glaring at Corrie and she knew that he, too, like Bill Houtaling, thought she was a jinx.

🎭 Chapter 26 🎭

Nov. 10. The days grow colder, and I think often of my baby, wishing often that his father took more interest in him—or her, whichever it is to be. But Avery can think only of gold now. It is the obsession of his life.

November had come, and it seemed to Corrie as if the sun-drenched days of summer had been only a dream, hardly real at all. The real season of the North was winter, savage and cold.

To have something to do, she had begun to keep a brief journal, jotted on a few sheets of the expensive paper which Mason brought her as a gift one day from town. The notations were somber, for she had no heart for gaiety.

Corrie looked back over the journal and reread some of her entries.

Sept. 22. We had our first snow, which turned to rain and fell miserably, washing away more of our roof. This morning the temperature, by the spirit thermometer which Mason keeps, fell to 32. We've had frost every night. Last night the aurora, incredible waving sheets of red, made me think uncomfortably of fire. I did not sleep well. . . .

Oct. 5. It was 7 degrees at 7 A.M.

Oct. 7. We had our first real snow today, which blanketed all the ground and covered up some of the ugliness of the tailings, but it all melted away by the afternoon.

The baby has not seemed so active lately; does he dread winter as much as I do? I have never experienced real, below-zero cold. Mason tells me of frostbite cases and men who have frozen to death. Avery refuses to hear of my leaving for home, and soon I shall not be able to, for the Yukon will be frozen again. Only the very hardy can travel on the frozen river.

Oct. 23. This week we heard the news of a big fire in Dawson which destroyed many buildings on Front Street. I have not yet heard how Li Hua has fared.

Four days after they received word of the fire, Avery decided that he had to go into Dawson City to buy a new saw blade and to see a doctor, for he had suffered another accident, skidding on a loose board and lacerating his right hand on the side of the mine shaft. Again he had been lucky, for he could have fallen headlong into the shaft, Corrie knew.

She begged to go with him, but Avery refused, insisting that the trip would be too rough to make in her condition. Corrie felt a pang. She longed to visit Li Hua, and to see Dr. Sebastian.

"I'll see them for you," Avery promised sourly. "Jouncing about on these rough trails in the cart, you'll only make yourself sick, and then I'd really have trouble on my hands. All I need is an ailing wife!"

Three days later Avery was back with a bandaged hand and news of Li Hua and Will Sebastian. The young doctor had furnished a small log cabin as his office, and established a busy practice in Dawson. He sent Corrie his best wishes and reassurances. She must come to Dawson two weeks before her expected confinement; then all would be well. By then, snow would cover the ground, and a sled could make a smooth passage.

As for Li Hua, her shop survived the fire and she was now running an establishment called the Princess Dance Hall. It was reputed to possess the prettiest girls within a radius of five hundred miles.

Corrie, surprised, could only stare at her husband. "But when I last saw Li Hua, she was running a hair-dressing salon!"

"And now she's branched out into a more profitable business." Avery's scowl ruined the symmetry of his patrician good looks. "Gold, Corrie—it's here, everywhere, for those who can find it. Some dig it from the ground, and others get it from the miners, that's all."

November. The days were mostly dark, the hills shaded in somber hues and the sky often a somber gray. Daylight was now only from about ten in the morning to two-thirty in the afternoon. The sun eased into a long twilight tinged with reddish-purple.

There were auroras almost every night. Corrie would step out of the cabin to watch them, standing awed under the ghostly spectacle of flickering waves and bars. Mostly the auroras were green, but a few times they were red, and the sight gave Corrie odd, uneasy thoughts of the brooch that Quade carried about with him, the brooch which had been worn by an eager, pretty girl who burned to death. . . .

On the nights of the fiery auroras, Corrie had nightmares. Once she dreamed that Donald Earle, dressed frighteningly in black, had stripped the dress from her body, each yank of the fabric accompanied by an odd, howling noise. She awakened with a stifled shriek to realize that the howling noise was made by wolves. Somewhere in the black bulk of hills, the trees were snapping from the cold.

On November twelfth, three inches of snow fell, and Mason told her cheerfully that the temperature was down to twenty degrees below zero. Without being asked, he had sealed all of the cracks in their cabin with soft moss, and poured water over the leaks in the roof. Their cabin, he said, would now be as cozy as any. And when deep winter came he would pile snow against the outer walls for further insulation.

Her time was near, and at last, on the fifteenth, she made plans to go to Dawson the next day. She felt dulled these days, not only by her cumbersome body, but also by a nameless foreboding. The mine was not doing well. Fires had to be built to thaw the earth so the men could work. Each day they panned out less "color," and Avery grew more restless and angry, barely speaking to her except in monosyllables. She knew that if it were not for her he would already have left the claim to go prospecting again.

She packed for her trip to Dawson City, knowing that

Mason would take her there, not Avery. Carefully she went through her belongings, bundling up the baby things, the soft flannel squares, the lacy gowns, and the infant's cloak which would be such a necessity here. Touching one of the flannel squares, she felt a squeeze of her heart as she remembered the moment when Quade, rummaging through her trunk, had found it. He had thought it was a towel. . . .

She smiled to herself, her eyes blurred with tears.

Doggedly, she continued to pack, her own clothes, her few books, her camera and case, photographic prints and chemicals, the brief journal. It looked, she thought suddenly, as if she was not to be coming back here.

But of course she would be, she told herself sharply. Whether she liked it or not, she had to. She was financially dependent on Avery now, at least until her passage money came from Aunt Susan. And that would not be until spring, when the ice left the river.

That night the red aurora haunted the sky, and again Corrie had a nightmare. This time she dreamed that she was back on the Chilkoot Pass, lying in the tent wedged against Li Hua, weighted down by snow until she could scarcely breathe. Somewhere in the dream, Quade was calling for her. She could hear his voice: *Delia, where are you? Little Delia . . . darling . . .*

She stretched out her hands and tried to call to him. But instead she could only moan hoarsely, as the snow continued to press against her. The pressure was strongest in a band across her abdomen.

Yes, she thought groggily, the snow was pressing in on her with such force that she had to groan aloud. . . .

She heard another moan and realized that she was awake. The air in the cabin was very cold, the stove nearly out. In his bunk across the room, Avery was snoring. The night seemed heavy, very black, pressing down on her eyes like a funeral shroud.

The pain came again, suddenly, twisting at her belly. Then slowly it subsided.

Corrie stiffened in her bunk. Wonderingly she put her hand down to the mound of her belly and felt the hard, muscular ball that it had become.

"Hello, baby," she whispered. *"I love you."*

Then the pain came again, strong and fierce and demanding, and she was no longer thinking of the baby, she was rolling from side to side, trying to contain the pain without screaming.

She screamed and Avery woke up.

❧ Chapter 27 ❧

She heard him crashing around in the dark until he lit the lamp. She could smell the sharp sulfur of the match. He held the lamp in shaking hands and stared down at her. In the shadows, his face looked more aristocratic and handsome than ever, his blond hair and mustache picking up the lamplight. He was like an ancient statue, or a mythical god in a painting, she thought wildly. But a god who has discovered something that he does not wish to see . . .

"You're not having that baby yet!" he shouted at her.

"I *am* having it, Avery. What am I going to do?"

Her voice rose; she felt like sobbing with fear. In a flash, she thought of a school friend who had died in childbirth, of her own mother who had perished while miscarrying. Of the whispers she had overheard among Bea Ellen and the other maids. Women did die having babies. They bled to death or they died of childbed fever, or the baby became wedged in the birth canal and would not emerge . . .

Dear God, Corrie thought wildly, she was going to have her baby right here in this cabin, right now! With no doctor, no midwife, and not even another woman to help her. With only Avery and his frightened face, which could barely conceal its horror.

"Avery—" She pushed herself up on one elbow and started to beg him to go to Dawson City to get Will Sebastian, even though it would take hours. Then another contraction hit her.

A first it was like a menstrual cramp; then it began to build. Pressure—grinding, twisting—gripped Corrie as if she were a piece of meat being chewed by a sled dog. Yes, that was it, she thought, choking off a high scream. She was a piece of caribou meat being devoured by dogs. She could feel their teeth now, shredding her . . .

The pain lessened, subsided, and was gone. As she lay back limply, she thought she could almost smell Avery's fear. Or was it her own? Perspiration was running between her breasts and down her thighs, and her hands and feet felt icy cold.

Avery, still holding the lamp, backed toward the cabin door. She could see his widened eyes, his flared nostrils. He was swallowing hard, and she realized that he was trying not to gag.

Anger filled her. How dare he be sick when it was she who was undergoing childbirth, she who was in pain!

"Damn you, Avery, don't you dare leave yet! Don't you dare leave me here in the dark! Come here!"

She could hardly believe it was her own voice, cursing as Papa had done. Avery slowly approached the bunk.

"Avery, I'm going to have it very soon." She arched her back as another contraction took her. "Don't go away, Avery." She gritted her teeth. "Don't you dare to leave me until I have some help."

"Help? But what help? My God, Corrie, I don't—I never . . . "

"I've never done it either! But I'm doing it anyway, whether I like it or not, and I've got to have some help—" Her words trailed off into a choked scream, and she had to wad great handfuls of the blanket into her fists. She pulled these to her mouth and bit down, tasting the fuzzy, greasy wool.

"But Corrie, I can't. I don't know what to do. I can't stay here . . . "

"I don't want you to stay here! I want some help, that's all. Get me Mason. That's it. Go and wake up Mason. He'll help me. He'll know what to do."

Avery fled, letting a blast of cold air into the cabin as he slammed the door behind him. Corrie was left alone in the smothering dark to cram the blanket into her mouth and bite off another scream. With a shudder she recalled Bea Ellen's stories of wooden blocks carved by midwives

for laboring mothers to bite down on. Of birthing stools.
Knives left under beds to cut the pain . . .

Good merciful heavens, she thought, tasting wool. How
could a knife under the bed help? How could anything
help against this? If only Avery had left her the lantern,
so she wouldn't be in the dark. Then at least she would
not have the sensation that she was lying at the bottom of
a black mine shaft, abandoned.

The door opened again. Lantern light flickered through
the cabin.

"Corrie? Are you all right? Avery said—"

It was Mason, puffy-eyed from sleep. He wore a shirt
hastily pulled on and buttoned crookedly, with no jacket
at all. His blond hair hung in his eyes, making him look
younger than ever. But Corrie had never been so glad to
see anyone.

"It's the baby," she told him, choking back a sob.

"I should have guessed. Avery was barely making any
sense at all." He approached her, his eyes assessing her.
"But it's nothing to worry about, really it isn't. Birth is a
simple process, very natural. Animals do it all the time
without making a fuss."

She closed her eyes. "But I'm not an animal. Mason, it's
coming, it's coming soon, I know it. The pains are harder
each time. I . . . I don't have time to send for a doctor,
do I?"

"I don't know. I don't think so. I'll send Bill over to the
Nugget, though. Miss Gilhooley might come back with
him. Then at least you'd have a woman with you."

"Yes, please, anything!" she gasped. "I don't care, I
just want this to be over."

Mason left the cabin for a moment and then he was
back. He took one of her hands in his. His skin felt very
smooth and cool.

"That's right," he said. "Clutch my hand, Corrie. I
don't care how hard you squeeze. You can break my
bones if you want to, although I'd prefer that you didn't."
She could sense him smiling at her. "The most important
thing is for you to relax after each pain is over. Just lie
there and let your muscles relax. . . . "

The next contraction came. Corrie gripped Mason's
hand and did indeed make every effort to break his fin-

gers. But at last the contraction subsided, leaving her this time with a dull ache in her back.

"That's right," he said. "Just hold on, Corrie. You're doing fine."

She licked her dry lips. "Mason, you act as if you'd delivered a baby before."

"I suppose I have. If a calf counts as a baby." He was grinning at her. "My father has a farm in Chelsea—that's near Ann Arbor—and I've always helped him. Do you know, Corrie, that when animals give birth they usually don't have any fear? They just lie there very quietly and calmly and do what they have to. Perhaps you should try that."

She suppressed a wild laugh. "I'm not a cow, Mason—"

Again the pain came, and this time it was deeper and more grinding, and centered somehow in her bowel. She felt as if something huge and malevolent were trying to get out of her, to shove its way directly through her flesh . . .

"Scream, Corrie. Go ahead and scream if you want to. I won't mind. But it would be better if you'd just try to relax. Really, I have delivered plenty of cows and I do know something of what should be done. . . . "

It all had a distorted, dreamlike quality. Shortly before the birth, Mason rummaged frantically about the cabin, found a first-aid kit Avery had bought in Skagway, and gave her a light dose of laudanum to ease the pain.

Dimly she could hear him yelling at her, shouting at her to push down. She pushed and the baby came. Later she remembered the odd, mewing quality of its cry, like a sickly kitten.

"Mason?"

"Corrie, you . . . you have a boy." Mason's voice didn't sound right, the thought came to her. No, he sounded choked, as if his nose was suddenly stuffy.

"Is he all right? His cry—"

Miraculously, the pain was all gone. She felt as if she were floating in a warm pool. She twisted her head about in an effort to see the infant Mason was holding.

"Mason, I want to look at him. Please bring him here so I can see him."

"He—he's not right. He was born with some deformities, Corrie. I frankly don't think he'll live very long. His face is very blue."

"Oh, God."

"Corrie, please. I'll give you some more laudanum so you can sleep. That would be the best thing for you. I think you should rest."

"But I don't want to rest! I want to see my baby!"

Mason stood on the other side of the cabin, wrapping something in one of the flannel squares and putting it into a wooden box he had found to use for a cradle. For a moment she heard the pitiful, mewling cry again, so faint. But then it stopped and there was nothing.

"Mason . . ."

"I'm trying to keep him warm and to get the mucous out. I'll do all I can for him. But these things happen, Corrie, and no one knows why. Farm animals are born like this sometimes, with . . . things wrong. They don't live, most of them. They die, and it's a mercy. God takes them, Corrie. And I think God will take your baby, too. He's very blue now and I know he can't last long."

From across the cabin, Mason sounded very old, and Corrie found it hard to believe that this was the same youth who had gripped her in his arms and pressed such passionate kisses upon her. But that had happened so long ago. In spite of the laudanum a crushing feeling pierced her chest, like shards of breaking glass.

"But it's my baby . . . Mason, I want to see him. I want to hold him. I—I want to know what's wrong with him."

"Corrie—"

"I want to know, I tell you!"

"Very well, then."

The lantern flickered, throwing shadows on the wall. Corrie saw Mason pick up something wrapped in flannel out of the wooden box and carry it toward her. He half knelt by the bunk so he could hold the baby out to her.

He was very small, with dusky-purplish skin and a forehead and eyes exactly like Cordell Stewart's. His little mouth was small and full and puckered.

"Pull back the blanket," Corrie ordered. The shards of glass were splintering in her, one by one, piercing her.

"But Corrie, I don't think you want to see all this—"

"Pull it back."

Slowly Mason revealed the baby. He was armless, his shoulders ending in little pulpy fingers of flesh.

"Corrie." Mason's voice had a glacial, empty, dreamlike quality to it, which seemed to come from an enormous distance, as far away as the aurora. "I think there's more wrong with him than just his arms. I think there are defects on the inside of him, too. I feel sure of it. This often happens with animals. He isn't breathing right, and I think his heart is damaged. Perhaps—perhaps it was something you ate, something that went wrong with the pregnancy, something we don't know about . . . "

She was pregnant when the carriage overturned and killed her father. Pregnant during those days when she lay unconscious, when they gave her heaven only knows what drugs and medications.

And Avery would not care. The knowledge stabbed inside her as sharp as a point of glass. He would probably be relieved if the baby died.

"Corrie, you mustn't look like that. Here. Hold the baby. Take him."

Dazedly she felt the infant being thrust into her arms. She had never held anything so small before, so weak and trusting. The eyes, so like Papa's, were watching her. They seemed to know her.

"Baby . . . oh, dear baby," she whispered to him. "Please live. Please breathe. It doesn't matter about your arms. I promise you I don't care about that. Just live. It's all I ask of you."

But the infant did not whimper. Its eyes fluttered shut, and its skin turned an even more dusky hue.

"Baby," she pleaded. "Baby . . . "

Half an hour later the baby was dead. Corrie sobbed silently, huddled in a ball with her back to the room, turned away from the hands which sought to give her more laudanum, to clean her up after the birth. Then, as if in a dream, she heard a voice screaming, and knew that it was her own.

"My gawd, she sure is carrying on, isn't she, poor thing," a new voice said, a woman's voice, and she knew that Miss Gilhooley from the Nugget was there, helping Mason.

Across the cabin Mason and Miss Gilhooley were talking. Not that Corrie cared. She didn't. She allowed the voices to go on, but forced herself not to understand their meaning.

"Well, we got to do something with her, and that's a fact," Miss Gilhooley said. "Can't let her stay like this, all crazy-like."

"She's not crazy! She's had a terrible shock, that's all. This was her first child. Besides, she's very young."

"Old enough to have a kid, though, wasn't she? And you drug me all the way over here for this? She don't want me, she don't want no one, from the looks of it. I coulda stayed in my blankets and got some extra sleep for all the good I'm doing here. What are you aiming to do with that dead baby, anyways? Send it back to Dawson City?"

"I don't know yet. I'll have to talk to her husband."

"Ask me, you ought to bury the filthy little monster right here in the ground and get it over with. Ugh. Thought I'd near like to puke when I saw the thing. No wonder she's screamin'. I'd scream, too."

"Look, would you just get out of here, Miss Gilhooley?"

"Well! Well, I never! Call me all the way over here in the middle of the night and look what I get. Backtalk from a kid barely out of short pants. You should be at your mama's knee, sonny boy, not out mining for gold."

"I said just get out of here."

"All right, all right, I'm going. You needn't get ornery about it."

Time passed and the cabin was silent. Then there was Avery's voice.

"Mason. Look, Mason, I— I can't . . . you see how it is, don't you?"

"No, I don't see." Mason's words were coldly angry. "She's just given birth and her child has died. She's had a terrible shock. She needs her husband here with her."

"But you know I can't . . . I haven't the stomach for . . . " There was the sound of retching, clear and distinct.

"For God's sake, Avery, go outside if you have to do that."

"I'll go. Should have done that a long time ago. Her and her demands. Couldn't she have waited? Waited until I could come back and marry her properly and buy her a house?"

"Where are you going? What are you doing?"

"I'm packing, that's what. I can't stay here, not with that—that *thing* buried here. Every time I walk past it, I'll throw up."

"That thing, as you call it, is your son."

"That thing is a piece of garbage, a piece of dog-carrion. God! Get a woman pregnant and what does she give you but a damned monster . . . "

"Avery! You can't just pull out of here like this and leave her flat."

"Jesus, I know that. Don't you think I'll think about it later and feel like a worm? But I . . . I can't . . . Every time I'd touch her, I'd start thinking . . . You do understand, don't you? I need time to think, to get away. She'll be all right. I'll leave her a poke of gold dust."

Voices buzzed past Corrie's ears like the ceaseless hum of summer mosquitoes. And then the voices were silent for a long stretch of time and she knew that all of them had left, all except Mason. He stayed with her, moving quietly about the cabin, thrusting wood into the stove, cooking, hauling water, lighting candles.

"Corrie." Mason's voice prodded her like a sharp stick. "Corrie, you've got to get hold of yourself. It's been five days now. I had to bury him. I went to the roadhouse and they knew of a preacher. We had the service yesterday. I wrapped him in that pretty embroidered robe you packed up . . . "

Silence. Long, long silence while light and shadow moved about the cabin and she slept and woke again, and slept some more. Odd, flickering dreams turned in her mind.

"Corrie, wake up! Corrie, you've been having another of those nightmares. You were screaming about fire, and about a brooch. And calling that man's name again, that Quade. Over and over you called him."

Mason's hands shook her shoulders, shook her until her teeth rattled and she had to flee from him, back into the core of herself.

"Corrie, why? Why are you doing this to yourself? Sure, you lost a baby in childbirth and yes, the baby was born deformed, and his death was a tragedy. I know that, and I'm sorry. But life must go on. Even I know that. You're alive, Corrie. Alive, do you hear me?

"No."

"Corrie, it's been eleven days!" Pain smacked at her face. Someone was slapping her mercilessly. "You can't go on like this, retreating from everything into a world of your own. Oh, God, oh, Jesus, how could I be doing this to you? But I am, and I've got to. Corrie, will you ever love me back? No, it's that Quade man, isn't it? He's the one . . ."

More slaps—stinging at her, making her cheeks burn.

Part 4

❧ Chapter 28 ❧

In later years Corrie would never know exactly what roused her out of her withdrawn state and brought her back to life, however somber a life. Was it Mason's slaps on her face, battering at her painfully? Was it the way Mason kept shouting Quade's name at her? Or was it simply her own healthy body, reviving because it was young, and could not mourn forever?

Whatever the reason, she did awake. Reluctantly, angrily, but at last fully aware, to find herself weeping hot, stinging, cleansing tears. Why would God have allowed such a damaged child to be born, only to take him away almost at once? What had the purpose been?

"We'll never know," Mason said. "My mother always used to say that God wanted an angel."

"Perhaps. But He needn't have taken my baby!" Corrie's eyes filled again.

"Why not your baby, Corrie? Why not anybody's baby?" Mason retorted and Corrie turned away from him, not speaking to him for hours. Anger consumed her—anger at God, or fate, whatever force it had been which treated her child so. Furiously she tossed the baby clothes and the wooden box which had briefly held her son out the cabin door and kicked snow over them. She didn't want to be reminded—she wouldn't be!

But then, hours later, she crept out and retrieved a small square of embroidered linen and a delicate gown trimmed with machine lace. She must have something, something to remember her child by.

A month passed. December crept on them like a gray cloak. Each day had only two hours of light, although the "afterglow," as Mason called it, lasted for an hour or so after sunset. Often they heard the howling of wolves, closer now and unbearably mournful.

"It's as if they were souls, lost and crying for their Maker," Corrie told Mason once, not adding that the eerie animal cries made her think of her baby. She hoped that, wherever he was, he was not lost and crying, and that his deformities were healed and he was made whole.

Although they waited, Avery did not return. He had talked of going north to Circle City, further upriver, Mason told her; discoveries had been made there on Birch Creek.

"He's not coming back," Corrie said dully one afternoon. It had been raining heavily for hours, the cold and ugly day matching the bleakness of her mood.

Mason nodded.

"He wanted to go all along," Corrie said. "He blamed me for holding him back. I suppose I was foolish to . . . " She let her words trail off.

"But what will you do now, Corrie? You certainly can't stay here. This claim is played out."

"I don't know. Go back to Dawson, I guess."

"Dawson!" Mason tossed his long hair out of his eyes. "You can't go back to Dawson City all alone, Corrie. Come with me. Be my woman. I . . . I love you. I'll take good care of you, better care than Avery ever did. And perhaps somehow we can manage to get you a divorce from him so that you can marry me and really be my wife—"

"Mason." She looked at him with pity. How eager he was, how capable and adventuresome. She really was fond of him, more than fond. And she owed him so much that she could never repay him. Still . . .

"Mason, oh, Mason. I can't be your wife," she said.

"But why not? I love you! And you need someone to take care of you. A woman alone here—"

"I'll always be grateful to you for what you've done for me. I'll never forget you, ever. But that isn't enough. I'm just not attracted to you in that way, not—not physically. You were so good to me when the baby came, but . . . "

She plunged on awkwardly, knowing that she was hurting him, but feeling that this had to be said. "I just don't think it would work for us, that's all."

"Why won't it work?" He gripped her shoulders. Behind them, on the stove, a rabbit stew was boiling over, but neither of them noticed it. "It might work if you'd try, Corrie. I know I'll always love you . . . "

How simple it would be, she was thinking, to say yes to him and to let him take care of her as he wanted to do. Yet she knew that she couldn't. She couldn't imagine being in bed with him. She would never be able to experience with him the intense feelings she had known with Quade.

No, if she went with Mason the passion would all be on his side. She herself would have only gratitude to bind her to him. And for her that would never be enough.

"Mason, I just can't. Really, you must understand, I— I'm very grateful and I'm very fond of you, but not in a man-woman way. I can't. That's all."

He let his hands drop from her shoulders. "I see," he said slowly. "It's that other man, isn't it? That Quade Hill man. When you were so sick you kept calling out for him."

"Mason, I'm so sorry."

There was a long silence while Mason looked at her, his face bleak. "What will become of you, then, Corrie?"

"I don't know. I think I will go to Dawson City and stay with a friend there, Li Hua. When spring comes and Aunt Susan sends the passage money, I'll go back to San Francisco, I suppose."

And never see Quade again, some little voice in her was crying out, but she pushed it aside. "So I won't have to trouble you any more, Mason. You can go about your prospecting without having to worry about me any further. After all, you know that you did come north for gold and adventure. Well, now that you're free of me you can go after it. Where do you think you'll travel now?"

He hesitated. "I might try Forty Mile. Perhaps I'll go along the Chicken or the Tanana. I heard . . . but first I'll see you to Dawson and see that your friend takes you in and that you're all right. And I'll give you some of my gold dust, too, so you'll have enough."

She was touched. "Oh, Mason, thank you so much, but I really couldn't take it. You'll need everything you have, with winter here. I'll get along—Avery left me a bit, and I think I can manage. At any rate, I'm sure I won't starve."

"But Corrie—" For an instant he seemed about to protest. Then his face changed and he said, "Very well. I'll take you to Dawson City as soon as the rain stops."

She touched his sleeve. "Mason, I want you to know I'll never be able to thank you enough for what you did for me."

"Oh, now—"

"No, it's true. And—Mason, I think I'll name my son after you. We never did give the poor little thing a name, did we? But I think it's time he had one. And we'll make a marker for him so that people will know."

They left the claim five days later, on a morning when the sky was a windswept clear blue and the temperature dropped to a crisp eight degrees. Snow squeaked under the runners of the sled and wind bit at the exposed skin of Corrie's face so that she had to pull a woolen scarf over her cheeks.

They left a board marker for the baby's grave, carved by Mason with a pocketknife: *Mason Edwards Curran, born 11-21-98, died 11-21-98.* Mason wanted to add more, but Corrie said that was enough.

"Words don't matter anyway," she told him. "It's what's in out hearts that counts. I'll always remember my baby—and you, too, Mason."

Dawson City seemed pinched and cold, with snow piled in the streets and dirtied by the passing of horses, dogs and mules. Men swarmed about on scaffolding, still rebuilding after the hotel fire. Outside each building were stacked huge piles of firewood, and it seemed to Corrie as if a mist hung in the air, comprised of wood smoke and vapor from human and animal breaths.

Before going his own way Mason delivered Corrie to Li Hua's. His eyes widened as he caught sight of the facade of the small cabin which was the hairdressing salon. Corrie, too, stared at the little salon in astonishment.

It had changed. Underneath the original sign, another

one had been installed. This one, done in oils, depicted a sinuous young woman dressed in the latest fashion. The woman's waist was small, and her bosom flared out exaggeratedly. However, it was her hair which had been given the most detailed attention by the artist. Her red hair had been swept up into a sumptuous knot and secured with a jewelled tiara, each stone carefully outlined. The size of the sign itself was at least six feet by four feet, and it dwarfed the little cabin which supported it.

But as if this were not enough, there were other changes, too. The structure to the right of the Pear Blossom Salon, previously a livery stable, was now a two-story building with two plate glass windows on either side of the door. Another huge sign announced, "The Princess Dance Hall, Loveliest Girls in the Yukon, Bar None."

Corrie stood frozen for a moment in front of the Pear Blossom Salon, feeling dispirited and out of place, the thought of her lost child a painful ache that seemed to penetrate to the very center of her bones. At last she made her way up the wooden plank walk and knocked at the door.

"Come in, we're open!" someone called.

She pushed open the door and entered. The small salon was full of girls. At least eight of them milled about, giggling, chattering, handling the combs and jeweled items which Li Hua had laid out on her table.

One girl wore a black taffeta silk waist, with rows of perpendicular tucks and a yoke of embroidery. Another was resplendent in red sateen, tucked and shirred and trimmed in matching satin bands. A third wore peau de soie. Carrie was transported by the delicacy of French lace, the sensuous rustle of silk and taffeta underskirts. All of these garments, Corrie knew, had been shipped up the river at great cost.

She glimpsed faces made rosy and alluring with carmine, lips reddened to a pout, eyebrows penciled into high, surprised wings. And their hair: it had been piled high in splendid creations of puffs, waves and spit curls. Some of the coiffures had been adorned with jet beads, combs or lace ribbons.

These were the dance hall girls, Corrie realized. Even

the plainest among them had been made pretty by Li Hua's skill.

Corrie's eyes traveled to a figure sitting on a pine stool in the midst of the hubbub of girls. It was Li Hua, of course, clad in a simple white shirtwaist and dark serge skirt. Her cast had been removed and she wore dainty black kid boots. Her glossy hair had been drawn up into a smooth pompadour, and her porcelain beauty was even more striking than ever.

"Corrie!" Li Hua looked up from the handful of beads she was showing to the girls.

"Li Hua— Oh, Li Hua—"

Forgetting the staring girls, forgetting everything, Corrie flew to her friend's arms, weeping against the crisp lace of Li Hua's blouse. "Oh, Li Hua, my baby, he d-died, and Avery's gone, and I . . . I had nowhere to go . . . "

Li Hua hugged her tightly. She smelled of soap and fresh linens. Then she clapped her hands together, thereby dismissing the dance hall girls, who trooped through the door in a flurry of giggles, emitting clouds of perfumed scent.

"There. They're gone, and we can talk. Oh, Corrie, you say you lost your baby? How terrible! I've thought about you so much, and wondered . . . "

Half an hour later, Corrie had told her friend everything, from Quade's visit to the hills near the mining site, to Avery's obsession with gold, his desertion of her, the birth of little Mason and his poignant burial.

"Oh, Corrie!" Li Hua embraced her again. "I'm so very sorry. You can stay here with me as long as you wish."

"I prayed," Corrie choked. "I begged God to save him. It didn't matter to me about his arms, nothing mattered, only that he should live. And now he's b-buried with only a wooden marker . . . "

A shadow crossed Li Hua's face, and Corrie remembered the horrors she, too, had endured.

"But you'll remember him," the Chinese girl said firmly. "You're strong, Corrie, much stronger than you know. God knows I had to learn that for myself. You can, too . . . "

Li Hua brewed some strong tea, and they continued to talk.

"What is that place next door?" Corrie asked. "Avery told me something about a dance hall."

"Yes, that's the Princess Dance Hall," Li Hua explained. "And it's mine—at least, partly mine."

"Yours?"

"I bought a share of it with the rest of Marty's money and what I could save from my shop. I manage it, too.. Do you like it? It's still in need of a good deal of work, and I'm planning to bring in some crystal chandeliers and build a new entertainment stage. But all that will have to wait until spring."

"A stage! Chandeliers! And that sign!"

"You like the sign? I had it painted especially for the shop. It's the Princess, the Princess of the Dance Hall, of course, and I thought it might lend a certain air, and make people notice us. Will Sebastian liked it quite well. He said that the sign painter, a man from Chicago, will be quite famous one day."

Li Hua was smiling. Corrie could not take her eyes off her friend. Never had the oriental girl looked more lovely. Her skin was perfect, nearly poreless. Her mass of blue-black hair appeared to be so heavy that it seemed to weight down her fragile neck.

"Why, it certainly is impressive! And, yes, I think that the artist will be famous one day."

"Oh, Corrie, in spite of your troubles, I *am* glad to see you. It's been rather lonely here. The girls—I don't like them, not really. I have no friends here save for Will."

"Will? Do you mean Dr. Sebastian?"

"Yes, he has been here to examine my leg several times." Li Hua flushed. "I limp a bit, but Will assures me that all will be fine."

Li Hua shrugged. "Besides, I don't have time to think about my leg. You'd be surprised at all there is to do with a place like this. And I have to earn my investment back. I virtually beggared myself to get in."

Corrie hesitated. "Are you truly happy here in a place like this, Li Hua? Is this really what you want to do?"

"Yes." The other girl said it defiantly. "Yes. I want to make money, and I have to do it now, quickly, before it's too late. I hear rumors. Someday this gold boom is going to move on, and everyone will leave Dawson City. They'll all go, and I'll have nothing left but a chandelier, some old whiskey bottles and an out-of-tune piano." She smiled faintly. "And Will," she added. "He'll be here, too."

"But what about—"

"Just don't worry about me, Corrie, please." Li Hua's fingers were cool on Corrie's hand. "I can take care of myself. Didn't I get myself north and then to Dawson? I can do anything that I want to do."

In February, influenza hit Dawson City, and Corrie was one of the victims. She lay dully on the rope-bottomed bunk Li Hua had had built for her in the back of the hairdressing salon, and the days slipped past without her caring where they went.

She sunk into a depression which seemed to have endless gray depth. Everything, every good part of her life, seemed to be dead. Papa, who had died nearly a year ago in the carriage accident. Her baby, little Mason Edwards Curran, whom she had buried under the hard Yukon sky.

Her marriage to Avery—that, too, was gone. Mason Edwards had disappeared into the vastness of the snow-covered hills and glaciers. And Quade was gone; that was the worst hurt of all. He had not even stopped at the Canadian Bank of Commerce to pick up her messages, as he had said he would do. It was as if, immersed in his own affairs, he had completely forgotten her, or had written her off.

He doesn't know about the baby. He thinks you are still married to Avery, a little voice prodded at her. *He told you that you belonged to your husband. He is an honorable man and would not interfere in a marriage.*

Besides, that same voice whispered, *his obligations to you are finished, aren't they? He transported you to Avery exactly as he promised to do. He saw you safely wed. He wished you luck.*

What more do you wish, Cordelia Stewart? What more?

Perhaps because of the influenza, which weakened her, there were days when she wished that she had died in childbirth along with her son. Li Hua, who welcomed

Corrie to her cabin warmly, made no secret of the fact that she was worried about her. Li Hua moved about the small, overheated cabin, preparing food over the sheet-iron stove. She brought Corrie a plate laden with slices of moose swimming in brown gravy, cranberry sauce, sour-dough bread, mince pie.

Corrie glanced at the plate and turned hastily away from the pungent smell of moose. "I . . . I can't, Li Hua. I wish I could; you've been so kind to me this winter . . ."

"No kinder than you were to me on the *Alki*. Corrie, you've had the sickness for three weeks now. If you don't eat, you'll never be cured. Do you want to starve away to nothing and lose all of your looks?"

"I don't care about my looks."

"Every woman should care about her looks!" Li Hua's hands were on her hips and her eyes flashed with anger. "Do you want me to take you over to the hospital for the sisters to nurse? I could. Or I could call one of the girls from the Salvation Army. They're likely to force-feed you. Would you relish that? To have food forced down your gullet whether you wish it or not?"

Corrie raised herself on one elbow. "You wouldn't do that. And neither would they."

"Maybe not, but I'd certainly like to." Li Hua's face softened for an instant, reminding Corrie of the girl she had known in San Francisco. "Eat, Corrie. This good food is going to make you strong again."

"I don't care about being strong," Corrie said stubbornly. But with a slow, wavering hand she took a forkful of the moose meat and put it in her mouth. Methodically she began to chew.

Li Hua sighed. "Well, that's a start. Now, mind, you've got to keep on eating or I will force-feed you, I swear it. I don't want you dying on me. How do you think it would look for the reputation of the Princess, to have one of its employees perishing of starvation?"

"Employee?"

"Don't you remember? You promised me you'd take some portraits of the men. They can send a picture home to their families. Or we can have their pictures taken with the girls, for the bachelors who'd prefer it. I've had the signs made for weeks, and when you're well enough,

I'll put them up. Who knows, Corrie, maybe you'll become as well-known here as Mr. Hegg!"

"I doubt it," Corrie said. But grimly she took another bite of meat.

"That's it, Corrie. Eat and get fatter. I'm sick of looking at you, all skin and bone and staring eyes. You need a bit of life in you!"

Dawson. If there was any town in the world more ill-suited to bring a person out of the throes of deep depression, Corrie did not know where it might be. It was as if she had been wrenched permanently away from sunlight and plunged into a midnight world of cold and gloom.

In the dark which lasted virtually twenty-two hours a day, the city of Dawson seemed to steam as clouds of vapor puffed up from chimneys and stovepipes. The ghostly greenish bars of the northern lights flickered across a dark sky; frost-racked timbers cracked like pistol shots in the cold. Frequently the howling of wolves could be heard.

Snow, mountainous quantities of it, blocked roads and paths, and was piled against cabin walls to serve as insulation. Saloon owners tunneled through it to reach their doorways. Frozen springs formed odd, contorted domes of ice over roads and paths and sometimes came welling up into buildings or cabins.

The cold, however, was the worst of it. Although Dawson City's climate was reputed to be milder than Fort Yukon's, that information was not comforting when the thermometer dipped to a frigid twenty or thirty below zero. Will Sebastian, who came to treat Corrie's influenza and called often on Li Hua, brought them ugly tales of frostbite. You must keep your hands and feet perfectly dry, he informed them, for the least amount of perspiration would invite freezing. Men, he explained, had to clip or shave their whiskers in winter, especially mustaches or nostril hairs. Otherwise, balls of ice would form there from their freezing breath. Only *cheechakos* here wore hair on their faces.

Often Corrie thought of Quade as she heard these stories. Was he taking precautions against the cold? How was he faring? She did not know. A letter left for him weeks ago at the bank, begging him to get in touch with her, had not been picked up. He could be a thousand miles away, and she would never know.

Cold. Never had Corrie realized its frightening power. At fifty below zero, you could not use a candle outdoors, as its wick could not generate enough heat to melt the wax. If you exhaled hard through your mouth, your breath would cause a soft roar. If you spat onto the snow, your saliva would freeze before it hit the ground.

Will told them of a man who, working outside, had thoughtlessly put a nail into his mouth. The metal froze to his lips and tore off a large piece of skin.

Corrie sensed the worst of the cold was past. It seemed to her that she could tell that each day the sun shone a few minutes longer. Summer was still a daydream, but one within the range of possibility, at least.

On the evening of February twenty-fifth, Corrie sat alone in Li Hua's cabin working on the accounts, which Li Hua had left for her in order to "stop her brooding." Li Hua was at the dance hall, supervising the constant piano playing and the serving of drinks. Waves of sound drifted over from next door: shouts, laughter, piano music, the sound of feet shuffling on wood.

The principle of a dance hall was simple. ("Never mind what the girls do in their off hours," Li Hua said firmly. "I won't think about that. I'm not running a bordello, and I've told them so.") Men wanted female company, would pay money to dance with a girl, often for hours upon end. The Princess charged one dollar for a three-minute dance, of which seventy-five cents went to the house. Bolo Mulligan, a former bouncer in a Chicago saloon, served as Li Hua's "caller off," and it was his job to get the miners to dance as often as possible. To do this, he would call or cajole them to join in a "real juicy waltz."

Corrie had watched this spectacle from the back of the room. She thought she would nearly suffocate from the choking, badly ventilated atmosphere of the place, with its warm air and strong human odors. The miners usually danced bootless, and the stench of rotten socks was strong as it mingled with the fumes from spilled whiskey, cigar smoke and perspiration. No wonder the girls bathed in perfume, Corrie told herself wryly. They needed it for self-defense.

After a few minutes the music would end in a crash of piano keys. Each couple was expected to promenade directly to the bar. Here the man would buy a shot of whiskey or champagne (at thirty dollars a pint) and the girl would get a white ivory chip—worth twenty-five cents—from the bartender as her commission for the dance.

"You could always try a turn or two yourself, Corrie," Li Hua suggested once, slyly. "You can waltz, can't you? You could make as many as a hundred and twenty-five chips by dawn—if your strength holds out."

"Li Hua!" Corrie was shocked and angered. "Surely you don't expect me to—"

"Of course not; don't be silly." Li Hua was laughing. "Where is your sense of humor, Corrie? Has it gone from you, too, this winter? Once you would have smiled at such a suggestion. Or at least tried dancing a time or two, just for the fun of it."

Yes, perhaps she would have. Now she cared about nothing.

She turned over a page in the account book and sighed, looking up as she heard a squeak in the snow in front of the cabin. Li Hua had promised to send some cake and pretzels over for her, another offering in her long campaign to "fatten" her up. It was probably brawny Bolo Mulligan, Corrie thought, come to deliver the snack.

There was a knock at the cabin door, and Corrie put down her pen and got up.

"Coming, Bolo. Just a minute!"

She opened the cabin door.

Quade stood there holding a lantern, his huge frame bundled in a sealskin coat on which crystals of snow sparkled like jewels. A snow-dazzled fur cap hid his hair, and the flaps were pulled down around his ears. His features were strong, his jaw blunt and ruggedly carved, his skin darkened by the winter sun. He smiled slowly, revealing a tiny dimple in his right cheek. His blue eyes seemed to pierce her, to stop her heart.

"Quade!" She stepped backwards, feeling the blood leave her face.

"Delia!" he said. "You're as narrow as a rail. What have you done to yourself, come down with scurvy?"

But she did not hear a word he said; she only knew that he was here, big and vital and smelling of arctic air. She threw herself into his arms, feeling the cold of the fur against her skin.

"Watch the lamp. And get in, my girl, back into that cabin before you catch your death of pneumonia."

He pulled her back into Li Hua's cabin and closed the door to keep in the warmth from the stove. He shed his coat and dropped his hat. She burrowed into the warmth of him, pressing herself against his rumbling heartbeat, weeping into the wool of his shirt.

"Quade, oh . . . " she sobbed. "You're here! And Avery's gone . . . "

He did not say anything to her, not real words, anyway, only a constant murmur as he stroked her hair with his big hands and held her to him. Once he stroked away her tears with his thumb.

"I was a fool; I should have come a long time ago," he muttered at last. He lifted up her chin. "Look at me, little Delia. I want a good look at that stubborn little face of yours."

Their eyes met. She had a full sense of him, so vital and strong and wonderful, too. Quade was a true man in every way. He was handsome, not as Avery was, too strikingly perfect, but rugged and real. Corrie felt her heart contract with her love for him. She adored him. She always had, perhaps ever since that day in San Francisco, when he first pulled her into his carriage.

"You're thin," he told her. "Skinny as a little bedpost. What's happened to you, darling? The last time I saw you, you were second cousin to an elephant. Or well on your way in that direction, anyway."

She lowered her eyes. "My baby—" Her voice caught. "He was born deformed, Quade. Without arms. Mason said he—he couldn't ever have lived. Mason delivered my baby, and we . . . we had to bury him . . . "

"Darling." Quade held her until she had control of herself again. "I'm so damned sorry, Delia. I can't tell you how sorry I am. If only I'd known what happened to you!

But I didn't. When I saw you last, you were well, and I merely assumed—"

You belong to him, Delia, not to me. You made that decision the day you married him.

As if from a distance, she heard Quade's voice go on. "I heard here in town that Avery had gone to Circle City. Naturally, I took it for granted that you went with him. After I saw you, I was in Forty Mile for a time, doing some interviewing, and then in Eagle—a beautiful, godforsaken place that is—and finally today I came back here to Dawson City. I stopped at the bank where I found your letter. I think—"

But whatever he had been going to say was never finished. He kissed her mouth now, kissed her in deadly earnest. She felt like swooning under the battering his mouth gave her, the sweet, hard power of his touch. Never during her months with Avery had she felt even an inkling of this wild joy. She wanted to cry out, to exult, to match Quade's passion with her own.

She was barely aware that Quade scooped her up and carried her over to the bunk, where he lay her down upon the woolen blanket. She only knew that she was in his arms, that she belonged to him.

Their bodies melted together, and she arched herself against him, moaning with pleasure. His hands delicately explored her, while his mouth sought her breasts. She gave back to him, barring him nothing, giving herself to him as a rose opens its fragrant petals.

"God," Quade groaned. "Oh, my God, Delia, my darling, my only—"

They sought each other, they gave, found and were renewed. Then, in a gathering burst of fire, they exploded, he together with her, both of them flying, rocketing, burning in the joy of their love . . .

❧ Chapter 29 ❧

Later, with the cabin door safely barred, they lay wrapped in one another's arms and talked. Corrie told him about having the baby in the little cabin with the help of Mason Edwards, who delivered the child as he might have done a calf.

"I kept telling him I wasn't a cow," she recalled. "I remember that, how indignant I was. He kept reassuring me that women and cows were both mammals and that, really, there were a great many similarities—no insult intended, of course."

Quade's eyes flashed with amusement, and Corrie gave a teary little laugh. "Poor Mason, he was in love with me. And now he's off prospecting along the Tanana or somewhere. I hope he's being careful. I'd hate to think of him getting frostbite. He meant to go back to the university and finish up his schooling. He wanted to be a doctor."

Quade sighed and stroked the soft skin of her left breast with one finger. "So you've had your adventures."

"Adventures? Yes." Corrie was silent, thinking of the baby, whose forehead and eyes had looked so much like Cordell Stewart.

She wiggled out of Quade's grasp and sat up. She was aware of his eyes on her, lingering on the curves of her body. Next door, the piano music was frenetic.

"God, but you're beautiful naked," Quade said. "Even thin as you are."

Corrie shrugged into the cambric and lace of her undergarments and stood there tying the ribbons, her face averted from him, feeling a deep blush staining her skin.

"I've rented a cabin," he said. "I want you to come and stay in it with me, Corrie."

"Oh!" Her fingers dropped the bit of ribbon.

"Please, Corrie. I love you. You know that, don't you? I want you to live with me and be my woman, and damn propriety. We've flouted it once and we'll flout it again. When spring comes we'll worry about a divorce. Or we'll live in sin."

"Oh . . . " She said it again, stupidly.

"Is that all you can reply?" Piano chords crashed the end of the song in the dance hall next door. The girls would be leading men to the bar and insisting that they buy drinks.

Quade's arms drew around her, removing her fingers from the soft ribbons of her corset cover and clasping them in his own. "You're coming with me, of course; I'll move your things over tomorrow. My cabin isn't as big as this, but it's clean enough, and we'll scrub it cleaner. I've got to have you all to myself, Corrie."

"But I promised Li Hua I'd take photographs—"

"You can still do that; I've no objection. But just live with me. I've been without you too long. I've had to give up making apricot cake, you know. Every time I start it I think of you and that funny, pudgy little belly of yours, and Lake Bennett. I want to make you pregnant, Delia. I want there to be another baby, yours and mine."

"Oh, Quade," her voice choked.

And now she was weeping, and he was gently stripping the undergarments from her. He took her again. She soared with him, far upward among the silent bars of the aurora, and shuddered in explosions of light, and knew that she was his, and he was hers, and nothing else would ever matter again.

Corrie packed her things and, with Quade's help, moved them over to his cabin, located on the outskirts of Dawson and comfortably furnished with hand-made pine furniture.

Two days later a miner passing through from Circle City left a crumpled letter with Li Hua to be given to

Corrie. The note was scrawled, almost illegible, but Corrie could tell it was from Avery. He was lying injured and penniless in a cabin near Circle City. His provisions had been stolen and he was living on charity from other miners. He needed Corrie's help.

Corrie's first reaction was anger. She took the letter, already bedraggled from its long transit, and crumpled it into a wad. Then she ripped the wad up into little pieces and flung them on the floor of Quade's cabin.

"What are you doing that for?" he asked her.

"Because! Oh, damn him, Quade. Damn him!"

Quade sat on a bench hewn from a halved log, smoking a cigar and staring intently at the blue wisps of smoke that curled upward. "I take it that letter is from your erstwhile husband?"

"Yes! He wants me to come to him. He's in Circle City, ill from some sort of accident, he says, and he has no one else to turn to." She choked on her fury. "He apologizes for the way he treated me, says he knows it was despicable, and he hopes I'll forgive him. He says—"

She lifted up a booted foot and gave a violent and furious kick at the scraps of paper, scattering them further. "He says he wouldn't turn to me if he had any other choice. But he doesn't have any. I'm his last resort."

"Well, and I suppose you are."

"What?" She whirled on Quade. "Oh, how can you just sit there and fiddle with that cigar and look so calm about it! The man deserted me! Left me to fend for myself! And now he expects me to come running to him just because he needs me!"

Quade examined the cigar rather closely, rolling it between his fingers. "Perhaps he does need you. And you did fend for yourself, didn't you? And rather well, I might add."

"Are you trying to tell me, Quade Hill, that I should actually *go* to him? Run to him like a dutiful little wife? After what he did to me?"

"And why not? You are his wife, aren't you?"

"Why . . . why, yes, of course, but—"

She sat frozen and watched as Quade unfolded himself from the bench and walked to the cabin's one window, made of crudely oiled canvas. Frost had condensed on its surface; Quade scraped at it with a fingernail, making circular patterns in it.

"Then you'd better go to him, Delia. I have a feeling the man might be dying."

"What? Dying! What makes you think—"

"This is a savage country, my dear, and it pounces on mistakes. Have you ever heard of a scurvy hut? Sometimes the miners build them when they are suffering with the disease, and then they just lie in them and tough it out. Sometimes they live through the winter and sometimes they don't. Men shoot off their feet, Delia, when they are cleaning their rifles. Or they're shot accidentally by a partner, or mauled by a bear, or caught in a snowslide. Or they simply fall on the ice and break a leg. And there's always frostbite. Snow blindness. A thousand possible accidents . . . "

She stared at him. "But Avery didn't mention . . . surely he can't be *that* ill."

"Why not?"

"Then you want me to go back to him. That's it, isn't it?" she asked dully. "You're tired of me."

"No. Of course I don't want you to go. You should know that." Quade's face turned into an expressionless mask. "It's just that, surprisingly enough, I have a sense of honor, if you want to call it that. I know what it's like to be out there alone in that hellish cold. Your Avery— I don't think he would write you at all unless he was pretty desperate. And I may be with his wife, but I don't want to be responsible for him. I don't want his life on my conscience. I owe him that much. So I'll take you to him, and then you can decide what to do for yourself."

Corrie drew herself up with a shudder.

As they left Dawson the sun was rising, a swollen red ball balanced on the horizon amid layers of purple-tinged clouds. It was a sunrise frightening in its cruel extravagance, Corrie thought, shivering. She could see why men loved the Yukon. But she could also see why they feared it.

Quade hired an Eskimo guide, a man named Alikammiq, who was short, cheerful, round-faced, and dressed in a soiled parka, his teeth darkened with chewing tobacco.

They made steady progress for the more than two hundred miles north. As the days passed, they skirted other mining towns: Forty Mile, Star City, Eagle, Nation. As the river neared Circle City, the close-pressing mountains seemed to recede, and the land grew flatter. This, Quade said, was because they were approaching the Yukon Flats. In the summer, he told her, once the river passed Circle City the land would look as if a mirror had shattered into a thousand shards of silver. Each bit of silver would be a lake, pond, swamp or slough.

Circle City was a little log-cabin town, its stovepipes sending up plumes of gray wood smoke into the cold air. They passed down its main street, lined with log buildings, many with slanting lean-tos added to the side. The city seemed bleak to Corrie, with its log fire department and its shedlike stores, one of them called the "N.C. Company." The jail offered a warning printed on its door: *All prisoners must report by 9:00 P.M. or they will be locked out for the night.*

"Not a pleasant prospect," Quade told her wryly. "When it hits thirty below, even jail might be a nice place to be."

"Oh, I don't care about that!" she cried. "All I want to know is where Avery is, so we can get this over with."

"Be patient. We'll make inquiries at a roadhouse. They're usually a center of town life. They'll probably know all about whatever is going on."

They did find a roadhouse, a log establishment named "The Place," its kitchen lean-to looking perilously as if it might slide down into its original heap of raw logs at any moment. A sign announced that the restaurant was run by "W. Rutnowski, Prop. ABSOLUTELY NO CREDIT." As they entered, they saw that another notice was nailed to the door. It informed them that those caught stealing would be punished by "whipping at the post and banishment from the country."

Corrie stopped in her tracks to stare at the notice, uneasiness pushing through her.

"Whipping at the post!" she exclaimed.

"Thievery is serious business here, Delia, on a level with murder. It could result in a man's death."

"I suppose so," she said faintly.

They made their way inside the building which, like most of these establishments, was crude, small, noisy and overheated, and smelled of food and wet boots and dogs. The proprietor, a big man with enormous shoulders and a lantern-shaped jaw, informed them that the menu consisted of bear meat, beans and pie, take it or leave it.

"We'll take it," Quade said cheerfully. "And a portion for our guide, too. He's in back tending to the sled dogs, but should be in shortly."

The man nodded, none too politely, and then went back toward the kitchen, stopping on the way to speak to a tableful of miners who were crammed together at a slab table, passing a whiskey bottle about and laughing uproariously. At another table three other men sat, absorbed in their full plates of food. But Corrie's eyes barely took in the scene of the diners. It was Avery who was on her mind. She felt apprehensive.

"Quade," she whispered. "Let's ask that man—Mr. Rutnowski, is it?—whether he knows anything about Avery."

"After we eat. Right now I'd like to enjoy a full plateful of food on a peaceful stomach."

"But Quade—"

"Bad news always sits better on a full belly; have you ever noticed that, Corrie? I smell dried apple pie. Or is it berry? Let's have some. And we can hope their cook ran out of shoe leather before he got to the crust."

"Oh, very well," Corrie said, sighing. She knew she had no choice but to go along with Quade's wishes.

Half an hour later they had completed their meal. Their Eskimo guide, whose habit of chewing tobacco was driving Corrie to distraction, came in and was given his meal in the kitchen.

Quade excused himself and went back into the kitchen lean-to. When he returned, his face was grim.

"Well," he said, "I got the truth, all right. And I'm not sure you're going to savor it."

An odd feeling pressed at Corrie's chest. "Go ahead. Please tell me."

"Well, it seems that our kindly friend Mr. Rutnowski does know of Avery. The whole town does. He has been prospecting about here, near Birch Creek mostly, but not

having much luck, since the good claims are virtually all
taken. It seems that Avery was the indirect cause of a
miners' meeting recently, the result of which was that sign
we saw on the door as we came in."

"That sign? About thieving?"

"Yes, I'm afraid so, Corrie. Avery came into town last
Thursday to pick up some provisions. On the way back to
his cabin it was snowing pretty heavily, and he was waylaid by two or three men, he was never able to tell exactly how many. The upshot of it was, they hit him over
the head, took his gold dust and left him to freeze to
death."

"Oh, my God."

"Don't worry, he didn't die. Your Avery is too tough
for that. No, he lay unconscious for a while and then he
came to. Somehow he managed to drag himself to his feet
and he kept on staggering down Birch Trail. Some miners
on their way back from a saloon in town found him. They
took him to their own cabin and thawed him out. But I'm
afraid he suffered severe frostbite anyway."

"Frostbite!"

"Yes. And, Corrie, it's pretty bad, I'm afraid."

"How bad?" she whispered, thinking of the hideous stories Will Sebastian had told.

"Both feet, both ears and his right hand."

"His . . . ears?" she said faintly.

"Yes. Apparently, he wouldn't let a doctor look at him.
He insisted on being taken back to the abandoned cabin
where he's staying. Your husband is a stubborn sort, I'm
afraid."

Across the crowded, overheated room, Mr. Rutnowski
was carrying a tray of well-laden plates to the drinking
miners; one of them belched loudly. At the back table a
man in a well-cut calfskin coat talked earnestly in a low
voice to his companions, his back to Corrie. None of them
were looking at her.

"Corrie, are you all right?" Quade asked.

"Yes—yes, I'm fine." Nausea pushed at the back of her
throat and desperately she swallowed. She couldn't be sick
here, she thought wildly. The rough, grainy wood surface
of the table seemed to rise, dip toward her and then move
away. Noise buzzed in her ears. All she could think of was

how handsome Avery was. His face always reminded her of a painting of one of the ancient gods. Women turned to stare at him; she had done so herself when first they met so many long months ago.

Now people would turn to gaze at Avery in horror.

For she knew full well—hadn't Will Sebastian mentioned this over and over?—that when the flesh got too badly damaged from the cold it must be amputated or the victim would die of gangrene. She had seen a miner in Dawson City once, limping about because of the amputation of his toes—

"No!" She felt Quade's arm about her shoulders, steadying her.

"Delia, take deep breaths. Go on, do as I tell you. Put your head down between your knees; you'll be all right in a minute or two. It will help . . . go ahead, my darling."

The table swayed again and numbly she allowed him to push her face downward. She felt the blood rush to her head, making it throb, and sensed the strength of his hands as he supported her.

"Better now?"

"A . . . a bit." She sat up again, dimly aware that the other diners were staring at her now. She tried to ignore them.

"Delia, little Delia, there's worse news to come. It seems the thieves, whoever they are, went back to Avery's cabin afterward and ransacked it. Threw things about, slit open sacks, tossed flour and sugar into the snow. They ruined everything. So now your husband is really in trouble: he doesn't even have a scrap of food except what the people here have given him. He's totally rejected the idea of surgery. Says it will make a monster of him. As I've no doubt it will, the poor devil."

Corrie stared at Quade, feeling her mouth suddenly go dry. This wasn't happening, she told herself wildly. It just wasn't. Of course she had been angry at Avery; who could blame her? But this! Never in her most furious or brooding moments had she ever wished such a fate on him.

"Wait here," Quade said. "I'll go and settle our check and then we'll leave. We'll go out and see your husband, and find out for ourselves how he is and what we can do for him. We owe him that, at least."

"Yes. All right."

Numbly she waited, only partly aware that the road-house owner was carrying a tray-load of pie slices to the back table where the three quieter men sat. Someone laughed, and a hand took a plate of pie. The man in the calfskin coat turned partly about in order to take a plate off the tray. As he did so, he looked up.

Corrie could not suppress her gasp. It was Donald Earle. Donald, here in Circle City.

For one horrid instant their glances met. And in those few brief seconds, Corrie knew that for Donald, nothing had changed. He still lusted after her, longed for her just as he always had . . .

She never knew later how she got out of the roadhouse. Upon seeing Donald, she acted instinctively. She grabbed her coat and other outdoor garments and jumped to her feet, racing toward the door.

"Delia!" Quade threw a bill at the owner and hurried after her. "Delia, what's gotten into you? Where are you going?"

"Did you see that man in there? Did you?"

"No. What man?"

"That was Donald! Donald Earle! He was in the road-house, Quade, at the back table. Eating here all of this time, in—in the calfskin coat. I didn't see him at first be-cause he had the coat on and his back was to us. . . . "

Quade's face hardened. "So. The tentacles of the Earle Mining Company seem to stretch all over the Yukon. I wrote a piece on him for the *Tribune*, you know. He's a hard, ambitious man, and will do anything he can to get what he wants."

Corrie wasn't listening. "But . . . he's here, here in Cir-cle! I don't understand. Unless—oh, Quade, do you sup-pose he *followed* us here?"

"Nonsense. I'm sure the man isn't following you about —how could he be? We didn't even know ourselves that we were heading for Circle City until we left. No, I don't like the man and I don't trust him, but I'm sure he's here legitimately. He's probably buying up good claims on the Birch; that's his usual procedure."

Her mind was working rapidly. "I wonder. Perhaps— oh, perhaps it wasn't us he followed, but *Avery*. Don't you see, Quade? Avery is my husband. You told me that he was waylaid by a group of men on the trail—"

A lantern hanging on a nail outside the roadhouse illuminated its entrance. In the light Quade's face seemed twisted, and heavy, even dangerous. His eyes narrowed throughtfully. But his voice, when he spoke, was quiet.

"Corrie, you're talking wildly, without any proof for what you say. *Do* you have any basis for what you're alleging?"

"Why . . . why, no, but I do know—"

"You don't *know* anything. Not for a fact. And neither do I. If I did—" Quade's lips pressed tightly together.

"But I do know Donald!" she cried out. "I know him, I know that he threatened Li Hua, I know what sort of man he is!" Her words were tumbling out. "It has been nearly a year since Papa's death. The will said that if I hadn't married Donald in eighteen months . . . Oh, Quade, what if Donald was *trying to get rid of Avery so that he could marry me?* If Avery died, I'd be left a widow. Donald could still marry me and inherit Papa's estate—"

"Hush, Delia." Quade had taken her arm and was urging her toward the dogsled, where the sled dogs slept in the snow, curled together in a mass in order to keep warm. "You're conjecturing, nothing more. Don't you understand, you have *no real proof against the man!*"

He helped her into the sled and wrapped the fur robes about her. "Stay here while I fetch Alikammiq. We'll go and find the local doctor and take him out to Avery's cabin. I have a feeling that his services are going to be sorely needed."

"But Quade, aren't you listening? Haven't you heard a word of what I've been telling you? Donald—"

"Just what is it that you want me to do? Take my rifle and go out and gun the man down, on the basis of what you've said? I can't. Don't you see that if I act on instinct, on feeling, or whatever you want to call it, then that makes me no better than he is? I would be just as amoral, just as evil." Quade's eyes were glinting savagely in the lantern light, glaring down at her almost with hatred.

"Can't you see, Corrie? I won't kill without proof. And until I get that proof . . . "

He left his sentence unfinished.

❧ Chapter 30 ❧

"Your husband, ma'am, is a very stubborn man," Dr. Kooning said as they set out into the early evening darkness. The doctor, who had a log building on main street, was a stout man in his late thirties with a wind-burned, plump face. He knew the way to Avery's cabin, he told them, and could take them there.

Corrie walked alongside the dog sled, shivering. The night with its opaque black sky and sliver of a moon seemed oppressive, crushing down on them. Corrie knew that she was not the only one who felt uneasy. She could sense the restiveness of the sled dogs, and even Alikammiq, their guide, hurried over the snow faster than was his habit, his habitually cheerful face glum.

This was her fault, she kept repeating to herself. If she hadn't come north, if she hadn't insisted on marrying Avery, virtually forcing him to become her husband—

"Do they often refuse surgery in cases like this?" she heard Quade ask the doctor in an undertone.

"Some do, if it comes to the question of a whole foot. Most don't balk at the removal of a few toes, though. A man can get along with a few less toes, or maybe a missing finger or two. Plenty of folks hereabouts have a few less digits than they started out with."

"Oh, do be still, the two of you!" Corrie heard herself call out sharply. "This sort of talk is making me feel . . . ill," she finished, swallowing hard.

"You'll feel a lot sicker when you see your husband, Mrs. Curran, if you'll pardon me for saying so," the doctor said. "Maybe you can talk some sense into him. God knows I couldn't. The fact is, he damn near threatened to shoot my head off if I came near him again. If you folks hadn't paid me a nice wad of bills, I wouldn't be going back, I'll tell you that. Matter of fact, I'm telling myself right now I'm a fool for going at all."

An hour later they came over a rise and saw Avery's cabin, dimly visible in the sparse moonlight, one of its walls half buried in snow. A stovepipe protruding from the flat, crudely sodded roof emitted a forlorn curl of smoke.

"He lives in somebody's deserted cabin," said Dr. Kooning. "I can see why they left it, too. It's not close to water, and it's smaller than most."

That was an understatement, Corrie felt. "It looks . . . like an animal burrow," she said, appalled. She clutched at Quade's arm.

"Man gets to *be* like an animal if he lives in this cursed cold long enough," Dr. Kooning opined.

Warily they approached the cabin—all except the guide, who hung back with the sled dogs. Corrie's breathing quickened. There was something wrong about this place. What was it?

Then she realized. There were no footprints leading away from the door. The snow, windblown into drifts, was pristine and untouched.

"No one's been here for a while," the doctor said, as if reading her thoughts. "He made it plain he didn't want nobody. Said he'd get through this by himself. So they left him some food and firewood and then went away."

Fervently, Corrie wished that she hadn't come. Avery, shut inside this ugly hut, squashed down under the heavy black sky—no, she didn't like this, not one bit.

"I guess we'd better knock, don't you think?" she asked.

Quade grimaced. "This is hardly the time for drawing-room manners, Delia."

"Whatever you two are going to do, make it snappy, will you?" said the doctor. "My hands are cold and I've got a woman in labor back in town; she's due to pop in a few hours."

They were all whispering, Corrie suddenly realized—

even this vulgar and rather insensitive little doctor. In the distance, they could hear a wolf's eerie, mournful howl.

"All right," she said. "I suppose—"

Quade knocked briefly and pushed open the cabin door. It swung loosely on rotten leather hinges.

"Avery! Oh, Avery, are you all r—" Corrie slipped under Quade's arm and darted forward into the dim interior of the cabin. She stopped suddenly.

A heavy smell was pushing out at her. A smell so strong that it was as if a hand halted her. It was a terrible stench, thick and horrible. It reeked of rotten flesh and human excrement, spoiled meat and other dreadful things. Desperately, Corrie swallowed, trying not to gag. She had never smelled anything like this before in her life.

"Oh, don't mind the odor," Avery's voice said. "You get used to it after a while. Besides, I have little choice in the matter. I'm not exactly walking very well."

With one hand over her mouth, Corrie forced herself to advance into the cabin. She felt Quade immediately behind her, his fingers pressing reassuringly on her arm.

The structure, so small that its four walls seemed to press inward, was in nearly total darkness. There was only a dull red glow from the stove, which had burned down and was obviously in need of replenishment. Probably, Corrie thought, there was no more wood.

"Avery?" Her voice was high.

"I'm over here, to your right. On the floor. There weren't any bunks in this place and I didn't have time to build myself one. I used cedar boughs."

His voice was faintly mocking; he could have been discussing the weather. She could see the light of the stove glinting on something metallic; slowly she realized that she was seeing the barrel of a rifle.

"Quade!" She clutched at his arm. "Oh, Quade, he has a rifle—"

"I see it. Stand away, Delia. Curran, don't be a damn fool. We're only here to help you. We won't even stay here if you don't want us to."

"Shut up, you." Avery's voice was losing its calmness; now it shook audibly. "Who are you, anyway? Some man Corrie picked up? I sent for my wife, not for her paramour."

Quade took an angry step forward and Corrie flung herself at him, dragging at his arm. "Quade, no. He's in pain, he doesn't know what he's saying, remember, the doctor told us?"

"All I know is that I'm not going to let him insult you."

"Quade, really. It doesn't matter." She turned toward the figure which reclined on the pile of boughs and blankets. Avery rose on one elbow. The entire length of the rifle barrel now caught the glimmer of the stove light.

"Avery," she said, swallowing. "I've come to help. Remember the letter you wrote me? You said you'd had an accident. You asked me to come."

"Did I?"

"Yes, you did. Avery, you sent for me and now I'm here, and I want to help you."

"Go back to town, Corrie. And take those men with you, or I swear I'll kill them. Coming here on their two good feet—" She saw the rifle barrel shaking violently.

"All right, I will go back to town, I swear it. But first I want to talk with you, Avery. Surely you'll grant me that much." She turned to Quade. "Please, just leave me with him for a minute or two."

His hand gripped her. "You little fool, he's turned mad. I won't leave you in a situation like this."

"Come on, ma'am," Dr. Kooning put in. "If the man wants us out, let's just get out. It's his funeral, not ours."

"Avery is my *husband*, have you both forgotten that?" Corrie's voice was low and furious. "I have every right to speak with him, and that's just what I intend to do. Please, both of you, just leave me here for a few moments. I'll be all right."

"Delia—"

Violently she shook off Quade's restraining arm. "I tell you, I have to talk with him. I do owe him that much."

"I won't let you. I—"

"Don't you understand? Whether I like it or not, *he is my husband.*"

She waited until the cabin door swung shut, then took a step closer to the figure on the floor. The rifle barrel glinted again, and she saw Avery lower it.

"Very touching," he said in the calm voice again. "Well, Corrie?"

"Avery, please listen to me, just for a minute. Dr. Kooning and I want to take you back to town so that you can be examined properly. He certainly can't help you here; there isn't even a proper bed or any wood for the stove. You've got to have some professional help. You must realize that."

"I don't want that man's fat hands on me."

"Avery—"

"Or that paramour of yours, either, whoever he is. I don't want him. Tell him to go fuck himself."

The gutter word, spoken in the closed space of the cabin, was ugly and brutal. Corrie recoiled.

"You're not exactly in a position to dictate to anyone what you want, Avery," she snapped. "Right now you're lying here in your own filth; your hands and feet are rotting away right on your body."

The figure on the floor gave a strangled cry, then was silent.

"You're going to die, Avery," Corrie said softly. "Can't you see that?"

"No I'm—"

"Yes. You're going to lie here in this wretched little cabin and you're going to die. Unless you get medical help."

"But . . . amputation," Avery said. She heard a rustle as the rifle dropped to the dirt flooring. "Amputation! My God, Corrie! How . . . how would I work a claim without . . . without any feet?" His voice cracked pitifully. "How, Corrie? Answer me that, will you?"

Pity filled her. Whatever his faults, whatever his obsession with gold, Avery *had* worked long, hard hours. He had pushed his physical strength to its limits. He was right. His mining days would be over forever.

"I can't. I don't know, Avery." She choked back a sob. "But I do know this. If you don't accept Dr. Kooming's care, you won't ever stake a claim again, anywhere, because you'll be dead. I'm sorry to be so brutal about it, but it's the truth."

The silence seemed to fill the cabin.

"Dead," Avery said. "My God, dead." A hand made a jerky movement and caught the light, and then Corrie heard the scraping, racking sounds of Avery's sobbing.

"Corrie? Oh, God, what am I going to do? I don't know. Without you, without you here, I'd have nobody. I—I'm sorry. Whatever I did to you, I'm sorry. I didn't mean it, I just wanted to get away and be able to think, be free to think. Oh, Corrie, help me. Tell me what to do. I . . . I don't want to die . . . "

His voice tore at a corner of Corrie's heart which she had not known existed. Once, long months ago, she had loved this man. She had traveled thousands of miles to be with him. She had married him and borne his child. And weren't his injuries really due to her? If it had not been for her, then Donald Earle would have no interest in Avery, and would not have tried to kill him. . . .

Corrie would never forget the trip back to Circle City, with Avery tied onto the sled and the sled dogs growling and snarling at the smell of him. Avery passively allowed her to take the rifle away from him, and he rode silently, not crying out, although Corrie felt sure he must be in pain.

"Don't let them turn me . . . into something horrible," he whispered to her as they loaded him. "Corrie, help me. You've got to help me."

It was on the way back to town, on the trail packed down by previous sleds, that Corrie began to realize what she must do. Avery needed a doctor. First she must see to that. Then she had to get him back to San Francisco, where he could see a specialist and be made as comfortable as possible. Artificial limbs would have to be made for him, carefully fitted so that he would walk again. There was no one here in the Yukon who could do such skilled work.

Corrie, help me. Without you I have nobody.

Avery's words rang in her head, seemed to be a part of the squeak of the snow under their boots, the snuffling and panting of the sled dogs.

Everything, she thought. Everything had changed.

❦ Chapter 31 ❦

"Delia! Delia, you little fool, you're not really going to do this!" Quade's voice was thick with fury and she thought she had never seen him look more savage.

Her voice was soft, despairing. "Yes, I am. I have to. Quade, I've thought and thought and I can't see any other solution."

"There is another solution! There must be! Do you realize just what you're doing? You're throwing yourself away. Throwing yourself away like trash, do you hear me? That man doesn't deserve you!"

"He also doesn't deserve what's happened to him. Partly through my fault."

"Your fault! How?"

"Because I . . . because Donald . . ."

Quade's grip on her arm hurt her, and Corrie felt the tears spring to her eyes.

"Listen," he said. "I've told you, you have no proof that Donald Earle was responsible for the men who attacked Avery. Avery himself said that he didn't recognize any of them. And Donald was at a saloon in town on that night; at least ten men can testify to it. I found out that much for myself."

"I don't care. I don't need any proof. I know he did it. And I also know that it's my fault. Avery is my husband—"

"For God's sake, Delia." Quade's voice went on arguing, attempting to persuade her. Stubbornly Corrie turned away. She wouldn't listen to him; she couldn't. If she did, she would weaken. She would throw herself into his arms and beg him to take her away from here.

Avery had undergone surgery, performed in two separate operations with the aid of chloroform and the assistance of the town dentist. Avery withstood the shock amazingly well, Dr. Kooning told Corrie afterward—his constitution was evidently very sturdy. And his loss was not as great as had first been feared. True, he had lost his right foot entirely, but only four toes of the left. He had lost all of the fingers of his right hand and most of both ears. His prognosis was good, for Dr. Kooning was certain he had gotten all of the damaged flesh. Of course, later on Avery would need further treatment by a specialist . . .

Numbly Corrie heard Dr. Kooning go on to tell her that he would keep Avery in his office for a few days for observation; Alikammiq could perform any necessary nursing chores.

"Delia—" Quade's voice brought her back to the present. She felt him grasp her by both shoulders and spin her about.

"Please, let go of me."

"Not until you listen to reason. Corrie, the man is your husband, I'll grant you that. But you don't owe a thing to him now. He seduced you; don't you recall that? He seduced you and left you pregnant. Then after you gave birth he deserted you again."

"I'm well aware of that," she told him in a soft, bleak voice. "But *you* are the one who made me come here. You're the one who told me he might need help!"

"So I did. He is a human being and I did feel we had some obligation to him. Well, now we've fulfilled that obligation. You've given Avery back his life and you've paid for his surgery. I will give him money for his passage home. Isn't that enough? What more do you want to do for the man? Do you want to sacrifice *yourself* for him?"

Corrie shook her head from side to side. She felt the same as she had the night her baby died; as if shards of broken glass were caught in her throat. If only she could fling herself into Quade's arms. If only she could say to him, *yes, I agree with you, I love you, I never want to see Circle City or Avery Curran again, as long as I live.*

"I'm only going to do for him what I owe him," she said as steadily as she could. "If he were well, things might be different. But he isn't well. He—"

Quade's eyes glittered at her. "You feel more for that bastard of a husband of yours than you do for me."

"No! That's not true! Oh, Quade, you don't understand. He *needs* me."

"*I* need you! *I* love you, Corrie. Can't you get that through your stubborn, willful little head?" His fingers cut into her shoulders. He shook her back and forth. Then abruptly he plunged his mouth down on hers. She felt his hard, angry lips.

She managed to twist away from him.

"Quade," she heard her own voice say. "I must do this. Don't you see, Avery is helpless now, almost as helpless as a baby. He can't even dress himself. And he doesn't have anyone else to be with him; his family is all gone. There's only me. And he—" She swallowed. "He does love me, in his own way, I'm sure of it. Otherwise he would not have been so jealous of you."

"He's a possessive, selfish—"

The words came from a solid block of agony within her. "He's my husband. For better or for worse. Why won't you admit it, Quade? I do have a responsibility to him. He has no one else, only me."

There was a very long silence. Corrie's eyes filled with tears, and through their blur she saw Quade stalk to the window of the hotel room to stare out at the main street of Circle City, where two men and a woman stood talking together, their breath rising in the air like smoke.

"I could ask you to stay with me," Quade said slowly. "But I won't. I'm not the begging type; that's not my way. You either love me and want me enough to go with me, or you don't. And I can see that you've made your choice. Very well. I hope you and your fine husband are very happy. As for me, I won't stay around here and watch. I'm leaving."

"But where—where are you going?" She started toward him and then stopped helplessly. She longed to reach out for him, but knew she could not.

"What do you care where I go?" he said harshly.

"I . . . I do care. I care very much."

"Like hell you do." He turned with a sharp scrape of boot heels. Then, with a furious motion, he dug into his pocket and jerked out a wallet. He peeled off a stack of bills and dropped a small leather poke sack.

"Here." He shoved them in her direction. "Take this; it'll help you. Well, what are you waiting for? Take it, Cordelia. God knows you'll need it."

She stared at the money. Her heart turned over slowly in her breast. "I can't take your money."

"You can't take my money! And just what in the hell do you think you're going to do up here, Cordelia *Curran*, sell your fair body in order to support your husband? Are you so naive as to think you can get him back to San Francisco without funds? Besides—" His voice was raw, lashing. "Besides, you earned it, after all. You, Cordelia, are a very good lay."

"What?"

He wanted to hurt her, she knew. Color stung her cheeks. She felt as if he had slapped her, as if his fist had slammed viciously into her flesh.

"I said, Delia, you're a good lay. And you deserve a bit of payment, right? So here it is. Two thousand dollars. That ought to keep you and Avery in crutches and bandages for a while." He tossed the money at her.

"Oh! How dare you!" Corrie reached down and snatched up the bills from the floor, thrusting them at him. "I don't want your money, Quade Hill, nor do I want your insults. Get out of this room, right now!"

"No. I won't." Fury seemed to emanate from him in waves. She could almost smell his anger, sharp, musky, acidic. His rugged face was twisted frighteningly. "I'll get out of here when I'm ready and not a moment sooner. Don't forget, my dear girl, *I* paid for this room and *I* paid for that husband of yours to get his toes lopped off. And I'm paying you now, too, for services rendered."

Corrie could only stare at him. Oh, how she hated him. She loathed him. She wished she'd never met him. Impulsively she lifted up the leather sack and flung it onto the floor as hard as she could. Gold dust spilled in a yellow streak on the floor.

"There! That's what I think of you and your money!
And this is what I think of your bills—I'll rip them up—"

His hand darted out and squeezed her wrist. Pain radiated up her arm in harsh waves. She felt her fingers loosening until the bills fluttered to the floor.

"You . . . you hurt me . . . "

"Did I? You temperamental, headstrong creature."
Quade's features darkened, his eyes blazed. "You said
you wanted to help your husband. How are you going to
do it? With a temper tantrum and a wad of torn-up paper
scraps? You need money, Cordelia, and you need it now.
And you're going to have to humble yourself for it."

"What—what do you mean?"

She started to back away from him, suddenly very
frightened of him.

"I want you to see what you're missing, that's all. Do
you think Curran is going to be able to make love to you
as I can? Do you think that he'll ever hold you close as
I've done—the two of us—"

"Quade, no—"

Slowly he advanced toward her. There was nowhere she
could flee. The hotel room was very small, with barely
room enough for a brass bed and a crude arrangement of
shelves.

"Come here, you beautiful, quixotic fool of a girl. Come
here."

"No. Keep away from me! I won't!"

He lunged at her and helplessly she beat at him with
her fists, knowing that it was futile, that nothing would
stop him. He brutally ripped off her clothes. Something
burned against her skin as he tore her clothing from her.

She was naked and still she fought him, clawing desperately at his face, drumming her fists against his chest, kick-
ing at him. It was as if he did not even feel her blows.
With one gesture, he picked her up under her arms and
flung her down on the brass bed. Then, before she could
kick out, he was upon her, tearing away at his own
clothes.

He entered her and she knew, abjectly, that he was rap-
ing her and that she was exulting in it. Wildly she knew
that she wanted and loved him, no matter what he did to

her in his pain, or how he did it. She would always belong to him.

Their bodies fought and shuddered together and Corrie found that she was matching Quade's passion with her own, thrusting violently toward him and accepting his returning violence with fierce desire. Nothing mattered, nothing except their gasps and cries and their pounding bodies.

She climaxed with a terrible, shuddering joy, and then, in the moments afterward, wept and clung to him.

For none of it, none of it, changed anything. Avery Curran was still her husband, her responsibility, and she had already made her choice.

✿ Chapter 32 ✿

"Corrie." Avery said querulously, beginning to stir from his drugged sleep. "Must we leave here? I demand that we stay. *He* left us enough money so that I can reprovision and hire someone to be my arms and legs. I could get Alikammiq, that Eskimo, to help me if I paid him well. Gold, Corrie. I can't leave here yet, not without finding my strike. I *won't* leave here."

It was four days later. Avery had been moved back to Corrie's hotel room and lay propped on the same brass bed where she and Quade had made love with such wild, bittersweet abandon. A blanket was arranged around Avery's legs. Bandages covered his ears, feet and right hand. Alikammiq came in daily to bathe Avery and change his dressings. Dr. Kooning gave Avery Dovers Powder—a form of opium—for his pain, and informed Corrie that her husband had the "constitution of a musk ox." Whatever that meant, she thought to herself despairingly.

She took three steps and found herself, for the hundredth time that day, staring out onto the main street, with its bleak log buildings.

"Corrie," Avery repeated. "Aren't you listening? I told you, I want to stay here and do some more prospecting. They've been making some more good strikes here. Dr. Kooning said—"

She jerked about. "I don't care what Dr. Kooning said!" Her shoulders sagged. "I'm sorry, Avery. I shouldn't have spoken so sharply to you. But don't you understand? We have to go home, back to San Francisco, just as soon as we can. Dr. Kooning said that you should see a specialist about your ears. And you have to be fitted with an artificial limb."

Avery drew his right leg restlessly up under the blanket, his eyes dreamy, as if he had not even heard her.

"I read of a new strike in the paper," he told her. "We could find it, you and I, a good, rich vein of color. We'd name the mine after you. How would you like that? The Cordelia Mine! The name has a certain ring to it, doesn't it?"

"Avery," she said quietly. "We have to go home. Dr. Kooning told me there's no way you can continue to do any mining."

"But Corrie, the gold here is—"

"Gold! I tell you, I don't want to hear another word about gold, not one word. That ugly yellow stuff, how I hate it! If it hadn't been for gold—"

She stopped abruptly and resumed staring out of the plate glass window, hating herself for saying these things to Avery, yet knowing that she could not stop herself. She had listened to Avery's grandiose hopes and plans and schemes for four long days. Couldn't he accept the fact that his mining days were finished? Mining was rough and often dangerous work even for a man in good health. But for a man with Avery's handicaps— No, she told herself. The whole thing was utterly impossible.

Her thoughts turned to Quade. When he left her his eyes were a cold, arctic blue, full of pain. "You've made your choice, Delia," he said.

"But Quade—you don't understand—"

"I do understand. More than you know. Well, good luck, Delia—or should I call you *Corrie*, your little-girl name? I hope self-sacrifice agrees with you."

"Quade!"

He turned on his heel and walked away, while she stood frozen, staring after him, wanting to scream out, to race after him and fling herself into his arms and beg him never to leave her.

But she had not done any of those things. She let him go. And in this big country, where men shifted from place to place like seeds blown in the wind, she knew it was likely she would never see him again.

So she was left with Avery as her responsibility.

Dully she heard her husband's voice mumble on ceaselessly about new strikes, nuggets, rumors, all as if he hadn't heard a word she'd said. He was growing to hate her, she knew. When once she offered to help him to eat, he flung the plate at her with his good hand. He spoke viciously of the crutches Dr. Kooning sold him, as if somehow he blamed Corrie for them. But most of all, she knew, he blamed her for keeping him away from the gold.

Had she really been in love with Avery once? She remembered the day on the wharf in San Francisco when she and Avery stood watching the Yukon-bound steamers. She remembered how he had tilted up her chin with his finger and for one wild moment she had thought he would kiss her. How long ago that had been. The girl who trembled under Avery's touch had been someone else.

Desperately, to distract herself from her thoughts, Corrie focused her eyes on the street. Daylight was nearly over. The shadows of the scattered buildings stretched out long and black, with a sort of harsh beauty. As she watched, four miners plodded past, their backs heavily laden with provisions. They were probably headed out toward the frozen creeks, she knew, buoyed by the hope that—perhaps this time—the pan of gravel would reveal rich, yellow color. She wondered dully if they would ever find it.

Then, almost on their heels, another man walked past. Corrie's heart began to pump in slow, painful beats. It was Donald Earle, wearing the same calfskin coat she had seen him sporting before. He strode rapidly over the packed snow dotted with animal droppings. His cheeks were reddened from the cold.

Donald, she thought. She had been here in Circle City for some days now, and he made no effort to contact her. But instead of reassuring her, this fact only made her more uneasy. It was not like Donald to stay away from her so meekly. She could not forget the look she had seen on his face that day their eyes met in the roadhouse. He still loved her, if that twisted emotion she glimpsed could be called love.

As she watched, Donald paused in the street to pull a cigar from his pocket and light a match. He stood poised for a moment staring into the red glow of the match, then deliberately touched it to the end of the cigar, drew in and tossed the still-smoldering match into the snow. He glanced briefly at the hotel where Corrie was staying. Then, casually, he sauntered across the street and went into the dry goods store opposite the hotel.

Corrie turned away from the window. She walked around the bed and picked up a novel from the shelf. She flipped the book open and rapidly scanned four paragraphs without even knowing what she had read.

She slammed the book shut.

"Good God, what are you so nervous for?" Avery asked. "Pacing about like a cat—reading standing up—can't you settle down for a while? Why don't you go out and see about getting us some provisions? That Eskimo Quade left us, he could do it—"

"Avery." Her temper flared, but she tried to keep her voice even. "Avery, I've told you. Alikammiq is going to do only one thing, and that is get us back to Dawson City so that we can buy passage on a steamer when the ice breaks."

Avery's face reddened. He raised his bandaged right arm at her as if he would like to strike her. "I hear you, slut. And I know what's the matter with you, too. You miss that lover of yours, that Quade Hill man. Isn't that right?"

Corrie lowered her eyes, feeling her face darken. We're devouring each other, she thought. Like two rats caged in the same room, gnawing away at each other's vitals, goading and taunting each other. Was this what their future together was to be like? This constant bickering and hatred?

"Never mind," she heard herself say. "It appears that you are recovering very well. I think you're almost ready to travel. We'll go back to Dawson as soon as I can make the arrangements. Perhaps tomorrow."

Avery pressed his lips together to form a thin, dry line. Bloodless and sunken, his face had lost any vestige of its good looks.

"Why can't we wait here until the spring break-up?"

"Because we can't," she told him. She was thinking of
Donald. She didn't feel safe where Donald was. "I have
my reasons. Besides, I hate this city. I want to get back
to Dawson. It will be more comfortable there for you."

"Nowhere is comfortable for me now," Avery said
suddenly. "Well, Corrie, I guess I'll have to do what you
tell me, won't I? Since you're the one with the money.
And the good legs."

He hated her for that, too. Corrie stared at him, feeling sickened. How had her life come to this, being trapped
in a hotel room with a man who hated her, and for whom
she felt an equal amount of pity and loathing? Would
things be any better after they were back in San Francisco?

Oh, Quade. The thought was like a wisp of wood
smoke, dissipating into the air.

"We're leaving tomorrow," she told Avery.

They left while it was still dark, dressing themselves
by candlelight. Avery would not speak to Corrie or look
at her. He gulped a spoonful of medicine and then shoved
her away fiercely when she attempted to help him pull
his shirt on. An odd mental picture came to her of a
ferret, or a cornered small animal, turning to snap at her.

"But Avery," she began. "I was only trying to help."

"I don't need your help! Just leave me alone, will you,
Corrie? I'll go to Dawson with you—I'll go that far. But
I don't have to take your interference, and I won't. And
when I get to Dawson—"

Corrie sighed. He pinned his hopes on being able to
change her mind when they reached Dawson City. He
would never give up, she knew, not while he still drew
breath. He would hound her and berate her, and seem to
agree with her, and all the while he would be making
his own plans, his dreamy, ephemeral plans . . .

They made their way out of the hotel, Avery somehow
managing (with what courage Corrie would never know)
to balance on his crutches. Alikammiq, bundled in a
dirty, bulky parka, was waiting for them with the dog sled.
As they came out he grinned at them.

The temperature was about fifteen degrees, Corrie

estimated—decidedly balmy after the below-zero weather
which they had endured for so long.

"Man ride sled. You walk," Alikammiq told her, spitting out a brown spray of tobacco juice. He seemed even
more short, squat and plump in his layers of furs. He was
truly cheerful and reliable, and Quade had assured her—
correctly—that she could not do without him.

"All right," she said. She turned to Avery, who was
leaning heavily on his crutches, his face beaded with perspiration. "Do you want me to help you get on the sled?"

"No!" He shouted it so loudly that a man passing in
the street turned to stare at him. "Damn you, Corrie, I
don't need coddling like a baby. I'm not helpless."

"Very well, then."

The dogs, rested and frisky, trotted effortlessly on their
short, sturdy legs. The sled squeaked in the snow. Corrie
found that she was savoring the physical exercise of walking after days of being inside the hotel in Circle City.
If she walked long enough, she told herself, she would
be too tired to think.

She was glad to see the huddled log buildings of Circle
recede from sight. Perhaps they should have stayed until
the spring ice break-up, she told herself. But she was filled
with an urgency to leave. Donald's presence seemed to
hover malevolently over the main street of Circle. Besides, she longed to see Dawson City again. Safe, cluttered,
crowded, dirty, cheerful, avaricious Dawson.

The light imperceptibly changed and turned pink. They
walked for an hour or so, and Corrie began to lag, finding it difficult to keep up with the brisk pace set
by Alikammiq. Up ahead two men approached from a
thick stand of spruces to their right, where the land sloped
down to the river bed. Avery, slumped under his fur wraps
and dazed by the opium he had taken, barely glanced
at them. Corrie, pricked by some feeling she could not
name, turned to stare as the two men approached.

The two men were dressed in heavy, nondescript jack-
ets. Both wore wool scarves pulled up over their faces.
Somewhere behind them she thought she heard a sled dog
barking.

"Say!" The taller of the two, wearing a mustard-
colored scarf, was waving at them. "Our partner back in

the woods has a broken leg. Could you stop and give him a lift to town?" The voice was educated, cultured.

Alikammiq hesitated, then slowed the dog team.

"Alikammiq, are you sure?" Corrie hurried forward, intending to caution the Eskimo, when the man with the mustard scarf walked in front of the sled, forcing the dogs to stop.

"I say, could you stop and lend us a hand? Our friend is in quite a bit of pain, and we certainly could use your help. I know it will inconvenience you a bit, and I apologize in advance for that—"

Corrie noted in some dim corner of her mind that the knitted muffler drawn up to cover his nose was not rimed from his breath. But she did not have time to think of the meaning of this, for both men, moving quickly over the snow now, were abreast of them.

It all happened quickly. The two men separated; the one with the mustard scarf approached Alikammiq and the other one, shorter, heavier, and wearing a black scarf, headed toward Corrie. Suddenly the first man drew something from his coat and made a quick, jabbing motion.

Alikammiq's knees buckled easily, almost gracefully, beneath him. He lay in a heap in the snow. A stream of bright red spurted out of the loosened neck of his parka. His blood pumped out as if a faucet had been turned on, a tomato red so bright that it could not be real.

A dog growled low in its throat.

Corrie stood frozen, staring at the blood, which steamed hideously in the cold air. But before she could scream, the black-scarfed man grasped both of her hands and jerked them roughly behind her.

"All right, now, little missus. I got a repeating rifle here, and my partner, he's got a knife, as you saw. All I want is your money. I ain't going to hurt you. Not if you're a real good little lady and does as you're told."

"What? Money? But—"

It was as if she could not take it all in, as if she could do nothing but babble senselessly. One minute they had been walking along in the snow. The next minute, this.

"Hush up, hear? Where do you keep your money?"

"In—in a sack." Her legs wobbled, she felt faint, and she tasted hot, raw vomit at the back of her throat.

Alikammiq lay on the snow in a puddle of blood, his face leached white, as if all of the blood in his body had been drained away. His eyes were wide open.

"Corrie!" Avery's voice sounded high, frightened and strangled. She saw the first man, the one who had stabbed Alikammiq, bend over Avery, concealing him from her view. Horror surged through her. She heard her own voice erupt in a scream.

"Please, oh, please don't hurt him! He's my husband, he—he's had an accident, he's been injured terribly. He can't possibly hurt you. Please, we'll give you our money. You can have it. Just don't hurt Avery!"

She sensed the man was smiling beneath the black mask. "Aw, now, don't worry none. We won't hurt 'im. All we want is your money. Where do you keep it, honey? Am I going to have to look for it?"

"No! It's in a leather sack. T-tied to my waist . . . "

"Well, now, we'll just have to see about that." His hands ripped at the front of her sealskin coat and fumbled at the waistband of the men's mackinaw trousers she wore. Corrie let out a little, choked cry.

"Stand still now, girl. Or I'll have to shoot you with this here rifle. You wouldn't like that now, would you? No, you wouldn't, not one little bit."

"I'll give you the money myself!"

"Mebbe you will. And mebbe you won't. Anyway, I got to look." He took off his heavy mittens to reveal stubby, hard, calloused hands. He thrust his rough hands under Corrie's heavy wool sweater and grabbed her breasts.

"The money is in my *belt*," she said coldly.

"Yeah?"

His exploring fingers moved downward, and Corrie stood rigidly, suffering his touch.

"Yes," she heard him say. "You're a pretty one, you are, and no mistake about that. But I got to take the money and get out of here, more's the pity. Yep, damn pity it is."

He fumbled with the strap which held the leather money bag. At last his fingers released the thong and pulled away the sack. The sled dogs growled menacingly, and Corrie felt her body tremble. Were they going to kill her too? Were they going to leave her sprawled in the snow in her own red, frozen blood?

She could hear the other man crunching about in the snow, and then a hand shoved her in the middle of her back, slamming her toward the sled with such force that she stumbled and fell against it. Avery, she saw dazedly, was still lying on the sled in his furs, his body very still. She thought she glimpsed blood dribbling out of his mackinaw.

God, she thought. Oh, dear God.

"Over there, little girl. Get over by that husband of yours and don't you dare to make a sound or a move. We still got some business to finish here."

She struggled weakly to her feet from her hands and knees. Avery's bandaged hand was dangling out of the sled, swinging a bit.

"Down, I said. Get down in the snow over there by the sled, girl."

"A-all right." Numbly she did as he asked. She stared up appealingly at the first man, the one with the educated voice. "Please, sir, we—we haven't done anything to harm you. We've given you our money. Just let us alone. Please!"

The man made a quick, impatient motion with his right hand. "Do you think I'd hurt you? A woman? We just have something more to take care of, that's all. Be patient; this won't take long."

The second man lifted his rifle and then there was an explosion in the clear, cold air, and the smell of gunpowder. With the first shot, Corrie's body stiffened, and she found that she was gripping Avery's hand, squeezing it until the bones cracked. The shots continued in a deadly necklace of sound. Gradually she realized that she was still alive, that they hadn't shot her.

She wasn't dead. But the sled dogs were. One by one they dropped in their harnesses. Corrie stifled a cry of horror and then remained where she was, huddled against the sled, afraid to look at the men for fear that she herself would be next.

"All right now. All you have to do, young lady, is to keep your head down and count to a thousand. If you don't, the same thing will happen to you that happened to the sled dogs. And it's a damn good waste of valuable dog flesh, too, if you ask me." The well-articulated voice stopped, then went on in a casual way. "And, listen, Circle is back in that direction." She sensed he was pointing. "All you have to do is follow the tracks of the sled. Retrace your path. You'll get back; you can't miss it."

They turned and walked away. Counting feverishly, Corrie heard their boots crunch in the snow. The sound of footsteps receded. Far in the distance she heard sled dogs barking and she knew that they must have concealed their own sled somewhere.

The Yukon sun burst over the tops of the spiky trees to suffuse the sky with light. Corrie stood stunned and dazed.

Avery, by some miracle, was still alive, although she was sure that he was injured severely. Frantically, she tore off her sweater and tried to bandage him as best she could. She piled fur rugs on him for warmth, knowing that he would have to wait here; the sled would be too heavy for her to pull alone. She knew she had to hurry. If she ran most of the way, surely she could reach Circle City and Dr. Kooning in less than an hour.

She staggered along the track left in the snow by their sled. Her lungs burned with the effort of sucking in each desperate gasp of air. As she ran, questions buzzed ceaselessly in her mind. Why had they killed the sled dogs? Why had they stabbed Alikammiq and Avery and not herself? And—most puzzling and frightening of all—why had the man in the mustard scarf taken such care to point her in the direction of civilization?

Why had she been left alive? Why? Why?

A stitch raked painfully in her ribs. A few moments later, she emerged over a rise. Then she saw him, walking slowly toward her over the sled tracks, picking his way carefully among the snowdrifts, as if he knew exactly where to find her, and in fact had come to meet her.

The rising sun caught Donald from behind, so that he stood dark and ominous against the white snow. He wore a calfskin coat.

"Corrie, is anything wrong? Do you need any help?"

"Donald Earle!" She stared at him, at his florid face and thick, black hair. Coldness washed over her, a dry prickling at the root end of every hair on her body. Donald was smiling at her, she noticed wildly. *Smiling.*

"You!" she whispered. "You were responsible for what went on back there, weren't you? You killed Alikammiq. You paid those two men to do it."

"What men? Who was killed?" Donald's full, red lips hung open, and Corrie felt a shiver convulsing her. Her hands and feet were suddenly icy cold.

"You killed Alikammiq," she said dully. "But you didn't succeed with Avery. No, he's still alive, and I bandaged him up and I have hopes that he's going to recover."

"What?"

"He isn't dead, I tell you! He's alive, and you've failed for the second time—or is it the third?"

Donald regarded her calmly, although there was a ruddy circle of red in each of his cheeks and his eyes were glittering at her. "You're talking nonsense, Corrie. I heard of your husband's accident, of course—what man in town didn't? But I had nothing to do with it. I was in the Nugget Saloon that night."

"Were you?"

"Corrie, are you telling me that some disaster has befallen your party? Why don't you come to my cabin—it's only a mile or so from here—and then I'll send someone out."

"No! I won't go with you! You planned all of this deliberately, didn't you? You wanted Avery dead, so you had him killed—or you thought you did. But there's something I don't understand. Why did you have to murder a man like Alikammiq? He never did anything to you. Or kill all the sled dogs? Your man shot them all, right in their tracks." She heard her voice rise hysterically.

"Corrie—"

"Oh, be still!" she cried. "I'm going into Circle City to get help for Avery. Just stand aside and let me pass."

Donald's full lips clamped together and she heard the snow crunch as he stepped forward. His fingers bit into her arms even through the layers of sealskin and wool she wore.

"Never talk that way to me, Corrie."

"I'll talk to you any way I wish! You're a murderer, aren't you? A cold-blooded murderer!"

"I'm no such thing. You're slandering me, Corrie. But then I suppose you can't help it. You're hysterical. Whatever you've witnessed must have been a terrible shock to you. What you need now is rest—rest and a hot whiskey to warm your insides. I'll send someone back and see just what's gone wrong. I'll take care of it for you, Corrie. You don't need to worry."

"I don't need whiskey or a rest. And I'm not hysterical; I'm not!"

To her horror she heard that her voice was high pitched. She beat against Donald's chest with her gloved fists, struggling against his strong, implacable arms which suddenly wrapped themselves about her.

"Now, Corrie, you'll have to get yourself calmed down or I won't be able to let you go. I can't have you accusing me of such wild things. You have no proof for any of them."

"But I must get a doctor for Avery—"

"I'll get a doctor for him. I've told you, I'll take care of it all. You don't have to worry about a thing."

"You won't," she babbled. "You won't do anything for him. You'll just let him die out here, I know you will, I know it. You wanted him dead. And now he's lying there on the sled—"

Donald's hands, stronger than she ever realized, pulled at her, forcing her to turn in a new direction. She wept, helplessly. She *was* hysterical, she thought wildly. She supposed she was. But she had witnessed so much horror. And there was Avery—he had only her to help him.

"Donald, please, you must let me go to Circle City and get Dr. Kooning. Dr. Kooning can help him."

"Corrie, haven't I told you not to worry? We have our own doctor, a man who is with my own party and is one of my own associates. Dr. Santee is a surgeon and he's well qualified to operate if that should be necessary. And it will be much faster than going back to town, since my cabin is only a few miles away. All we have to do is go there and fetch Dr. Santee, and he'll go right back to your husband and give him the medical attention he needs . . . "

She was forced through the trees toward a path

trampled by tracks and littered with the droppings of sled dogs.

"Do you really think that I would not offer you my help when you needed it, Cordelia Stewart?" Donald's voice was soft, soothing, almost crooning. Only his hands were sharp. One of them gripped her right upper arm; the other prodded at her ribs.

"I don't want to go with you—and my name isn't Cordelia Stewart," she sobbed defiantly. "It's Cordelia Curran, don't you remember? Avery is my husband!"

"Yes, so he is."

"I don't want your doctor to treat him, I want Dr. Kooning. I insist on going back to Circle for Dr. Kooning."

"Do you know, Corrie, I think you're going to need quite a long period of rest before you're quite right again. Oh, yes. You're quite hysterical, you know."

🏶 Chapter 33 🏶

Whiskey in a tin cup was forced between her lips. She had to swallow it down or choke. It tasted harsh, with a suggestion of some other bitter taste she could not name. She coughed, nearly gagging.

Donald's voice said, "Go on, drink. It'll help you to rest, and God knows you need it after what you've been through. They must have been bandits. They've been seen in these parts lately: the miners have called meetings about it. Didn't you see the sign on the door of the road-house?"

"They were not bandits!"

"Drink," Donald commanded. "Just drink. I'm going to take care of you, Corrie. Everything is going to be all right."

They were in a cabin—dark, overheated, and smelling of a mixture of damp logs, food, wood smoke and perspiration. Somehow this didn't seem quite the place where Donald Earle would choose to live, she thought half-hysterically. But here they were, and Corrie was too dulled by shock and by the exhaustion of her long run through the snow to offer Donald more than token resistance. She glimpsed two other men as she entered the cabin. One of them was evidently Dr. Santee. He was tall and gawky, with long, spidery arms and legs, and unkempt reddish hair. The other man, Artie, was shorter, with a large slit of a mouth and a face pitted by acne scars.

"Of course it was bandits," Donald repeated, as if she

347

were a child. "Who else would it be? But you needn't worry; I've sent Artie and Dr. Santee back there. They've a good dog team and should have your husband back here in short order." He prodded at her lips with the rim of the metal cup. "Now you'd better take another drink. It's local hooch, but at least it's potent and it will help you to sleep. In this bitter country a man needs some protection against the chill—I've learned that. And I suppose a woman does, too."

"But I don't want anything to drink. And I don't want to sleep. I want to—"

But before she could finish her sentence, Donald's right hand forced her head back and she swallowed and coughed.

The liquid burning down her gullet was redolent with alcohol fumes. She started to retch, but managed to stop herself. She looked frantically about her. The cabin was like most here in the Yukon, made of moss-chinked logs and fitted with two greased-cloth windows solidly rimmed with frost. Even in daylight, the cabin was dim. To her left, two candles burned on a slab table.

Her eyes moved rapidly about, looking for two scarves; one mustard-colored and one black. Although there were various articles of clothing scattered about, she could not see any scarfs. Had she been wrong? Had she falsely accused Donald? Oh, if she could only think clearly. Her brain seemed fuzzy, sluggish. The cabin was tilting slightly, first to her right, and then to her left.

"You're feeling faint," Donald said. "Or is it sleepy? At any rate, you'd better lie down. There's a bunk which is comfortable enough. It's only a wood slab, but we've padded it well with blankets."

She felt herself being carried, and struggled to open her eyes. Why was the cabin getting so dark? It seemed to whirl about her, to pitch dizzily.

"There. You ought to rest very nicely now." Donald's voice reverberated from very far away.

"No . . . " she muttered. "What have you given me . . . in that whiskey . . . "

"Given you? Nothing but whiskey and a little laudanum, a tincture of opium, meant to make you sleepy. You needed it, I must say. You're quite hysterical, my dear. You need to calm down. We can't have you raving like a madwoman, saying all sorts of impossible things."

"Not impossible . . . "

"Oh, yes, Corrie. Quite impossible. To accuse me of—but it doesn't matter. You're with me now, and I'll take care of you until you're well. As long as I'm here you won't have to worry about anything."

"No, please. Oh, God."

Corrie could feel the weight of her eyelids pressing down on her eyes like pennies. She felt as if she were floating, floating on a sea of darkness. Or was it a soft calfskin cloak . . .

At first her sleep was still and silent, as if she was a stone dropped into a pit of soft tar. Then she began to dream, jagged, frightening images that swirled in front of her mind, then receded before she knew what they were about.

More blackness came, heavy and thick. An indeterminate time later she awoke to find that it was vaguely light inside the cabin. Donald sat on the edge of the bunk attempting to spoon something into her mouth. It tasted like soup. She swallowed it thirstily. Her throat felt dry and the flesh of her mouth leathery, as if she had been sleeping with her mouth open for many hours.

"Well, you're awake, are you?" Dimly she was aware that there were others in the room. Men, talking in low voices. The clink of forks against metal plates.

"Avery—" she managed to gasp.

"I've told you, Corrie, you're not to worry about him."

"But I want to know. I have to know. Is he all right? Is he alive? Please, I'm sure I'd be fine if only you'd—" But the thought abruptly seeped out of her mind so that she could not remember what she had been going to say.

"Drink your soup," Donald said.

"No." Blindly she pushed at the spoon and felt the heat as the liquid spurted across her chest.

"All right," Donald said. "Another dose of laudanum then. That's what you need, my girl."

Again the metal cup pressed hurtfully against her dry lips. Again the harsh, fiery stuff burned her palate with a bitter taste.

"That's it," he said. "Swallow it down. After a while you'll understand your situation and then you won't need this. You're a very sensible girl underneath that haughty exterior of yours."

Corrie wondered what he was talking about. "Avery," she mumbled. "My . . . my husband. Where is he?"

"I said you're not to concern yourself about him. We'll talk about him when you're better."

"But . . . I am better . . . oh, please!" She struggled to sit up, but was instantly pushed by Donald and fell back on the blankets. She had no strength—she could not fight him even if she wished.

"Tomorrow," Donald said. "Then we'll see."

Again Corrie dreamed, this time of Quade. His eyes were hot blue chips of anger. *Well, good luck, Delia . . . . I hope self-sacrifice agrees with you. . . .*

She drifted in and out of consciousness. Sometimes she was vaguely aware of others in the cabin, and at other times she sank downward to the most profound darkness she had ever known. From time to time, she heard voices.

Earle, I may be a renegade and I may be an abortionist, but you're a damned fool, did you know that? And that's worse.

So? You got all of her money, didn't you? You got her guide and her sled dogs. She's helpless. What else can she do now—

She looks stubborn and difficult.

Stubborn, yes, but tractable enough under the right circumstances. I've waited years for her and then I delayed too long and almost let her slip out of my hands. I should have killed him before, when—

Words, phrases without meaning sifted down onto Corrie's bunk like fine, granular spring snow. Her brain was so fuzzy. Once she tried to sit up—or was that, too, only a dream? The cabin shifted about her so savagely that she knew she would fall and was forced to lie down again.

Periodically a metal pan was thrust under her body by unknown hands and she would perform the functions of nature, because she had to—there was no other way—and she could not lie in her own filth.

One morning she awoke and discovered that her eyes could focus on the interior of the cabin and pick out the details of the room. There was a crack in the oiled cloth of one of the windows, she discovered, with a westward, upside-down, cuplike curve rather like that of the Yukon River. Crude shelves held pots, pans, a metal strong-box. Clothes hung on nails: mackinaws and woolen garments such as she had seen hundreds of times before.

"Good morning, Corrie," Donald said. She turned her head and saw that he was sitting on a crude stool beside her bunk.

She licked lips that were dry and cracked.

"Avery . . . " she whispered in a voice gone strange from disuse. "He was my . . . responsibility. What happened to him? Donald, you must tell me. I must know."

"He died."

"D-died?"

"By the time Dr. Santee got to him he was dead. He must have died soon after you left him. He did have a knife wound; he probably bled to death, Dr. Santee says, or died from the shock. And of course you do know that you were robbed, don't you? We found your leather money bag thrown onto the snow not far from the sled. They took everything you had. You haven't a penny, Corrie."

She was silent, her tongue touching her lips. Poor Avery, she thought with a sharp pang. Now he'll never find his big strike. She lay there feeling numbed, her eyes focused blindly on the crack in the window cloth.

"We brought his body back here and buried it," Donald's voice was saying. "In an old mine shaft, because the ground is frozen so hard. If you don't believe me, I'll be happy to have Artie dig him up for you. Of course, he's bound to be rather an ugly sight and he just might throw you back into your hysteria again."

"That's not necessary," she said dully. She turned her face to the wall. Of course, she told herself. They were not forced to murder Avery—not exactly. All they had to do was to leave him lying in the sled until he died of shock, loss of blood or exposure.

"He wasn't much of a husband to you anyway, was he, Corrie?" she heard Donald go on. "You were a fool to marry him. But I knew I could wait. I knew you'd eventually turn to someone who could help you, who could take care of you and treat you the way you're meant to be treated."

Corrie shook her head, trying to clear the awful fuzziness that clouded her thoughts. His eyes, she thought wildly. There was that look in them again, that heavy, devouring look.

"Cordelia Stewart." He said it musingly. "The beautiful, haughty Cordelia Stewart who couldn't even spare one smile for me when I sat at her father's table. Do you think that I've forgotten that? Oh, no, I've not forgotten, not at all. I vowed years ago that I'd have you, I'd have that smile of yours and I'd have everything else, too."

His hand was on hers, squeezing her fingers so hard that she wanted to cry out.

"You haven't got any money, Corrie. Did you realize that? No, you haven't an ounce of gold to your name now, nor even a single penny. And even an aristocrat like you must realize that it takes money to survive here. Food is scarce and nothing is free, not even here in this charming settlement of Circle City.

"No, there's only one kind of legal tender you possess at this moment, my love, and somehow I don't think you're the sort of woman who would willingly whore herself. So you've got to depend on someone. And I'm that person, Corrie. You've no one else now, only me."

Three more days passed and still she was being drugged by the medication which Dr. Santee kept locked in the metal strongbox. The red-haired doctor gave her laudanum, a bitter powder mixed in an alcoholic solution. He watched her, hawklike, until she had no choice but to swallow.

Corrie was convinced it was Dr. Santee who had given her the bedpan when she had been lying on the bunk all those days. His gray eyes seemed to burn at her, but he was polite enough, and had even rigged up a curtain, behind which she could retreat when she wished privacy to wash or dress.

And it was because of Dr. Santee, too, that they lightened the drug dosage. She heard Donald and the doctor arguing about it one night. *Do you want the girl addicted to the stuff, for Christ's sake? Where is your sense, Earle? Then she really will be mad, you fool!* She could walk shakily about the cabin. But her thoughts still felt thick and somehow distant. She slept a lot, her slumber heavy and deep.

Someone was always with her. Donald, Dr. Santee or the shorter pock-marked Artie, whose husky voice was so familiar that Corrie was convinced he was the assassin who had worn the black scarf. Hadn't Dr. Santee worn the mustard-colored one? If only she could get out of this cabin and breathe some fresh air so that she could think!

"Madness!" She drew herself up as haughtily as she could. An odd, warm, ripply feeling ran down her arms; was this one of the effects of the laudanum or whatever it was that they gave her? "Donald," she told him. "You know I'm not any more mad than you are. It's just this medicine that Dr. Santee keeps giving me. It—it makes me feel so fuzzy . . . " She pressed her right hand to her forehead. "If only I could think clearly! I wish you would just take me back to Dawson City. I want to see Li Hua so much. And I want to go home."

She was suddenly crying.

"You'll go to Dawson soon enough. I'll take you there. Artie is going to Circle this afternoon to fetch someone and then we'll be ready to leave."

"Fetch someone? Who?" She looked at him suspiciously.

"You'll see soon enough."

"But I want to know! Who is coming?"

"Don't get in a temper, young woman. You'll learn what is happening fast enough. And you'll go along with it, too, I'll wager. After all, you're very lucky. Few men would want a madwoman, a girl who raves all sorts of impossible things no one would ever believe, a girl who wakes up screaming in the night."

"I—I never woke up screaming."

"You did. You shrieked out all sorts of strange things. And you've been calling out for someone named Quade. Quade! What an ugly name. A newspaperman interviewed me when I was at Bonanza—he had that same name, and an ugly sort he was, too, asking all sorts of prying questions."

Donald's lips pulled back in a smile. "Are you aware, Corrie, that the manager of your hotel in Circle told me that a man named Quade Hill left for Forty Mile right after your husband's surgery? And do you know something else? I heard in town that they've had a big hotel fire in Forty Mile. Three people were killed. And one of them just happened to be a journalist from Chicago."

Shock slammed through her like a wash of freezing Yukon water. "No!" she gasped. "No, you're lying."

"Am I?"

Nausea pushed at the back of her throat. "But . . . you must be. Quade can't be dead. He can't be."

"You're growing hysterical again, Carrie. Your eyes are as big as plates. You would think you'd had some sort of emotional shock."

"Don't—don't make fun of me! I think you're lying! Quade . . . he can't be . . . "

"Dead? Of course he can be dead. How many journalists from Chicago do you think are roaming about these parts? Not many, I'd wager. Lie down, Corrie, or I'm going to have Dr. Santee mix you another dose of laudanum. A good, strong one, so you'll sleep."

Quade dead. No, it couldn't be. It was impossible! She thought of the day near Avery's bench claim, in the field of wild roses, when Quade had held her so fiercely, so lovingly, the feel of him next to her so warm and strong. She remembered the night when he had appeared at the door of Millie's cabin, his clothes and hair flecked with snowflakes. How glad she had been to see him then! She remembered the touch of his lips on hers, his tender kisses on her throat, her breast . . .

Fear licked through her like little, hot flames. No, she wouldn't let Quade be dead, she refused to think of it! He was too alive, too real.

"I don't want to sleep," she heard herself protest to Donald.

"You'll sleep if I desire you to."

Corrie abandoned herself to weeping.

After the sun had gone down that afternoon and the lamps were lit, Artie stamped into the cabin, dropping chunks of snow all over the floor, his wide frog mouth triumphant. He had brought someone with him, a short, rather cowed-looking little man in a shapeless parka. He introduced Corrie to Reverend Rudge.

"Reverend!" Corrie struggled up from the bunk where she had been lying in tear-sodden misery all afternoon.

"Reverend Alex Rudge," the man repeated uncomfortably. "I'm bringing the word of God to the people here; we're trying to build a new church and your husband-to-be has helped considerably with the building fund. Or he will have, when the ceremony is complete."

The preacher shifted his booted feet about, gazing everywhere but at Corrie, and she realized that Artie must already have told him about her "madness." Reverend! she thought in numbed shock. Surely this couldn't mean— but she knew it did.

She brushed frantically at her rumpled hair, which was sticking out in tangled snarls. How long had it been since she combed it? She couldn't even remember. She must look a fright. Worse even than Mattie Shea, the madam who had died on the *Alki* after uttering her frightening prediction. Yet Reverend Rudge *was* here, by some stroke of luck, and he was a representative of the sane, ordinary, outside world. She had to enlist his help.

"Whatever this man told you, don't believe it," she began rapidly. "I'm not hysterical at all, not really; I've just had a—a shock. You see, I lost my husband . . . these two men stabbed him and then they put his body down a mine shaft . . . "

"Yes, yes, yes." The preacher nodded his head but at the same time backed away from her.

Corrie took a step forward. "Please, you must listen to me. Everything they tell you is a lie. You see, Donald has been waiting years and years to marry me—he even charmed my Papa into liking him . . . "

She started toward the little man, intending to throw herself on his mercy, to beg him to listen to her. But Dr. Santee interrupted her.

"Now, Corrie, you know you're getting excitable again."

"Leave me alone!" she cried, shaking off the red-haired doctor's hand. "Please, sir, you mustn't pay any attention to him. He killed Alikammiq! Killed him with his knife!"

The little minister looked alarmed, and he moved hastily away from Corrie as if she was a wild animal.

"Corrie," Dr. Santee said firmly, grasping her by both arms again. "I'm sure the Reverend doesn't want to hear you babbling on like this. As you can see, she is still quite ill," he added to Reverend Rudge.

"Alikammiq was her favorite sled dog, you see, and unfortunately we had to kill him because he'd turned bad and wouldn't get on with the other dogs. We had no other choice. But she'd made a pet of him, and took it badly. She's newly widowed; her husband died of typhoid not long ago, and Mr. Earle here volunteered to take her back to Dawson . . . "

"That's a lie!" Corrie screamed. "It's all a lie! They're keeping me a prisoner here, can't you see that?"

"She has a vicious temper, too, when she's upset," Dr. Santee informed the trembling visitor as if she were not even present. "She really must be taken back to the States. As you see, she's in no condition to endure this harsh northern country. And my friend here is ready to marry her and take care of her. Believe me, very few other men would be willing to do such a thing."

Reverend Rudge's eyes widened and Corrie knew that he was agreeing wholeheartedly.

"L-let's get on with it," he said. "I've things to do back in Circle City, a sermon to prepare. And—and so forth."

"*I'm* ready," Donald said. His voice was low. He had been standing near the stove all this time, Corrie realized. In her fury she had not noticed him.

"Then I suppose . . . we should begin."

"No!" shouted Corrie. "I don't want to begin! I don't want to marry Donald! I have no intention of doing so! I hate him! Hate him! Don't you hear me? I hate him!"

"She's had a relapse," Dr. Santee said, shooting an angry look at Donald. He went to the shelf where he kept the metal strongbox. Taking a key from his pocket, he opened it and took out a small bottle. He splashed liquid into a spoon and approached Corrie with it.

"No!" She uttered a shriek and knocked it out of his hand. Liquid splashed on the slab floor among the clods of snow. The Reverend Rudge shrank back, his eyes widened as if he had glimpsed a snakepit of hideous rattlesnakes.

"Really," he said suddenly. His Adam's apple wobbled. "I don't think . . . I don't think I should go through with this. She . . . she is mad, she has no awareness of what she's doing. Really . . . "

Donald moved forward and grasped the preacher's upper right arm. "I'm paying a good deal of money for this ceremony," he said softly. "Enough to build your cursed church from foundation to steeple. That's what you want, isn't it? And now you have to do something a bit unpleasant to get it. Well, you needn't let your conscience bother you. This woman is insane, true enough, but she will be well taken care of, and I plan to place her in the finest asylum as soon as we get back to San Francisco. She'll have everything, every comfort, every medicinal help known, the best doctors. But she must be my wife. Surely you see that, don't you?"

"I . . . I don't know . . . "

"Of course, I *could* give that gold to someone else. Perhaps the Baptist Church would relish receiving it. *They* would know what to do with it."

The minister licked his lips. "I tell you, I don't know . . . "

Donald pulled him toward the center of the cabin. "Then you'll do it. Pull out your Bible and let's get on with it. Santee, give her another swallow of medicine. Enough to quiet her. You and Artie can be the witnesses. We want this nice and legal, with no questions later. Do you understand?"

Dr. Santee, tall and gawky like a stork, gave Donald another scowl. "You'd better hold her still, then. I don't want her spitting in my face. She's a little cat, this one is. You'll have your hands full with her, I can tell you that. If I were you, I'd let her go to work in a brothel and forget about her."

"Just do as you're told," Donald snapped.

"Very well, then. But as I say, you'll have to hold her down. She's like a little vixen."

As Donald approached her warily, Corrie crouched down, knees bent almost like the wild animal they accused her of being. Fright gave her a sort of wily cunning. She backed toward the stove and the shelf behind it where they kept the cooking utensils. She would fight, she told herself desperately. Quade might be dead (Oh, merciful heavens, but he couldn't be, he wasn't, she wouldn't let him be), but she would not marry Donald. She would kick and scream and struggle until she died. If Quade was really dead, it didn't matter whether she lived or perished.

"Now, Corrie. Cordelia, listen to me." That was Donald, facing her, looking big and repulsive, his willful lips twisted, the ugly scar on his hand standing out. His black hair hung in his eyes, which were hard, ugly stones of hate. He still held the drug bottle, and she knew that he planned to force its entire contents down her throat.

Well, let him try, she thought.

She backed into the corner nearest the stove. She could feel the heat emanating from its sheet-metal bulk. She fumbled behind her for the shelf, and the tin pot in which they brewed coffee. Her fingers closed on its handle. Then she hurled it at Donad. She had the satisfaction of seeing it hit him in the temple. Blood began to dribble down his cheek.

"Damn you! You little wildcat!" His cold black eyes were slits of fury. "Haughty little bitch—you always defied me, didn't you? Throwing away my expensive diamond ring as if it had been trash—oh, you'll take your medicine, my girl, and you'll swallow every drop of it. And you'll be my wife, too. My nice, meek, mild, *insane* wife."

"No!" she shouted. She threw another pan at him. It sailed over his shoulder. She saw the Reverend Rudge's mouth drop open in shock and dismay.

"Coward!" she shrieked at the preacher. "Coward!"

She no longer heard what she was yelling. She only knew that her voice was filling the cabin, that Artie was creeping up on her left and was grasping her arms and twisting her. Artie threw her to the floor so roughly that her nose hit the wooden slabs and began to bleed.

"No! No!" she screamed. "No—"

They poured the laudanum into her mouth and someone's palm clamped itself across her lips so that she couldn't spit. She was forced to swallow the fluid or choke to death. She swallowed. And then in a few minutes the lassitude began to creep over her, the terrible, drugged relaxation, so that she no longer cared that Reverend Rudge was staring down at her with wide eyes, or that he had pulled out a black Bible and was fumbling with it nervously.

"All right, then," Donald said. His voice sounded as if he were speaking from the bottom of a very deep and resonant well. "Get on with it, man, what are you waiting for? Don't just stand there shaking in your boots. Do you want the money for your building fund, or don't you?"

Five minutes later she and Donald were husband and wife.

✿ Chapter 34 ✿

She was later to wonder what had happened to Reverend Rudge. Had they let him go back to Circle City with his extraordinary tale of the raving, screaming, drugged girl who was being forced to marry a man she did not want? Or had they killed him to silence him, a possibility that filled her with horror.

She was never to know. She saw no one, she was not given any newspapers, and they left two days later for Dawson City, avoiding all roadhouses in the vicinity and preparing their own food over camp stoves.

Numbly, Corrie did as she was ordered, knowing that she had little other choice. If she rebelled, more laudanum would be forced down her throat. Her only hope now, she realized, lay in keeping her brain clear. She was not strong enough to fight back, so she would try to cooperate. She would be docile and obedient, and lull them into thinking she was harmless. Perhaps, if she were very lucky, her chance would come.

The fact that they were heading to Dawson seemed hopeful. Donald could not keep her away from other people forever, could he? Resolutely she pushed aside the remarks he had made about her being insane, and his statement about finding an asylum for her when they reached the States. I wouldn't let that happen, she told herself. I'll be gone from him by then.

Dawson, she reassured herself, meant she'd be near Li Hua. In Dawson there were red-coated Mounties and a post office, and—when the ice broke—the river steamers would arrive. Her camera gear, too, she thought longingly, was still at Li Hua's; perhaps Donald would allow her to go there and get it. Perhaps she could somehow blurt out her predicament to Li Hua . . .

They had only been traveling for an hour or so, however, before something happened to horrify her and destroy all of her optimism. Donald, walking ahead of the pair of sleds, strolled casually toward the edge of the trail and gave a kick to some dark object which lay there. Corrie, wrapped in fur robes and riding on the sled, glanced at the objects as she passed by. She drew in her breath in a quick gasp.

Jumbled into a snow-drifted mound, as if someone wished her to see them, were two scarves, one black and one mustard-yellow. Scarves belonging to Avery's murderers.

Even under her heavy layer of furs, Corrie began to shake convulsively. She was sure that their discovery of the scarves had been no accident. Not the way Donald was glancing deliberately back at her, as if to see whether or not she had absorbed the message.

She raised her chin and stared stonily toward her left at the endless vista of trees and hills and partly melted snow. She would pretend that she had not seen the scarves. And she would not reveal her fear.

The journey continued. At first Corrie rode in the sled, but after a few hours she got out and walked. She observed Dr. Santee giving her a sharp look, but he said nothing, and grimly she forced herself to stagger on through the soft snow. She knew she had to start building up her strength. The long days of inactivity, the lassitude of the drugs, had left her weak. And she couldn't be weak, not if she wanted to get away.

"I'd rather you rode in the sled," Donald told her, turning back from his position at the head of the two sleds. He put his arm around her possessively.

"And *I'd* rather walk," she told him sharply. "I'm getting cold sitting in the sled. Some exercise will warm me."

"Very well." Donald fumbled in the pocket of his coat for a cigar. He paused, hunching to get out of the wind, to pull out a small metal box, from which he extracted a sulfur match. He lingered over the flame, at last tossing the match away to hiss out in the snow.

He was fascinated by fire. Fire in any form . . .

Corrie hurried ahead, trying not to look at him. *He is enraptured by fire and flames, obsessed by them in a terrible, terrible way . . .* Corrie remembered Li Hua's words. Corrie had not known the full horror of it, not until her wedding day . . .

The consummation of her marriage had been nightmarish. As soon as the ceremony—if such a travesty could be called that—was completed, Artie and Dr. Santee hustled Reverend Rudge out of the cabin door.

"Stay away for a while," Donald ordered as they left. The pock-marked Artie gave Donald a lascivious wink, and even Dr. Santee cast a long, hot, assessing look toward Corrie. Then they were gone, and Donald walked to the cabin door and bolted it shut.

He turned to her.

"All right," he said. "You're going to pay for all those high and mighty looks of yours. Now you're going to be mine, all mine."

"No . . . " she had babbled, scarcely aware of what she was saying. She felt drugged and unutterably sleepy. She could barely keep her eyelids open. The cabin started to whirl about her.

Donald quickly stripped off his garments. Months ago, in San Francisco, his body had been soft, pudgy about the waist, reflecting a man who does little physical labor and enjoys eating. But now he was different. His belly was thick but flat, the muscles of his chest were rounded and taut and his sex organ was blue-veined and distended.

"What are you looking at?" he asked sharply. "You were a married woman. Haven't you ever seen a naked man before?"

Weakened by the laudanum, she began to cry.

"Well, you're seeing one now, aren't you? And you're going to like it. You'll like it and worship it before I'm through—worship it, do you hear?"

She felt his fingers on the crown of her head, grasping her hair and pushing downward so that her neck ached under the pressure. Slowly, slowly, he forced her to kneel.

"No . . . " she sobbed.

"Worship," he commanded.

"No! I won't! I can't! I—"

"Oh, yes, you will. You'll do just as I say."

Minutes passed, unbearably slow moments when she was forced to follow Donald's instructions. To her dismay, he did not find satisfaction in what she did for him. When at last she pulled back from him she saw that his face was contorted, his hard black eyes almost pleading.

"Take off your clothes, Corrie. Take them off . . . "

Donald gave her whiskey and she drank it eagerly, wanting for once the feeling of oblivion that it would bring. "Hooch," they called it here, and it was harsh and raw, but it sent a warmth burgeoning through her, removing her even further from what was happening. Hours passed. She was never to be sure how long. The medication and the liquor made everything seem very distant and unreal.

She did not know how many times Donald had her. But after each time his erection seemed not diminished but increased. Again and again he could not reach orgasm. He thrust angrily, roughly, his features contorted. He was bathed in sweat, yet there was no release for him.

"Please, Donald, stop. I . . . I can't go on. Please—" Corrie felt weak and powerless, caught in a nightmare that went on and on.

"Corrie. You've got to— It's the only way for me— They'll do it for me in the whorehouses in Dawson if I pay them enough. It's the only way I can get relief."

She watched numbly as he went to the stack of split logs by the stove. He picked up one of them and wrapped a rag around its end, knotting it securely. Then he splashed the rag with lamp oil and thrust the sapling into the orange-red maw of the stove. Instantly the torch flamed alight. It was an oddly barbaric sight Donald made, his big body flat-muscled, holding up the wavering, smoking torch as if he was a naked warrior.

"Take the torch," he told her, "and lie down with it. Hold the flames close to your face."

She stared at him. "What?" she said stupidly.

"I said lie down with it."

Trembling, she did as he asked, the slivers of the rough pine slabs on the floor piercing her skin. She tried to hold the torch as far away from herself as she could. It smelled of smoke and pine pitch; she could hear the crackle of its burning, feel the heat of its flames. This was only a dream, she told herself unbelievingly. A crazy, distorted dream from which she would awaken at any minute.

"Please—" some remaining instinct of self-preservation made her beg. "Please, you'll set me on fire—"

"Closer," he commanded. "Bring the torch closer to your face. I need the flames. I need to see them in your eyes." His voice was husky and urgent.

His erection grew huger, monstrously distended. Then he plunged himself into her, thrust fiercely, and it was over in seconds. Warm liquid spurted down her leg. Donald's heavy body sagged against her, and then he rolled away. He grabbed the torch from her violently trembling hands just as she was about to drop it.

He walked naked to the stove and thrust the torch into its interior.

"Get dressed," he said shortly. The nightmare was over.

They stopped to eat one night at a roadhouse, predictably named the Klondike, near the outskirts of Forty Mile. In the darkness, the wind whipped savagely past them, burning at any exposed skin. But the roadhouse, small and hot and packed with customers, was a haven, and Corrie entered it with a feeling of relief.

Her relief, however, was short-lived. Even though the roadhouse was full of people, she was not given a chance to speak to them. Artie and Dr. Santee stayed with her, and Donald kept urging more moose stew upon her until she wanted to strike out at him in her desperation.

Among the diners were two young women evidently on their way to Dawson City from Forty Mile. Corrie overheard snatches of their conversation. Apparently they were dancers, and had been touring the makeshift theaters in the area and entertaining the miners. When the two got up to visit the privy located behind the roadhouse, Corrie saw that one of them was Cad Wilson, the dancer for the Eldorado Kings.

Corrie stood up.

"Where are you going?" Donald demanded immediately.

"I have to go outside," she snapped. "Do you object?"

"Then Artie will go with you."

"Artie!"

"If you want to go, he'll have to accompany you."

"Very well." She was dismayed, though of course she should have expected nothing less.

She and Artie pushed their way through the filthy, cluttered little kitchen lean-to, out the back door, and through the tunnel of snow which led to the outdoor bathroom. Outside the small shack, she found Cad Wilson patiently waiting.

"It's busy, honey. You've got to wait your turn and hope you don't freeze to death." Cad was rosy-cheeked and kittenishly pretty in a sealskin coat with matching fur hat. Her soft mouth was set in a pout. Corrie could picture her on some tiny stage, turning and pirouetting in a brief costume while men hooted and whistled and tossed gold nuggets at her feet.

Artie took up a station at the far end of the walkway near the kitchen door, where he could watch Corrie and still get some of the kitchen heat.

"That your man?" Cad asked curiously.

"No—"

"Kinda ugly, isn't he? A little short, too. I like 'em big and tall and rich." Cad threw back her head and laughed. "Those're the only ones I'll even look at!"

"Please," Corrie said quickly. "I heard you talking and I know that you just came from Forty Mile. Could you tell me if there was a hotel fire there? A fire in which three men were killed?"

"Sure enough. A big one it was, too. I forget the name of the hotel where it was at. But three of 'em died, all right, and some others was took bad from the smoke, and from falling on the stairs. They said it was started by some damn fool smoking a cigar in bed."

Corrie felt herself swaying, and the blood left her face. So the story about the fire was really true. It had not been one of Donald's lies. She clutched the folds of her coat about her; the chill of the night air seemed to seep through the fur directly into her bones. She licked her dry lips.

"Can you tell me if a man, a journalist from Chicago, was one of the ones who died in the fire?"

"Listen, honey." The smoky eyes of the dancer widened in sympathy. "I'm sorry, but it's rough country for a girl up here, rough and ugly. I don't know a damned thing about those men who were killed in that fire, and I don't want to know, either. Unless they've got them a big poke of gold, I don't care a damn for any of 'em, and that's the way it is."

Cad gently put her hand on Corrie's sleeve.

"You'd ought to forget him anyway," Cad said. "Men! They'll use you and toss you away. What do they care?"

But Corrie did not hear Cad's last words. Blindly she turned, tears running down her cheeks, and stumbled back into the roadhouse.

By mid April they had been back in Dawson for some weeks. New rumors of gold strikes were as plentiful as the men who poured into the city. Gold had been found in a desolate place called Nome, hundreds of miles away on the coast of the Seward Peninsula near the Bering Straits. The precious metal, it was said, lay on the beach, which stretched for fifteen fabulous, sandy miles. All you had to do was to find a vacant spot and start digging. Gold was everywhere, in "ruby sand," in "ruby" mixed with black, and at bedrock.

Corrie didn't care whether they found gold in Nome by the ton. Even Dr. Santee was speculating about it, but she turned sourly away from such talk. What did she care about gold? She was torn by uncertainty over Quade's fate. *Had* he died in the hotel fire? *Dear God,* she prayed. *Let him be alive.*

Donald's plans, she learned, were to remain in Dawson for a few weeks after the spring breakup in order to sell or consolidate his interests before finally leaving for San Francisco. Once they were actually home . . . Corrie remembered his talk of an asylum and shivered. When they registered at their hotel, she overheard Donald telling the manager that his wife was subject to nervous attacks and had recently had a breakdown; the manager was not to be too alarmed if he heard odd sounds coming from their room.

The first day in Dawson, as she passed out of the hotel in the company of Dr. Santee to buy some clothes (Donald insisted she be fashionably dressed), she tried to smile at the dark-skinned little manager, to show him that she was perfectly normal. The man gave her a startled look and dropped a huge ink blot onto his registration book.

How easily people believe in insanity, she thought bleakly. All it took was a few words, a hint or two. And the louder you protested, the more insane you appeared. She was sure that, given enough time, Donald could even convince Aunt Susan of her madness, if he wished to do so.

Gradually a shade of her natural optimism came back. Surely, she told herself, something good would happen soon to lift her spirits from despair. Quade was not dead, she was sure. He was far too tough, too vital and alive, ever to die so uselessly. Meanwhile she was here, in Dawson, and Dr. Santee had actually gone over to Li Hua's to pick up her camera and photographic supplies. Donald would not permit her to take any photographs, but at least she could look at the prints she had already taken, and experience the bittersweet memories. So many of the pictures she had taken while in the company of Quade . . .

Dr. Santee also brought her news of Li Hua. The Chinese girl was well, and her dance hall was doing a splendid business—so good, in fact, that she had opened an annex next door. Her hairdressing establishment was constantly busy and she had hired an assistant.

"Oh, Donald, please, couldn't I go and visit her?" begged Corrie. "I miss her so much. She is my only friend here in Dawson now that Millie has gone."

Millie would have been able to help her, she thought with a pang; Millie would have known what to do. But Millie was far away, in Seattle, happily married.

"No," Donald said. "I want you here. My wife is to be a lady. She is not to mingle with prostitutes and dance hall girls."

"But Li Hua isn't a prostitute! She—"

"She certainly is no lady! Be still, Corrie; I'll decide what's best for you." As she began to protest, he added,

"Do you want another dose of laudanum? You can be sure that Dr. Santee is still amply supplied with it."

Corrie, defiant, would not be stilled. "I *will* visit her! She's going to wonder why I haven't come. She knows I'm here in town—she'll begin to ask questions!"

"Let her ask them. Dr. Santee had already informed her of your mental breakdown due to the death of your first husband. That should silence her."

"But I haven't had a breakdown! I'm perfectly well! You know that I'm as sane as you are!"

"*Do* I know that?" He turned to look at her, his eyes glittering, and Corrie shrank away from him, frightened by something in his eyes. She said no more about Li Hua.

In spite of herself, during the days of virtual imprisonment, she came to know Donald better. Or, rather, she learned that she would never know him really well. He was extremely reticent, saying little about his personal feelings or background. If he had ever had a childhood, it was lost in the dim mists of the past.

Then one night he returned from the Red Feather saloon reeking of whiskey. Each day he seemed to be drinking more heavily, and Corrie hated it, for sometimes he wanted her, and the routine with the torch was now a regular part of his sexual practices. It seemed he had given up trying to function sexually in the normal way. He had to see the flames reflected in her terrified face; without the stimulation of fire he could not have an orgasm.

But tonight, to Corrie's vast relief, sex was not on his mind. Instead, something else was. He muttered about a woman he had seen, and even Dr. Santee shot him a wary look as he left their room. She heard Dr. Santee click the lock Donald installed on the outside of the bedroom door, and then she was alone with her husband.

"Black hair and fat arms and face—God, but she made me think of *her*," he mumbled as he took off his boots and dropped them with a thump on the floor. "Murdered, Ma was, by one of her johns. And then eaten by rats. I was only six then. There wasn't any food and she wouldn't get up. At first I thought she was sleeping. I hit her and I kicked her and I screamed at her, but still she wouldn't get up. And then the rats came. Have you ever seen a corpse eaten by rats? The flesh hangs out like half-chewed meat . . . "

He swallowed noisily and she sensed that he was on the verge of vomiting. "I . . . I couldn't keep them away. I'd scream and yell at them, but they'd keep coming back . . . "

He staggered over to the ewer and was noisily sick; then he fell across the bed and she thought he had gone to sleep. In a few minutes he stirred. He began to talk again, of a woman and a child living in one cramped room and sleeping on mattresses of straw beside an enormous, filthy stove with so much laundry draped in front of it that you could not see its front.

"She'd spread her legs for anything or anyone and it didn't matter who was watching while she did it. I watched her. Dozens of times . . . she didn't care . . . "

At last he fell deeply asleep and Corrie sat by him, feeling stunned. What was this horror Donald had come from? How on earth, she wondered, had he emerged from it to the respectability of the shipyard? But he had. What effort, what grim determination had it taken?

The next morning he was quiet and sullen, and Corrie was careful not to mention the things he had told her. It had been like a brief lifting of a curtain, a glimpse she knew she was not likely to have again.

At the end of April, another fire swept through Dawson. The conflagration destroyed building after building in the business district—banks, stores, hotels, warehouses. Corrie and Donald were forced to evacuate their hotel. They stood on Front Street at a safe distance, watching the ragged flames engulf Dawson, silhouetted against the dark bulk of hills and sky. Men shouted and scurried about with buckets, vainly trying to stop the blaze.

They had watched the fire for some time when Corrie heard a noise coming from beside her. Donald stood staring at the fire as if hypnotized by it. A low, growling sound came from deep within her husband's throat. She turned, startled, to see him staring at her, his eyes eerily lit by the flames.

"Corrie . . . "

Instantly she knew what he wanted.

"Donald! Oh, no, not here, we can't—"

He did not even hear her protests. Instead she felt herself being dragged behind a smoldering building. Her skirts were ripped up, her undergarments brutally torn away. Then, in full sight of some men running past with buckets, he threw her to the ground and raped her. His frenzy ended in a violent convulsion, and at the height of it Corrie had the spooky thought that somewhere nearby a girl was screaming, screaming silently . . .

Later, people said that the fire had started in the room of a woman living over the Bodega Saloon. Speculation was that she had either been smoking or curling her hair with a hot iron, and had grown careless. There was a board of inquiry which could not decide on the girl's guilt, but did decree that the "soiled doves" of the town should be forbidden to enter all public buildings except licensed hotels.

Corrie barely listened to this sort of talk. What did it matter now how the fire had started? It had happened. She and Donald had to find another hotel and Li Hua, she learned from Dr. Santee, was rebuilding her dance hall as fast as she could, utilizing old nails pried out of the wreckage.

In late May came the spring breakup, a spectacle so full of grinding and crushing fury that Corrie, even depressed as she was, took pleasure in it. Men placed bets on the exact time the ice would go out. When it did, roaring like freight trains, the sound was greeted with shouts of joy or dismay, depending on whether the miner had won or lost his bet.

Then, to Corrie's joy, the steamers began to arrive from where they had wintered: the *Bella*, the *W.K. Merwin*, the *Alice*. An impressive boat named the *Susie* brought her a letter from Aunt Susan. Dr. Santee picked it up for her at the post office. She took the letter and thanked him.

"Don't thank me. I've already appropriated the money out of it for your husband to keep. It seems he doesn't want you to get any ideas about buying steamer passage on your own."

In a less joyous mood, she opened the letter and began to read the words penned in Aunt Susan's precise, feminine handwriting.

. . . am fine and well. I am marrying a man named Thomas Cartendon. He is a stockbroker here in the city, and has three half-grown boys. I am moving to his home as soon as I can get my things sorted and packed. I will have the house here kept open, of course, until your return. Mrs. Parsons and Jim Price are staying on. Do be assured that I will always be near you as before, really only four blocks away. But the house has seemed very empty, and I will relish having young people about me again . . .

Corrie put the letter down and turned away so that Dr. Santee could not see the pain on her face In her thoughts her aunt had always been as she had last seen her. It had never occurred to her that Aunt Susan might remarry, move away or change.

Finally she read the rest of the letter. *I have not heard from you in so long, and repeated news of shipwrecks in the passage has come to us. I do not even know if you have received the money I sent previously. Have you? I hope that you are well and that Avery is fine also. Was your baby a boy or a girl? I think of it so often. I am enclosing more money in this letter. I am sure you will find good use for it. When are you coming home? Surely that cannot be long now. Yours with all love and affection, Susan Raleigh.*

Corrie's eyes filled. If only Aunt Susan knew!

A week later she found the clipping. She did not know exactly why she had decided to search Donald's things, only that it had been on her mind to do so for some time. Donald was very careful with his possessions, particularly his money belt and the Colt pistol he carried. For days she had been waiting for the right opportunity.

It came on a sunny Tuesday morning. They had had sex the previous night, a session even more terrifying than usual, for Donald had been careless with the torch and dropped it, igniting the bedclothes. Corrie doused the flames with water from the ewer. Then Donald, his restless desire temporarily sated, left the room. He was gone for hours—drinking, Corrie was sure.

Just before dawn he returned to the room and stripped off all of his clothing as if it itched him unbearably. He fell across the bed, naked, and began to snore. Light came and still he slept, sodden. Hesitantly Corrie covered him with a blanket. A shaft of early sunlight, golden as ingots, was slanting through the plate glass window.

Corrie got up cautiously from the bed, her lace nightgown rustling. She looked down at the floor where Donald had flung his clothes. His leather money belt, worn to softness, lay tangled among his undergarments, the heavier leather poke sack, which contained gold dust, beside it. From beneath the folds of his shirt protruded the blunt nose of the Colt.

Corrie's eyes narrowed. The pistol . . . She did not dare to touch it. She was not sure she would be able to kill. She had never used a pistol before and could not even tell if it was loaded. Besides, the room was locked from the outside, and Dr. Santee, who occupied the room next door, was a light sleeper. He would hear any noise and come in at once. For all of his small kindnesses, she had seen what those skilled fingers could do with a knife . . .

She focused her eyes on the money belt. Papers stuck out of it, and she realized that Donald must use it as a kind of file, as well as for money. Softly she crept toward it, freezing as Donald expelled a loud sigh and turned over on the bed.

He began to snore again and Corrie's hand darted toward the belt. The papers were mostly meaningless to her. She found a few business cards, receipts, a membership card in a private gambling club in San Francisco, some scribbled notes. She gently put the belt down, and a thin scrap of paper fluttered out.

It was a newspaper clipping which had nearly disintegrated from age. She smoothed it out as best she could and held it under the shaft of sunlight, trying to read it. Most of the print had been obliterated. However, she was able to catch a name and a few key phrases. *Miss Ila Hill . . . body identified by . . .*

She let the clipping fall from suddenly icy fingers.

Miss Ila Hill! Vomit surged up at the back of her throat. She rushed over to the porcelin ewer and threw up. She prayed that the sounds of her retching would not awaken Donald.

Could it possibly be true?

Corrie felt sure that it was. *Donald* was the office clerk who, in an effort to conceal the funds he had embezzled, had poured kerosene over the Hill office and ignited it, burning Ila Hill to death in the process.

Corrie sank to the floor, her lace-edged nightgown crumpled up about her thighs. Under its soft cambric, her skin felt unbearably clammy, and she could feel perspiration running down her ribs.

Donald, she thought. Donald killed Ila. *Donald is the man Quade Hill is searching for.* Involuntarily her eyes fastened on the still-sleeping form of her husband. As he slept, he tugged unconsciously at the blanket with one hand, drawing in his breath in a sharp, half-moaning shudder. At that moment, Donald looked as vulnerable and helpless as all sleeping people do. It was incredible to think that he had—

With enormous effort, she stopped the thought. She knew that mere possession of an old newspaper clipping was no real proof of guilt. Was it? Surely anyone could cut something from a newspaper and carry it about with him; there was certainly no law against that. Still . . .

Feverishly her mind began to go over the facts. Donald originally came from Chicago, where the Hills lived. He had come approximately six years ago, in 1893, the year in which Ila Hill died. Donald started his work at the Stewart Shipyards as a clerk, the same position he held in Chicago. He never seemed lacking for funds while in San Francisco, although he could not have been paid much by Cordell Stewart, who was not noted for his generosity in paying his employees. He explained once to Corrie that he was in possession of a "legacy."

Furthermore (here her hands began to feel so cold that she had to thrust them under her armpits for warmth), Donald was obsessed by fire. He could only enjoy sex when burning flames were reflected in a girl's eyes.

With a physical gesture she shook off the picture this brought to her mind. Her heart was thudding heavily. If Quade were alive, he would surely want to know about this.

Or did Quade somehow know already?

Corrie drew in a sharp breath as memories began to flood over her, bits of talk she recalled from the months she had known Quade. His hints that he had come north on an instinct, a feeling. His talk of a man he had seen on the street, a man who looked familiar. She had never wondered at finding Quade in Dyea the day she arrived there. But Donald had been there also. Was it possible that Quade had *followed Donald from San Francisco?* That *Donald* had been the "man in the street"? That Quade was tracking him as relentlessly as any bloodhound would sniff out its quarry, driven by nothing more than a hunch, an instinct, a gut feeling emanating from—she hesitated, then grimly continued the thought—emanating from a burned brooch that he carried in his pocket?

A brooch, guiding Quade here?

Oh, but that thought was wholly fantastic! She was crazy to believe in such a far-fetched thing.

Nevertheless, the picture of the brooch with its pale, carved cameo face was distinct in her mind, as clear as if she actually cupped it in her palm. She remembered the odd feeling she had when she touched it, as if it somehow held hatred and fear, an actual physical presence.

Her perspiration felt cold on her forehead, and moisture streamed down between her breasts like iced water. She inched over to the money belt and thrust the clipping back into a hidden fold of the leather as carefully as she could. She must write to Quade, she told herself. Transmit the message to him somehow, on the wild chance that he might still be alive . . .

Half an hour later, scribbling feverishly before Donald awoke, she completed the letter. She blurted out as much as she could of her own situation, all of her confusion and love and fear, the known facts (they were few), and her own conjectures. It was, she knew, a fantastic mixture. And perhaps she was writing it all to a corpse, to a man who could not help her because he had been in his grave for long weeks.

She dressed herself in the skirt and delicately ruffled and shirred shirtwaist which Donald preferred, and tried to occupy herself by reading. At last Donald awoke in a surly mood and sent down for luncheon from the restaurant next door to the hotel, an establishment which catered to the "Comstock Kings" and their lady friends. While they waited for the food, Corrie paced nervously about, uncomfortably aware of the letter tucked into her bosom. If Donald should decide to make love to her again—

She had no appetite for the meal when it arrived, a rich *omelette au rhum*, Klondike grayling, pâté poulet. She pushed bits of egg around on her plate, her mind going over her plans feverishly. How exactly was she to dispatch the letter? She had no money. She was watched constantly. Artie or Dr. Santee was with her when Donald wasn't. She was not even allowed to go to the privy, but used the chamber pot in the room.

Perhaps she might drop the letter out of the window and hope it would be found. No, she decided. That was far too risky. Could she slip it to the boy (he had eyed her admiringly) who brought their food? No. How could she do that with Donald not three feet away?

"What are you thinking about?" Donald asked her suddenly through a mouthful of fish.

"N-nothing," she said nervously. Involuntarily her hand went to her bodice and touched the letter.

"Well, you look as if you found a tarantula in your food. Is that why you're barely touching it? I paid good money for it. Do you realize what fresh eggs cost here?"

"No, it—it's fine. Nothing is wrong. I . . . I'm tired, that's all."

"Tired? Why should you be tired? I'm the one who came in late, not you." His eyes on her were sharp.

"I didn't sleep very well, I guess . . . "

"Your hands keep going to your blouse, Corrie. What have you got in it?"

"Nothing!" She took an involuntary step away from him, trying to smile. "Nothing, of course. There is nothing in my shirtwaist but . . . but me."

"Let's see 'you,' then."

"But I've told you . . . " From somewhere she found the strength to make her smile brilliant, and she gave a saucy little pirouette, whirling her skirts. As if to demonstrate her innocence, she ran her hands down her bust-line.

"Strip off your clothes, Corrie."

Her heart contracted as if pressed between giant bellows. "Surely you can't mean—"

"I said get them off—at least your blouse. I want to see whatever it is that you've got hidden. And I mean to see it. I'm your husband, Corrie. Have you quite forgotten that?"

✿ Chapter 35 ✿

"What nonsense," Donald said, ripping the letter in half. "Do you really believe this drivel?"

Corrie was stubbornly silent, pulling the blanket from the bed more tightly about her shoulders so that her nudity was concealed.

"You're being very foolish if you do believe it," Deliberately, Donald ripped the letter into smaller strips. He tore these across, letting the small, white scraps flutter to the floor like leaves. Then he gave them a negligent kick.

Corrie stared at him. The only sign of emotion on Donald's face was a slight reddening along his cheekbones. Otherwise he seemed perfectly calm. "Of course I believe what I wrote," she told him. "I think you killed poor Ila Hill and I think you killed my husband Avery, too. Not to mention Alikammiq, a boy whose only crime was in being hired as a guide. Even those poor, harmless sled dogs—"

He gazed at her levelly. "Then your hysteria is showing, Corrie, and you know what that means."

"Oh, yes, I know! You plan to drug me again! Isn't that it? Drug me so I'll keep quiet, so I won't be able to tell people the truth—that you're a murderer!"

She shouted it now, forgetting that she was naked and at this man's mercy, with only a blanket to shield her.

"Letting a girl burn to death—how could you, Donald? How could you be so inhuman?"

"Nonsense. I assure you I'm quite human. I don't know what you're talking about."

He took a step toward her. "But I do think it's time for your laudanum again. We certainly can't have you shouting and carrying on like this. What would the other people in the hotel think? That you've gone completely mad? As for your allegations, they have no basis in fact whatsoever. You have no proof."

"I have a clipping!" Too late she remembered that the clipping was in Donald's possession, not in her own. "And—and I'm not mad at all; I'm perfectly sane, as you very well know. You're the one who is mad! Do you call it sane to lust for a woman all of these years, to turn your whole life inside out in order to get her? To—to need fire in order to enjoy being in bed with her—"

"Enough!"

"No, it isn't enough! I won't stop talking, you can't shut me up, nothing will shut me up now—" She was shouting out wildly, sobbing in her anger and fear, for she knew that she was beaten. Already the door had opened and Dr. Santee stood there, his eyes riveted on her nakedness. He held a small bottle in his hand. She did not have to be told what was in it.

"No!" she screamed. "You won't drug me again; I won't let you! I—"

"Oh?" Donald took another step toward her. Now he was flanked by Dr. Santee whose eyes, some terrified corner of her mind had time to note, were regarding her body appreciatively.

Desperately she backed away, trying to put the bed between them. She knew, though, that she was only delaying the inevitable. The room was small and the two men blocked the door; there was nowhere for her to go. In a few seconds they would have her trapped in the corner beside the bed.

"You're certainly in no position to decide what's best for you, Corrie," Donald said almost pityingly, as if she really was a madwoman. "And here I thought you were coming along so well. I had such hopes for you."

"Hopes!" she screamed. "What about Ila Hill? What about her hopes! Perhaps she didn't want to be burned up in your fire! Perhaps she—"

"I said that's enough!" Donald's mouth twisted. "Let's get her, Santee. We can't have her rousing the whole place. They know about her, of course, they know she's mad, but still it's very awkward."

"All right."

They moved closer to her with the small bottle and she knew that screaming would not be of any use.

Corrie opened her eyes, shaking her head to clear the spider webs that seemed to be draped in gray swathes across her mind. Her eyes felt unbearably gummy, almost crusted shut. Her mouth was dry and tasted leathery. How long had she been asleep? It seemed forever.

She tried to stir in the bed. Her legs, however, would not move. Her arms, too, felt strange. Something was cutting into her wrists, and her ankles felt raw.

Panicking, she tried to lift her head, but she knew already what she would see. She was tied to the bed with strips of blanket which had been torn and used as crude restraints. To her relief she was no longer naked—at least they had spared her that indignity, and had pulled her nightgown on.

"Well, sleeping beauty. I see you're finally opening your eyes."

She twisted her head about, trying not to moan with the effort. "Donald?"

"Yes, it's me, your husband. Are you going to be quiet now, Corrie, or are we going to have to force more medicine down your throat? I'm getting tired of dosing you like a sick horse. Dr. Santee tells me you'll become addicted to the stuff if we keep on giving it to you long enough. Do you want that to happen to you?"

"No . . . of course not." She blinked her eyes, feeling unbearably stiff and exhausted. "How long have I been asleep?"

"Long enough. More than twelve hours."

"Twelve hours! Would you please untie me? And let me have a drink of water? I'm so thirsty."

"Perhaps. If you behave."

"I—I will. I promise you."

Her tongue moved thickly over the lie. Hatred surged through her like river ice. She should have used the Colt pistol when she had the chance, she told herself. Why hadn't she? She had wavered with foolish scruples and doubts over whether she could kill, whether she could use the pistol, whether or not Dr. Santee would hear. And look where hesitating had gotten her. Her situation was a thousand times worse now.

"Lift your head," Donald was saying. "I'll get you some water."

She did as he asked. He spooned cool liquid into her mouth, and she swallowed thirstily. The water felt heavenly on the parched membranes of her mouth.

"More," she croaked.

"Very well."

He held her gently and continued to spoon water into her mouth. What an odd, tortured, complicated man he was! And how many ways had she seen him—angry, cold, businesslike, sullen, weeping, lusting. And now this, an eerie gentleness.

"What are you going to do with me?" she asked at last.

"We'll go back to San Francisco and I'll see about the shipyards. There's much work to be done there, and I must see if that manager I hired has been cheating us."

Us. Yes. She supposed, according to the will, she and Donald owned the Stewart estate jointly now. Her papa had, after all, had his wish.

"What did you tell them here in the hotel to explain my screaming?" she asked at last, dully.

He was at the window now, looking down onto the main street. They could hear the sounds of men shouting to each other as they worked on a bank across the street. The air rang with the sound of men hammering. The world of normalcy, Corrie thought.

"I told them the truth—that you'd had a mental breakdown and were under a doctor's care. It's not so strange. Women do go mad here, some of them. They can't take the cold and the darkness and the hardship. It's happened before."

She let her muscles sag against the lumpy mattress and did not try to fight her bonds. The room started to whirl slowly about her, and Donald's voice faded. His voice seemed to recede into a drugged buzz, then throb forward again to fill her ears.

" . . . you do know, don't you, Corrie, that a wife is

not allowed to testify against her husband in a court of
law?"

"I . . . I hadn't thought of it . . . "

"It's true."

The room gave a dip to the left and she clutched at
the bed, feeling as if she was going to slide off it onto
the floor.

"I'll still talk," she whispered. "You'll never be able to
stop me. Never."

"Be still, slut! If you talk much more I'm going to start
remembering that letter you were sending to a dead lover,
and I'm going to start recalling what a little wanton you
are."

"I'm not a wanton! And Quade is not dead! He isn't,
I know he's not. Just because there was a hotel fire—"

"He is dead. If he weren't, wouldn't he have tried to
contact you himself?"

Corrie, lying dizzy and trembling in her bed, had no
answer for him.

Several days passed. Three? Four? It was as if all of
her careful gains over the more than three months had
been negated, as if she were once more back in the cabin
near Circle City, being drugged until she no longer knew
or cared what day it was, or what hour. At some point,
they removed the strips of blanket. She was dimly aware
that Donald was sleeping on a mattress on the floor.
Sometimes she heard voices in the room—Dr. Santee and
Donald, conferring. Or Artie's low, hoarse laugh. She had
ugly dreams, some of the brooch gleaming up at her from
a circle of flames. *Nonono not me oh God,* a voice seemed
to scream hideously from the brooch. *I hate I hate I
hate . . .*

But always, even through the worst fogs, a grim little
kernel of determination remained alive in Corrie's mind.
She was going to escape. She didn't know how, but she
was going to do it. It was her one thought, the lifeline
which allowed her to hold on to her sanity. She was going
to escape and find Quade if he still lived, and nothing
was going to stop her. Nothing.

She said little, trying not to anger Donald. Twice when
Dr. Santee came to give her the medicine, she remem-

bered a childhood trick and managed to hold it in her mouth until he had turned, then spit it into her hand and wipe it on the blanket. Dr. Santee seemed preoccupied, and did not notice.

Another day. The June light was long now, the street noises more intense, as if men were trying to cram all of their preparations for winter into a few brief days of sun. Dr. Santee fed her breakfast and lunch. Donald appeared briefly, spoke in an undertone to Dr. Santee and then left.

Corrie pretended to nap. She could sense Dr. Santee's restlessness, hear the snap of paper as he turned the pages in an old magazine. She opened her eyes a crack and observed that the light in the room had grown a bit dimmer. Dawson's fleeting sunset was beginning. Below, from down on the street, the faint sound of a piano reached them.

Corrie stirred and gave a soft, sleepy moan as if she were just waking up.

"Dr. Santee?"

"Yes, I'm here. I've been here all day." The doctor tossed his unkempt red hair out of his eyes and sighed.

She stretched and yawned. "What time is it?"

"Getting late. You slept through your supper."

"Oh." Corrie sat up in the bed, pulled the blanket up about her shoulders and wished that she looked more presentable. "Will you please bring me my hairbrush?" she asked.

Silently he found it and handed it to her. She began to work at the snarls in her hair, her eyes watering with pain. Dr. Santee's long legs straddled the room's one chair as he watched her.

"You're a very beautiful woman, did you know that?"

"Worth killing for?" She said it sharply and was rewarded when he flung himself out of the chair and strode jerkily toward the window.

"Shut up, Corrie. There are reasons, motivations you don't understand—"

"No, I guess I don't understand them." But she sensed that this was not the proper approach. She forced herself to smile at him, making her smile as provocative as possible. He stared at me naked, she remembered. A few times he had been kind to her. He liked her . . .

"Dr. Santee, I—I'm hungry. And I'm feeling so much better. Couldn't I get dressed and maybe go outside for a walk? If I don't get some exercise I think I'll die. Perhaps we could even stop at a restaurant . . . "

He stretched and fidgeted, then yawned loudly. She knew he must be restless, for he had been sitting here in the room most of the day. She finished brushing her hair and shook it about her shoulders in a swirl of chestnut-gold. Glimpsing herself in the mirror, she saw a girl with skin flushed to apricot from suppressed excitement. Her eyes held a defiant fire.

"I'm not supposed to take you out."

"Why not? You won't be letting me out of your sight. And he did allow you to take me out before, didn't he? I'll behave. I've learned my lesson. I can't fight Donald any more. He's too strong."

She could sense him wavering.

"Oh, please," she begged. "I'd be very grateful. I need a friend, Dr. Santee. Someone I can lean on and depend on. And you're the only one who . . . " She stopped delicately.

"Oh, all right. But five minutes, no more; do you hear me? And don't tell him you went out. Let it be our secret."

She made him turn his back while she dressed, and sensed his reluctance to do so. He was attracted to her, that was plain. Perhaps he had been for a long time. Why hadn't she seen it before? What sort of a fool had she been? But at least she'd discovered it now. She would use him, ruthlessly.

Her fingers flew over the buttons of her blue sateen dress—one Donald insisted she buy—touching the lavish rows of tucks, tiny buttons and embroidery. She pinned up her thick hair with a few swift gestures and grabbed her sealskin coat, which was too warm, but was the first wrap that came to hand. Her heart began to hammer with excitement.

As she pulled on the coat, she managed to turn her back and slipped the hairbrush into her pocket.

They descended the stairs of the hotel, Dr. Santee behind her. "Remember, I'm watching you. And I have a knife in my pocket, too."

"How could I forget that?" she said dryly. She caught herself. "Oh, but I'm so grateful to you for giving me the chance to get out and breathe some fresh air. That room is so stuffy! And my stomach is growling frightfully with hunger—"

She let herself chatter on, saying the first words that popped into her head. They moved through the lobby where the owner, a tall, thin man with a head of thick, oily black hair, eyed them.

"Oh, hello," she said to him. "Isn't it a wonderful night? I've been sick for a week with influenza and this is my first time out." She flashed him a brilliant smile and could sense Dr. Santee relaxing beside her.

They were out on the street. Dr. Santee held her elbow and guided her over the boardwalk, tilted and awkward with the ravages of the permafrost, which had pushed some sections up and pulled others downward.

"Which way shall we go?" she chattered. "Oh, it feels so wonderful to be free again!"

Desperately she looked up and down the street. A cart, mired in the mud, stood abandoned in the road. To her left a group of men thronged out of a dance hall, laughing and shouting and shoving at each other, a companionable group of revelers.

Before Dr. Santee could react, she turned toward the saloon. She strolled along the boardwalk, holding daintily onto his arm, forcing her movements to seem relaxed, although she was terrified that the doctor would sense the excitement boiling up in her. The dance hall, with all of its activity: this was her chance—surely the only chance she would have.

As they neared the dance hall (a sign proclaimed that it was the "Yukoner"), she slowed her footsteps. She stared boldly at one of the men, a plump, red-faced *cheechako*, hoping desperately that he would meet her eyes. He did.

"Say, hello there," he said. "Looka the pretty lady."

To Corrie's delight, he was thoroughly drunk, evidently having engaged in a great many dances and indulged in the drinks that went with them. "You're pretty," he added, leaning toward her and hiccuping. "Prettier than any of them pigs in there."

The others turned to look at her. Corrie flashed them a smile, too, and began to sway her hips languorously, like the prostitutes she had seen. She established eye contact with another man, moistening her lips as sensuously as she could. She had never been a flirt; desperation made her one now.

"Corrie, what are you doing? Wait a minute—" Dr. Santee began to realize that something was wrong. She felt his fingers dig into her arm.

"Oh, I'm just being friendly," Corrie said lightly. She saw that the men, instead of moving on, began to cluster in front of the dance hall. She reached into the pocket of her coat, extracted the hairbrush, and in a sudden violent movement, smacked Dr. Santee across the bridge of the nose with it. He let out a strangled cry.

She twisted away from him and shoved at one of the miners with a strength she had not known she possessed. Drunk and poorly coordinated, he lurched into another man, and the two of them staggered into a third. Someone hit someone else. Instantly there was a melee of pushing and shoving.

Taking advantage of the confusion, Corrie ducked under someone's arms and yanked open the front door of the dance hall. She ran inside.

The interior of the hall was dark and smoky, filled with the stench of whiskey fumes and sweaty human bodies. A piano blared out, and from a side room could be heard the click of a roulette wheel and the buzz of low, tense voices. From behind a long, polished bar a white-aproned bartender stared at her.

The front door burst open and Corrie ran blindly, pushing her way toward the dancers. She shoved ruthlessly against soft, plump, perfumed bodies, and heard a man's indignant bellow; another man laughed. Someone tried to grab her but she twisted away, skidding on sawdust, some instinct driving her toward the back of the building.

A boy in a white coat came hurrying across the floor carrying a tray laden with plates of food. He gazed at her goggle-eyed.

The kitchen! Corrie thought. Of course! It would have a back door.

She flew past the boy, shoving the tray as she did so. Dishes clattered to the floor. She raced in the direction the boy had come, toward the swinging kitchen door black with fingerprints. A fat Chinese cook turned to stare at her and then she was out in the open again, stumbling among boxes and barrels of trash. A rat scurried, and she tripped on a board laid over the mud and nearly went sprawling.

She kept her balance and kept on running.

Li Hua pulled on the black satin wrapper, fastening its glittering jet buttons with fingers that trembled—whether from joy or excitement, she didn't know. It was nearly midnight, time for the sun's eerie brief dip to the horizon before rising again. If she lived here a hundred years, she thought, she would never get used to that. From next door, piano music could be heard; someone shrieked with laughter.

Life at the Princess Dance Hall went on.

And her own life? She flung into a carved, upholstered parlor rocker she'd recently ordered for herself. The Stewarts had owned a similar one; perhaps that was why she had bought it.

She and Will Sebastian were going to be married. She could scarcely believe it.

In fact, she was filled with doubts. Ever since Will had proposed two hours ago, she had done nothing but pace back and forth across the little cabin, barely seeing its hand-made table, the hair pomades and restorers, the pompadour comb and curling iron, the wigs and Parisian bangs and alice waves and all of the other beauty paraphernalia that lay about.

"Li Hua." Will had called her name in a low voice, sitting here in the cabin looking masculine and uncomfortable among such female fripperies. "Li Hua, you know I can't offer you much. My leg—I'll always limp a bit, I have no illusions about that. As for my medical practice, I've decided to stay here in the North as long as there are people who need me. I like the North. And I want a woman to share it with me." His hand found hers and squeezed it hard. "I want you."

"Me?" She could only stare at him, her heart thumping. "Me?" she repeated stupidly.

"And who else?" Will's gentle mouth curved in a slight smile. "You are the one I love, Li Hua, and have ever since that day at the Chilkoot Pass when I set your poor leg and you clung to me, trying desperately not to cry out from the pain. You are a very brave person, darling, in so many ways."

The sound of her swallowing was loud in the room. "But . . . but I'm not, not really. I—I've whored myself, Will. I told you that; you know what I am."

"Yes. I know what you are."

She lowered her eyes, for she could not look at him. "Then . . . ? To wish to marry me, surely that's ridiculous!"

"It's not ridiculous at all. Li Hua, you are fine and courageous, and I love you and want to live with you for the rest of my life." Will Sebastian's face darkened. "Do you think that *I'm* perfect? Do you think that I have not made mistakes in my life, too? Perhaps big ones? Ah, God, darling, I've made a few. And will probably make a few more, too. It's you I love, Li Hua. Will you have me?"

"Yes," she had whispered, unable to speak further. "Oh, yes, Will."

They would live in Dawson, where their marriage would cause little gossip. Will would practice the medicine he loved, and she would run the dance hall as long as there were miners to patronize it. Eventually, she might open a small clothing shop.

Li Hua continued pacing, scarcely able to contain herself. Would Will later be sorry he had married her? Would he regret his decision?

She knew *she* would never regret marrying him. Ever.

A frantic knocking at the cabin door dispelled her reverie.

"Who is it?" she called, alarmed.

"Me! It's me, Corrie! Oh, for God's sake, let me in, Li Hua! You've got to help me! You've got to hide me!"

* * *

"Now, tell it all to me again," said Li Hua. She practically had to hold Corrie upright, her friend was so hysterical. Corrie's eyes were wide and stunned, her chestnut-gold hair tumbling wildly down her shoulders, pins dangling from it.

"I can't! I haven't time! Oh, don't you see, Li Hua, Dr. Santee knows I know you, he knows you're my friend. He'll come here, I know he will, maybe he's even on his way here now . . . Oh, you've got to *hide* me. Please—I can't let Donald find me—"

Li Hua looked sharply at her friend. Yes, Donald Earle was a monster; didn't she herself know that as well as anyone? Still, perhaps Corrie *was* mad. She certainly looked it at this moment, with her wide, frantic eyes, her heaving chest, and her fingers that clutched and shook.

"But Corrie," Li Hua said, drawing a deep breath. "Surely you must be exaggerating some of this. Laudanum! Drugs! Murder! And what do you mean by a brooch and a girl screaming in it? It doesn't even make any sense."

"Oh, Li Hua, I'll tell you later if only you'll hide me. If Dr. Santee comes here—" Corrie was grasping, tugging at her. "Li Hua, if you're my friend, you'll help me. Or he's going to . . . I don't know what. You've got to hide me. Please."

"But you certainly can't stay here. My cabin is too small; there's scarcely room under the bunk, and I have the girls coming in. He'd find you at once."

Corrie's eyes darted around the cabin. "There's got to be somewhere else, somewhere I could go—" Her eyes fastened on the hair paraphernalia, and then her hand shot out and snatched at one of the wigs, a black pompadour used by a girl named Aubergine.

"Put that wig on me, Li Hua," Corrie cried. "I'll go over to the dance hall. You must have some little cranny over there where you could put me for a day or so!"

"Well, there is the theater. It's almost finished now, and—"

"The theater? Then hurry!"

"All right." Li Hua moved quickly. With a swift gesture, she gathered Corrie's long hair into one thick hank and twisted it about, securing it with four big pins. Then she pinned on the black wig. Corrie was instantly transformed.

"That's good, but you'll need something different to wear. He'll recognize you in those clothes. Here, take my wrap."

She stripped off her own black satin robe and thrust it at Corrie. "Wear this—it'll change your looks completely. Go out and through to the dance hall," she ordered. "Tell Jim—he's the bartender—that you're auditioning. Tell him to put you in the theater dressing room. I've just put in a new theater; we open on Tuesday. Jim won't think anything about it."

With the satin robe carelessly buttoned so that a good deal of white breast was showing, and the black pompadour to cover up her hair, Corrie did indeed look like a dance hall girl, pretty and frivolous. Li Hua tossed a black lace mantilla at her.

"Pull that over your face, Corrie; it'll hide your features. Now go, Corrie. Go!"

Corrie swallowed. "Li Hua, I can't thank you enough—"

"Don't thank me now. Go on! Hurry, before it's too late!"

Corrie rushed out the door. Less than one minute later, Li Hua heard another knock on the door and knew that Dr. Santee was there.

When Corrie saw Dr. Santee coming up the boardwalk, looking like a bony red spider, his hair untidy and his face grim, she thought she would vomit. She felt like screaming and was tempted to break into another frantic run. She forced herself to walk slowly, and wiggled her hips languidly. A goodly length of leg showed where the satin robe gaped in front. Casually she reached up and adjusted the mantilla so that it hid most of her face.

Dr. Santee barely glanced at her. He went directly to Li Hua's door and began to pound on it. Her body shaking, Corrie continued to stroll toward the dance hall. She pulled open the door and stepped inside.

The Princess Dance Hall was crowded; no one noticed her right away. To her left was the bar, a big mahogany structure charred in several places from the fire, with a

huge, cracked mirror pasted over with liquor advertise-
ments. The bartender, a sleek young man of twenty-five,
was handing out chips to three girls.

"Yeah?" He looked boldly at Corrie.

"Where is the theater? Li Hua told me to . . . to wait
in the dressing room. I'm here for an audition."

"Yeah?" His eyes traveled down to the spot where her
breasts emerged from the black satin. "You might do. It's
right this way. I'll show you myself, personal-like."

"All right." She was too frightened to do anything but
follow him. There was a door to the right of the bar opening onto a corridor. At the end of the passage a little
theater was under construction, with crude seats of
boards on sawhorses, and a miniscule stage draped with
a blue velvet curtain trimmed in gold braid. There were
six steps directly in the center of the stage.

"The seats ain't come yet," he informed her. "We've
got them on order, though. She's going to be a beauty,
ain't she? We'll play to a full house, I'll wager, if she
signs *you* on. You dance? Or sing?"

"I—I sing," Corrie said bravely.

"There's where you wait, in that room there—up the
stairs and behind the stage. You sure you don't want a
bit of company?"

The dressing room was really a closet furnished with a
bare table, slab stool and a small mirror tacked to the
wall. Some wood chips still lay on the floor.

"Company? No, thank you . . . "

"Aw, why not? I'm a man, all right. A real man. I can
please you." Suddenly he thrust his hand into the folds
of the satin robe and grabbed at the swell of Corrie's
breasts.

She shoved at him angrily. "Get away from me! Get
away, do you hear? I'm here to audition and that's *all*."

"Yeah? A pity, that is."

But the man drew back and then, ludicrously, he
winked at her. "Take care, now, honey. And don't let
that bitch Li Hua scare you none. She's only twice as
tough as she looks."

As soon as he was gone, Corrie sank down on the
rough stool. Her body was shuddering.

✿ Chapter 36 ✿

She spent two days in the little dressing room on a mattress which Li Hua had the bartender, Jim, drag in for her. A girl brought her some embroidery and Corrie spent time doing the satin stitch and the cross stich on a design of flowers and fruit. She had managed to send Dr. Santee away, Li Hua assured her, so Corrie was not to worry.

Li Hua told her of her plans to marry Will Sebastian, and Corrie listened with growing delight.

"Oh, Li Hua, oh, that's wonderful news! I'm so happy for you!"

"I'm happy, too." The other girl's black eyes were soft, the way they had been in San Francisco, before all the ugly things had happened to harden their expression. "He knows me, Corrie, and loves me as I am."

"Will you go back to San Francisco with him, then?"

"No. I think we belong here, Corrie, in the North. Even after the gold fever is over, there will be people left in Dawson who still need Will, and he'll stay for them. And I—I'll stay, too. At least I can be free here."

Corrie, her eyes welling with tears, could only hug her friend. "You were always free, Li Hua, don't you know that? Perhaps you taught me to be free, too."

During the long hours when Li Hua was busy with the affairs of the dance hall and the hair salon, Corrie busied herself writing long, desperate letters to Quade. She mailed them to as many places as she could think of: Circle City, Tanana, Dyea and Eagle, all in care of general delivery. Even if he was still alive, there was a slim chance that he would receive them, but, she told herself, at least she was doing something instead of merely sitting, waiting. She sent Jim out to purchase a steamer ticket to Forty Mile for her. She would go there and ask questions, she decided. No matter what she found out, it would be better than not knowing anything.

She awoke very early on the morning of the third day, her mind already full of plans. Shortly after noon her steamer, the *J.P. Light,* would be leaving and she had to bathe and make preparations.

She got up, rolled her narrow mattress into a cylinder and stuffed it under the table so that she would have room in the cramped cubicle to move about. The dance hall was silent; at this hour the girls were asleep in their rooms, resting from the night's strenuous waltzing. The piano was silent; even the street sounds were muted. Somewhere a bird called raucously.

Corrie restlessly smoothed the folds of her dark blue skirt, now thoroughly wrinkled and soiled from her head-long flight. If only she had a flatiron so she could press it! And a bath: she absolutely had to have one, she told herself. She felt soiled and sticky beyond endurance.

Cautiously she pushed open the door of the dressing room, intending to steal into the kitchen area and draw a basin of water. If her luck was good, she told herself, she would have time to put the water on the stove and heat it . . .

Wincing as the door creaked, she tiptoed across the little stage and down the six steps which led to the main level of the floor.

"It's not much, is it? This place, I mean. We have theaters a thousand times better than this in San Francisco, don't we, Corrie?"

"Donald!" She suppressed a shriek.

He was leaning against the footlights at stage right, impeccably dressed in a dark wool cheviot suit, and wearing a clean shirt and stiff collar. He could have stepped off the cable car at California street, Corrie thought hysterically, so citified did he look.

"Surprised to see me, Corrie? But you shouldn't be. Surely you must have realized that your bartender friend,

Jim, harbors hopes of going to Nome. He wanted a grub-stake. I wanted you. It was very simple."

Wildly Corrie looked about, but there was nowhere she could run. The stage did not have a back entrance and Donald blocked her way. He moved toward her and grasped her upper arm, squeezing it until she wanted to weep with pain.

As they left the dance hall, they encountered Li Hua walking past the bar with a sheaf of papers under her arm, intent on some business of the day. At the sight of Donald, the Chinese girl's eyes widened with horror, and her face paled to the color of bleached linen.

Her reaction was swift. Instantly she started toward the polished bar, where Jim kept a loaded pistol.

"Stop where you are, you little yellow bitch!" Donald shouted.

Donald pulled a gun from his own belt and brandished it at both girls. "Corrie is mine, and no little piece of Chinese meat is going to stand between us!"

Li Hua froze, two spots of color staining her cheeks. The two girls' eyes met, and Corrie could see the shock and dismay on her friend's face. Li Hua's effort to help her had been futile. As Donald dragged her away, both girls knew they might never see each other again.

"Li Hua—"

Corrie reached out to the other girl.

"Corrie, be careful . . . "

But before Corrie could reply, Donald yanked her past a horrified Li Hua and out the door of the dance hall.

Despair weighed Corrie down heavily as she stumbled through the streets beside Donald. At the hotel room, Dr. Santee was packing a trunk with her clothing, camera and photographic prints. Clothes and books were strewn all over the bed. He looked up resentfully as she entered.

"Well, so the little runaway is back."

"W-where are we going?"

"Back to San Francisco, I think," Donald said. "Perhaps we'll move into your father's house. I always fancied that place. Now that your aunt is no longer living there, it should be quite cozy. Perhaps we won't have to ship you out to an asylum after all. No, I'll have Dr. Santee with me—he has agreed to come and act as our personal physician—and I'm sure he'll be able to care for you quite adequately."

"To be my keeper, don't you mean?" she snapped.

The red-haired doctor shot her another resentful look, then left the room.

"And when we get back to the States," Donald continued as if she had said nothing at all, "I'll buy you another diamond to replace the one you so carelessly 'lost.' It will be a very large one, and I'm sure it will look quite handsome on you. You'll be so proud of it. Eventually, when you've quite accepted me, we may even move into society again."

This time Corrie knew enough to remain silent. She walked over to the window and looked out. The street was crowded with miners, carts, drays and horses. Over all of the bustle arched a blue sky, so pitilessly clean that it almost hurt the eye. A V of wild birds soared to the right, cutting across the brilliant sky. *Alaska,* Corrie thought dully. What a hard country it was, gigantic and terrifyingly beautiful and uncaring.

"Would you do one thing for me before we leave?" she ventured at last.

"And what is that?"

"Would you please make an effort to find out what happened to . . . to my friend Quade Hill?"

Donald's face jerked as if she had struck him, but Corrie floundered on. "You must know that was why I bought a ticket to Forty Mile. I wanted to find out about that hotel fire. I had to; I— Oh, Donald, you don't have to tell him where I am or give him any message from me. I just want to know whether he is alive or dead." Her lips were dry when she licked them. "If you will just find that much out for me, I'll be a good wife to you, Donald. In every way. I . . . I swear it."

Donald stared at her. A wash of anger stained his cheeks, and there was a flicker of pain in his cold, dark eyes.

"So you love him that much."

"Yes. I do love him." She said it defiantly. "And I always will. You'd never understand that, would you?"

His jaw was squared at her, his eyes veiled. "I, too, can love, Corrie. Did that ever occur to you?"

"Love! You don't love me. You only want to own me."

"Perhaps the emotion I feel isn't the same as the one you feel. Yet to me it's love. . . . Did you ever stop to wonder who was the man who changed your bedpan and took care of all your private needs when you lay unconscious in my cabin at Circle?"

She stared at him. She could feel her mouth drop open. "You! But I thought . . . Dr. Santee . . . "

"Do you think that renegade would soil himself taking care of someone else? He may abort women, but that's as far as he goes. No; he didn't want to, and I wouldn't have allowed him to do it anyway. You are mine, Corrie; you belong to me. So I did it."

"Oh, I hadn't realized . . . " She felt an absurd blush cover her face and spread over her cheekbones to her forehead. She did not know where to look or what to do or say. To think that Donald . . . An act so intimate, so private that . . . She felt stunned, more shocked than if he had slapped her across the face.

He gripped her shoulders, pressing her toward him, and she knew with incredulity that this odd scene was as close as Donald would ever come to really making love to her. Love, so twisted and wrong. She felt a brief spasm of pity for him, that this was all he could know.

"Donald. I know you . . . love me. But if that's the case, then you must allow me this one small thing. Find out for me what happened to Quade Hill. Please. It's the only thing I'll ever ask of you. I must know. For my peace of mind, one way or the other."

He stared at her, his eyes narrowed. "You're not to love any other man but me."

"Please. I'll never think about him again if you'll do this for me."

Donald's face was stony, closed.

"Very well," she said, turning away. "You won't do it, will you? I was a fool to ask."

"Yes, you were a fool. And if I ever hear that man's name again I won't be responsible for what I do. Is that clear to you, Corrie?

Corrie was silent.

Abruptly Donald was all business again, issuing orders to Dr. Santee to hurry with the trunks, going next door to shout something to Artie. Corrie could only stand there and wonder if the previous scene had all been some sort of wild, crazy dream.

Donald, making love to her? Could murderers love, even in a twisted way? Could a killer care tenderly for a woman's most personal needs?

Oh, Quade, she thought, desperately. Her throat felt choked, filled with all of the tears she did not dare to shed. Quade, am I going to leave the Yukon without knowing whether you are alive or dead?

Donald purchased tickets on a steamer called the *Hannah.* They rode the short distance to the waterfront in a horsecart. The *Hannah,* Donald informed her on the way, was the "peer of the entire Yukon fleet." It was 225 feet long and had elegant appointments rivaling anything that might be found on the Mississippi. There were actually electric lights in the cabins, and the pilot house possessed a searchlight which could be shone out over the water to detect snags, sandbars or other boat traffic.

It was a brilliant late June day. The air was clear, the sun so strong that every leaf and tree, every rock in the hills which loomed over the city, stood clearly outlined. The Yukon was in one of her golden, intensely beautiful moods . . . A brisk wind pushed at the folds of Corrie's skirt, molding it to her body.

In spite of her fear and depression, Corrie could not help glancing about her curiously. Dawson's waterfront had always been hectic, crammed with boats, scows, dories and rafts full of logs brought upriver to be sold for fuel. All were moored in hopeless confusion. But now she saw that the row of flimsy tents and cabins along Front Street had been rebuilt. A row of electric light poles bristled along the river, their glass insulators gleaming. Electricity had come to the city.

Interspersed among all the larger boats in the harbor, moored almost bow-to-bow, were hundreds of small, homemade crafts. With their rectangular sails, they looked exactly like bath toys assembled by a rather clumsy boy, and then crammed with men and provisions. Somehow the scene reminded Corrie of Lake Bennett. The air was filled with the same sense of urgency, reckless adventure and excitement.

Of course, she thought. Nome. Lured by tales of the fabulous strikes there, men were beginning to stream out of Dawson as fast as they could. There was gold excitement in the air, brash, alive and careless.

Abruptly her mood plummeted. What did all of this matter to her? She wasn't a part of it any more. She was going back to San Francisco, and virtual imprisonment.

"Come, Corrie." Donald nudged her. "What are you goggling at? Haven't you ever seen boats before? Get out of the cart. I want to see our trunks on board."

She stood numbly while Dr. Santee and Artie wrestled with the luggage. Donald kept a firm grip on her arm. As they went up the gangplank she couldn't help looking over the water. The small boats were everywhere. She could not imagine how the steamer was going to pull out without damaging some of them.

Halfway up the gangplank she froze.

"Well, go on," Donald said, shoving her in the back none too gently. "For God's sake, Corrie, go on aboard, will you? Why are you stopping?"

"I . . . " Perspiration sprang to her face. She hesitated, then slowly began to walk again. "I just was looking at the boats, that's all. I thought I saw something."

"A lot of fools going to Nome, that's what I see," he told her. "Move along now, will you?"

Corrie heard Donald say something in an undertone to Dr. Santee, and then glance at her. Evidently, he wished the doctor to dose her again with laudanum.

Dr. Santee looked annoyed. "I've told you, Earle, what will happen if you give her too much of that stuff. This whole thing has gone entirely too far, if you want my opinion. Why don't we just dump her and—"

"Keep your voice down, you fool. And I've told you, I don't want to lose her. I've lost her one too many times and I don't like it. A little laudanum won't hurt her. Thousands of people take it."

"But laudanum is a—"

They moved slightly away fron her, and Corrie could

no longer hear their whispered wrangling. She didn't care. A feeling of hopelessness overwhelmed her, so sudden and disabling that she wanted to sink to her knees with despair. Instead, she forced herself to look along the boiler deck, where a few passengers lingered, and a neat row of cuspidors along the rail invited cleanliness.

Her mind had been playing tricks on her, she told herself harshly. For one wild instant on the gangplank, she thought she'd seen Quade—the side of his head at least—as he sat at the tiller of one of those ridiculously small, homemade boats.

But the boats, a shifting pattern, moved unsteadily, and the man she had seen was lost to view. It could not have been Quade anyway, she told herself firmly. She had been thinking about him so desperately that her mind manufactured a picture of him. That was all it had been.

"Well," Donald said. "We're on board, and now all we have to do is pray that the food is good and the weather holds."

A woman wearing a dowdy black dress brushed past them, and for a moment Corrie thought she recognized Eulalie Benrush. Then the woman turned, and Corrie saw the young, plump face of a stranger. She felt herself shivering. Ghosts . . .

"Couldn't we stand here by the rail and watch the steamer leave?" she heard herself asking Donald. "I'd like to see it."

"Why not? As long as you behave yourself, my girl. I have no intention of being a cruel husband. Just a possessive one. What do you say we take a turn or two around the deck first?"

As they walked, Donald pressed her arm tightly to his ribs. Corrie felt as if she could not endure his touch, yet she forced herself to continue walking with him, aware, ironically, that they appeared like any other happy husband and wife out for a stroll on shipboard.

She heard Donald tell Dr. Santee and Artie to go to their cabins and check to be sure everything was prepared. Then, as they made another circuit of the deck, the wind pushing at their faces, Donald began to talk to her about the plans he had made for the Stewart Shipyards. He would switch entirely to the manufacture of steamers, he told her. The days of the sailing ship were over. From now on, all ships would have engines.

Corrie didn't listen. She stared out at the crowded river. All around them the small, homemade craft surged, almost bow to bow. Somewhere up ahead there had evidently been a mishap, for she could hear men shouting. Some of the occupants of the boats leaned out of their craft to shake their fists in the direction of the tie-up.

One boat in particular caught Corrie's eye. Its shape was square and blunt, and its stern was labelled with a hand-made sign: "Gnome or Bust." Its skipper, a youth of nineteen or twenty, caught her eye and waved cheerfully.

Corrie smiled back at him, blinking away a sheen of moisture which threatened to spill from her eyes. The boy, with his blond hair, looked absurdly like Mason Edwards. Mason, smiling and trying to keep her spirits up as he delivered her child . . .

"What are you brooding about?" she heard Donald say. "And what a log jam. Damn those idiotic little boats anyway. Half of them aren't seaworthy and the rest look dubious. And worse luck, I think we're stuck here for a while, unless the captain wants to run some of them down."

Corrie ignored him, fixing her eyes on the boats and willing herself not to cry. She wouldn't cry, she told herself. She just would not. She would simply have to stop thinking of her baby, and of Quade . . .

The engine of the *Hannah* roared and the paddlewheels rumbled as the captain tried to maneuver a few feet away from the wharf, perhaps in the hope of scaring away some of the boats. As the steamer's wake tossed the little boats, their occupants shouted indignantly. Again Corrie found that her eyes were fastened on a man who sat in one of the larger craft, lounging nonchalantly at the tiller, a soft hat pushed back from his forehead as if he were rather enjoying this confusion. He was a big man, she saw, with broad shoulders that seemed far too wide for the red plaid shirt he wore. Corrie squinted but the sun glared too brightly for her to distinguish his features.

"It seems that there is always some delay, isn't there?" Donald was impatient. "How dare those men block river traffic like this?"

Corrie did not hear one word he was saying. Her eyes were fastened on the features of the man in the boat. Again she strained to see him, concentrating against the brilliance of the sun.

Just then the man turned to stare calmly up at the steamer, and Corrie's heart gave an enormous leap.

"Quade!" She screamed, shaking off the surprised Donald's grip. She rushed over to the whitewashed rail. "Quade! It's me! Corrie! Oh, Quade!"

Her voice soared over the water. She was totally unaware of Donald behind her, trying to pull her away from the rail, or of heads tilting up as the men in the boats began to realize that something was happening.

"Quade! Quade!" Corrie yelled desperately.

For one wild instant their eyes met. She saw shock cross his features. He seemed to shake his head in surprise. Or did he? Damn the sun, she thought furiously. She couldn't see!

"Quade, it's me! Corrie! I'm here, I'm here!"

She had never screamed so loudly or so joyously in her life. Faces were tipped up to her; some of the steamship passengers turned to stare at her as well. A man in one of the dories gave a whistled catcall, and she felt Donald's fingers like metal gripping the soft flesh of her upper arm. He tried to drag her away, down to the prison of their cabin.

"No," she panted. "No, I won't go yet." She dug her heels into the deck, grabbed for the rail and clung to it like a barnacle. Donald cursed and yanked at her.

Quade was shouting back at her—at least she thought he was, for she could see his mouth moving. She couldn't hear a word he said, for the men in all the other boats were yelling, too. Bored and irritated by the enforced wait, their interest fastened on the pretty, distraught girl yelling at the man out on the water. Some of them started to whistle at her. Others waved, and one youth, standing precariously in the bottom of his boat, gestured an eager semaphore.

"Come on, honey," he shouted up to her. "Toss *him* over the side and try me!"

"Me!" another one shouted.

"How 'bout me, baby?"

They were having marvelous fun, and Corrie, gripping the wood of the rail until her hands ached, felt sudden tear prick at her eyelids. These men, these wild, crazy, wonderful stampeders—in this moment she loved them all, for Quade was alive, he hadn't died at all, and he was only a few hundred feet away from her.

The steamer lurched forward, nearly knocking Corrie over. She felt a smack of pain, and realized that Donald had slapped her hands, trying to loosen her grip.

"What in hell do you think you're doing, Corrie?" His voice was low and furious. He added a vicious, gutter curse. He shook her, rattling her back and forth until her teeth cut into her lip and she tasted salt from her blood.

"Don't! Donald, please—"

The men, caught up in this small drama, howled to see a pretty girl being treated in this way. And now Quade, too, was standing in his boat, waving at her.

Corrie drew in a sharp breath. She had an instant's careening feeling, as if she were caught on some mad, whirling carnival ride, where everything was happening violently, and much too fast. Again Donald slapped her. The pain, worse this time, jolted through her, loosening her grasp on the rail. He was going to drag her away, she thought chokingly. Drag her down to their stateroom and drug her. She would never see Quade again . . .

Without thinking, she jabbed her elbow into the soft area of Donald's belly. He expelled an involuntary grunt of pain and staggered backwards. Driven by anger, pain and a wild, growing hope, Corrie lifted her skirts and flung her right leg over the whitewashed rail of the steamer. She threw her left leg over the rail.

For one horrid instant she dangled. Then, before she had time to scream or to be afraid, she gave an outward push.

The miners in their flotilla of homemade boats screamed with joy at the sight of a pretty girl leaping over the rail of the steamer, her skirts flying in the air to reveal petticoats, flesh and stockings. Corrie caught a brief glimpse of a man's open mouth. Then something hard slammed up at her, something so horribly solid that it seemed as if it would drive her bones up into her mouth.

She was laughing and crying and she felt cold water splash her and arms reaching to grasp her.

"My God, girl," someone said.

She blinked her eyes. She realized that, by some accident, she had landed in the bottom of one of the small boats, nearly capsizing it.

"Please . . . " Was that her own voice, gasping and weeping? Her entire body hurt from the force of the landing. Had she broken anything? She didn't know.

"Please," she gasped again. She felt her right arm move and point in the direction of Quade's boat. "Please . . . help me . . . I have to go to him . . . "

"Him? Won't I do?" The boy grinned at her.

"No— Oh, please, hurry . . . Donald will find me if you don't hurry . . . "

"Never let it be said that I wouldn't help a damsel in distress," the youth said, making a face. "All right, miss. This way. You'll go hand over hand, and maybe you won't get too wet. How about it?"

"Yes . . . yes."

She felt the first of the many pairs of hands shuttle her over the water as if she were a sack of provisions.

Part 5

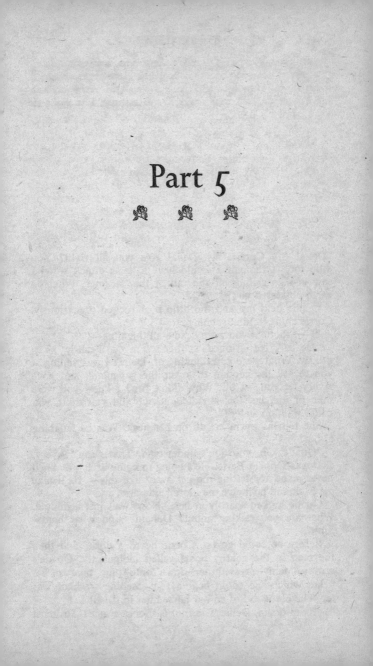

❧ Chapter 37 ❧

"Delia! My Corrie, my Delia! Are you all right? You little fool, I thought I would have a heart attack when I saw you go sailing off the rail of that steamer. What on earth possessed you?"

Quade held her and the little boat rocked precariously. Corrie clung to him, sobbing.

"I—I thought you were dead—all this time—"

"Dead?" He grinned at her. "I'm as healthy as a grizzly. What were you thinking of, Delia? I was yelling at you to ask the captain to lower the gangplank and have Avery let you get off. Why didn't you? I knew you were fond of me, but this is ridiculous. Or did you think you could walk on water?"

She felt his warm breath on her neck. Was he laughing at her?

"Quade. Oh, you don't understand. That wasn't Avery; that was Donald Earle. He's going to come after me. He'll never stand for letting me get away like this— He'll take me back and he'll give me more laudanum, and—"

Quade looked sharply at her. "Now, wait just a minute. What are you talking about? Donald? And what laudanum?"

Before he could go on, Corrie heard a noise, and then the men in the nearby boats yelled indignantly. Quade's arm suddenly pressed her down onto pine boards, beneath which she could hear a foul-smelling wash of water. The blunt end of an oar jabbed her in the ribs.

"Keep down, Delia. The fool is shooting at us. He must

be winging at us from the deck of the steamer. And he's got damned good aim. We're still in range, too, worse luck."

"He . . . he'll kill us," she choked.

"Then you'd better tell me what this is about. Where's your husband?"

"My husband?" Corrie gave an hysterical giggle. "Donald *is* my husband."

She could hear shouts as the men in the boats around them scattered to get out of range. There was another loud report from Donald's Colt.

"Donald!" Quade exclaimed.

"Avery died and I married Donald and Donald is the one who killed Ila," she blurted.

She felt Quade shifting his position beside her. "Dammit, never mind," he told her harshly. "I haven't time to listen now. Doesn't that man realize he's going to kill someone? There are hundreds of people on this water. If he doesn't get us, he's going to get someone else."

There was another loud explosion.

"Why don't they *stop* him?" Corrie said nervously.

"God only knows. Maybe they think he's shooting at ducks." Quade edged forward toward the bow of the small boat, which was partly covered by a crude wooden structure built to shelter some of his provisions. It also contained a small stove for cooking.

"What—what are you doing?" Corrie screamed. "Don't get up, Quade, he'll see you! He'll shoot you!"

"And what do you think he plans to do anyway? Do you want us to sit here in this boat like birds on a nest until he finally gets us sighted properly? Move, Corrie. I'm hoisting the sail. It's plenty windy enough; we're going to push our way out of here."

"But how can you? The river is full of boats. Nobody's going anywhere!"

"We are. And we're going damn fast."

Cautiously Quade reached up and began maneuvering the crude rigging of the boat. The canvas sail slowly bellied with wind.

"This is going to be tricky, I'm afraid," he said. "There isn't much sailing room and I may have to jab around a bit with the oars. I want you to stay down, do you hear me? No matter what happens or what I do."

They began carefully curving through the water, their bow smacking into the side of another craft.

"Hey! Watch it, will you?" protested its owner.

"Let us through, you fool. Let us get out of range, or maybe you want to get shot too?"

From her crouched position Corrie could glimpse Quade's face, twisted with concentration as he forced their way through the crowds of boats, ramming some, threatening others, once taking out a pistol of his own to wave it menacingly. None of the miners protested, for the big, craggy-faced man, his eyes narrowed with anger, looked formidable indeed.

At last they were past the tie-up, which had been caused by two dories capsized by a big log raft. Men, dogs and provisions all bobbed in the water as bystanders tried to rescue the swimmers and fish out tons of provisions.

"Well, it looks as if you're coming to Nome with me," Quade said lightly.

"Nome!"

"I'm a wanderer, Corrie, remember? I plan to write a chapter about the rigors of boating on the Yukon. It should be quite informative."

The river stretched before them, its surface dotted with boats further ahead, the choppy waves brilliant with the glare of the sun. Green trees leaned out over either side of the river. The rows of Yukon hills were blue-green touched with gray. Overhead a few cottony clouds scudded across blue skies. For the first time Quade drew a deep breath and sank into a more relaxed position, his hand light upon the tiller.

Corrie sat up. "I thought you told me you couldn't sail." Her belly felt as if it were filled with jellied aspic. She felt like laughing and crying all at once.

"I never said that. I said I didn't *build* boats. There's a difference. I lived in Chicago, remember? We used to sail quite often on Lake Michigan. We had a very nice sloop rig once."

Quade squinted into the sun. "As a matter of fact, sailing was one of my favorite occupations. I bought this boat from a man who built her at Lake Bennett. She's crude but effective. Do you like her? I think I'll christen her *The Delia*. After you, my dear."

Corrie couldn't smile back at him. "How can you sit there so calmly? You've just been shot at—we both have. And here you sit, talking about naming a boat!"

"What else shall we talk about, then? Life? Fate? The Great Beyond?"

"Don't make fun of me, Quade Hill. Donald Earle is nothing to laugh about. I'll wager he has already stopped the steamer and is coming back after us. And you don't know about Dr. Santee, do you? Dr. Santee carries a knife. And Artie, Artie is a killer, too. They all are. They killed Avery. And Alikammiq—"

"Enough, Delia girl. I do realize how serious this is. I'm sorry if I was flippant about it. You just looked so helpless and frightened, on the verge of howling at any minute, that I wanted to cheer you up, that's all."

"Cheer me up! I'd feel a lot more cheerful if we were away from here!" She lurched to her knees and reached out for Quade, intending to clutch at his arm for balance.

"Sit down!" His voice was sharp.

"But—"

"I said sit down, Delia, and I meant it. The last thing I need right now is an hysterical woman, especially one whose husband likes to take pot shots at her and at anyone she happens to be with."

Angrily Corrie lowered herself among the spare oars and bags of provisions. Never had her body ached in so many places. Her ankle throbbed, her right arm hurt, and her shoulder felt as if it had nearly been pulled out of its socket. In the morning—if she lived until then—she was sure her skin would be a mass of welts and bruises.

"All right," Quade said. "We have time. You can tell me about it."

She drew a deep breath and, forgetting her anger at him, began her tale. As she spoke, Quade's face grew paler, and by the time she was done, his eyes glistened tensely. His mouth was a grim line.

"So he's the bastard who killed my sister."

"Yes."

"The bastard who poured kerosene over my father's office and then put a match to it. They said she must

have died from being burned, not from smoke inhalation.
Can you imagine how exquisitely that must have hurt?
How she must have shrieked?"

"Quade . . . don't . . . "

"I will if I wish." His face was white, the blood gone
from his lips. "Do you know, Delia, the minute I saw
him, I *knew*. Not in any rational, thinking part of my
brain, but deeper, in some atavistic part of me that isn't
civilized and never will be. Later I told myself what a
fool I'd been to come here, what a gullible, emotional
fool."

Quade's eyes were distant, fixed on the thick bristle of
trees which lined the river. "And now," he said softly,
"I'm glad I stayed."

She looked at him. In this moment his skin seemed
stretched too tightly over the rough, cragged cheekbones,
giving him a cruel look. She found that she was shivering.

"Quade," she said. "We've gotten away, haven't we?
For all practical purposes? Surely it's all over with. We
can . . . forget him now and go on with our lives."

"Can we?" His eyes glittered at her, cold and pale and
flat. "Nothing is over, Delia."

"But—it *is*. It is for me. I—I'll go back to San Francisco and divorce him, and I can even have him put in
prison—"

"For what? Come now, Delia, you have no proof—
nothing that would hold up in a court of law, anyway. A
newspaper clipping! I can just hear the judge now, laughing at you. But we know he is guilty. I know it, deep in
my guts. Every instinct tells me so. And you know it,
too. It doesn't matter about legality; I have the proof *I*
need, the proof *I've* been waiting for, and I'm satisfied.
This man murdered my sister."

"Quade—"

"Delia, you think that by going back to San Francisco
and forgetting this, you'll be rid of him? Well, you won't
be. Don't you realize what a persistent tormentor he is?
If what you've told me is true, I believe he'll follow us
to the ends of the world if necessary, and believe me,
Nome isn't very far from that point. He'll never let you
go. Not so long as there is a pulse of life in him."

Corrie shivered again. She pulled her knees up and

wrapped her arms about them, wishing that her clothes weren't damp and she had a sweater. It seemed very odd to her that the sun was shining brilliantly.

Quade took something out of his pocket. It lay in the palm of his hand, winking in the sunlight. The brooch. He had carried it nearly six years now, she thought with a sick feeling. The profile of the girl seemed to be staring directly at her, the eyes mute and pleading.

"Don't you hear her?" Quade said.

"Hear . . . her?"

"Why, she's screaming, Delia. Screaming at us to help her, to avenge her so that she can rest. And I plan to do it. I'm going to kill him."

Later, in Quade's tent, somewhere past Fort Reliance, Corrie learned more about what had happened to Quade since she had last seen him. He *had* been a victim of the fire in Forty Mile, he explained. That, at least, had been no lie of Donald's. Shouts had aroused him from his sleep and he awakened choking and gagging on thick smoke. He staggered out of his bed and ran to the next room, to a dormitory where twelve men slept. Before him was a scene of wild panic and confusion. Men were shouting, shoving or jumping out of the room's one window. An elderly man lay spread-eagled on the floor unconscious, whether from smoke or from drink, Quade was never to learn.

He scooped the man up and hoisted him on his shoulders. He decided to brave the staircase rather than the window, which was jammed with frightened men. Halfway down the narrow stairs, he was jostled from behind by men trying to get out. He fell, along with the man he was carrying. Both survived, but Quade broke a bone in his arm, and the doctor who treated him advised him to stay in Forty Mile for a month or so, and to avoid doing any heavy work. Otherwise he might be permanently injured.

"Besides," he told her, winking slowly. "I had lost you, hadn't I? You were married to Avery and you'd chosen him over me. I was angry at you, and lonely and depressed, and I really had nowhere to go anyway. I only knew that I didn't want to leave the North yet; I couldn't, there was still something here that I had to finish. So . . . " He shrugged. "I stayed. There was even a girl in one of the dance halls—you may have heard of her. Cad Wilson."

"Cad Wilson!" She was the smoky-eyed girl who danced for the Eldorado Kings, wearing a belt of gold nuggets. Corrie had met her outside the Pear Blossom Salon and in the roadhouse when she was with Donald. She could not conceal her jealousy. "Did you think she was pretty? She told me that she—she preferred her men big and tall and rich!"

Quade laughed. "Indeed she did."

"Then why didn't you stay in Forty Mile with her?" Corrie snapped. She wrenched away from Quade, her back stiff. "If you found her all that appealing!"

Again Quade chuckled. "Did I say that I found her appealing? She is an embittered girl, Corrie. I felt pity for her. I was her friend, that's all. Don't tell me that *you're* jealous! Jealous of me, and here you've had two husbands since you've been here in the Yukon and neither of them has been me."

She lowered her eyes, shamed. "That was different," she whispered.

"Different? I don't see how. At least I had the sense not to marry Cad."

"Oh . . . be still!" She tossed her head and started to get to her feet, but instead he pulled her back down to the groundsheet, his arms encircling her.

"For God's sake, Delia, you're the only one I'll ever love, damn you, and don't you ever forget it. Ever. Do you hear?"

They made love, urgently, as if grasping at something that might slip away from them at any moment. Each kiss was electrifying. Never had Corrie felt so alive, so full of life and joy. The fact that Donald might be coming after them lent a preciousness to the minutes they shared together. Never again might she lie in a tent safe in Quade's arms, with his mouth on hers and his hard body against her own. In a day, or a week, she might be dead, or Quade might be dead, or both of them could be.

So they would make love now, and they would not

think about the future, about the fact that Donald was certain to be following them. They would pack all of their living into these few days in case there was to be no more for them.

If was a curiously sad and final kind of loving, and Corrie awoke in the middle of the night to pillow her face on Quade's shoulder, her cheeks streaked with tears.

"What's wrong, Corrie?" He awoke as lightly as a cat, his muscles tensed. "Did you hear something?"

"No."

"Then what's wrong? Did you have a nightmare?"

"Yes . . . Oh, I don't know. I only know that I love you, Quade, and I have this feeling, this terrible feeling that something is going to go wrong for us. I'm too happy; I love you too much—"

He held her tightly. "Never say that you love me too much."

"But I do, I do. Something's going to happen. *Something*. I can feel it."

"Don't think that way, darling. Just relax. I've told you that everything is going to be all right, and it will be."

"Oh, Quade," Corrie sighed.

"Hush, now." His lips were on her, soft and gentle. "Hush and go back to sleep. Here, fit your body into mine. Let's be spoons."

Obediently she nestled against him and closed her eyes. Soon she was peacefully asleep.

The river seemed to cup the sky and reflect it back. The sun glittered on its waves and on the trees which crowded to the water's edge.

Two days passed. Corrie and Quade continued to work their way north, seeing nothing more formidable than a moose cow with her calf browsing along the water at dusk, the calf spindly legged, the mother majestic in her bulk and dignity. Water fowl filled the river, at first by the dozens, then by the thousands. There were snow geese, Canadian geese, sand-hill cranes (Quade called these Alaska turkey and said they tasted delicious), green-winged teal—more birds than Corrie ever imagined could exist—and surprisingly, Quade knew the names of most of them.

They sailed past Circle City and into the Yukon Flats, an endless expanse of level land blanketed by timber. Here the river spread out over the land into a thousand sloughs and bogs and swamps, all of them, it seemed, infested by blood-thirsty mosquitoes. And everywhere was water, shining in the sun and mirroring back the faultless blue sky.

It was beautiful. Or it would have been if Corrie wasn't so frightened. Each time a boat passed them, she wondered if it might not contain Donald and Dr. Santee. She was sure that Donald was following them. So was Quade.

"He'll come," Quade had said. "And when he does, I'll be ready."

"No! Quade, I don't want you to do this. I won't let you. Horrid as Donald was, I think it's got to stop somewhere. What if he killed you? Haven't I grieved enough for you already? I don't want you to be dead, Quade. I couldn't bear it."

"I won't die. I have no plans to lose you, Corrie, to death, to Donald Earle, or to anything else. But this is something I've got to do."

"Why? Why must you?" she raged. "Why? I can't understand! Hasn't there been enough killing, enough terrible things done already?"

"Corrie, I realize that this doesn't seem reasonable to you, this obsession of mine. And perhaps it isn't; I don't know. But it is what I have to do. Ila won't rest in peace until the man is dead. She hates him and she'll keep on hating him until he dies. That's why she has kept after me the way she has."

"Kept after you! Oh, what nonsense! A sensible man like you, a journalist, who should pay attention to *facts*, believing in ghosts and goblins!"

Quade's face turned somber. "You believe in a few ghosts, too, Delia. I saw your face when you looked at that brooch."

They continued to progress toward Nome, following the trail of hundreds of others who had gone before them, getting lost in the Flats and finding their way again, guided by guesswork, instinct and an occasional sign made by someone who had been over the route before. The weather was ideal; eighty degrees and balmy, the Yukon in her most benign humor. Flowers grew to water's edge, thousands of tiny dots of color.

Corrie felt an increasing respect for Quade's boating skills. The square, ungraceful sail of the homemade boat was not designed well and did not catch the wind efficiently. Often they were becalmed and had to use the two sets of oars. Or the opposite was true. Sometimes there was too much wind and current, and they faced the danger of capsizing. Once, in fact, they had come perilously close, and Corrie held her breath ready for the plunge when Quade managed to right the sail. It had been a close call, and she did not doubt that there would be more to come.

They passed Fort Yukon, a bleak town crouched at a wide point on the river's shoreline. They passed the little settlement of Beaver where, it was rumored, quartz gold had been discovered on the upper Chandalar.

As the Yukon Flats came to an end, thousands of muddy channels flowed together, and the banks of the river narrowed into a series of deep gorges known as Rampart Canyon. With frightening velocity, the Yukon plunged through high cliffs not fifty yards apart. The little town of Rampart looked incredibly lonely and isolated under the wide, blue sky.

They stopped to eat at a roadhouse. Corrie was frightened when she heard Quade tell the owner their names and where they had come from. They were camping at night along the river bank, he told the man casually.

Corrie barely tasted their meal of caribou, sourdough bread and beans. As they left she clutched Quade's arm. "Why did you tell him who we were? Don't you realize that Donald might stop here too? He'll be asking questions about us!"

"That's exactly what I want him to do. You may not have noticed this, Corrie, but we've been taking our time. I *want* him to catch up to us. There are people along the river, true—towns and trading posts and wood stops—but basically we men are only like fleas on an elephant's back here. There is still plenty of elephant. And plenty of wilderness, too, deep, true wilderness, more than enough for my purposes. The land doesn't talk; it doesn't tell what it sees."

"Quade! You can't mean that!"

"I do mean it. You can't know how much I mean it."

That night they debarked at a rather flat, gravelly spot which Quade told her made a good natural harbor. Beyond the tops of the spruces the sun dipped low, giving an orange-pink haze to the line of clouds at the horizon. In the distance the trees were shaded with purple, and the entire scene had a melancholy cast to it as the shadows of evening crept toward them.

Corrie caught her breath. In a clearing sat an old, deserted trading post. In the last gleam of sunlight, its weathered boards appeared silvery, almost ghostly. On the old trellis beside the front door climbed a rose vine covered with golden blossoms. More shoots sprang up from the grass itself and had begun to run wild.

Wild roses, Corrie remembered with a squeeze of the heart. Quade had once held her among a patch of such unutterably sweet blossoms . . .

She walked closer. Who had planted those rose cuttings? Who had lived here, waiting patiently by the water in hopes of customers traveling upriver? A few yards away she could see the wreckage of another cabin, and the stumps of felled trees. Had this once been a wood stop for the river steamers?

But no one lived here now. The evening wind lifted up the petals of the roses, scattering them like flakes of purest Bonanza gold.

"Quade! Look! Wild roses!" She pulled Quade's old shirt closer about her shoulders, and shivered in the evening wind.

"Probably planted by the wife of the storekeeper," Quade said cheerfully. He whistled as he finished beaching the boat, the knotted muscles of his shoulders moving with ease. "Bringing with her a bit of home, no doubt, to look at when she felt lonely here."

As they finished carrying in the food (Quade decreed that they could leave their tent and much of the other gear still lashed in the boat) she got a better look at the deserted store. Its weathered log front was still festooned with items once for sale: pots, pans, tools, a washboard, a gold pan, a hoe. Over the door was nailed a faded sign: "Roses-of-Gold Camp, L. Bannon, Prop."

She wondered who L. Bannon was and where he and his wife had gone and why. To the right of the door was a small window leaded with twelve small panes of glass, two of which were broken. Mrs. Bannon probably kept the panes polished so that she could stare out at the river. Maybe she also plucked long stems of roses to put in a vase to brighten the dim interior of the cabin.

"Come, Delia," Quade said. "You're daydreaming. Get to work. I don't tolerate lazy women." Quade's eyes smiled at her, belying his words.

"I'm not lazy!"

"Then start working, girl, or I'm going to wish I'd dumped you in the river as breakfast for the trout."

"I don't think I'd make anyone a tasty breakfast, especially not a trout," she giggled. Some of the thoughtlessness of her mood was gone, and she began to unload more quickly.

Once inside the old store, however, with their things arranged on shelves, firewood cut and the creaking old bunk made up, a feeling of bleakness began to settle on her. This abandoned old store was not a good place for them to be. It held only danger. She knew it, and feared what was to come.

❧ Chapter 38 ❧

"Yep, this here river's about the prettiest in the world, bar none," Billy Watkins said. He shifted the big wad of chewing tobacco to his other cheek and swatted at a mosquito.

"Is that so?"

"Yep. The Yukon's got more birds, more mountains, more trees, more gold, more mosquitoes, and more just plain damned wildness, than any other river I know."

"Really."

Donald Earle was thoroughly tired of this middle-aged, gray-haired, talkative guide they had hired in Dawson City, along with his boat, to get them up river. The man considered himself an authority on the Yukon, and pointed out more sights along the river than Donald cared to look at. He had a bad case of verbal diarrhea, Donald thought sourly. Why hadn't they had the brains to hire a deaf-mute?

Beside him Dr. Santee whistled tunelessly through his teeth, and at the stern of the boat Artie Shultz trailed one hand in the water as if he was a child on an outing.

Donald felt like hitting all three with his fist. He looked down at his right hand, his fingers clenched on the splintery gunwale of the boat. He was almost quivering with his desire to lash out, to smack into flesh, to make blood run and feel bits of broken teeth.

Damn her.

Why in the hell did this have to happen just when he had her and she was starting to relax and accept him?

Engraved on his retina was the image of Corrie as he had last seen her, huddled up like a floozy in the bottom of Quade Hill's boat, fearful of getting shot. Anger surged up in Donald, so strong and corrosive that he could almost feel it eating away at him. That little bitch, he actually started to confide in her. He even told her that he loved her! And now she had done this, betrayed him like the whore she was, and whore they all were, all of them.

"What's the scowl for, Donald? Aren't you enjoying the tour?" Dr. Santee's voice was light, mocking.

"Shut up," Donald growled. His throat hurt, his whole chest, with the feeling of losing something precious, of being cheated beyond all redemption.

"Come, come. Even if a man has lost his lovely wife, he should not give up hope. Women always change their minds; she'll come back to you."

"I said shut up, damn your hide, and I mean it!"

Dr. Santee chuckled, then began to whistle again. Donald stared at him coldly. Someday . . . But he couldn't afford to lose Santee yet. He still needed him. Thank God the man was in this as deeply as he was. If he was not . . .

Donald moistened his lips, thinking back for the dozenth time to his stunned surprise when Corrie screamed out about Ila Hill and the clipping. He had not remembered anything about a clipping.

Later he realized that she must have searched his things, so he had gone through them, too, pocket by pocket, trying to discover what she had found. Old, stuck in a fold of the leather, and nearly disintegrated, he discovered the clipping in his money belt. He couldn't even remember cutting it out. How had he ever had the colossal foolishness to carry that thing about with him all of these years?

He had taken such care to obliterate everything of his past. He put on weight. He changed his name and his hair style, even gave up the wire-rimmed spectacles that he needed for reading. He moved to a new city and took a new identity and a new job. But he didn't change the money belt because it was old and soft and comfortable and he was attached to it.

Donald shivered slightly in his dark suit and shifted about on the hard board floor of the boat, where a folded

tarpaulin served as a rough cushion. If a man believed in
ghosts, he might start thinking that the hand of the dead
girl had thrust that clipping into his belt. Fanciful thinking
by a man who knew better, a man who lived in the world
of power and money and facts and figures.

He had better face it, he made a mistake with Cordelia
Stewart. He was carried away by his damned desires, and
he had allowed himself to become obsessed with her. And
now she had given him this, this gut-wrenching, nauseat-
ing anger that clamped at his vitals, which ached as if they
were about to explode.

"Not too much farther, I'd say." The guide shot out
another long, brown stream of tobacco juice into the
muddy waters of the Yukon. "Just around this bend, maybe. There's a pretty good little harbor, too. The steamers
used to stop there for fueling before Bannon left. I suppose they could be there. It's a good place for stopping.
Especially for a couple that's not in a hurry."

"Yes?" Donald's shoulder muscles tightened. He felt
himself tensing.

"Yep, he used to sell just about everything. To the
Injuns or the miners or anyone."

"Who did?"

"Why, Bannon; who else did you think I'm talking
about? Had a little blonde wife. Went half-crazy, she did.
Had to take her back to Seattle. Nothin' there now but a
bunch of them wild-growin' yeller roses. Only gold on the
place, too."

Billy Watkins cackled. Donald stared at him with dislike. He was the best guide they could find on short notice,
and he accepted their story that Donald was looking for
his runaway wife and her lover, who had stolen ten
thousand dollars in gold dust from him. Later, of course,
the poor man was going to run into a little problem with
his boat. Accidents; they happened with regular frequency
here; any fool knew that. One more would not surprise
anyone.

"Yep," Billy said. "You know, though, there is one thing
that kinda puzzles me a bit, just a little bit, about this here
man that ran off with your wife. He sure don't take no
care to cover his tracks none, does he?"

"No, he doesn't."

"Funny he'd be that way. Now me, if I'd run off with some pretty gal, I'd hide and I'd run and nobody'd ever see me again unless I wanted 'em to."

"Well, he seems to be different than you are."

"Yep. He sure is. More of a damned fool, too, I'd say." Watkins spat into the water.

Or smarter than we guess, Donald thought uneasily. Again he dug his fingers into the splintered gunwale as tension began to creep through his body, stringing his muscles as tight as sun-dried rawhide.

It was two days later, two days of interminable waiting. Corrie filled the time weeding the golden roses and propping up their vines, thinking of the unknown woman who once had loved them. She was washing their clothes in the river, and periodically stopped to pace the clearing and stare out at the ceaseless wash of the water.

Wearing an old serge skirt, she knelt gingerly on a bed of sharp pebbles and wrung out a woolen shirt, thinking with deep regret of her camera, and of all the photographic prints she had abandoned on the *Hannah*. Quade had promised her that once they reached civilization again, he would write a letter to the steamship company. There was a slim possibility that Donald had stored their luggage somewhere until he could return for it.

She hoped so. She would gladly pay any amount in bribes or storage fees, if only she could get her camera and prints back. Not to mention her few, pathetic momentos of her baby . . .

She looked up to see Quade approaching. He had taken a walk along the river bank to the south, another of the restless sorties he kept making—watching, she knew, for the boat that would bring Donald to them.

"Why are you washing those things?" he asked her. "You're only rearranging the sand, you know."

"Perhaps. I know the river is muddy, but at least this gives me something to do. I've scrubbed out that old store about fifteen times, and my hands ache. I think I've remade our bunk five times. Or is it six? If this place was ever haunted, I'm sure I've washed the ghosts out by now."

Quade gave a bitter laugh. "Yes, and I've started my article about Nome at least five times, too. When I left Dawson City I thought I would write something colorful about how it felt to struggle upriver in one of these home-made boats. Instead I find myself embarked on an adventure I can't even begin to write about, because my readers would never believe me."

She nodded.

"Delia." He reached down and pulled her to her feet. "My Delia, are you sorry you came with me?"

"Sorry! No, I'll never be sorry for that."

"Are you sure?"

"Yes. Absolutely." She let the damp woolen shirt drop from her fingers and pressed her body against his. She closed her eyes, savoring his musky, male scent, his bulk and vitality. Then she lifted her lips to his and they kissed.

"There," she said. "Does that answer your question?"

They kissed again, passionately, hungrily.

"I know this is a terrible wait for you. I should have left you in Forty Mile and done this alone," he said after a moment, turning to face the curve of the river. On one of the banks a clod of dirt washed into the water; it landed with a soft, liquid plop. Somewhere a bird was calling hoarsely. Water glittered in the sun.

"No! I want to be with you, no matter what. I'd hate it there," she told him fiercely.

"I imagine you would, at that, especially if Cad Wilson ever got after you." For an instant Quade threw back his head and laughed. But then the smile was gone, to be replaced by an expression of alert watchfulness. His eyes narrowed as he turned to stare out at the river again.

"Oh, Quade, would you stop looking at the water?" she said suddenly, sharply. "He isn't there and I don't think he's going to be. Six boats passed today and none of them was Donald. I wonder if he's coming at all."

"He is. I want you to learn how to use a pistol. After the noon meal I'll teach you. That will give you something more useful to do than scrubbing out shirts."

"But I've told you, I don't want—"

"You don't want more bloodshed. Yes, yes, I know. But I want you to learn to use a gun." His hand went under her chin and tilted it up. She looked into his eyes and saw that they were pale blue, paler and colder than the river.

Again she kissed him and clung to him. As they separated from their embrace, she saw the square of a white sail edge around the deep green curve of trees.

"Quade. Another boat."

He put one hand to his forehead to shade his eyes as he squinted in its direction.

Corrie stared, too, her eyes watering against the glare of the sun. She could feel her heart begin to thump a bit faster. It did that with every boat they saw.

Finally she relaxed. "Only one man in it," she said with relief. "So it can't be Donald. He never goes anywhere without Dr. Santee and Artie, and I'm especially sure he wouldn't come upriver alone. He's a city person."

Quade nodded. "Well, whoever he is, it looks as if he sees us. I think he's waving at us."

Minutes later the boat was upon them, large, squarish and better built than most of the river craft, with a good canvas sail. Its bulky load was carefully covered by a tarpaulin and stowed under the front structure to protect it from wetness.

The man at the tiller was about fifty, with a stubbled gray beard and weathered skin. His face, however, was agitated, and his clothing was soaking wet. Streams of moisture ran out of his hair into the collar of his sodden shirt.

He furled the sail and rowed the craft closer to shore.

"I see you got wet," Quade called.

"Yes. Say, you wouldn't happen to be a doctor, would you? Or know of one near here? My partner, he fell out on some rocks at the last bend and I had to go in and pull him on shore. His face is terrible smashed. He's screaming something fierce and wouldn't even let me pull him in the boat. I think I'm going to need some help with him."

Corrie looked at the man closely. His face *was* frightened and anxious, and his clothing was certainly wet, which bore out his story. A homey quality in his voice reminded her of Jim Price, Papa's driver.

"Help? Why, of course, we'll do what we can," she assured him quickly. She didn't like to think of a man lying all alone at the river's edge, screaming with pain and wondering if he had been abandoned.

"Sure would appreciate it, ma'am."

"Corrie—" Quade said it warningly, in a low voice.

"Oh, but Quade, a man has been hurt. I think if both of us went back with him, we could at least lift him into the boat without hurting him, and bring him back here. I can cut some of our shirts up to make bandages. You have a first aid kit, don't you?"

Quade's fingers dug into her arm. "No, I don't like this."

She twisted away from him angrily. "This man has nothing to do with Donald; I've never even seen him before. We owe it to him at least to—"

"We don't owe anyone anything." Still Quade started toward the water, where the man was now beaching his boat, one hand hovering near the holster where he carried his revolver.

"Say, my partner really does need help; I'm not lying!" the man said rapidly. He grinned at them, and Corrie, who was walking behind Quade, suddenly paused. Hadn't all of this somehow happened before? Perhaps Quade was right. Certainly they weren't being very cautious—

Then it happened. The bulky canvas tarpaulin suddenly flew off and the boat seemed to rock under the burden of the three figures who were leaping up and jumping into the shallow water, rifles aimed in their direction.

"Delia! Delia, for God's sake, wake up! Please, darling—"

The voice seemed to come from a very long distance away, as if it had been shouted through a long series of solid oak doors.

Corrie—or was her name Delia now? *Delia darling*—stirred and heard someone moan. Her head felt strange, as if it was stuck in glue. Each time she tried to move it, the glue pulled. She felt like there was a long metal stake embedded in her skull; each time she twisted the stake would twist, too, shooting pain through her.

"Delia! Damn him. Wake up, will you? Wake up. Oh, darling, why did I get you into this . . . it's my fault . . ."

The voice—was it Quade's?—prodded at her. Corrie felt as if she were swimming in that glue, her arms and legs weighted down. She could barely move.

She heard another moan.

"That's it, sweetheart, struggle out of it. Damn them, they banged you on the head. Damn their souls. But you're going to be all right. Just let yourself wake up; it's going to hurt, but try to move a bit. It might help you."

She began to realize that the voice did belong to Quade, and that it was filled with a thick, husky anger.

"Darling. Darling, I know it's hard, but you've got to wake up. You've been out ten minutes now, and they've already—" His voice broke off.

"No . . . " she said incoherently.

"Listen, Delia, you've got to be ready to help yourself when the time comes. My leg . . . I'm going to need your help or we won't make it, darling. . . . "

She groaned again, fighting the heaviness of the glue, and heard his voice push at her again, mercilessly. Urging her. Demanding that she wake up, open her eyes, be aware.

The light hurt her eyes, her body ached and the stake in her head would not quit turning. She twisted about again, wondering why the glue seemed to have hardened about her arms and legs. Something was wrong. She wouldn't think of it now, she told herself. Not yet. First she would go to sleep. That's it, she would dive back into that warm, cozy corner of her brain, away from the pain . . .

"Delia! Dammit, girl, wake up!"

"No . . . don't want to . . . "

"You must. You little fool, I know it hurts, I know it's hard, but that doesn't matter now. *You must wake up.*"

Increasing, desperate urgency now. Words yanked at her, pried her up from sleep as if she was a clam being brutally scraped out of a shell. Her eyelids fluttered. She caught quick, tilted glimpses of weathered logs. Chinks of moss. A bouquet of golden blooms. Quade's plaid shirt hanging on a nail. They were inside the old trading post.

"That's it. Open them, Delia. Open them wide. It's our only· chance, precious little as that is at this moment . . . "

Again her eyes fluttered. This time they stayed open for a few seconds longer.

"What—what time is it?" she asked thickly.

"It's only been about ten minutes, maybe twelve." Quade's voice was thick, strange, almost unrecognizable. Dimly she wondered why. Wrong . . . something was terribly, terribly wrong. . . .

"Do you remember anything?" he was asking her. "Do you remember what's happened?"

"I—I don't know . . . "

"Think, Delia, think!"

Think. How could she, when her brain was filled with thick gray-yellow glue? When glue pushed down her body, pulled at her limbs, paralyzed her?

Think. She shook her head again and clenched her jaws tightly together until her teeth hurt. Gradually she began to look about herself with more awareness.

She was in the store, lying on the floor about four feet from the sheet-iron stove, which still glowed from the wood they had fed it when they prepared their morning meal. She had gone out to wash some laundry in the river, that was it. Quade had come back from his walk. They had talked. She had kissed him. And then . . .

Now it was coming back to her, rushing toward her so fast that she wanted to scream. "No," she moaned. "Oh, no . . . "

The horror came back to her in brief, ugly flashes. Herself facing Donald, screaming at him in fear and defiance. Donald's hand slapping her across her left cheekbone, a blow so powerful that it numbed her cheek and made her drop to her knees.

And then the flashing movement when Quade drew his pistol and lunged toward Donald. The sound of a shot. Her own scream, high and silvery in the soft summer air. The glimpse of the butt of Donald's rifle, descending toward her, and the final white flash of pain in her head.

She struggled to sit up, fighting the ropes which held her.

"Quade—they shot you—"

"Easy, Delia, easy. I'll live; it's just a thigh wound. Try not to struggle too much, or you'll hurt yourself. I'm afraid they've trussed both of us up like Sunday chickens."

"But—the rifle—they *shot* you, Quade," Corrie insisted.

"Yes, they certainly did," Quade agreed. "Or, rather, your husband did. But it seems I was lucky. The bullet just winged me in the fatty part of the thigh. Oh, I'm going to have a nasty scar there, but your friend Dr. Santee assured me the wound looks clean and the bullet made a nice exit. He was kind enough to pour whiskey over it to cleanse it."

"I can't believe—Dr. Santee cleansed your wound?" Delia felt as if her head was swimming with the strangeness of it. With difficulty she twisted about to look at Quade, and drew in her breath sharply, in dismay. He lay sprawled only a few feet from her, bound also with ropes, a bloody cloth wrapped about his thigh. His face, drained of color, was an ugly gray-white. He must have lost a good deal of blood, she thought dazedly. Yet here he was, reassuring her . . .

"Yes," Quade was saying. "Dr. Santee bandaged me, don't ask me why."

"I still can't—"

"Delia, I don't know, I'm not sure of anything. All I know is that they dragged us in here and tied us up. The red-haired one, your Dr. Santee, gave me some rudimentary medical attention. Why he did it, I don't know. Maybe he felt that flowing blood is untidy. Maybe he remembered his Hippocratic Oath. I'd say it's rather useless, though, to give me medical care now, considering what plans they have for us."

"What plans?" Corrie said sharply.

"They certainly haven't any intention of escorting us to Nome and grubstaking us to a claim on the beach," Quade said heavily, slowly, as if it took a great effort to talk.

"You don't mean that they plan to . . . " Corrie could not complete the sentence. Her mouth felt curiously like boot leather, dry and acrid. She tried to swallow and discovered that she had no saliva whatsoever.

"Delia, about five minutes ago, I heard a cry. I think they were disposing of the gentleman who hailed us for help. They probably picked him up somewhere. I have a feeling that they're trying to decide what to do about us —about you and me. I heard them arguing a few minutes ago."

"Oh, God."

Corrie felt light-headed. Of course, she thought. What else could Donald do now but kill them? Corrie knew of his guilt, had witnessed two of his killings and knew of others. For a time Donald evidently thought he could keep her quiet as his wife. By daring to escape, she made it plain she would never be silenced. And now, worst of all, she had involved Quade.

"I'm so sorry," she said. "I didn't mean to bring you into this."

"I was already in it," he told her bleakly.

For a second their eyes met and she saw the love in his. A fierce warmth leapt between them. Their glances held; she felt as if she was swimming in his eyes, drawing strength from them.

The cabin door was pushed open. "Well, well, well. My dear wife. I see you've regained consciousness, more's the pity. I was hoping you would stay out for a while."

Donald stood in the open doorway, his body silhouetted against the green pleasantness of the summer day. Corrie could only stare at him, horror rushing through her. This was her husband, she thought wildly, this big, heavily built, muscular man who many women would find exciting. She found him very frightening. Especially now, for she sensed a tension in him, tightly drawn, near to exploding. Never had she seen Donald like this, his face suffused with color, his hands clenched into trembling fists.

She found her voice. "Donald, where is the man in the boat, the man who hailed us? What have you done with him?"

"Never mind." Then, oddly, Donald shook his head. "Now I know; you look like *her*," he muttered under his breath.

"Like who? Oh, Donald, was that man your guide? I'd like to talk with him, if I may."

"He's gone. You can't talk to him. I have something for you, Corrie. Something to relax you."

"No, please. No more!"

She did not need to ask what he meant. He held up a bottle of laudanum.

Laudanum! Corrie felt her muscles tensing, straining against the ropes which held her, cutting into her flesh. Laudanum contained opium—it would make her sleep. But why should Donald want her to sleep? She felt perspiration running down her forehead to her temples, and then into her hair, making her chilly.

"Donald, you must listen to me. Couldn't we just talk? In a normal, civilized way? If only you would untie us—"

"No."

"You bastard," Quade said. Corrie saw his body jerk against the ropes; more blood flowed from the wound in his leg. "You murdering bastard. You killed Ila. *You killed her.*"

"Yes, I did," Donald said slowly. He took a step toward them, and Corrie saw that his fists were trembling violently.

"Why?" Quade asked. "Why? Just tell me that. She was a young girl, not even a woman yet, with all of her promise still before her. She was pretty and talented and bright. She could have done so much."

Donald's face was sullen. His eyes avoided Quade's, and darted around the trading post as if searching for something. But what? Corrie wondered with a sick feeling. Somewhere in the deepest part of her mind, she already knew . . .

"It was an accident," Donald said. His mouth was twisted out of shape. "I didn't want . . . didn't want to do it. Do you think I'm a monster? But she—I didn't know she was there. I didn't see her until I had already poured out the kerosene. She was in this little back room . . . Oh, God, just standing there, with her mouth open. She was screaming . . . "

Donald licked his lips, his face the color of brick. His eyes were wide and staring, his nostrils flared. Corrie knew he was reliving what happened.

"She—she just screamed and looked at me and screamed. I could feel her hating me. . . . The flames, they were in her eyes, shining in her eyes . . . and then I . . . "

Now Donald made an odd gesture. He slapped at the scarred back of his right hand as if it, too, were burning. Corrie watched him, mesmerized by the terrible words he was uttering in a strange, choked voice.

"Fire . . . My God, I can't believe it, fire . . . burning in her eyes . . . "

"Stop it, man. Stop it! Snap out of it," Quade said, so sharply that Corrie knew he, too, was caught up in the eerie horror of this moment.

"Fire—more fire—in circles about her. So red, so bright, so warm . . . " Donald grabbed his groin. He rubbed himself violently. His body stiffened as his eyes fixed blankly on Corrie. He seemed totally unaware of where he was. Corrie knew that he was not seeing her at all; he was seeing someone else. A girl with a face as pale and lovely as the one on the burned cameo—

"Donald! Look at me," she cried. "I'm not Ila Hill, I'm Cordelia, I'm your wife, don't you remember? Come back, Donald, come to your senses. You know you can't kill us. People would—they would find us, they would know what happened. You'll be caught—"

"Ila," Donald called. "I won't be caught, Ila. Not this time."

"I'm not Ila, I'm not, I'm Corrie—"

Donald did not seem to hear her protest. He moved toward the stove and bent down to pick up a piece of firewood.

"Donald, what are you doing? You can't—"

He was. Methodically, as if he was alone in the room, he moved about the cabin, making his preparations. He pulled Quade's shirt off the nail where it hung. He wrapped it securely about the thickest end of the stick of wood. He reached for a metal container, the one which contained the kerosene for Quade's lamp.

"Accident," he mumbled. "It's going to be an accident, Ila. Like that other time. Only this time you won't scream. I couldn't stand that."

With quick movements, his hands no longer trembling, Donald picked up the tin of kerosene and poured the liquid over the torch he had prepared. The liquid sloshed out and some of it spilled onto the floor, leaving dark splashes. Kerosene fumes were heavy in the air.

"You screamed at me," Donald said. "You screamed and you screamed and you screamed . . . "

"You!" said Mattie Shea, the madam Corrie had encountered on the Alki. She pointed a finger and said in a deep, hoarse voice, "You watch out! I can see it! I see . . . Oh, God, I see fire, flames. Flames licking and burning—watch out! Watch it! They'll burn you. They'll burn you alive!"

What?" Corrie involuntarily shrank back as far as she could get from the dying woman. "What do you mean?"

"I said fire! I said fire and burning and black, charred flesh! I said watch out, Cordelia Stewart!"

The voice of Mattie Shea seemed to whirl around the small log building, spinning in and out of Corrie's mind until she thought she would go mad. This isn't real, she told herself. This is a nightmare, a strange, opium-induced nightmare. It couldn't be true that in a few minutes she would die. And Quade, too, her beloved Quade. No, none of this was happening.

Numbly she watched as Donald completed the last of his preparations. He forced laudanum down Quade's throat exactly as a veterinarian might cram medicine down the gullet of a dog. As Corrie watched in shock, she saw Quade abruptly relax. He lay limply in his ropes.

Asleep? Dead? Corrie thought her heart would pound itself out of her chest.

Donald took out a small knife and cut Quade's ropes. Corrie knew why he was doing it, of course. When their bodies were eventually found, there would be no ropes, no trace of force. Their deaths would look accidental. Cabin fires were common here; wood-burning stoves were not always safe and men grew careless. She and Quade would not be the first to die in such a way. . . .

Released from the ropes, Quade's body rolled slightly, each muscle relaxed and limp. Thick snores filled the air. He would die sleeping, Corrie told herself in mounting panic. Mercifully, he wouldn't know . . .

Donald cut her bonds away. Her arms prickled as the blood flowed back into them.

"Donald—" she pleaded feverishly. "Donald, you've got to listen to me—"

He continued to work on the ropes on her legs, at last tossing them petulantly toward the stove. Corrie tried to think. If only she could edge away from him, crawl even, before he remembered to give her the laudanum. But of course, she thought frantically, there was Quade. Quade sprawled unconscious on the cabin floor, helpless to save himself.

"Donald, you—you said you loved me. Don't you remember that day? Would you do this thing to someone you loved? Would you, Donald?"

"Too late, Ila. It's too late."

"But I'm not Ila! And it's not too late! Oh, Donald, don't you see—"

Donald regarded her. With one hand he rubbed the corners of his eyes with his knuckles, as if he were a child, a tired, lost and despairing little boy.

Dr. Santee, Corrie thought desperately. Where was he? If he were only here, perhaps he could talk sense into Donald.

"*Donald.* If you'll only untie me, I—I'll be a good wife to you, I swear it! I won't laugh at you, I won't run away any more—"

"No. That's right. You won't run away." The childish expression faded from Donald's face, and was replaced by a fixed look.

She saw Donald reach into his pocket, but instead of the laudanum he drew out a little metal container painted with an advertisement, the box where he kept his sulfur matches.

He slid off the lid and fumbled inside.

The match head gleamed as he held it. Then, slowly, he lifted the sole of his boot in order to strike it.

"*No!*" Corrie screamed. "No!"

Donald lit the match.

A flash of flames, a roaring, sucking whoosh filled the room. Then she felt a hand grasp her arm, and drag at her with such fierce strength that she knew her shoulder socket would ache for days.

Corrie was never to remember the details clearly. She only knew that somehow Quade had lunged to his feet and that they staggered out of the trading post together, supporting each other, dragging themselves away from the terrible flames.

She was in his arms, racked with sobs.

"Quade— Oh, I thought— You were asleep, the laudanum—"

"Not me. Hate the stuff. Always refused my medicine as a child."

They held tightly onto each other, Quade swaying with exhaustion and pain. Dimly she heard the old store explode. The river bank was empty, with only their own boat moored there. But none of that seemed to matter: the only reality was Quade, the feel of his arms about her.

"I . . . think I'm a bit drunk, D-Delia," he mumbled. "I tried to make a squirrel pouch out of that blasted laudanum and not swallow any. Knew his plan. Faked it, faked being . . . asleep. Don't you think I was . . . clever at it? But I think some slipped down anyway . . . think I'm pretty tired . . . "

They swayed against each other.

"Look at it," Quade said. "Look at the place . . . "

They turned to stare. The old trading post was bursting with flames, its center a wave of muddy, dark-gray smoke. The structure burned hungrily, its dried moss and old logs fueling the flames. Yellow blooms withered and were gone. Corrie closed her eyes, feeling suddenly nauseous. She thought she heard a scream.

"Man . . . a man's in there." Quade leaned against her so heavily that she staggered. "Dying, Delia. He's burning up. Funny . . . now that it's happened . . . makes me feel sick. . . . "

She fell under almost the whole of Quade's weight and she knew that at last the laudanum he had swallowed had taken effect: he had gone to sleep standing up.

Twelve hours later the wreckage of the old store was still smoldering, the logs caved in on each other, grisly and charred. Only one rose shoot had been spared, and still grew among the ashes, green and valiant. Going down to the river to get water, Corrie found the body of the middle-aged boatman, the back of his head crushed in from a heavy blow. She managed to drag him ashore and pull a blanket over him; later, when she felt stronger, she would attempt to bury him.

She found a tent among the supplies Quade had left stored in the "cuddy" of his boat, and she managed to put it up so that they would have shelter from the night. Quade awakened, and she helped him to crawl into the tent, where the late sun, brilliant as gold bullion, streamed through the open flap. She even managed to prepare a crude supper with some dried fruit and flour she had found in the boat.

After they ate, Quade gave a little sigh and turned to her. He put an arm across her shoulders.

"Well, I guess you haven't forgotten the cooking lessons I gave you, Delia. How long did I sleep? Most of the day? It seems forever. My leg is beginning to throb."

"I—I'm sorry. I don't have anything for it. I don't think there is any laudanum left."

They both shook with wild, half-hysterical laughter, and clung to each other.

"Donald, dead," Corrie said at last, brushing back hot tears. "I just can't believe that all of this has really happened."

"It did, though. *I* certainly believe it," Quade said, looking down at his thigh.

"I wonder where Artie and Dr. Santee went."

"To Nome, I'd wager. They say there's gold there by the ton, right on the beach for the taking. All a man has to do is sink in his shovel."

"But why?" Corrie said. "Why would they desert Donald like that? I don't understand."

"Who knows? Perhaps Dr. Santee finally got tired of all the killing. Perhaps he knew that Donald's mind was going at last. It probably finally occurred to him that he and Artie would be next: they had to be. Donald certainly couldn't allow them to continue to live, knowing what they did."

Corrie fell silent, listening to the sounds of the wilderness, the rustle of the tall weeds in the breeze, the distant call of a duck. Overhead the sky was a pure, incredible blue.

"I know I hated Donald," she said at last. "But to think that he had to die like that. Burning alive—how terrible. No matter how guilty he was, surely no man deserves to meet such an end."

"Yes." Quade's voice was low, and Corrie sensed that he

felt as shaken as she did. "Do you know, Delia, I think that he wanted to get out. I'd completely forgotten him—I was only thinking of you. I knew the fire would reach you in a second and all I wanted to do was to get you out as fast as possible." He shook his head. "I think I felt him behind me, trying to get out, too. No one could have wanted to stay in that inferno."

Quade's words stopped, then went on again, almost inaudibly. "He must have skidded on the burning kerosene. I heard him fall. His death was really an accident, if you want to call it that."

"Slipped? But—" Corrie was silent, thinking of the girl in the brooch. *Had* Donald's death really been an "accident"? They would never know. And somehow she didn't want to.

"Quade." She ran her hand gently over his hair, over the face so rough and battered and dear to her. "Quade, the brooch. Now you can stop carrying it about. Donald is dead at last. And your poor sister can rest in peace, wherever she is."

"Yes." Quade's hand cupped itself around Corrie's breast, his flesh as warm as life. A little vein in the hollow of his neck was beating strongly. "Do you know something, my Delia? I looked for that brooch later, after I woke up, while you were putting up the tent. I couldn't find it. I believe that it's still there in the burned store."

"W-what?"

"Yes. In the ashes. That's the best place for it, don't you think? Now we can all be at peace. You and I can get on with the rest of our lives. Put your arms around me, Delia girl. I want to hold you. I want to feel you."

Corrie did as he asked, and the feel of his embrace was sweetness beyond measure.